Bed of Leaves

Lemuel McRorey

To my friend James
Best wishes always
Lem McRorey

Copyright Information

The characters, incidents, and dialogues in this book are fictitious. Except for biblical facts, every word written is the product of the authors imagination and not to be perceived as real. Except for biblical facts, any resemblance to actual events or persons, living or dead are completely coincidental.

Table of Contents

Chapter 1

Bright Light

5

Bed of Leaves

The morning air was cool. Birds flying in the sky announced their arrival as they landed on the branches of one tree, then announced their departure as they took off to land in another tree. Each made its own music, but all the birdsong together couldn't compare to the music that softly rolled out of the cracks and windows of the small town Baptist church-the same church that claimed ownership of the trees the birds played in.

Inside, the children sang. Their innocent singing pleased their families and friends. A smile was on every face.

"This little light of mine, I'm gonna let it shine. This little light of mine, I'm gonna let it shine. This little light of mine, I'm gonna let it shine, let it shine, let it shine, let it shine. Jesus gave me light, now I'm gonna let it shine. Jesus gave me light, now I'm gonna let it shine . . . "

It would be hard to figure out who were trying to please God the most, the children or the birds.

In a pew at the back of the church sat a middle-aged man, sobbing softly to himself. Jim had been to church several times in the past, but never by himself, and certainly not in tears. Nobody noticed as Jim held his head in his hands; they didn't see the tears running through his fingers. At that moment, nobody else in the church could have felt the loneliness that Jim felt. Never before had Jim sat in self-pity, and never before had he felt so helpless.

Unaware that the children were close to finishing their song, he looked up at the ceiling with tears in his eyes. "Lord, help me," Jim whispered.

Suddenly, the children's singing faded, and the room became dim. He heard a low humming sound that grew louder, as though amplified through speakers. As the humming got louder, it started to pulsate. Up near the ceiling, a glowing light appeared. In the middle of the glow, the paint of the ceiling seemed to peel back to reveal a window, open into heaven.

In the center of the window was a bright light in the shape of a man. The brilliant light sparkled as the figure stretched its arms out toward Jim, filling Jim's body with the spirit of God. The humming sound started to fade.

A voice that could only be that of the son of God gave Jim the hope he was searching for. *"I am the way, Jim. Let me come into your heart and you will never be alone again."*

With this, the image disappeared. The humming sound grew faint, and the window closed. As quickly as it had formed, the glow on the ceiling vanished. The vision was over.

Jim looked around. He realized he was the only person of the congregation who'd witnessed this miracle. Tears still ran down his cheeks, but now they were tears of happiness as he bathed in the spirit of God. He knew he had found everything he'd been looking for. Excited by the vision and the knowledge he'd received, with a mental image of God sitting on his throne in heaven, Jim gave thanks through prayer and praise.

"Father," he prayed, "please forgive me of my sins and Lord, please have mercy on my soul. I know I'm a sinner. Thank you," he said, "for Jesus, who died on the cross for my sins. I praise you, Father, for all that you have done for me, and thank you for the vision you have shown me. Please guide me every day in the way you would have me be. In Jesus' Holy name, I pray. Amen."

The children had finished their song. Reverend Cox stepped up to give a sermon about Moses and the Ten Commandments. He spoke about the golden calf and God's punishment for Moses. Jim listened eagerly to every word. He wanted to learn all he could about the Bible.

7
Bed of Leaves

Reverend Cox ended the sermon with a prayer. "Lord," he prayed, "forgive us for our sins; our righteousness is as filthy rags. Speak to your children, Lord-every single heart-and may those come to you who will do your bidding. In Jesus' name, amen."

The congregation began singing, *"Just as I am without one plea, and that thou bids me, come to thee . . . "*

Without hesitation, Jim slipped from his pew and walked down the aisle toward the altar, tears still in his eyes. Jim had never been so happy in his life. He knew now that he was a child of God. He approached the altar with his heart lifted and his sins forgiven. The love of the Holy Spirit completely filled him.

Reverend Cox reached out to shake Jim's hand. Jim clasped it. "Brother Cox," Jim said, "as I sat in the back of the church, I saw a vision."

Reverend Cox hesitated. He stared at Jim. "Jim, are you sure it was a vision?"

"Yes, Brother Cox," Jim replied firmly. "A window opened up into heaven and I saw Jesus as a light that sparkled. He held his arms out and spoke to me."

Reverend Cox didn't really know how to respond to Jim's revelation. Even though he loved God with all his heart, Reverend Cox had never had a vision, nor had anyone else in the congregation. He thought the congregation wouldn't understand, so he decided not to say anything about the vision Jim claimed to have had.

Reverend Cox gave Jim guidance through literature, advice, and prayer. Still confused by his experience, Jim hardly heard a word he said. He did hear Reverend Cox say that the baptism would be next Sunday night.

Reverend Cox offered prayer, and then asked the congregation to come up and welcome Jim to his new home.

Jim realized that Reverend Cox was not going to tell the congregation about his vision. "Brother Cox," he said with tears in his eyes, "I want to tell the congregation about my vision."

Jim's and the preacher's eyes met, and both men stood looking at each other for several seconds. Neither Jim nor Reverend Cox said a word.

Not a sound could be heard from the congregation. Silence filled the church. The congregation didn't understand what was going on, but everyone could tell that Reverend Cox was uncomfortable about what he was going to say.

Glancing toward the congregation, then back to Jim, Reverend Cox put his right hand on Jim's left shoulder. "Jim, at this point, I don't have the right to forbid you to tell anyone about your vision."

Reverend Cox removed his hand from Jim's shoulder and lifted the microphone to his mouth. When he spoke, it was as though he was talking to Jim and the congregation at the same time. "I pray this is a vision from God," he said, "and that it will be a blessing for the congregation." Reverend Cox put his hands together as if to pray. He turned from Jim to look at each and every face in the congregation. "Brothers and sisters in Christ, Brother Jim had a vision here in our church today, and now he's going to share it with you."

Reverend Cox smiled at Jim and handed him the microphone, then quietly moved two steps to Jim's left side. Both men stood looking at each other, then Reverend Cox, with a gentle smile on his face, nodded for Jim to begin. Jim stood still for a few seconds with the microphone held up to his mouth. The congregation was quiet, sensing the tension.

Bed of Leaves

Jim put his mouth in motion, but not a word came out. Choking back tears, Jim tried to speak again. Nothing. This time he couldn't control himself; tears ran freely down his cheeks. Then, receiving strength from the Holy Spirit, Jim opened his mouth to try to speak again.

"Please forgive me," were the first words the congregation heard.

With his hands still clasped together as if to pray, Reverend Cox said, "Amen." Reverend Cox's motto for the church was *Father, please forgive me*. It pleased Reverend Cox to hear Jim say the words.

Three other voices in the congregation echoed Reverend Cox's "Amen."

Jim, still drawing from the strength of the Holy Spirit, was now able to hold back his tears. As he searched for the right words to say, God opened Reverend Cox's eyes so he could see the Holy Spirit working in Jim. What Reverend Cox saw left goose pimples all over his body.

A thin black outline formed around Jim and began to glow. With a low hum, the thin outline expanded outward from his body. As it expanded, it changed color from black to a soft blue aura that completely engulfed Jim. When he moved, the aura moved with him.

Reverend Cox's vision of Jim seemed to last for several minutes, but in fact it only lasted a few seconds. It was as if everything happened in slow motion. As Jim spoke, the aura remained with him, but only Reverend Cox could see it.

"I saw a vision today," Jim said, "as I sat in the last pew at the back of the church. A window opened up into heaven, and I saw shining, glittering lights in the shape of a man. He held his hands out toward me." Jim looked around the room as he spoke. "It was Jesus. He said if I asked him to come into my heart, I would never be alone again."

He could tell by their faces that no one else had seen the vision, and because they didn't see it, they couldn't understand how Jim could. He lowered the mike and reached out to hand it to Reverend Cox.

Reverend Cox again invited the congregation to come up to the altar and welcome Jim as a new member. No one believed Jim had had a vision, but no one thought he was lying, either. They thought Jim had imagined everything he saw. They all were cheerful and friendly as they went up and walked past him in single file, shaking his hand.

The last person to shake Jim's hand, an older woman, congratulated him on his decision to become a Christian. She told him she was glad he was now a member of the church. She said what she felt obligated to say and then released Jim's hand and shook the preacher's hand. Then she left the church, walking behind the others who were leaving.

Reverend Cox and Jim now stood alone at the altar. Reverend Cox shook Jim's hand again.

"Jim," Reverend Cox said, "as you spoke to the congregation about your vision, I saw a vision of my own." He paused. Jim waited to hear more. "I saw a blue aura around your body, Jim, and I'm convinced God has something special for you to do."

Jim thought about that. "Brother Cox, do you know what God wants me to do?"

Reverend Cox looked at him. "No Jim," he said gently. "God revealed nothing to me, other than the blue aura around your body." Reverend Cox noticed the confused look on Jim's face and added, "Jim, I don't know what God wants you to do, or even if he has anything for you to do. I just wanted you to know what I saw."

Visions and auras were new to Jim. He didn't know how to react. "Do all Christians have visions and auras?" he asked.

"No Jim," Reverend Cox replied, "I don't, and I've never known anyone who has." Realizing Jim's life was about to change, he added, "If you ever need consultation or someone to talk to, feel free to call on me. I don't know if I can answer all your questions, but I'll try."

"Thanks, Reverend Cox," he said.

Reverend Cox and Jim walked down the aisle toward the front door. They shook hands again and said good-bye. As Jim stepped out onto the church porch and shut the door, a calmness came over him. He looked up toward the sky. It was a beautiful day. The sun shone on his face and a gentle breeze ruffled his hair. The church was surrounded by tall trees and a manicured lawn with a church sign in the front and a parking lot beside the church. A sidewalk ran from the church to the street.

Jim formed a mental picture of God sitting on his throne. He closed his eyes to pray. "Father," he said, "from now on, I will serve you however you will use me."

Jim slowly walked toward the only car left at the curb. He opened the door and slid into the driver's seat. He started the motor, but didn't put the car in gear. He sat there, thinking about God and what heaven was like. He had never felt more content in his life. Jim sat there for over an hour with the motor running, lost in thought. All he could think about was heaven and life after death. He was familiar with the Bible, but had never read it. Now a desire to read the Bible was turning into a hunger.

Jim put his car in gear and drove toward his apartment, where he spent the rest of the day reading the old Bible his dad had passed down to him.

Chapter 2

Vision Of Africa

13

Bed of Leaves

Monday morning, Jim walked through his company door and past several offices on the way to his own office, offering his usual "good morning" to employees working at their desks.

Jim's secretary walked out of the break room and stopped at the water dispenser on the outside wall of the break room. She placed a glass in the automatic water dispenser and waited while ice cubes clinked into the bottom of the glass. She was waiting for the water to fill as Jim walked toward her. "Good morning, Mary," he said, then smiled and added something extra for the first time. "You really look nice this morning."

Mary blushed. "Good morning, Jim," she replied, then added, "you look nice yourself." That didn't really describe what she meant. After a little hesitation, Mary blurted out exactly what she wanted to say. "Jim," she said, "you really do look nice this morning. There's something different about you. You look happy and content."

Jim's smile widened. "Mary, I found the Lord yesterday and I'm really excited about it."

"Sounds great, Jim," Mary quickly responded. "I'll get you a copy of the quality production report. I'll be right back." Mary professed to be a Christian, but anytime the subject of religion came up, it made her uncomfortable.

When Mary returned with the quality production report, Jim took the document and entered his elegant office. Crossing the thick, soft carpet, he laid the document on his desk while he removed his jacket and hung it on a coat rack. As he sat in his chair and picked up the quality production report, the spirit of God suddenly filled his body.

The room became dim. As he had in church the day before, Jim heard a humming sound that progressed from soft to loud. The humming sound began to pulsate. After a few seconds, it faded, then ceased. Jim saw a glow appear on the ceiling. In the middle of the glow, as if the paint were peeling back, a window appeared, open into heaven-into what looked like the throne room of God. In the center of the window was a bright light.

A loud voice boomed as though amplified, *"Jim, you have been chosen by God."*

The voice startled Jim. He dropped to the floor, knocking his chair out of the way. He fell flat on his face, shaking all over, and pressed his forehead against the carpet. Elbows out to his side, he covered the back of his head with his hands. Fear drained all of his strength. Jim could hear words coming from his own mouth: "I'm scared, Father. I don't know what to do."

"Jim," the voice thundered, *"I am but a servant of God. I was sent to deliver you a message. Fear not, for no harm will come to you."*

Jim heard what the voice said, but remained with his face against the floor.

"Jim." God's messenger beckoned. *"Sit up and view what comes forth from heaven."*

Jim rose to his knees and covered his face with his hands. Fear made his heart pound. He slowly removed his hands from his face and opened his eyes.

He had been removed from his office. He now sat on green grass. Around him were strange-looking buildings constructed of bamboo framework, with straw roofs. He was made aware, within himself, of the purpose of each building. On his left, a small hospital had a porch on one corner and several windows along its side. A paved road with curbs and streetlights ran in front of the hospital, and across the road were several blocks of African-style houses. The houses had no garages or driveways. All the streets were paved. Streetlights dotted the entire residential area.

Jim looked to his right, across another road with curbs and streetlights, and saw another large building that he knew was a dining facility. His eyes slid along this building to the public meeting building in the village park behind it. He saw several shaded picnic tables scattered throughout the park, and a play area with swings, slides, and a merry-go-round in one corner. At the opposite end of the park was a beautiful flower garden with bordered plots.

Many black people were walking in and out of the buildings and along the streets. Jim watched one man approach him and then pass right through him as though he was a ghost.

The little village faded away and Jim found himself back in his office. "I don't know what all this means," Jim said. "It's all strange to me."

"Jim," the messenger replied, *"God wants you to go to Africa and be a witness to thousands of people who have never heard of the Bible."*

Jim knew if he went to Africa, he would have to leave his business and the only way of life he knew. "But sir," he argued, "why does God want me to go to Africa? Aren't missionaries already there?"

"You told God you would do whatever he asked of you," the voice thundered. *"Yes, there are missionaries all over Africa. But God has a place there for you, too."*

"Sir, does God want me to go to the village you showed me?"

"Jim," the voice boomed, *"God wants you to* build *the village you saw. He wants you to feed the hungry, clothe the poor, and house the homeless."* The voice hesitated, as if the speaker noticed Jim's confusion. *"Jim, God knows your heart. He knows you will do what he asks of you."*

With this, the window into heaven closed. Jim heard the soft humming sound that grew louder, then began to pulsate. After a few seconds, it faded away. As quick as it had started, the glow on the ceiling vanished and the vision was over.

Slowly Jim reached up to the corner of his desk and pulled himself up from his knees. He righted his chair and sat down with his elbows on the desk and his hands covering his face. He sat for a long time, thinking about all that he had seen.

Jim was a wealthy man-a multimillionaire. He owned the South and West Tool Company, with over one thousand employees. As president of the company, he appointed dependable and trustworthy people to top positions, including his board of directors, so he had the freedom to come and go as he pleased. With his newfound Christianity and his mission from God, it was even more important that he have trustworthy people running his company.

God's plan for Jim would take him thousands of miles away from his company, to a place that was totally different from the world he grew up in. Jim had never been to Africa, but it didn't matter. He would do what God asked of him.

Jim knew money very well. He had over eight hundred million dollars in the bank. Eight hundred million dollars would feed a lot of hungry people. The continued profits from his company could keep them fed.

17

Bed of Leaves

Jim spent most of the day planning his trip to Africa. He contacted the company pilot and set up meetings with his board of directors. He sent his clothes to the dry cleaners and made calls to the US Embassy in Africa. Charged with a new sense of purpose, Jim was eager to get to Nairobi, to learn where to purchase large amounts of groceries and how to get them shipped. Every day that went by meant another day people would go hungry. Many of them would even die.

Jim had never thought about hungry people in the past, much less cared. Now he couldn't make things happen fast enough. He knew people were starving to death and he knew he had wasted so much of his life in his lust for money-money that didn't even bring him happiness. He felt as if it was his fault that there were hungry people in the world.

He spent the next week meeting with his board of directors and getting his travel arrangements completed. He learned all he could about Africa.

A week after Jim professed Jesus as his Lord and Savior, he glanced at the Bible lying on his desk and smiled. He'd always thought Christian people were very strange, but now he was acting just like them. He had already read most of the Bible, and planned to finish reading the Bible and to study it thoroughly. He loved the Lord. Jim had never been happier in his life.

His luggage was packed and loaded in the company limousine. The chauffeur was on alert and waiting for Jim's call. Jim put his coat on and walked to his office door, then paused. Something had caught his attention.

Jim's office was as appealing and comfortable as any office in the world. As he looked around the room, as if for the last time, his eyes fixed on the trophy case that was built into the wall directly in front of his desk. The case contained trophies he'd received for playing sports in high school and college. Jim stepped back inside his office and walked over to the trophy case for a closer look.

Mary knocked lightly on the door.

"Come in," Jim said absently, eyes still on the case.

As she entered the room, Jim noticed who it was. "Mary," he said, "do you see this trophy case?"

"Yes."

"I had it built there," he said, "so I could look back on my achievements in high school and college."

Mary walked over to stand beside Jim. She bent over and looked inside the case.

"The trophies look pretty in the case," Jim mused, "but I've always been too busy to notice them."

Mary seemed puzzled. "Jim, I don't understand. Why does that bother you?"

"The trophy case doesn't bother me," he replied, "but it reminds me of something I did; something that does bother me."

Mary frowned, not understanding what Jim was talking about.

Bed of Leaves

"Mary, I hurt someone who was very close to me." Tears welled up in Jim's eyes. "I was cruel to Christine." Christine was Jim's ex-wife. "I loved Christine with all my heart, and I still do." Jim paused to wipe the pooling tears from his eyes, then continued in a voice that had become shaky and weak. "She was beautiful, and I built her a beautiful house. She was my trophy in my trophy case, but I was too busy to notice her. Now she's gone." Jim hung his head in shame, and when he spoke again, the words came out in a whimper. "She married a man whose wife died three years ago."

Mary could see the pain in his face. "Jim," she said, "everyone makes mistakes. You can't change the past."

Jim composed himself and wiped more tears from his eyes. "I wish I could. I would spend every minute of every day with her." He thought about the years he and Christine had spent together. "My road to success collided with my marriage. It left Christine with no direction for her life."

Jim thought about what he'd just said. "Mary," he exclaimed, suddenly excited, "Christine searched for a new direction in the church. The man she married six months ago is a preacher!"

Mary looked confused. "And you're happy about that, Jim?"

"Yes! Don't you get it? I'll be with Christine in heaven!"

Mary didn't want to talk about religious things, so she changed the subject. "Jim, I came in to wish you good luck on your trip to Africa. We'll all miss you."

"Thank you, Mary," Jim replied. "I'll miss everyone here, too."

Mary smiled at Jim and left the room. She closed the door behind her.

Lemuel McRorey

Jim sat at his desk and all he could think about was beautiful Christine. He was well aware that beauty is only skin deep, but Jim knew Christine was beautiful on the inside, as well. He sat and thought about Christine until the grandfather clock clanged several times, waking him from his reverie. He needed to get to the airport.

He picked up the phone and pushed a button. "Mary," Jim said when she answered, "I'm ready to go to the airport. Tell Raymond to park the limo out front." Then he picked up his Bible and walked out of the office. He closed the door behind him. It was time for Jim to start his new life in Africa.

He walked out into a sunny day. A light breeze soothed his body. Raymond was already parked in the driveway and standing beside the company limousine. Raymond observed Jim walking through the door and opened the passenger door on the driver's side. "Good morning, sir."

"Good morning, Raymond," Jim responded, then asked about the man's wife and four children. "Is all well with you and the family?"

Raymond smiled, pleased with his boss's new attitude and friendliness. "Yes sir, my family and I are doing well. How are you?"

"Raymond," Jim replied as he slipped inside the limo, "I'm going to Africa and I don't know what to do when I get there." He smiled at the chauffeur still waiting beside the open door. "I feel in my heart that God will be with me."

"Sir, I know why you're going to Africa," Raymond replied, "and I, for one, think you should be commended for it."

"Thank you Raymond. But I should have done this years ago."

Raymond shut the door, walked around the front of the car and opened the driver's door, then ducked his head and slipped into the driver's seat. He started the car, checked the mirror to make sure Jim was ready, then pulled out of the driveway.

Jim's office was just a few blocks from the freeway. On the way to the airport, Jim studied the horizon, paying close attention to the line where the sky met the ground. The horizon went on and on forever, he realized, fascinated. It was like heaven, and life after death. After you die, Jim theorized, your body is dead, with no feelings or thoughts. Your dead body decays, but your soul instantly goes to heaven. It would be as fast as the twinkling of an eye. Jim knew he could be wrong, but it didn't matter. If your body lay in the grave for ten thousand years, it would only seem like a split second before you were in heaven. And after you woke up in heaven, just like the horizon, life would go on and on, forever.

The thought of living forever in paradise left goose pimples all over Jim's body. He whispered to himself, "Why did it take me so long to understand how great God is?" He thought about people who didn't know Jesus.

"Raymond," he said, "as a new Christian, I want to lead people to Christ. If I say the name Jesus, people do everything they can to get away from me. I don't know what to do to be an effective witness."

Raymond's reply surprised Jim. "I'm a Christian myself, and I think God already gave you the answer to your question."

Jim thought about what Raymond said. "I don't understand."

Raymond looked at him in the rearview mirror. "Maybe God thinks, if you feed a hungry man's stomach with food . . ."

Jim understood what Raymond meant. He finished the sentence Raymond had started. "Then maybe you could feed a man's hunger that he didn't know he had. A spiritual hunger."

Raymond nodded. "You got it, boss."

"Thank you, Raymond." Jim lowered his head and gave thanks to God.

As the company limo got closer to the airport, Jim opened his window so he could get a better view of a jet coming in for a landing. The giant's wheels gently touched the ground, and it rolled down the runway and stopped. Seconds later, another jet taxied down the runway to start its flight.

The only thing separating the airport from the highway was a chain-link fence. Outside the fence was a graveled area where people could pull off the road to watch planes take off and land. Jim asked Raymond to stop the car, and the chauffeur immediately complied.

Jim owned a small twin engine plane. As a pilot, he enjoyed watching other pilots displaying their skills. Now as he watched, he remembered the few times he and Christine had flown off together on vacation. That was the only quality time Jim and his wife had ever had. He hadn't flown his plane since his divorce eighteen months earlier. He watched several planes take off and land, then, anxious to get to Africa, he instructed Raymond to proceed to the airport.

Bed of Leaves

When the limo stopped before the company jet, Mike, the mechanic, was doing some last minute repairs on the jet's door latch. The pilot and copilot were already in the cockpit studying the flight route, making some last minute safety checks, and preparing to warm up the plane. Mario, the pilot, clambered down the steps and crossed the pavement to greet Jim through the window of the limo. Behind him, the mechanic hurriedly put his tools in his toolbox and started down the steps too. When Mike noticed Jim watching him, he stopped and waved.

"Chuck's still checking out equipment," Mario said, referring to the copilot.

Jim nodded, watching Mike walking away. Ever since he'd become a Christian, people treated him differently. They seemed friendlier, more comfortable around him. He didn't know it was because he treated them with more respect.

Raymond unbuckled his seat belt and slid his seat back, saying, "I'll be right there to open your door, Jim."

Before Raymond could get to the back door, Jim was standing beside the limo. Raymond stopped, looking puzzled. "Sir?" he said uncertainly.

Jim smiled. "Raymond, I can open my own door. From now on, I don't want any of my employees to do anything that would be demeaning or give the impression that they're expected to wait on me.

"Raymond, your job is to drive company personnel safely from point A to point B, and to keep the limo in peak condition and appearance. Nothing more and nothing less." Jim shook Raymond's hand. "From now on, I want you to be more than just my chauffeur, I want you to be my friend."

Raymond's face showed more respect for Jim than it ever had before. "It would be my honor to count you as a friend," he replied. "You will always be welcome in my home."

Jim released Raymond's hand and turned to walk toward the plane, Bible and briefcase in hand. Before he could take a step, Mike approached him.

"Good morning, Jim." Mike reached out to shake Jim's hand.

Jim slipped his Bible into his other hand so they could shake hands. "Good morning, Mike."

As Jim and Mike talked about the plane's minor mechanical problems, Raymond took Jim's bags out of the limo's trunk and carried them onto the plane. Before Jim and Mike finished their conversation, Mario joined them.

"Will your family be OK for a few days while you're in Africa?" Jim asked him.

"Yes sir," Mario replied. "Pat's brother will be here if she needs any help."

"OK then, if you're ready, let's go to Africa." Jim put his hand on Mario's shoulder and jokingly spun him around, and they both climbed up the stairs to the plane.

Raymond waited at the door of the plane. Jim put his hand on Raymond's shoulder. "Thanks, Raymond, for carrying my bags on the plane."

Raymond grinned and left.

Chapter 3

Africa Bound

Within minutes, the company jet was in the air and slowly ascending to 33,000 feet. Mario leveled the plane and set the speed at 525 miles per hour. The plane settled into a smooth flight pattern.

Jim looked out the window and noticed God's handiwork filling the sky above and below the plane. Below, white, puffy clouds looked like snow-covered mountaintops. When they occasionally cleared, Jim glimpsed distant green trees, lakes, and roadways. Above, all he could see was clear sky.

Chuck, the copilot, walked back to where Jim was sitting. He leaned over and placed his hand on Jim's shoulder. "Is everything OK, sir? Can I get you anything?"

"Thanks Chuck," Jim replied absently, still looking out the window, "but I'm fine."

"Nice day," Chuck said. "Why don't we all just go fishing?"

Jim turned and grinned at Chuck. "I've been looking out across the sky and it keeps me thinking," he said, and turned back to look at the sky again. "It fascinates me, how big space is. Space is a mystery that man will never have all the answers to solve."

Chuck sounded uncertain when he replied, clearly not understanding where Jim was going with this. "To me, space is just what it implies. Nothing but space."

Jim looked back at Chuck. "Space is more than that. Space is planets and solar systems. People think about the sun, the moon, and all the stars and occasionally they think about the vastness of space. What people don't think about is that space has no stopping point." He shook his head. "It's hard for me to understand that space goes on and on, with no end to it. Everything earthly has an end, but not space. Everything that is spiritual has no end to it. Could it be that space is a part of heaven?"

Bed of Leaves

Just as Jim finished his last sentence, the plane hit an air pocket. It jerked up and down as if it were hitting chug holes or bumps in the sky. Chuck smiled. "Jim, I think everyone has their own theories about space. As for me, I just don't know." He looked toward the front of the plane. "Mario might need my help. You may want to fasten your seat belt."

Jim located his seat belt and fastened the ends together. Chuck started walking toward the front of the plane. When he got close to the cockpit, the plane hit another air pocket and lunged. Chuck disappeared through the door.

Tired, Jim laid his head back against the seat. Within minutes he was in a deep sleep. As he slept, a foggy black image appeared in his mind. As he observed the blackness, a white dot appeared in its center and grew bigger and bigger until it completely overtook the vision. Suddenly the image exploded into a blueness filled with a hundred white and black dots.

Even in his dream, Jim was curious. What did it mean, or did it mean anything at all? The black and white dots turned into the faces of men, women, and children, people of every race, every religion, and every country.

Jim knew he was dreaming, but he was still without understanding. He could hear himself shouting in his dream, "Father, are you trying to show me something or is this just a dream?"

The dots with faces in them began to click into different faces. The faces began flashing in rapid succession.

A booming voice entered Jim's dream. Jim knew it came from heaven. The dots with the faces kept changing.

"Jim," the voice thundered. Immediately Jim could see a small image of himself standing in front of the blueness and the dots with the faces. *"The blueness you see is heaven. The dots with faces in them are people whose names will be written in the Lamb's Book of Life. The faces are those of the people who will be led to salvation because of the work God sent you to do in Africa. Many of them will find Jesus directly because of the food they receive. Many more will have their eyes opened because of the influence of the news media and word of mouth."*

Jim was dumbstruck, but found the energy to ask, "Sir, I conclude that you are not God, but you are . . . of the heavenly host?"

"I came not to deceive you, Jim," the voice replied. *"I am not God; I was sent to reveal these things to you. To help give you strength to do your work diligently and without faltering."*

"Sir," Jim replied, "I don't know what to do when I get to Africa."

The voice boomed, *"Be not concerned; God will show you the way."* With that, the voice was gone, and the dots with the faces disappeared. The image of him vanished. The blueness was all Jim could see. Even that began to fade, as if it were becoming transparent. Jim glimpsed something else behind the blueness.

Bed of Leaves

Suddenly he found himself on the opposite side of the blueness, looking at a small image of himself. The image was viewing two angels in the sky as they descended toward him. The angels carried something between them, each holding one end of the object. As the angels got closer to the image of himself, Jim could see they were carrying a small bed-nothing more than matted leaves laid across two poles. Laying on the bed of leaves was a young black girl. Her knees hung over the edge of the bed of leaves. When the angels reached the image of him, they laid the bed holding the young black girl at the feet of his image.

Jim knew there was something special about this girl. Her body was almost lifeless. As the image of himself looked at her, Jim could see that she was in a state of poor health. She lay on her right side, too weak to rise. Her arms and legs were thin and appeared twisted. Her bones were covered with loose, discolored skin. Scabbed-over sores were evident above her right eyebrow and under the left side of her lower lip. The young girl's hair was thin and matted. Her stomach was swollen from hunger.

Jim saw the image of himself looking at her face. Her sunken eyes opened and a tear ran down the side of her face onto the mat. His dream image dropped to his knees and covered his face with his hands. Tears ran through his fingers. Tears also ran down the sleeping Jim's cheeks, dripping onto his shoulder, as he watched the dream image of himself crying.

The two angels ascended back to heaven. As Jim looked on, the image of himself gently slipped his hand under the young black girl's head, then bent to kiss her on the forehead. A sick feeling came over Jim as he watched his dream image lower the young girl's head down to the mat. His dream image rose and put his hands together as if to pray. He lifted teary eyes toward heaven and shouted, "Father, how could you allow this young girl to suffer so?"

A booming voice interrupted the vision. *"Jim,"* the voice said, *"the vision you see is yet to come. She will be the first to be delivered to you. Many more will follow."*

The voice paused. Jim considered what the voice said.

"The girl's name is Rhasha and she lives in Africa. Remember her, Jim. She will be a blessing and an inspiration to you for the rest of your life."

Jim looked at the image of himself and the young black girl, wondering what part she would play in his life. The voice spoke no more. The image of Rhasha on the bed of matted leaves faded away. All that remained of the vision was the image of himself. Within seconds, the image of himself disappeared too.

Instantly, Jim found himself high in the sky, looking through the windows of a small plane. Jim could see the propellers on the engines turning rapidly; he heard the deafening noise the twin engines made as they pulled the plane through the sky. Inside the plane he saw a girl, and he was made aware that this was also Rhasha, even though the girl Jim saw in the plane was nothing like the Rhasha he'd seen with the angels. This Rhasha was healthy and pretty. Her face was like that of an angel. She was crying, and she appeared to be praying to God. A light blue aura surrounded her. Jim marveled at her beauty.

He could see a mountain range coming into view through the windshield, and knew Rhasha's tear-filled eyes couldn't see the mountains looming in front of her. He knew that if Rhasha didn't turn the plane, she would crash.

"Rhasha, turn the plane, you're going to crash!" Jim yelled, forgetting this was a dream. "Rhasha, please turn the plane."

Jim watched in horror as the plane crashed into the mountain. The plane burst into flames and rolled down the side of the mountain.

He saw the image of himself again, sobbing. “Rhasha,” his dream image said, “I love you.”

Sadness filled Jim’s heart and tears welled in his eyes. He couldn’t understand why the image of himself said he loved Rhasha.

Jim fell back into a deep sleep and saw no more dreams. He slept soundly for several hours. When he awoke, sunlight streamed through the window onto his face. The sound of the jet engines was no more than a low, whistling hum on the inside of the plane. The temperature was a comfortable seventy degrees. He was slumped down in his seat. He sat up straight, straightened his clothes, and hand brushed his hair. Then he looked out the window and downward. He could see the ocean.

Still tired despite the nap, he laid his head back against the seat and closed his eyes. Then he remembered the dream he’d had, just hours before. Jim was sure it was more than a dream. It was a vision. Jim could remember every detail as if it had really happened.

The young girl who crashed in the plane-what did it mean? The voices told Jim what every vision meant except for that one, the fiery mountain collision. Was the young girl, Rhasha, going to die? Jim couldn’t get it out of his mind. Why was Rhasha by herself in the plane when she crashed? Why did his dream image say “Rhasha, I love you”?

Little did Jim know that these questions would haunt him for the rest of his life.

Several times during the next few hours, Chuck or Mario checked on Jim to see if he needed anything or to let him know the flight status. Several times Jim got up to stretch, use the rest room facilities, or wash his face.

Hours later, the wheels of the plane gently touched down on the runway in Nairobi. Jim waited patiently until it came to a complete stop in front of a rented hangar. Chuck opened the door and steps automatically unfolded out from the plane.

Jim rose and met Mario and Chuck in the cockpit. "Mario, bed the plane down in the hangar and make sure that everything is locked up. I'm going to the hotel. I'll send a taxi back to get you and Chuck."

As Jim turned to leave the cockpit, Mario stood to escort him off the plane. "Jim," he asked, "what are our plans at this point?"

Jim thought for a moment. "You and Chuck stay here in Nairobi for a day, and get some rest." Jim's brow wrinkled as he thought. "I'll be busy at the embassy, so the day after tomorrow, I want you to take the plane back to Dallas."

Mario nodded. "Don't worry about the jet, we'll get it back to Dallas. I wish you the best of luck, here in Africa."

Chuck jumped in before Jim could comment. "If you need any help, Jim, you know Mario and I would be glad to stay."

"No," Jim insisted, "they need you two back in Dallas."

"All right, we'll see you on the next trip. You be careful. Africa can be a dangerous place."

Jim shook Chuck's hand. "I will. And I'll see you when you come back to get me."

Mario reached out to shake Jim's hand, and they said good-bye. Then Jim gathered his bags and walked down the ramp to the taxi waiting to take him to the hotel.

Minutes later, the taxi deposited him at the Ambassador Hotel. Jim asked the driver to return to the airport to get Mario and Chuck, then checked into the hotel.

Bed of Leaves

He hadn't seen much of Africa, but what he had seen so far didn't look too bad, Jim mused as he waited for the desk clerk to give him a key card for room 214. He was happy to learn that Kenya's primary language was English.

He followed the bellhop who took his bags to his room, then thanked him for his help and gave him a tip. He didn't stay in his room, though. He was tired and hungry-he had to get something to eat. He closed the door to his room and rode the elevator back down to the first floor, ate a chicken-fried steak in the restaurant, then returned to his room to relax for the rest of the day. He could start his work the next day, fresh and relaxed. Jim fell asleep before Mario and Chuck got to the hotel.

Chapter 4

2000 Acres

Bed of Leaves

Early the next morning, Jim hired a guide to drive him everywhere he needed to go. His first stop was the American Embassy. He needed information about Africa-specifically, the value of land in the area, and the name of a good realtor. The Embassy personnel contacted sources in the region and sent Jim to one firm after another. Nobody had what Jim was looking for.

Jim talked to Mario and Chuck only once before they boarded the plane to go to the United States. That was the last time he saw them.

At the end of the week, Jim was awakened by the high pitched tone of the ringing telephone. Pushing the covers back and dropping his legs over the side of the bed, he turned on a lamp, then picked up the phone. "Hello," he mumbled.

"Good morning, sir," the hotel manager replied. "I'm so sorry to wake you at six o'clock in the morning, but I have a man here who insists on speaking with you."

Jim rubbed the sleep out of his eyes and scratched his nose. "It's all right," he said sleepily, "but who is the man, and what's his visit about?"

The manager cupped his hand over the phone while he asked the man the questions. Jim could hear a muffled conversation, then the manager uncupped the phone. "He says his name is Jackie Short and he wants to talk to you about a land deal."

Jim stood up with the phone in his hand. "Tell him I'll be in the lobby in about fifteen minutes."

Jim didn't have time to take a shower. He quickly donned a pair of comfortable, sloppy jogging pants and a pullover shirt, brushed his teeth, then rode the elevator down to the first floor.

The lobby was large and elegant, with several sofas, end tables, and lamps scattered over a beautiful plush carpet. Near the door was a large picture window with long, thick curtains. A fairly well-dressed white man who appeared to be in his mid-forties stood looking out the picture window. He was the only person in the lobby, so Jim walked toward him. Jim was halfway across the lobby before the man turned around, saw Jim walking toward him, and met him in the center of the lobby. Both men shook hands.

"Good morning, Jackie," Jim said. Jackie returned the greeting, but then seemed reluctant to speak further, so Jim continued. "I understand you have some land for sale?"

Jackie eyed the sloppy clothes Jim was wearing. "Can you afford two thousand acres?" he asked.

Jim looked down at his clothes and then looked at Jackie's clothes. He smiled. "Jackie, if the price is fair and the land suits my needs, I have money to buy it."

Jackie looked embarrassed. "I don't own the land," he said, "but I represent an elderly gentleman who does." He held up a small map of the area and pointed at a handwritten X. "This is where the land is located. If you have the time, I can show it to you."

Remembering that he needed a shower, Jim suggested, "If you could come back in one hour, I'll have cleaned up. We could get some breakfast together and be on our way."

"OK," Jackie said, "shall we meet in the restaurant at about seven-thirty?" He gestured toward the entrance to the hotel's restaurant.

"That's fine."

Both men shook hands, and Jim returned to his room to shower and shave. When he finished, he still had about twenty minutes before he was supposed to meet Jackie, so he settled into a colonial-style chair and read through some pamphlets about Africa. His excitement grew. Soon, perhaps, he would have the land he needed to build his village.

At seven-twenty he went down to the restaurant and looked around for Jackie. The dining room was very modern, with highly polished hardwood tables and chairs. A few large plants accented several half walls that cut inward to make little hideaways. He finally spotted Jackie sitting at a table by himself in one of the hideaways.

He walked over and sat across the table from him. "Hello Jackie," Jim said as he pulled his chair closer to the table.

"Howdy partner," Jackie replied, knowing Jim was from Texas. Both men smiled.

"Have you ordered yet?" Jim asked.

"Not yet," Jackie replied, "I just got here, myself."

The waitress walked up with a "Good morning" and handed them menus. "Can I get you something to drink?"

"Yes ma'am," Jim replied. "I think . . . I'll have a glass of orange juice this morning."

The waitress pulled an order pad and pen out of her apron pocket. Jackie ordered coffee, then looked at Jim, smiling. "You're from Texas," he said, "and you ordered orange juice?"

"Sure," Jim replied. "The rest of the world orders coffee, but true Texans always order orange juice."

The waitress looked at Jim with the pad and pen in her hands. "Do you know what you want for breakfast, sir?"

Jim thought about it for a second. "I think I'll just have a bowl of oatmeal," he replied.

"I'll see if we have any oatmeal, sir." The waitress looked at Jackie. "And do you want oatmeal also?"

"No ma'am," Jackie said, "I'll have two eggs over easy, bacon, hash browns and toast, please." Again Jackie looked at Jim and lifted a skeptical eyebrow. "You're from Texas, and you ordered oatmeal for breakfast?"

Jim grinned. "The rest of the world orders eggs and bacon . . . "

All three of them laughed. The waitress put the pad and pen in her apron pocket and took the menus from Jim and Jackie.

"So Jackie," Jim asked when he'd finished his breakfast, "can you tell me anything about this property?"

Jackie had just bitten off a piece of toast with grape jelly on it. He chewed quickly, swallowed, and took a drink of coffee. "Jim," he said, "when I heard about you and the work you plan to do, I knew this land was what you needed. In the center of the land is a large cleared area. It's a perfect location for a village."

They waited while the waitress deposited a tray containing Jim's change on the table, then Jackie leaned forward. "A dirt road runs across the middle of the land and connects with a main road that leads to a village."

"Tell me more," Jim insisted as Jackie ate the last of his hash browns, then drank what coffee was left in his cup. "How far is it from that village?"

"It's only fifteen miles away, but it's a small village. Jim, you just have to see it; you won't be disappointed."

"It sounds like what I need," Jim confessed. "So how much will it cost me?"

Jackie pulled a land survey document from his back pocket. He laid it on the table and slid it toward Jim. As Jim unfolded it, he could see the price of the land handwritten in the left bottom corner.

"The price seems reasonable," Jim said. "Is this in American money?"

Jackie smiled. "Hmm. I'm sure the owner would take American currency, but I don't think you want to do it that way."

Jim chuckled. He liked Jackie's personality. "Are we ready to go?" he asked.

"I am, if you are, Jim."

They left tips, Jackie retrieved the survey document and put it in his back pocket with the map, and the two men walked out to the parking lot and got into Jackie's car.

A jeep pulled up behind them, blocking them in. A heavyset black man who looked like he didn't worry too much about personal hygiene got out of the jeep and walked up to Jim's side of the car. Jim recognized his guide, Fishman.

Fishman bent over and laid his arms along the opened window. "Good morning, Jim," he said, "where you headed?"

Jim hadn't seen Fishman walking up to the car, so the man's voice startled him. "Oh, good morning, Fishman. I'm glad you're here."

The smell from Fishman's armpits almost gagged Jim. Fishman wore sloppy, dirty clothes and the stubble on his face indicated that he hadn't shaved in several days.

"We were just on our way to find you, Fishman," Jim continued. He had to hold his breath as he spoke. Every now and then, he turned his head away from Fishman and breathed-inconspicuously. "Jackie's going to show me some land, so you take the day off, with pay."

Fishman straightened up and backed away from the door. Jim began to breathe freely again. Jim didn't like to be rude, but he wanted Fishman to smell better before he rode with him. "That might give you time to take a bath, Fishman," he added.

Fishman ignored Jim's remark. "OK," he replied. "So do you want me to meet you here tomorrow at the same time?"

Jim thought about it for a second, then nodded. "Be here about eight o'clock, with clean clothes on and your face shaved."

Fishman turned and walked toward his jeep. "I'll be here boss. I'll see you in the morning." He got back in his jeep and drove away.

Jackie drove his car out of the hotel parking lot and onto the main road. Within seconds, he accelerated to the little car's top speed. The car top was down, and the wind blew through Jim's hair. The car hit every pothole in the road. Jackie had the pedal on the floor, but all the little car could do was forty-five miles an hour. Jim wondered if they would ever get to the property.

"How long will it take to get there?" Jim asked.

"At our present high rate of speed," Jackie shouted, "a little over an hour."

Jim returned Jackie's smile. "I noticed you had the afterburners kicked in."

During the next hour, Jim and Jackie discussed and solved all of the world's problems. Jim was really happy when he found out Jackie believed in Jesus Christ. He finally told Jackie what he had been thinking about all morning. "Jackie," he said, speaking from his heart, "I hope in the future you and I will become good friends."

"I'd like that," Jackie replied. "I have a lot of respect for you and what you're planning to do. I'm also glad to know that you and I will continue to be friends in heaven."

Jim was pleased. "A friendship that will extend past a lifetime and into eternity."

41
Bed of Leaves

As the car chugged, rattled, clanged, and occasionally even backfired along the road, Jackie finally found what he was looking for. "Jim," he said, "just ahead is a big tree on your right. Do you see it?"

Jim strained to see which tree Jackie was talking about, but there were several tall trees. He saw one tree with a much thicker trunk than the others. "Are you talking about that short, fat tree next to the road?"

"Yes," Jackie replied, "the one with the big branch that shoots straight out from it. That tree marks the corner of the property."

Jim was excited. This land, he thought, might be the land he would do God's work on. He surveyed the picturesque landscape, with a green forest full of wildlife and a breathless blue sky above. Birds flew all around the trees. Jim could imagine the future, with healthy Christian children playing all through these woods.

The car slowed as Jackie prepared to turn right onto a narrow dirt road. He sped a short distance down the dirt road, then ground into a lower gear and pulled to the right side of the narrow road. A large tree trunk lay partially in their path.

"As I told you," Jackie said, "This road runs through the middle of the property. Soon we'll come to a clear area that's large enough for you to build a small community." He pulled around the tree trunk and continued driving.

When the clearing came into view, Jim nodded. "Jackie, from what I see, this land is perfect. Tomorrow I want to check out the geography of the area and talk to the locals. I'll let you know the day after tomorrow if I want to buy it."

"That's fine, Jim," Jackie replied, understanding that Jim wouldn't rush into a deal of this scope. "But I think you'll take it, so I'll spend tomorrow getting the paperwork together."

Jackie brought the car to a stop in the center of the clearing, and they got out to stretch their legs and look around. After a few seconds, Jackie leaned comfortably against the fender of his car and gazed into the distance, deep in thought. His mother was in poor health, and he was worried about her. When he finally came back to earth and looked around, he saw Jim about a hundred feet away on the opposite side of the car. A light blue glow surrounded Jim as he knelt on the ground with his hands clasped together, deep in prayer.

The Holy Spirit suddenly filled Jackie's body. His ears went deaf. Not a blade of grass was blowing. Everything seemed to move in slow motion, and the sky grew dim. He heard a humming sound that progressed from soft to loud. The humming sound began to pulsate. After a few seconds, it faded, then ceased.

Jackie looked up at the sky. At an angle well above Jim's head, angels held a window open into heaven. He could see the throne room of God, shining with a radiant, sparkling light. As Jim prayed, a foot-wide beam of light shot upward from his head, tapering to a thin line as it entered heaven.

Jackie could see every word of Jim's prayer form at his lips and expand to the width of the beam. Every word seemed to snap out of Jim's mouth to ascend to heaven on the beam of light as if it was on a typewriter, being typed one letter at a time.

Jackie looked around. He saw many beams of light ascending from the ground at different places all around Africa. Each beam of light ended at the same point in heaven. Jackie knew the beams of light were the prayers of God's people. Each beam of light had a prayer written on it and the words scrolled toward the light in the throne room.

Jackie read the words "In Jesus' name, Amen" as they formed at Jim's lips and scrolled to heaven, then only the beam of light was left. It disappeared and the four angels pulled the window to heaven shut. The sky went back to normal, and Jackie could hear again. The light blue aura around Jim's body shrank to a thin black line and disappeared. Jackie again heard a humming sound that grew louder, then began to pulsate. After a few seconds, it faded away. Jackie felt a light breeze ruffling his hair. The sky became bright and everything returned to normal motion.

Jackie knew what he'd seen was a vision. It was the first vision he had ever seen.

Jim was still kneeling on the ground. He opened his eyes and reached down to pick up a handful of dirt, unaware that Jackie was watching him. While sifting the dirt through his fingers, Jim lifted a small rock and rolled it around in his other hand. Finally he stood up and flung the rock across the clearing. He dusted off his hands and walked back to Jackie's car.

Jim noticed a strange look on Jackie's face. "What's the matter, Jackie?"

Tears welled up in Jackie's eyes. "Jim, could I ask a favor of you?"

Jim saw the anguish in Jackie's face. "Jackie," he said gently, "all you need to do is ask."

Jackie cupped his hands over his face and spoke in a whimper. "The next time you pray, would you say a prayer for my mother?"

"I'd be happy to," Jim replied.

"Tell God I love my mother very much," Jackie said. "Ask him, if he must take her, could she go to sleep without much pain?" Jackie ran the tips of his fingers underneath his eyelids to wipe the gathered tears away.

"Jackie, we'll both pray for her on the way to the hotel."

Jackie wiped his wet fingers on his pant legs and opened the car door. He slid into the driver's seat and slammed the door. The door didn't latch tight so he slammed it again as Jim got in on the passenger side. Jackie started the car and put it in gear. As he drove, Jim prayed out loud all the way back to the hotel.

In his hotel room, Jim lay back on his bed, thinking about the land and what he needed to do next. He realized he didn't have any plans for the rest of the day. He wanted to get out of his room and do something, but he didn't know what. All he'd eaten during the day was a bowl of oatmeal, but he still wasn't hungry. Then he recalled seeing a large, heated, indoor swimming pool across the lobby from the restaurant. No one seemed to use the pool during the day. Jim decided to go for a swim. He cut off a pair of old blue jeans about knee length and changed into them and a pullover shirt, then hung the dress suit he'd been wearing in the closet. He picked up a towel and his key card, and headed for the hotel swimming pool.

Jim threw his towel and key card on a chair, then walked to the edge of the pool. He thought about God sitting on his throne with Jesus at his right hand side. Jim dipped his foot in the water to check the temperature. Satisfied that it was warm enough, he entered the pool at the shallow end, planning to slowly work his way toward the deep end.

When Jim entered the water, he could see the texture change. It felt smooth, like oil. When the water got too deep to walk, Jim swam to the middle of the deep area. A blue glow filled the swimming pool. It extended out and over the pool like an egg-shaped dome.

The glow made Jim want to talk to God. He closed his eyes. "Father," he prayed, "I love you and I praise your holy name." He could hear the humming sound, growing louder, then pulsing. After a few seconds, it faded away. Jim stopped swimming. He felt his body being pulled out of the water until he knelt on its surface. It felt like a cushioned floor. "Please forgive me of my sins," he said, "and have mercy on my soul."

A warmth entered his body. It tingled all over. His soul was now one with God. Overcome with the feeling, Jim began to cry. Tears ran down his cheeks. "Father, I want to please you more than anything in the world. Please love me, Father," he whimpered, "and let me always feel the love I feel right now." Eyes still closed, he raised his arms as if he were reaching for God.

The warmth Jim felt inside began to envelop him on the outside. Something that felt like arms wrapped around him and held him tight. Jim could hear a voice softly whispering in his ear, *"Jim, I love you so much that I gave my only son for you, and I will always love you."*

Jim lost all his strength and his arms fell down to his sides. All that held him up was the warm love that surrounded his body. He was aware of his surroundings, but he felt like he was somewhere else. It felt like heaven. Jim bathed in the warmth of the Holy Spirit.

"Father," Jim said, "I appreciate what Jesus did for me and I will always love him, too. I pray these things in the name of Jesus. Amen."

The Holy Spirit released Jim's body so he could slip back into the pool. Jim began treading water to stay afloat. He could hear the humming sound rising, thrumming for a few seconds, and then fading to nothing. The soft blue glow remained, but Jim thought it was a reflection from lights somewhere around the pool. He continued to feel the warmth of the Holy Spirit. He didn't realize it then, but he would have that warmth for as long as he lived.

The pool didn't have a life guard and no one else was around. Jim had the pool to himself. He began to play in the water. He floated on his back for a while, and swam a few laps around the pool. Finally he swam to the shallow end and sat on a step to think about what heaven was like. After a while, he got tired of the water and decided to get out of the pool and relax. The minute his foot left the water, the glow vanished and the egg-shaped dome dissipated.

Jim walked to his chair, dripping water onto the concrete. When he glanced behind him, he saw his wet footprints on the concrete, glittering like silver. Jim frowned, then shrugged. *It must be a reflection,* he thought. He picked up his towel and dried off, taking special care to dry his hair. Then he settled into a lounge chair and relaxed for about thirty minutes.

After his workout in the pool, Jim's stomach told him it was time to eat. He went back to his room and showered and changed, then ate a good meal in the hotel restaurant and returned to his room and slept until six o'clock the next morning.

Bed of Leaves

The next day, Jim had Fishman drive him out to the proposed property so he could talk to people in the area and check out the terrain. He mostly wanted to get an insight into the unemployment rate in the area, but he also wanted to find out if there were any homeless people there. Jim wasn't sure if this would be the best location to care for hungry people, but he liked the area. *When needy people hear about the village,* he finally decided, *they will find a way to get here.*

Chapter 5

Building A Village

Bed of Leaves

Jim met with Jackie to pay for the land and transfer the deed. It didn't take much time to finalize the transaction. The next item on Jim's agenda was to hire a company to drill a water well. A second company would set up a pump and build a water tank. He also hired a company to set up a small but permanent electric generator system.

Jim visited the Davis Construction Company of Africa and hired them to pave all the roads around the hospital he planned to build, and to widen and pave the narrow road that ran to the main road. He contracted the Buju Excavation and Construction Company to build permanent public rest rooms and showers and to clear all the undergrowth from under and around the trees. They would also start the foundations for the hospital and dining hall. Once the hospital and dining hall were completed, Buju agreed to build thirty small houses and later, a church, swimming pool, and the park. Work would commence in three weeks, when workers had been hired and the necessary equipment and building materials had been delivered to the job site.

By Friday, Jim was happy with the way things were going. Some of the work would begin on Monday, he'd been told. But when he arrived at six-thirty Saturday morning, he found workers all over the place, and saw six jeeps and trailers loaded with workers, driving toward the wooded area to begin clearing the undergrowth from under the trees. Wanting to impress Jim, Bujugy of Buju Construction had hired anyone who had a strong back and was willing to work, instead of waiting three weeks.

Jim instructed his guide to pull off the road and park so he could watch all the activity. Fishman did as he was asked.

A drilling truck was at the location where the water well would be drilled. Workers were raising a small derrick from the back of a truck. Other workers were putting up warning signs. Still others were staking out the routes for the paved roads. Near the center of the clearing, workers were taking measurements, driving in stakes, and running strings from one stake to another for the foundation of the three room hospital. Other workers were unloading shovels and picks from the back of a pickup truck. Foremen in different areas were going over blueprints, bosses were pointing out places where workers should drive stakes, and trucks hauling heavy equipment were pulling into the job site and parking in their designated areas to unload.

People were everywhere. Everybody was busy. Everything was organized. Jim noticed that he wasn't the only one watching all the activity-local residents stood along the tree line, observing all that was going on.

Jim saw workers on the edge of the clearing unloading undergrowth from trailers and throwing the wood into large piles. Foremen set fire to the piles of rotted wood and undergrowth. Red, searing flames and smoke billowed into the sky. Six such fires burned wildly, all around the outer edge of the open area. Smoke filled the sky. Workers continued to bring undergrowth out of the woods and throw it onto the burning piles. A breeze began to blow, fanning the flames higher and higher to mingle with the dust blowing all across the job site.

Jim was anxious to get all the work done, but his first priority was completing the hospital. He had made arrangements with eight doctors in outlying communities to be flown in on a daily basis, at a substantial wage. This was a temporary arrangement until Jim could find a permanent doctor at a more reasonable cost.

Noticing the owner of Buju construction talking to his foreman and pointing to a group of workers, Jim got out of the jeep and walked over to join Bujugy. Fishman followed him. Bujugy saw them coming and met Jim with a handshake.

"Good morning, Bujugy."

"Good morning, Jim," Bujugy replied, then reached out to shake Fishman's hand. Fishman and Bujugy knew each other, but Fishman stayed true to his bad attitude. He didn't say a word and he didn't shake Bujugy's hand. He just turned his head and walked back to the jeep to wait for Jim.

Jim didn't care much for Fishman's bad attitude or his foul language, which Jim had already warned him about three times. At one point, Jim even threatened to get a new guide. But Fishman said he really needed the job and assured Jim that he wouldn't talk that way anymore. Jim let him stay and Fishman had so far stayed true to his word.

"I have two twenty-six foot travel trailers back in the company yard. Neither one of them are being used," Bujugy said as he rolled up his blueprints and put them in a round canister. "I'm bringing one trailer out here to use for an office. I thought maybe you could use the other one to live in until we get your house built."

"Thanks, Bujugy," Jim replied. "That way, I won't have to go back and forth from the hotel every day."

"That's what I was thinking."

Jim looked down the road and saw the dust rising from a utility truck pulling the twenty-six foot trailer destined to be Bujugy's office. When the driver stopped to get instructions from Bujugy, Jim turned to watch a 'dozer operator start his engine. Black smoke blew out of the exhaust stack. The driver dropped the gearshift into reverse and began backing the 'dozer off its trailer. The tracks rolled evenly until the 'dozer was hanging halfway past the end of the trailer. Then the back half of the 'dozer dropped down onto two ramps that ran from the trailer to the ground. When the 'dozer was firmly on the ground, the 'dozer operator lifted the hinged ramps straight up in the air one at a time until they fell flat on the trailer, secured them, then moved the truck out of the way.

The ninety foot by forty foot foundation for the hospital was laid out. Now five workers kicked their shovels into the ground and pulled out big clods of dirt that they tossed inside the marked area before kicking their shovels into the ground for another load. Within minutes a trench began to form. Jim watched their progress while Bujugy was pointing out to the truck driver where he wanted the trailer.

Beyond them, the water well workers had dug a good-size pit and lined it with plastic. A driver backed a water truck up to the pit and pulled the latch. Water gushed out the back of the truck into the pit. When the truck was empty, the driver latched the lid back and drove off to get another load of water.

When Bujugy finished giving instructions to the utility driver, he came back over to Jim. "Jim," Bujugy said, "after the driver unhooks from this trailer, he's going back to get your trailer."

"Good deal," Jim replied. "While he's gone, I'll go back to the hotel and get my stuff."

"OK, but I'll be gone when you get back," Bujugy told him. "When the driver unhooks from your trailer, go ahead and move in. It will be parked near my office trailer."

Jim thought about it and decided he didn't want to live next to the office. "I think I'd rather have it parked out by the tree line."

Bujugy shrugged. "If that's what you want, that's where we'll put it."

Jim and Bujugy said their good-byes. As Jim climbed into Fishman's jeep and fastened his seat belt, he told Fishman to go to the hotel. Fishman nodded, started the jeep, and stomped on the accelerator. The jeep sped down the road. Everyone knew they could only drive ten miles per hour down the road, or the breeze would pick up the dust and blow it all over the area. Fishman had no respect for anyone. As he accelerated to forty miles an hour, dust rolled off his tires and blew across the construction site. Jim could hear men yelling, "Slow down, clown!" as they dusted themselves off.

Very irritated, Jim said, "Fishman, stop the jeep." When Fishman brought the jeep to a stop, he insisted, "Now turn the jeep around and drive ten miles per hour over to the drilling rig." Again, Fishman complied with Jim's demand, and moments later parked beside the drilling rig.

Jim got out of the jeep and walked over to talk with the driller.

"Hi," the driller replied when he approached, "can I help you?"

Jim could tell that the driller didn't know who he was. "I'm Jim Brown," he said. "I own this land. Do you have some kind of sprinkler system that you could put on the back of your water truck?"

"Yes sir, we have a bar that goes across the back of the truck, and the truck has a pump."

"Good. I'd like your driver to spray the dirt road down so it won't be so dusty," Jim said, then added when the driller hesitated, "Don't worry, I'll pay extra for it."

The driller brightened. "OK. We need this next load of water, but I'll send him back to get some more."

"Where is he getting water from?" Jim asked.

"He's loading at the river. We have a pump down there."

Jim nodded. He thanked the driller and got back in the jeep. "Fishman," he said, "let's go to the hotel, but take it slow."

As Fishman drove them slowly through the construction site, Jim counted eight fires blazing. Dust and smoke filled the air. Several workers had covered their noses and mouths with pieces of torn rags. As they passed through the wooded area, Jim saw workers chopping away at the undergrowth while others dragged the brush over to pile it on a trailer.

Jim and Fishman had very little to say to each other as the jeep turned left onto the main road and sped up to fifty miles per hour. When they got to the hotel, Jim left Fishman in the jeep while he went to his room, packed his bags, and went down to the main desk to check out. On the way back to the construction site, Jim had Fishman pull into a local grocery store and wait while he purchased several bags of groceries. Once he'd deposited the groceries in the back of the jeep, they continued the drive to the construction site, and arrived at the entrance of Jim's property about an hour later.

As Fishman turned onto the narrow dirt road, Jim could see that it was still dusty. He looked ahead and saw the water truck coming slowly toward them. As it got closer, Jim could see water spraying out from the back of the truck. Behind the truck, the dust had settled.

Bed of Leaves

There was no sign of Jim's trailer. The utility truck was gone, so Jim knew the driver was on his way to get it. Jim and Fishman sat in the jeep and watched the fires burning. The smoke made Jim's eyes tear.

"I've had enough of this," he finally said under his breath. "Something's got to be done about it."

Jim got out of the jeep and walked over to Bujugy's foreman, Randy. Randy stopped what he was doing when he saw Jim coming.

Jim said, "We have a problem with all these fires."

"I know, Jim," Randy replied, his tone slightly apologetic, "but we have to burn all that undergrowth."

"I understand that, but does it have to be today?"

Randy frowned. "What do you mean? If we burn it today or tomorrow, it doesn't matter. It still has to be burned."

"Yes, but wouldn't it be more comfortable for everyone if we didn't have all this smoke?" Jim could tell that Randy was puzzled. "Randy, the workers can pile the brush up as high as they can, and in a couple of weeks, we could set it on fire. It would all burn in one day and we wouldn't have to put up with all this smoke every day."

Randy's brows rose in comprehension. "OK Jim, I'll see if the water truck driver can spray water on the fires."

"Thanks," Jim said. He returned to the jeep to watch the work around the construction site.

After about an hour, he saw the utility truck coming toward them. "Fishman," he said, "let's go talk to the truck driver."

"Where do you want this trailer, Jim?" the driver asked when Fishman pulled the jeep up next to the driver's door.

"Turn around and follow us." Jim asked Fishman to drive to the entrance of the clearing. When they got there, he said, "Turn left and drive along the tree line. I want to find a place where there's a big gap between fires."

The utility truck driver followed the jeep until Jim found a place he was comfortable with. The driver unhooked from the trailer and set a portable generator nearby. He ran a heavy-duty extension cord between the trailer and the generator. Then he drove away to other duties.

Jim unloaded his bags and groceries from the jeep and put them in the trailer. Before he finished unloading, another truck pulled up. It was loaded with a small water tank that the driver set down near the trailer, then hooked up to the trailer with a water line.

Jim didn't need a guide anymore. He paid Fishman what he owed him, thanked him for his services, and let him go. Jim was now without transportation. He hung around the trailer for the rest of the day, watching the activity.

The next day, no workers showed up for work. It was Sunday, and Jim had put a clause in all the contracts that gave workers Sundays off. He did this to ensure that all workers had one day a week in which to go to church or to spend with family. By choosing Sunday as the contracted day off, he assured that most workers would be off on their day of worship.

Jim believed Saturday was God's holy day, but most people went to church on Sunday. According to the Bible, God had sanctified and made the seventh day of the week holy. It seemed strange to Jim that, in Old Testament days, Saturday had been the day of worship, and in the days of the New Testament, most people worshipped on Sunday. Did Satan somehow trick the whole world into making God's holy day, Saturday, a day of eating, drinking, and drunkenness?

Jim believed Saturday was the day God sanctified, but he had one philosophy: *Believe in the name of Jesus Christ, and thou shalt be saved.* Jim had been baptized in a Baptist church that worshipped on Sunday. In Jim's opinion, any church that taught that Jesus Christ died on the cross for our sins *could* lead souls to heaven.

Nevertheless, Jim had no transportation; he knew *he* couldn't go to church this Sunday, and he felt bad about that. This was the first Sunday since he'd become a Christian that he would miss church.

Jim sat in the doorway of his trailer and created a mental picture of God sitting on his throne. "Father," he prayed, "Please forgive me for my sins and have mercy on my soul." Jim started every prayer with those words. "Father, please forgive me for not going to church this morning and for not having the foresight to arrange transportation."

As Jim prayed, he heard a car stopping nearby. The motor ran for a few moments, then it stopped. Jim kept his eyes closed. He heard a car door shut. "Father," Jim said, "thank you for your many blessings. In Jesus' holy name, I pray. Amen"

Jim opened his eyes and found Jackie standing in front of him. Jackie didn't even give Jim a chance to say hello before he blurted excitedly, "Jim, the Lord spoke to me this morning. The Lord has never spoken to me before."

Jim became excited too. He stood up. "Did he say anything you can share with me, Jackie?"

Jackie began to calm down. He nodded. "I was having breakfast and I said grace. Before I could open my eyes, a voice spoke to me!" Jackie shuddered. " 'Jackie,' the voice said-He called me by my name, Jim!"

Jim was anxious to hear what God had said. He gestured quickly for Jackie to continue. "OK Jackie," he prompted, "so what did God say?"

"He said, 'Jackie, Jim moved into a trailer house on his land and he has no transportation to church this morning.' The voice blasted loudly at me! 'Go tell Jim you were sent to take him to church,' God said. 'You don't have time to go back to your church, so take him to his church.' "

"Jackie," Jim said, "I'm sure the voice you heard was not God, but a messenger for God."

"Jim, he called me by my name! I couldn't even eat breakfast! The Holy Spirit has been with me all the way out here!"

"Praise God, Jackie," Jim said, "you're a dear friend. Let me get my Bible and we can go."

When Jim got back to the car, Jackie was already in the driver seat. "Jackie," Jim asked as he climbed in on the passenger side, "how is your mother doing?"

"You wouldn't believe it," Jackie replied. "The doctors can't understand it. She is completely healed. You can't tell she was ever sick." Jackie looked like he was going to get emotional, but he managed to control himself.

"I'm really happy for you and your mother," Jim exclaimed. "Isn't God great?"

"He certainly is," Jackie agreed with much feeling.

The car spit, sputtered, and sometimes backfired its way to church. Jackie seemed to be deep in thought. Jim guessed he was thinking about his mother and how God healed her. Jim sat quietly in the passenger seat, enjoying the breeze blowing through his hair.

Finally Jackie broke the silence. "Jim, my mother had cancer and God healed her. He's been good to me and now I have a strong desire to show him my appreciation."

"God knows your heart," Jim said. "He knows you love him."

"I know," Jackie said, "but I want to do something to show God I love him."

"What do you have in mind?" Jim asked.

Jackie hesitated for a second. "Jim, I want to help people. I'd like to be a part of the work you're doing. If it's OK with you."

"Jackie, I'm glad you asked. I need a good friend, one that would also find pleasure in helping people."

They continued toward church without any problems, even though Jackie's car sounded like it was going to blow up.

"Jackie," Jim asked after a few minutes, "are you busy tomorrow?"

"Not really. I thought I would come out to see all the work going on."

"I'd like that. While you're here, could you take me to buy a car?"

"Sure, that wouldn't be a problem."

"Good," Jim said. "And after I buy a car, we can put your car in the shop. You can drive my car until you get yours fixed."

Jackie nodded. "I have the commission I made from selling you the land."

"No Jackie," Jim insisted, "let me pay for it."

Just as Jackie was getting ready to argue with Jim, his car backfired and the motor began knocking. Jim and Jackie immediately heard the now-familiar humming sound. It progressed from soft to loud, then began to pulsate before fading away a few seconds later. The sky became dim, and everything seemed to go into slow motion. Sparks began popping all around the car, like sparklers on the Fourth of July. Blue lights trailed outward from the each spark. They trailed from the hood of the car and along the sides. The car was vibrating all over.

Jackie pressed on the brake to stop the car. His brakes worked in slow motion. The car finally came to a stop. Jackie and Jim jumped out of the car. The fireworks around the car ceased and the vibrations stopped. Movement returned to normal and the sky brightened. The humming sound rose, pulsed, then after a few seconds, faded.

Jim and Jackie looked at the car in amazement. The car had been transformed from an old, worn out clunker into a newer version of itself. It was clean and sparkling where before it had been dented and dirty. Not a scratch was on it. Even the tires looked new. Even the door Jackie always had to slam shut and latched properly. It was as if the car had just rolled off the assembly line.

Jim and Jackie got back in the car and continued down the road. The engine purred like a kitten. Not a spit, rattle, or clang could be heard.

"We must have scared the car when we talked about putting it in the shop," Jackie said in a voice soft with shock.

Jim laughed. "I don't think that was it. I think God just wanted us to get to church this morning."

Jackie grinned. He accelerated to fifty-five miles per hour and maintained that speed until they arrived in Nairobi. Before long they were sitting in a church pew.

The church services were rewarding, and the Holy Spirit warmed every soul. The music was beautiful and the sermon spoke to every heart. Jim and Jackie left the church with their hearts lifted and their faith stronger than ever.

They returned to Jim's trailer for lunch, then drove down to the river and sat on a steep bank under the shade of the trees. They let their shirttails hang out and rolled up their pant legs so they could hang their bare feet in the water as they spent the rest of the day talking about whatever subject came up. God seemed to be on both their minds a lot.

Jackie stayed the night in Jim's trailer. Both men were awakened in the early morning by the sound of trucks driving onto the site. By six o'clock all the workers had arrived and by six-thirty, the site was bustling with activity, as it had been on Saturday.

Later Jim and Jackie walked around the job site, talking to construction workers. When Jim mentioned to one of the foremen that he was looking for a car to buy, a young black man overheard and eased over to speak to Jim.

"Boss man," he said, "I know someone that has a jeep for sale."

"That's what I need," Jim replied. "I might have to go pick up sick people sometimes. They could be in places that are hard to reach."

"It's a real nice jeep," the man went on, "and he has a fair price on it."

"Good enough. Where can I find him?"

"Boss man, he works for the Roby Sacks Lumber Company. You can find him there until seven o'clock tonight."

"What's his name?" Jim asked.

"Everyone calls him Shorty. He works in the shipping department."

Jim didn't know where the Roby Sacks Lumber Company was, so he asked Jackie for directions.

Jackie replied, "Everyone around here knows where the lumber company is."

"Can you take me over there?"

"Sure. Are you ready to go now?"

"Whenever you are, Jackie."

Jim looked back to the young black man and thanked him. He placed the equivalent of twenty dollars in the man's hand. The young man thanked him as he stuffed the money into his pocket and went back to work.

Jim and Jackie walked to Jackie's car, and Jackie slipped into the driver's seat as Jim went into the trailer to get some money. Moments later they were turning right onto the main road.

Little did Jim know that the lumber company was seventy-five miles away. When he found out how far it was, he stuffed money into Jackie's shirt pocket to cover gas. He hoped Jackie wouldn't argue, but Jackie said, "Jim, I'm not going to take that," and dropped the money into Jim's lap.

"Jackie, I'm a wealthy man, so let me give you something to show my appreciation."

"If I can't help a friend without getting paid for it, what kind of a friend would I be?" Jackie countered.

"I'm using your gas and I want to pay you for your time and trouble."

"Look at it this way, Jim," Jackie argued. "I well overcharged you for your land and made my client a wealthy man."

Jim laughed. "Jackie, you got me a good deal on that land and you know it."

Jackie laughed too. "Yes, Jim, I got you a good deal on the land, and now I want to take my friend to buy a car."

Jim gave up. "OK, Jackie. I appreciate your help. Maybe someday, I can return the favor."

When they arrived at the entrance to the lumber company, Jim could see stacks of logs all around the yard. Heavy equipment unloaded more logs on one side of the yard, while forklifts loaded evenly cut planks onto trucks on the other side of the yard. Jim realized it was a mill, with the sole purpose of cutting whole logs into planks. Jackie told him the planks were shipped to other companies, to do the finishing work.

A long roof protruded from a large warehouse in the center of the yard to rest on wooden poles. Building and roof sat on a two foot high slab of concrete. In the center of the floor under the roof, a large saw blade spun, squaring off tree trunks. Dump trucks waited at a nearby dock to be loaded with the sawdust that blew across the factory floor. On the other side of the sawmill, flatbed trucks waited at another dock to be loaded with planks. Forklifts raced back and forth with stacks of wood.

Jackie pulled his car up to some stairs next to the loading dock and they got out and walked over to a forklift operator who stopped to see what they wanted. Jim asked where they could find Shorty and the forklift operator pointed to a small black man on a different forklift. Jim and Jackie walked toward the thin man, who was loading lumber on a flatbed truck. When he saw them approaching, he stopped what he was doing, shut off the forklift motor, and waited for them on the forklift.

Jim and Jackie shook hands with him, then Jim asked, "Are you Shorty?"

"Yes sir. What can I do for you?"

"I understand you have a jeep for sale."

"I sure do," Shorty replied, "would you like to see it?" He led them a short distance to the company parking lot and pointed to a nice looking jeep parked off by itself. Shorty started the motor and let it run for awhile while he and Jim discussed the price.

"OK," Jim said, "so where do I pick up the title and the jeep?"

"I have the title with me. You can take the jeep with you." He fumbled through the glove compartment, looking for the title.

"Shorty," Jim asked, "if I take the jeep now, how will you get home tonight?"

"My brother can give me a ride home," Shorty replied. "He's the man you talked to when you drove in."

"Are you ready to go, Jackie?" Jim asked when Shorty had pocketed the payment and returned to work.

"I need to check on my mother," Jackie told him, "and it would be closer for me to go home from here."

"OK, I'll see you soon."

"I'll be back in a few days," Jackie told him as he got in his car.

Jim watched him drive out of the parking lot, then climbed into his new jeep and carefully backed out of the parking place. He hadn't driven for several months, and it had been years since he'd driven a vehicle with a standard transmission. As he let off the clutch, the jeep lunged forward. The motor died. Jim started the motor and let out the clutch slowly. The jeep crept forward, then Jim ground into second gear. As he turned onto the main road, he felt more comfortable. He shifted into third, and then fourth. He accelerated to fifty and maintained that speed until he was back on the job site.

As he pulled onto the job site, Jim noted the cement truck parked in front of the hospital foundation. The foundations for the public rest room, the hospital, and the dining room had all been dug and rebar had been erected and wired together inside the trenches. Braces held twelve-inch forms straight on all the outer walls of the trenches. Workers were lowering a trough from the truck to the trench, preparing to pour the contents of the concrete truck inside the forms.

Along the tree line, workers continued to load trailers with undergrowth. Other workers pulled the trailers to big piles of wood and unloaded them. Front-end loaders scooped dirt from between the stakes marking the twenty-foot-wide roadbed bisecting the clearing and hauled it away.

As the weeks went by, the front-end loaders finished digging the roadbed to a depth of a foot, and the road was filled with caliche. A water truck went back and forth, spraying the entire road. Heavy rollers packed the caliche tighter and tighter. A big rain soaked the road thoroughly. As it dried, heavy packers compressed it one last time.

For the next two weeks, workers were allowed to drive on the caliche to help pack it tighter. Then sand was hauled in to cover the caliche. Oil was sprayed on top of the sand and left to harden. Finally, a four inch slab of asphalt was laid over the oil-soaked sand and a white, broken line was painted down the center of the pavement. All the other roads were finished at the same time.

Jim watched as wood poles rose like skeletal frameworks for the thatched panels that formed the walls of the hospital, dining room, and church. The paneled walls could easily be loosened at the bottom and pushed out and up to be braced open. The roofs were built on top of wooden A frames and thatched with straw. Before long, doors and windows accented the structures. The ceilings were nothing more than horizontal poles laid across the vertical wall poles and covered by bamboo strips. Jim followed this rural African design for all the public buildings, so the people that gathered in them would feel more at home.

The foundations for the rest room area and ten houses had been poured, and workers completed these next. The houses were also made of sturdy bamboo frames and thatched straw, with wooden floors above the concrete foundations. Twenty more houses remained to be built.

A large water tank now towered above the empty village. An electrical generator had been installed and wires run underground to all buildings. A few streetlights had been added, mostly around the hospital, dining hall, and residential area. The swimming pool and park area were now complete. The forested area had been cleaned up and the piles of undergrowth burned. Finally, a truckload of food was delivered and shelved in a storeroom next to the dining hall.

Jim stood in front of the hospital, admiring the finished buildings. He had waited a long time for this moment. He knelt on the ground and prayed, "Father, please forgive me of my sins and have mercy on my soul. Father, the important buildings are finished, and ready to receive the needy. We have a doctor and nurse on staff, but no patients. We have a cook, a preacher, and a pilot. We have food, medicine, and vacant houses. Father, all the hospital beds are empty and the storeroom is full. If it be your will," he pleaded, "send us the hungry and the homeless, the sick and the helpless. Father, I pray for these things in the name of Jesus Christ. Amen."

Chapter 6

Rhasha's Bed

Jim stood up and looked down the road, as if he expected God to answer his prayer immediately. In the distance, he could see two black men walking toward him. They carried something between them, each one holding an end. As the men got closer, Jim could see that they were carrying a small bed, really nothing more than matted leaves laid across two poles. A young black girl lay on her right side on the matted leaves with her knees hanging over the edge.

The two black men laid the bed holding the young black girl at Jim's feet. Her body seemed lifeless. Loose, discolored skin covered the twisted bones of her thin arms and legs. He saw scabbed-over sores above her right eyebrow and below the left side of her lower lip. Her hair was thin and matted, her stomach swollen from hunger. As Jim watched, her sunken eyes opened slightly and a tear ran down the side of her face onto the mat.

Jim dropped to his knees and covered his face with his hands. Tears ran through his fingers. The two men stepped to the side, out of Jim's way. Jim knew there was something special about this girl. He gently slipped his hand under her head and bent down to kiss her on the forehead. A sick feeling came over him as he lowered the young girl's head down to the mat.

Jim stood up and put his hands together. He lifted his tear-filled eyes toward heaven. "Father," he said, "how could you allow this young girl to suffer so?"

Jim looked at the girl on the bed of leaves. "I've seen this girl before," he whispered. He looked at the two men. "Is her name Rhasha?"

"Yes, " the taller man replied, "but how could you know that?"

Jim put his hand on the man's shoulder. "I saw her in a dream," he said, "and God's messenger told me her name."

Bed of Leaves

Jim gently lifted Rhasha from the matted leaves and carried her inside the hospital.

Thirty empty beds lined the walls of the hospital. Rhasha would be his first and only patient. The doctor and nurse hurried to her side as Jim laid her in the first bed. The nurse quickly stripped off Rhasha's tattered clothes and washed her body with cool, clean water. She put a clean gown on her and washed her hair. The doctor put an IV in her arm and nutrients trickled through Rhasha's veins.

The two men who had carried Rhasha to the hospital watched from the entrance. Both men were tall and very thin, their stomachs swollen from hunger, their faces gaunt. They leaned on the door frame, as though they had very little strength.

"Jim," the doctor said, pulling his attention back to the girl on the bed, "a few more days, and this girl would be dead."

Jim heard a *thunk* and quickly looked toward the entrance. One of the men had collapsed in the doorway. The other man was helping him up. Jim and the doctor rushed over to them. The fallen man had tears in his eyes. Jim knew he'd overheard what the doctor said about Rhasha.

"Are you Rhasha's father?" Jim asked.

The man tried to answer Jim's question, but he broke down, and covered his face with his hands. Tears ran through his fingers. "Please don't let my little girl die," he sobbed, "I love her so much."

"Rhasha will not die," Jim assured him, then asked in a gentle voice, "What is your name?"

"Thamish." The man regained control of himself and wiped the tears away. His eyes were on the bed. Jim turned to watch as the nurse took Rhasha's temperature, checked her blood pressure, and took a blood sample. The doctor went into his office to get some medication.

"Thamish," Jim said, "is there anyone else in your family?"

"My wife Thasha," Thamish replied. "And I have a son."

Jim looked at the other man. "What is your name?"

"Rantutu," the man said. "I have a wife and a three-year-old son."

"Where are they?" Jim asked.

"Out by the big road," Thamish replied, "sitting under the trees."

Jim immediately rushed out of the hospital and jumped into his jeep. He sped to the entrance at the main road. On the left-hand side, Jim saw two women sitting with their backs against a tree, and a teenage boy and a baby sitting on the ground beside them. They were all very thin, with sunken faces and swollen stomachs.

Jim pulled the jeep up in front of them and yelled, "Come, get in. I'll take you to get some food."

They were all sick and weak. Jim helped them into the jeep, then raced back to the hospital.

Rhasha's mother's face was creased with worry. "Is Rhasha . . . " She started crying, fearing the worst.

Jim wished he could put his arms around her and make all her fears go away. "Rhasha is doing good," he said, "and soon she will be a very beautiful girl."

Jim drove past the hospital and stopped in front of the dining hall. "Rhasha is in that building over there," he said, and pointed across the road to the hospital. "She's sleeping right now, so let's all go in here and get some food." Jim helped everyone out of the jeep. He picked up the baby and started walking to the dining hall.

Thasha wasn't walking very fast. She continued looking toward the hospital.

"I promise you," Jim said, "Rhasha is doing fine. Come in and let's get something to eat."

Bed of Leaves

Jim finally got all four people inside and asked the cook to get them some food. He then ran across the road to the hospital and convinced Thamish and Rantutu that Rhasha was getting good care. He walked slowly with them to the dining hall. All six people ate, but only small amounts. Jim knew that once they were eating three meals a day, they would have more energy and bigger appetites.

"Is everybody full?" Jim asked once everyone finished eating and the cook had cleared off all the dishes. They all nodded. "OK," Jim said, "you will all probably be sick tonight. The food will throw your bodies into shock." Jim knew they wouldn't understand this, but he wanted to warn them. When they woke up sick in the middle of the night, he wanted them know why. "The food will go through places in your body that are shut down right now. Food will open up these places, and it will be very traumatic for you on the inside. You probably will feel very sick.

"I have houses for you," Jim went on. "The houses are small, but they will protect you from the weather. All the houses have three bedrooms, a living room, a kitchen, and a bathroom."

Jim led them across the road and assigned the two families houses next to each other. He explained to them that they could live there as long as they wanted to, or until they could support themselves. "You can use the swimming pool anytime you desire," Jim said. "I only ask that at least two adults be present when children swim. I'll buy new clothes for you in a few days. OK," Jim said, "these are your homes. Feel free to go inside."

Thamish and Rantutu thanked him and shook his hand. The new tenants went inside to check out their new homes.

Jim went back to the hospital and pulled a chair next to Rhasha's bed. He clasped her left hand between both of his hands. Her eyes were closed, so he didn't talk to her.

About fifteen minutes later, Rhasha's mother, father, and brother walked through the hospital entrance. Jim didn't hear them come in. He was holding Rhasha's hand and praying. A light blue aura surrounded Jim's body. He was saying words that were strange to Thamish's ears.

"Father," Jim said, "Rhasha is a sweet girl who could be a blessing to you, here on earth as well as in heaven. I'll teach her all about you, Father. I'll read the Bible to her whenever I have a chance."

Thamish and his family stood quietly and listened to Jim pleading for Rhasha's life. "Father, someday she could have children that could serve you through eternity. If you would heal her, even her family would know your love. Father, without a miracle from you, she will die."

Jim didn't know Rhasha's family was there or he would not have said that.

Tears flowed from the eyes of Thamish and his wife and son. Thasha moaned in sorrow.

Jim heard the sounds of sorrow and remembered what he'd said. He immediately got off his knees. The blue aura left his body. He rushed over to Thasha, put his arms around her, and kissed her gently on the forehead. "God will heal Rhasha," Jim said. "He has shown her to me in a dream."

Rhasha's mother looked straight into Jim's eyes. Tears ran down her cheeks.

A humming sound filled the air, growing louder and louder. It began to pulsate, then, after a few seconds, it grew softer and softer until it ceased. The hand Rhasha's mother lifted to wipe her cheeks moved in slow motion. The room became dim. A glow developed around Jim and Thasha. Their eyes were locked onto each other's.

Bed of Leaves

Two bright white beams of light shot from Jim's eyes and hit Thasha's eyes, knocking her head slightly backwards. The beams carried a message from God, delivered through Jim to Rhasha's mother. Everyone in the room could see words written between the two beams, but the words were written in a language that no one, including Thasha, could read. The words went into Thasha's head through the bridge of her nose. Once the words were inside her head, she smiled in sudden understanding.

Once she'd received the message, the two beams faded away. The humming sound rose again, pulsated for a few seconds, then waned. The lighting brightened and everyone's movements returned to normal speed. Sounds could be heard in the room again.

Jim looked at Thasha's face. Her tears were gone. She appeared calm and relaxed. He knew the message from heaven had told Thasha that Rhasha would not die.

All along, Thamish had looked like he couldn't figure out if Jim was a con artist or just a good person. Thamish didn't know God, but he believed that Jim cared about Rhasha.

He led his family over to her bedside. They looked at her face. Rhasha's eyes were open. She had been awake the whole time.

Drained by the emotional experience, Thamish and Thasha and their son soon left. They slowly walked across the street to their new home.

Jim stayed with Rhasha and read the Bible to her. The doctor and nurse had been in the doctor's office, watching everything that happened. When Jim started reading the Bible, they came out of the office and pulled up chairs to listen. Jim read the Bible for three hours. Rhasha, the doctor, and the nurse listened to every word he read.

The doctor finished his ten hour shift at eight o'clock and went home. When Jim finished reading, Betty, the nurse, picked up the Bible and went into the office to read more by herself. Jim sat in a chair next to Rhasha and held her hand between both of his. Rhasha didn't sleep; she seemed curious, as though she wanted to see what Jim would do next. She lay with her face tipped toward him.

"Rhasha," Jim said, "you have very pretty eyes. You're a pretty girl. Sweetheart, you're very special to me." He hesitated and gazed into her eyes. "Rhasha, for a few days we're going to feed you through your arm." He wanted her to understand that her body was getting liquid food. "When you get stronger, we'll put you on soft food."

He kissed Rhasha on the forehead, then placed his hand on her cheek. He could feel the warmth of her skin. "Angel, from this day on, you will get stronger and stronger. Soon you will be able to walk, and before you know it, you'll be running all over this place."

Jim talked to Rhasha for an hour. She hung on his every word. Finally he stopped talking. He knew she wasn't going to sleep. Jim had an idea. "Rhasha," he said, "I'm going to leave for a few minutes, but I'll come back. If you're asleep, sweetheart, I won't wake you up. I'll let you sleep, but I'll see you in the morning. OK?" He gently squeezed her hand, and kissed her on the cheek.

Jim ran to his house, grabbed an old guitar that he'd been given, got a drink of water, and ran back to the hospital. When he got inside, Betty was checking Rhasha's blood pressure. After she finished, she gave Rhasha some medication, placed Jim's chair back where he'd had it, and turned to return to the office. As she passed Jim she whispered, "Rhasha's doing real good, Jim."

Rhasha's eyes lit up when she saw Jim. He sat in his chair and rested the guitar in his lap. "Rhasha," he asked, "do you know any songs you want me to sing?" Jim knew she couldn't answer him, but he wanted her to feel like she had a say in what he played. "Do you want me to pick one?" It seemed to Jim that Rhasha might have moved her head slowly up and down to say yes.

Jim slipped his thumb into a guitar pick and lifted the instrument up to his chest. He looked into Rhasha's eyes and began to strum the guitar. Music filled the air. *"This little light of mine, Lord, I'm gonna let it shine. This little light of mine, Lord, I'm gonna let it shine. This little light of mine, Lord, I'm gonna let it shine. Let it shine, let it shine, let it shine."*

In the office, Betty heard Jim singing to Rhasha. She pushed the Bible back and listened.

Jim could tell Rhasha loved the song. Her eyes glittered, and she smiled.

"Jesus gave me light, now I'm gonna let it shine. Jesus gave me light, now I'm gonna let it shine. Jesus gave me light, now I'm gonna let it shine. Let it shine, let it shine, let it shine."

When Jim finished that song, he started another.

"My mommy told me something that every kid should know. It's all about the devil and I learned to not like him so. He certainly causes trouble when you let him in your room."

Happiness and contentment filled Rhasha's face. Her eyelids became heavy. She tried to stay awake, but the soothing music pulled them shut. Before Jim finished the second song, Rhasha was in a deep sleep. Jim set the guitar on the floor and leaned it against the side of the bed. He leaned over and kissed Rhasha gently on the cheek. He knew she had been through a lot of pain in her life.

Sleepiness pulled on Jim's eyelids. He yawned and raised his arms in the air to stretch. Still seated in the chair, he laid his head on the bed beside Rhasha. Soon he was sound asleep. He slept that way until the next morning.

As the bright sun broke through the early morning fog and birds began to echo cheer all around the village, Jim opened his eyes and lifted his head. His eyes met Rhasha's. She had been awake for some time, looking at the top of Jim's head. She smiled when she saw Jim's face.

When Jim saw Rhasha looking at him, he smiled. "Good morning, sunshine," he said.

The nurses had changed shifts, and now Pepper sat in the doctor's office, going over Rhasha's chart. She walked into the patient section of the hospital when she saw Jim talking to Rhasha. She checked the girl's temperature and blood pressure. While Pepper took care of Rhasha, Jim picked up his guitar and leaned it against the wall. He asked Pepper if she would help him turn Rhasha over so she could lay on her other side.

Rhasha was laying on her right side, with her feet pulled up. Pepper took her shoulders while Jim lifted Rhasha's knees to try to roll her over, but her position made the maneuver complicated. "Wait, nurse," Jim said. "I'll put my arms under her body and as I turn her over, you turn her head." Ever so gently, Jim turned Rhasha over as Pepper turned Rhasha's head over at the same time.

When the task was finished, Pepper filled a bucket with lukewarm water and washed Rhasha's face, arms, and hands. Jim turned around so Pepper could wash her breast, stomach, and private parts. Pepper completed Rhasha's bath by washing her legs and feet. She put a clean gown on her and partially covered her with a sheet.

"I'm finished, Jim," Pepper said. "You can turn around now."

Jim turned around. “Sweetheart,” he said, “you have such pretty eyes.” Rhasha’s face seemed to glow.

Pepper was filling out Rhasha’s medical chart. When she finished, she looked up at Jim and said, “She’s getting stronger.” Then she went back to the doctor’s office to do some paperwork.

Jim moved his chair to the other side of the bed. He leaned over to kiss Rhasha on the forehead. Rhasha watched every move Jim made. Jim clasped Rhasha’s hand between both of his and started talking to her again. “Rhasha, I feel so lucky. I’m holding a very pretty girl’s hand.”

As Jim talked to Rhasha, he remembered a calendar hanging in the doctor’s office. The calendar contained twelve large pictures of cowboys sitting on horses. Below the pictures, in large, black, italicized letters, were captions describing what the cowboys were saying. “Sweetheart,” he said, “would you like to look at some pictures?” Jim released her hand and walked into the doctor’s office. He returned a moment later with the calendar and flipped it open to January. Holding it where Rhasha could see it, he pointed to a cowboy riding a bucking horse. “See this, Rhasha?” he said. “This cowboy is waving his hat wildly through the air. He’s yelling, ‘I’m breaking him in.’” Jim watched Rhasha’s eyes move up and down as she looked at the picture. “See how the horse’s back is humped? He’s trying to buck the cowboy off.”

Jim flipped the calendar to the next page. The February picture was a cowboy sitting on a beautiful white horse. Rhasha’s eyes brightened when she saw this picture. “See this? The cowboy is waving at everyone, and he’s yelling, ‘Howdy partner.’ That means the same thing as hello.”

Jim flipped the calendar to the month of March. A young girl, about five years old, sat astride a small pony. She was dressed in children's western clothes, complete with vest and cowgirl hat. "See what she's saying, Rhasha?" Jim pointed to the caption. "She's saying, 'Let's go, little horsey.'" The picture made it obvious that the little girl was gently kicking the pony's sides with her heels.

In the April picture, a horse reared at the sight of a rattlesnake on the ground, and the cowboy had his pistol drawn. "In this picture," Jim explained, "the cowboy is getting ready to shoot the snake." He knew Rhasha probably didn't know what a gun was, so he explained that when the cowboy shot his gun, a bullet would come out the end of the barrel and kill whatever it hit. Jim formed his hand into the shape of a gun and cocked his thumb back as if it were the hammer. "Sometimes," he continued, "when a cowboy shoots his gun, he blows the smoke off the end of the barrel." Jim demonstrated by blowing on the end of his finger. "See this?" He pointed at the caption. "The cowboy's yelling, 'I'm gonna shoot the varmint.'"

Just as Jim flipped the calendar to the month of May, he heard a commotion outside the hospital entrance. He looked up to see if someone was coming in. He waited, but the door didn't open, even though he could see movement through the glass. Whoever it was, couldn't get in.

He rushed to the door to see what the problem was. When he turned the door knob, the door wouldn't open. He looked down to see if it was locked. Someone had inadvertently turned the lock lever to the down position. He pushed the lever up and opened the door.

Standing at the door was a tall, slender, black man. A young black woman and two children lay on the hospital porch. Jim could see they were in a poor state of health. They were in the same condition Rhasha had been in when she was brought to the hospital. Flies irritated the open sores on their skin.

Several other people were standing on the ground, waiting to see what Jim would do. It was obvious that the woman and two children would be the hospital's next patients.

"Man," the tall, slender man at the door said in a deep, gruff voice with a distinct African accent, "we heard you help people."

By this time, Pepper was standing behind Jim, looking around his shoulder. "Nurse," Jim said, "let's get them in beds."

Pepper rushed to the office to get a stretcher. Jim and the slender black man carried the children in and laid them on separate beds. The nurse returned to the porch with the stretcher. She rolled the young woman on her side and slid the stretcher close to her back. With the stretcher in place, Pepper rolled the woman back to her original position, so the young mother was laying on top of the stretcher. The slender black man picked up one end of the stretcher as Jim picked up the other end. They carried the woman into the hospital and eased her off the stretcher and onto the fourth bed.

The doctor wouldn't arrive for two more hours, but Pepper knew what to do. The people standing outside the hospital now stood inside. They watched as the nurse slipped an IV into the woman's arm. The mother appeared to need medical attention more than the children.

Jim asked the bystanders to have a seat in the waiting area-nothing more than several chairs lined up against the wall at the entrance, in the same room as the hospital beds. They all did as he asked.

Pepper hooked IVs to the children and quickly went back to work on the mother. Jim began cleaning one of the children. Pepper checked the mother's blood pressure and temperature.

"Jim," she said, "the mother's not going to make it."

Not knowing what to do, Jim stared despairingly at the young woman. He hadn't considered the fact that people would die in his hospital. He knew he would have to tell the woman's husband. He walked over to the slender black man, who leaned against the office wall with his arms crossed. "Are you the woman's husband?" Jim asked.

"No, man," the black man replied, "my son was playing in the woods outside our village and found them lying together. We don't know who they are. We heard about this hospital," he added, "and thought maybe you could help them."

"We can help the children," Jim replied, "but we think the mother might die."

"That is sad," the man said in his deep bass voice. "The children won't have anyone to take care of them."

"The children will be taken care of," Jim replied. "If you wish, you can leave them with us."

The man nodded. Jim shook his hand. "Thank you for bringing them to us," Jim said. "Any time you know of anybody who needs help, please let us know."

The slender black man motioned for the others to get up, so they could leave. "It's good to know that we have someone to turn to, if we need help," he said.

Jim invited them to eat breakfast at the dining hall. They all accepted his invitation and left the hospital.

Jim returned to the sick woman's bedside. Pepper rolled a heart monitor from the office and positioned it beside the woman's bed. She plugged the electrical cord into the wall socket and taped the monitor wires to the woman's chest, then she turned the monitor on. It was an old-style monitor with a black and white screen. A thin black line ran through the middle of it. Jim and Pepper waited for the monitor to receive information from the woman's heart.

The thin line continued to scroll horizontally across the screen. Suddenly the line shot upward slightly to a peak and then settled back into the straight line. Another peak followed, and another, following the woman's heartbeat.

Jim looked at the woman. The heart monitor was hooked up and the IV was in her arm. An oxygen mask covered the woman's nose and mouth. Nothing more could be done until the doctor arrived.

As he looked at the woman in the bed, he realized more construction needed to be done to the hospital.

Pepper finished giving the woman a sponge bath and covered her with a sheet. She frowned, noticing that Jim was deep in thought. "Jim," she asked, "what are you thinking about?"

Jim sat down on the fifth bed. "Pepper, we need a four wheel drive ambulance and paved driveway to the back of the hospital. And we need to build an emergency receiving area with an unloading dock. The dock needs to be the same height as the floor of the ambulance." Jim looked at the children. "We also need an orphanage, with lots of toys."

He looked back at the dying woman and added solemnly, "We need a small morgue and, regrettably, a cemetery."

The nurse looked into Jim's face and her expression softened in sympathy. She put her hand on Jim's cheek and gazed into his eyes. "Jim, we can't save everyone who comes to us." She took her hand away from Jim's cheek. "Let's grieve for the people that die, but let's celebrate with every life we save. I believe we'll celebrate much more than we'll grieve."

"Yes, Pepper," Jim replied. "I agree with you. And in the process, maybe we can lead many of them to Christ."

Jim walked over to Rhasha's bed and leaned over to kiss her cheek. Her eyes were wide open. He picked up the chair and carried it over to the dying woman's bed. Jim sat in the chair and put his elbows on the edge of the bed. He closed his eyes and cupped his hands together, to pray. "Father," he said, "please forgive me of my sins and please have mercy on my soul. I know I'm a sinner."

Pepper walked over to stand beside Jim and bowed her head. She placed her hand on his shoulder and closed her eyes.

"Father," Jim continued, "I don't know this woman, but I know she has two small children. I'm sure they love her very much. Lord, I know you are the Father of mercy and I know you are the Father of miracles." A tear ran down his face. "I give you all the praise and the glory for everything that is good and decent. You are the Father of love, and you are the Father of healing. Father, we beg you for all of those things, here, today." Jim hesitated for a brief second as he thought of the right words to say. "Father, we need your mercy. We need your miracle and we need your love. We need your healing tears to touch this woman. In Jesus Christ's holy name I pray, amen."

Jim kept his eyes closed and his head bowed. He studied a mental picture of God sitting on his throne. In his vision, Jim could see tears running down God's cheeks.

Pepper looked up to check the heart monitor. The woman's heartbeat was faster and stronger than before. She looked down at the woman's body and saw a blue glow completely engulfing the woman. The glow also covered the two children. The woman's breathing became stronger. One of her fingers moved and then her eyes opened. The sick woman was conscious, but unable to move. She still had a long way to go before she would be completely well.

Pepper couldn't control herself. Tears flowed down her cheeks, and everything blurred. She looked at the children through tear-filled eyes, then wiped away the tears with her fingers. As her eyes began to focus, Pepper stared at all four patients in disbelief.

A white, transparent figure stood on each side of each patient, eight in all. The bright white figures were angels, dressed in long flowing gowns.

Pepper had never seen a vision before. All her strength left her body and she fell to the floor. Tears ran down her cheeks. She sobbed loudly. Jim heard Pepper crying and looked up to see what was going on. When he looked up, the blue glow disappeared.

Jim could see Pepper sitting on the floor, crying. He rushed over to her. "Pepper, what happened? Are you OK?"

Pepper regained her composure. "Jim, don't you see the angels?"

Jim looked at the four patients. "No, Pepper," he said, "I don't see them."

The transparent figures were gone. Pepper jumped to her feet and looked around. "I saw an angel on each side of each patient," she declared. "Please believe me, Jim! I know they were there."

Jim put his arms around her. "I believe you, Pepper, and I believe the angels are still there. We just can't see them now."

Jim felt her shoulders relax and released his hold on her. She excused herself and moved to check the young mother's pulse. Jim looked at the mother and saw tears running down her face. He looked at Rhasha and could tell she had been crying, too. He knew Rhasha and the young mother had seen the angels also.

He walked over to the mother's bed and kissed her on the cheek. Pepper had finished checking her pulse. "Jim," she said, "she's much stronger now. I think she's going to make it."

Jim smiled. He lifted the mother's hand and held it between both of his hands. "You're going to be OK. God will take care of you." He kissed her hand and laid it along her side.

He winked at Pepper and walked over to Rhasha's bed. He kissed Rhasha on the cheek. "Did you see the angels, sweetheart?" he asked. "God sent them to take care of you." Jim knew Rhasha couldn't answer him, but he wanted her to know that what she saw was real. "You rest now, sweetheart," he added, "God is watching over you."

Jim formed a mental picture of God sitting on his throne. "Thank you, Father."

The doctor was half an hour late. One of Jim's fears was already becoming a reality.

Moments later, he heard the sound of a plane flying overhead. He ran out of the hospital and drove to the hangar located at the end of the runway.

Charlie, the pilot, spotted Jim's jeep as he landed the plane. He taxied to the hangar and shut off the engines. By the time he'd unhooked his seat belt and climbed out of the plane, Jim was standing next to the wing.

"Charlie, where's the doctor?"

"He didn't come, Jim," Charlie replied. "He said he was to busy today."

"OK, Charlie," Jim said, "go see if you can find another doctor somewhere. We have three new patients in the hospital."

"I'll see what I can do." Charlie climbed back in the plane and started the engines. Moments later, he was airborne. There wasn't anything else Jim could do, so he drove back to the hospital.

While Jim was gone, Rhasha's family had been in to check on Rhasha. Pepper told Jim that the family was sick. She'd given them some medication and sent them to get some breakfast.

Jim walked over to Rhasha's bed. He leaned over and kissed her on the cheek. "Hello, pretty girl," he said.

Rhasha made no movement, but Jim could see a gleam in her eyes. He knew she was getting better and soon she could be put on soft food. He carried his chair over from beside the sick mother's bed and set it beside Rhasha's bed. He sat with her and talked about God and read the Bible to her. During the day, Jim also spent some time talking to the mother and her children. When he read the Bible to Rhasha, he read loud enough for everyone to hear.

At the end of the day, Jim picked up his guitar and sang three Christian hymns to Rhasha. Rhasha kept her eyes open as long as she could, but the music was soothing and she soon went to sleep. Jim leaned his guitar against the wall and said a prayer for all the patients. He kissed Rhasha on the forehead and held her hand between his hands. Then he laid his head on the edge of Rhasha's bed and went to sleep.

Every day, Jim told Rhasha how pretty she was, and talked to her and read the Bible to her. Every day, he brushed her hair and sang to her. Every day, he held Rhasha's hand between his. Every day, he prayed for her and went to sleep in the chair next to Rhasha's bed.

During this time, Buju Construction Company finished working on the last twenty houses. Jim hired them to build an emergency unloading dock. He hired Davis Construction Company of Africa to pave a driveway from the street to the unloading dock, and he bought an ambulance and hired a driver with E.M.T. (Emergency Medical Transporter) experience. Jim also contracted Buju Construction to build an orphanage and a small morgue. Buju agreed to build fifty more houses identical to the first thirty houses.

Jim knew people would need new clothes, so he contracted the Buju Construction company to build a facility where new clothes could be stored. The store would become known as The Factory, because so many people would get free clothes there. Finally, Jim hired a female doctor, just out of medical school.

Jim gave a house to anyone who didn't have a place to live. He gave food to the hungry and clothes to those who needed them. He sent anyone who needed medical attention to the doctor. Word spread all over Africa about the work Jim was doing, and more people were added to the hospital. The village grew. Children ran and played in the park and swimming pool. The public rest room and shower facilities had frequent visitors. Happy people could be seen all over the village, playing and cutting up. All Jim's houses were now occupied, and construction was under way on another fifty houses. Some people went to church on Sunday morning, but they did so mostly to please Jim.

87

Bed of Leaves

Eventually the doctor put Rhasha on soft food, along with the young woman and her two daughters. Jim spoon-fed Rhasha every day while the nurse spoon-fed the other three. A week later, the doctor allowed Rhasha's parents to take her home. Rhasha was still bedridden, but the doctor said there was nothing more she could do for her. The mother and her two small children were doing equally well. The doctor would have released them, but they had no one to take care of them.

Chapter 7

Jim's Promise

Bed of Leaves

Jim continued to go to the hospital every day. He prayed for each of the patients and talked to them, one by one. Even though Rhasha was out of the hospital, Jim visited her at her house every evening. He prayed for her and talked to her. Every day, he took food to her and spoon-fed her until she began spitting it out.

The first thing he always said was, “Rhasha, you have such pretty eyes.” He held her hand and sang to her. Every night he went to sleep in a chair beside her bed, and every morning he woke up to find Rhasha already awake and watching him. He’d kiss her on the cheek and say, “Good morning, sunshine.”

Even though Rhasha couldn’t talk yet and could only make grunting sounds with some effort, Jim could tell she loved the attention he gave her. She liked hearing him say he loved her as he brushed her hair. She liked falling asleep every night to the sound of Jim’s singing, knowing he would be there when she woke up. Sensing that Rhasha was becoming too attached to him, he decided one evening not to go to her house. He thought it would be better for Rhasha if she started depending on her parents more.

Thamish didn’t agree when Jim told him his idea. “I understand what you’re saying, Jim,” he replied, “but I think Rhasha will grieve deeply if you stop coming over.”

“Let’s try this tonight,” Jim said. “If there are any problems, let me know.”

That evening, after his visit to the hospital, Jim went to the dining hall to eat with his other guests. When he finished eating, he went home.

Jim had a hard time getting to sleep. He missed Rhasha very much. He thought about her until his eyelids finally dropped shut and he fell into an uncomfortable sleep. At about eleven o’clock, Jim was abruptly awakened by someone shaking his shoulder.

“Jim, wake up,” someone cried.

Jim forced his eyes open. “OK, I’m awake, what’s wrong?”

As his eyes focused in the dark, he could see Rhasha’s parents standing beside his bed. They were both crying.

Thamish said, “Jim, please come to our house.”

Thasha, beside him, pulled on Jim’s wrist.

Jim wasn’t completely awake yet. “What’s wrong, Thamish? Is something wrong with Rhasha?”

“Rhasha’s crying,” Thamish said. “Her pillow is soaked with tears and she’s shaking all over. She’s scared, Jim. She doesn’t understand why you didn’t come to see her tonight. We tried to explain it to her, but she wouldn’t stop crying.”

All Jim could think about was how fast he could get to Rhasha. He jumped out of bed and ran out the front door in his pajamas, not taking the time to change his clothes or put on his shoes. He ran across the pavement, heedless of the rough surface that bruised and cut his feet. When Jim got to Thamish’s house, he flung open the front door and dashed to Rhasha’s bedside. He sat on the edge of her bed and, putting his arms around her, he hugged Rhasha tightly. Without thinking, Jim kissed her on the lips. Tears ran down his cheeks as he held her in his arms. They both cried as if a close relative had died.

Jim gently laid Rhasha down on the bed, but kept his arms around her. He felt bad about hurting Rhasha and begged her to forgive him. In his haste to make it up to her, he was careless about his choice of words. “Rhasha,” he said, “I promise you I will be by your side every night, until you ask me not to come. I will never hurt you again. You have my word on the Bible,” he added.

Trusting Jim never to break a promise, Rhasha stopped crying. She still had tears in her eyes, but a slight smile formed on her lips. For the first time, Rhasha slowly raised her arms and dropped them around Jim's neck. Jim pulled her close and kissed her gently on the cheek.

Jim didn't realize what his promise meant to Rhasha. He only meant that he would be by her side every night until she was completely healed. To Rhasha, it meant she and Jim would be together until they died.

Rhasha was still very weak. *It's a miracle she can raise her arms,* Jim thought as he laid Rhasha down on the bed and slipped his arms out from under her back. Her arms dropped from around his neck. Jim picked up Rhasha's hand and prayed.

"Father, please forgive me of my sins and please have mercy on my soul. Please forgive me for hurting Rhasha. You know I only wanted to help her."

By this time Rhasha's parents were standing at her bedroom door. They could see a blue glow around Jim and their daughter.

"Father," Jim continued, "I promised Rhasha I would be with her every night until she tells me not to stay. I pray this will make up for the pain I caused her, and Father, I make this same promise to you."

Rhasha and her parents heard every word Jim said. Thamish and Thasha could see the blue glow expanding out from Jim and Rhasha until it filled the whole room.

"Father, I promise never to hurt Rhasha again. If I do, I pray you will punish me severely."

When Jim heard himself make this promise to God, he realized what he'd promised Rhasha. Jim hesitated as he thought about the words he'd said to her.

"Father, I pray you will heal Rhasha soon so she can go on with her life. In Jesus' holy name, I pray. Amen."

The soft blue glow disappeared as Jim opened his eyes. His feet, abused during his barefoot run down the road, didn't hurt anymore. The cuts and bruises were completely healed.

As Jim gazed into Rhasha's eyes, he heard a humming sound. Her eyes widened-Rhasha and her parents could hear it, too. The humming got louder, then began to pulsate. After a few seconds, it faded away. Sparks flashed from Rhasha's eyes, like sparklers on the Fourth of July. Jim stood up and backed away from the bed. He knew God was performing a miracle for Rhasha. As he and her parents watched, sparks flashed all over Rhasha's body. Lightning-like streaks shot out in several directions. The flashes finally stopped. Rhasha lay quietly on her bed.

Her body had been completely transformed into that of a beautiful girl. She looked just like the Rhasha Jim had seen in his dream. She was unconscious, and wore only a thin hospital gown. Slowly Rhasha's body was elevated until she hovered twelve inches above her bed. She floated away from the bed to hang in the air, about thirty-six inches above the floor. As she levitated, her body slowly began to rotate until she was in an upright position with her feet six inches above the floor. Then she descended until her feet rested flat on the floor.

The humming sound rose, pulsated for a few seconds, then faded away. Rhasha was now conscious and standing in front of Jim.

She smiled at him and held out her arms, beckoning him to come to her. Jim walked up to her, but didn't know if he could touch her. When Rhasha put her arms around his neck, he slipped his arms around her waist. She pulled Jim close to her.

Her bright eyes gleamed. Tears formed in Rhasha's eyes. For the first time, she spoke. "I love you," she said in a voice so beautiful, it threw Jim completely off guard.

He had no strength left in him. "Rhasha," he said, "you'll never know how much I love you."

They held each other tight. Rhasha's parents eased toward her. They touched her on her shoulder and back. Jim and Rhasha released each other. As Rhasha kissed Thamish and Thasha, Jim lowered his head. He closed his eyes and gave thanks to the one and only God.

Rhasha's brother Robby had remained in bed. Now, attracted by the strange sounds coming from Rhasha's room, he ran into the room to see his beautiful sister standing in the middle of the floor. Tears streaming down his face, Robby ran toward her. Robbie couldn't understand what had happened to his older sister, but he hugged her tight for a long time, as though he didn't want to turn her loose.

A spiritual feeling filled the room. Thamish, Thasha, Robbie, and Rhasha sat on Rhasha's bed with their arms around each other's waist and began to talk about the past. They each had memories to share, laughing over the happy ones and growing quiet over the sad ones. Some of their memories included Jim, who sat in his chair across from them.

After a while, Thamish noticed Rhasha and Jim looking at one another and realized that they wanted to be alone. He told Robbie to go get some sleep, and Robbie kissed his sister and returned to bed. Thamish and Thasha kissed their daughter and went to their bedroom. Jim suspected neither Thamish nor Thasha would get to sleep.

Jim and Rhasha sat on the edge of her bed and held each other's hands. Finally, Jim released Rhasha's hand. He picked up his guitar and began to sing. *"This little light of mine, Lord, I'm gonna let it shine. This little light of mine, Lord, I'm gonna let it shine. This little light of mine, Lord, I'm gonna let it shine. Let it shine, let it shine, let it shine."*

Smiling at her surprise, Rhasha began singing with him. She'd learned all the songs Jim sang to her every night. *"Jesus gave me light, now I'm gonna let it shine. Jesus gave me light, now I'm gonna let it shine. Jesus gave me light, now I'm gonna let it shine. Let it shine, let it shine, let it shine."*

In their bedroom, Rhasha's mother heard her daughter's beautiful voice singing and began to cry.

"Everywhere I go now, I'm gonna let it shine. Everywhere I go now, I'm gonna let it shine. Everywhere I go now, I'm gonna let it shine. Let it shine, let it shine, let it shine."

When they finished singing, Jim leaned his guitar against the wall and kissed Rhasha. He moved his chair next to her bed, so they could go to sleep. Rhasha lay down on the bed and slid to the opposite side. She pulled on Jim's arm, inviting him to join her.

Jim looked at Rhasha. He wanted her, but he knew she was too young for him. "Rhasha, I can't do this," he said, "you're only eighteen years old and I'm forty-five. Besides, God wouldn't approve of it."

Tears ran down Rhasha's face. "Jim, you promised me you would be with me every night. I don't want you to sleep in that chair anymore."

"Rhasha," Jim said excitedly, "do you mean . . . just to sleep?"

"Just to sleep, Jim." She smiled. "But could you hold me?"

Jim smiled as he crawled into bed next to Rhasha. He put his arms around her. "Sweetheart," he said, "I don't think God will get angry with me if I just put my arms around you and hold you every night."

They slept all night with their arms around each other.

The next morning when Jim woke up, he found to his surprise that Rhasha was already awake. Her face was no more than six inches away from his, and she was staring into his eyes with her hand on his cheek. She kissed him on the forehead. "Good morning, sunshine," she said.

Jim chuckled. Rhasha was saying the same words to him that he greeted her with every morning. "Good morning, sunshine," he replied.

Rhasha placed his hand between both of hers. She had a serious look on her face. "Jim," she said, "you have such pretty eyes."

Jim grinned at Rhasha. She grinned back. Jim knew what she was doing. Jim heard giggling behind him and turned to see Rhasha's parents standing in the doorway. They knew Rhasha wasn't flirting with Jim, but showing him her appreciation.

Thamish asked if they slept comfortably, and Rhasha said that they had. Jim was afraid Rhasha's parents might have gotten the wrong impression. He couldn't explain fast enough.

"Thamish," he said, "all we did was sleep."

Thamish walked over and sat down in the chair. "Jim," he replied, "if it wasn't for you, Rhasha would not be alive today. I know you wouldn't do anything to hurt her."

"It was God who healed Rhasha, but you're right, I would never knowingly hurt her." Jim put his hand on Thamish's shoulder. "Thamish, I want Rhasha to marry a young man and live a normal life."

Rhasha didn't want to hear what Jim was saying. "You promised you would be with me every night until I said not to stay," she protested.

"Rhasha, I will never break my promise to you," Jim told her, but he sensed she might be thinking of marriage. "If I were twenty years younger, I would be on my knees begging you to marry me." Jim could see that Rhasha didn't understand. "Sweet girl, I have no desire to leave a young widow behind when I die."

"I love you, Jim," Rhasha said. "I don't care about your age."

"I love you too, Rhasha," Jim said, "but I'll only get older."

Rhasha argued, "People lose husbands and wives every day. They don't lose their love or their memories."

Jim was impressed by her wisdom. "Rhasha," he said, "we can show each other love, but we can never get married."

Jim and Rhasha stared into each other's eyes.

Finally Rhasha replied, "As long as we can be together, that's all I ask."

They kissed passionately and held each other tight.

Jim threw his legs over the edge of the bed and stood up. Rhasha climbed out on the same side and stood beside him.

"What are you doing, Rhasha?"

"I'm going with you," she replied.

Jim looked at Rhasha's hospital gown. "But you don't have any clothes."

Rhasha looked at Jim, then she looked around the room. "Where are your clothes?"

Jim was still in his pajamas. Remembering he'd left his clothes at home, he popped his forehead with the palm of his hand. "Oh no!" he groaned.

Rhasha smiled at Jim. She looked as though she'd come to a brilliant conclusion. "Hmm," she said, "it looks to me like neither one of us is going anywhere."

Jim smiled as their eyes met. "Sweetheart, I think I liked you better when you couldn't talk."

Rhasha laughed.

"Thamish," Jim said, "could you go to my house and get my clothes? They're hanging in my closet."

"Sure Jim, I'll be right back."

Jim smiled at Rhasha and winked. "Thamish," he added, "could you also go over to The Factory and ask them for some clothes that would fit a slender teenage girl?"

"Sure, Jim." Thamish left to get Jim and Rhasha's clothes.

Jim kissed Rhasha passionately and held her tight. When he released his hold on her, he closed his eyes to pray. Rhasha and Thasha didn't know God but they closed their eyes as Jim thanked God every way he could think of, for healing Rhasha. "Amen," Jim said, and opened his eyes. He picked up his guitar and began strumming. Jim and Rhasha's voices joined together to the sing hymns Jim had sung to her every night.

Thasha thought about all the pain her family had been through. She'd long ago given up all hope of having a happy life, but as Jim and Rhasha sang, tears of happiness ran down Thasha's cheek's. She knew now that her family would at least survive.

Jim and Rhasha smiled at each other as their voices filled the room.

A half-hour later, Thamish returned with Jim and Rhasha's clothes, and Jim took his clothes into the bathroom to change. When he opened the door to the bedroom, he found Rhasha standing in front of him, wearing her new clothes. The only clothes The Factory had in Rhasha's size were five pairs of denim shorts and five button-up shirts.

Jim's eyes opened wide. "Rhasha!" he exclaimed, "you're beautiful!"

"If it pleases you, Jim," she replied, "this is all I'll ever wear."

"Rhasha," Jim said with feeling, "it doesn't matter what you wear-to me, you're the prettiest girl in the world."

Rhasha blushed as she exposed a sheepish grin.

Jim couldn't help but notice Rhasha's long, beautiful, black legs and her small, feminine feet. She was wearing sandals that looped around her heels. She'd run a scarf through the belt loops on her shorts and tied it on one side, and she'd tied the two ends of her shirttail in a knot above her waist. The gap between her shirt and shorts left her belly button exposed. Jim was breathless as he looked at her beauty. He wished, as he admired her long, silky black hair, that he was twenty years younger.

Jim put his arms around Rhasha's waist and pulled her close to kiss her. "I'm going home to take a shower," he told her. "Before I go to the hospital, I'll come back for you."

"But Jim, I want to go with you."

"It will be faster if you take your shower here, and I take mine at home," he replied, then suddenly realized what Rhasha meant. "Rhasha, do you mean you want to live with me?"

Rhasha didn't say anything. She looked like she was afraid to. He looked at Rhasha's face, and she hung her head. Jim decided, no matter what, he would never hurt Rhasha again. He tucked two fingers under her chin and gently lifted her head up until their eyes met. He kissed her on the forehead. "Angel," he said, "let's go home."

Rhasha's sadness quickly turned into excitement. Her smile warmed the whole room. As Rhasha hugged her parents and said good-bye, Jim picked up his folded pajamas and said good-bye to Thamish and Thasha. Rhasha held onto Jim's arm tightly as they walked through the bedroom door. They left the house through the front door and started walking across the yard. Suddenly, Rhasha stopped.

"Wait," she said. She released Jim's arm and ran back inside the house.

While Rhasha was gone, Jim thought about all that had happened. He remembered his dream on the plane. God's messenger had said Rhasha would be an inspiration to him for the rest of his life. Jim also remembered the vision of Rhasha in a plane crash. He knew he could never tell Rhasha about that part of the dream.

When Rhasha came out of the house, she was carrying all her new clothes. She looked at Jim with a smile on her face. "I just wanted to put something that belongs to me in my new home."

Jim understood why and hugged her. Thamish and Thasha were standing in the doorway. Jim and Rhasha waved to them as they crossed the yard.

When they reached Jim's house, Rhasha quickly found an empty drawer for her new clothes. While Jim went to the bathroom to take a shower and shave and brush his teeth, Rhasha looked around the bedroom, and happiness filled her heart. She suddenly had an impulse to throw herself backwards onto the bed. She lay there with her legs spread wide and her arms spread across the bed, and felt good all over.

"This is the happiest day of my life," she murmured. She was the only person in the room, but she was sure that the whole world could hear how happy she was.

Jim had left his bed unmade the night before, so Rhasha got up and pulled the covers back into place. She then put the pillows neatly on top, at the head of the bed.

Jim came out of the bathroom, wearing his bathrobe. Rhasha rushed up to him and grabbed his hands and pushed them out to each side. She used her body to push Jim's body against the wall. With his head against the wall, Rhasha had to stand on the tips of her toes so she could kiss him. "Mister," she said, "I thought you would never finish."

Rhasha peeled herself off Jim, then disappeared through the bathroom door.

Jim watched her go. He loved her teenage energy and her fun-loving humor. *Rhasha,* he thought, *is going to be a handful.*

He took off his bathrobe and put his dress suit on. Then he knocked on the bathroom door. "Rhasha," he said loudly, "are you going to take all day?"

"Go away," she yelled, knowing he was teasing. "You're bothering me."

While Jim waited for Rhasha, he stepped out into the front yard. He could see children playing ball in the street. Down the street, a family was walking to the dining hall. People stood in front of the hospital, talking. Everywhere Jim looked, he could see healthy African people, laughing and playing.

The sky above the village was clear, but in the distance, he saw heavy rain clouds. He gazed across the village at the tops of the houses. The thatched straw roofs and bamboo frameworks stood as monuments to Jim's love for God. *People seem to be happy as they live life one day at a time,* Jim thought.

Jim was happy with the way the village had turned out. No one did without food or clothing and everyone had a place to live. People were donating their time to help in the dining hall. Others helped in the hospital. Goodwill seemed to be everywhere and anger was rarely seen.

Jim formed a mental picture of God sitting on his throne in heaven. Silently, he thanked God for sending him to Africa. He praised God for all He had done. When Jim opened his eyes, he saw six small children running to meet him. None of them could have been over ten years old.

As two of the boys roughhoused, pushing each other around playfully, a young girl looked seriously at Jim. She seemed to have something on her mind. “Mister,” she said, “my Papa told me you’re a good man. Are you?”

Jim was ready with an answer. “Sweetheart, God causes me to do good things for people.” He knelt on the ground so the children could gather around him.

One little boy put his arm around Jim’s neck. “My Mama said you take care of us and you give us food.”

Before Jim could answer, the first little girl eagerly added to her friend’s comment, “Not just food! My Mama said he gives us a house and clothes and even gives us smiles.”

Jim had a chance now to tell the children what he wanted them to know. “God does all those things for you,” he said, “and He lets everyone think I do it.”

The children didn’t understand about God, because they never saw him. They believed what their parents told them. A shy little girl built up the courage to have her say. “Mister,” she said in a timid voice, her head lowered, “my big brother said you care about us, like you’re everyone’s papa.” She slipped away from Jim.

Jim knew the little girl didn’t have a papa. He put his arms around her and kissed her on the forehead. “I love each and every one of you with all my heart,” he said.

Slowly, the shy girl raised her head and her eyes met Jim’s. “I love you, too, Papa,” she said.

There were a few seconds of silence, then all the children began yelling, “Can we call you Papa, too?” They jumped up and down. “Can we, Papa, can we?”

Jim didn't want to upset the children's parents by letting them call him Papa. "You can all call me Papa," he said, "if your mamas and papas say you can."

All the children took off, running down the street. Jim could hear them yelling at other people, "He said we can call him Papa."

Jim turned around to find Rhasha standing behind him. She threw her arms around his neck and crushed her body against his as she kissed him passionately.

"Papa," she said, and smiled. "Everyone will call you Papa, now. It's so honorable for people to call you Papa."

Jim put his hands on Rhasha's waist. "Sweetheart, you wouldn't ever call me Papa, would you?"

A sheepish grin formed on Rhasha's face. "I might," she replied, "whenever I feel like honoring you . . . Papa."

Jim and Rhasha walked arm in arm to the hospital. When they entered, the doctor and nurse were tending to patients. A volunteer stood at the back door, talking to the ambulance driver. Sara, the doctor, was giving a little girl in the first bed some medication. She saw Jim and Rhasha walking through the door and stopped what she was doing. She came over to talk to Jim.

She noticed Rhasha had her arm around Jim's waist. "Who's your friend?" the doctor asked him.

"This is Rhasha." Jim replied.

Sara looked at Rhasha with curiosity written all over her face. "Rhasha," she said. "That's a very pretty name. Have you known Jim long?"

Jim knew Sara didn't recognize Rhasha. "Doctor," he said, "this is the girl you released a few weeks ago. She was in bed one."

Sara shook her head. "That's not possible. That was a little girl. Besides, there's no way she could have recovered so quickly."

"This is the same Rhasha," Jim insisted. "I was in her bedroom last night when God healed her." Jim pulled away from Rhasha and pointed toward her with both hands. "Did God do a good job, or what?"

"I can't believe it, Jim!" the doctor said, looking at Rhasha. "You're so pretty, dear. I'm really happy for you."

"Thank you," Rhasha said, "and thank you for being so kind to me when I was sick." There were tears in her eyes when Rhasha hugged Sara.

Sara hugged her back, then excused herself and went to her office. Jim and Rhasha walked over to bed one.

Every morning, Jim started with bed one and worked his way around until he'd visited with each patient. A very young girl had taken Rhasha's place in bed one. As Jim walked over to the bed and kissed her on the cheek, memories rushed back to Rhasha. Rhasha was watching Jim at a different angle this time, but it was as if she was looking through the little girl's eyes. She could see Jim leaning over toward her and feel the kiss Jim placed on the little girl's cheek. She could hear Jim telling the little girl she was very pretty, and it felt like Jim was talking to her. Rhasha could feel his hand when he picked up the little girl's hand and placed it between both of his. Tears ran down Rhasha's cheeks as she watched Jim stroke the little girl's hair with a brush. Rhasha could feel every stroke. When Jim picked up his chair to carry it to the next bed, Rhasha could feel the disappointment the little girl felt. She knew the little girl didn't want Jim to leave.

The little girl was too weak to talk, but Rhasha knew what the little girl would say to Jim, if she could talk. Rhasha knew the little girl loved Jim.

Chapter 8

Talking Eyes

Jim went to the next bed and kissed another young girl on the cheek. As he began talking to her, Rhasha found a chair and placed it next to the little girl in bed one. She leaned over and kissed the little girl on the cheek. Tears were in her eyes. She placed the little girl's hand between both of hers. Rhasha didn't have a brush so she stroked the little girl's hair with her hand. "Sweetheart," Rhasha said, "you're such a pretty little girl. You have beautiful eyes."

Rhasha could see the little girl's eyes watching her. She knew what the little girl was thinking. "Did you know," Rhasha said, "when I first came to this hospital, I was sick, just like you? I was in this very same bed."

The little girl gave her a smile filled with love.

"Sweetheart, I know you want to talk and walk and play. In a few months, you'll be able to do anything you want to. Just wait and see, nyou'll be very happy." Then Rhasha leaned over and whispered in the little girl's ear. She didn't want Jim to hear what she said next. "I know what you would tell Jim, if you could talk. Would you like for me to tell Jim something for you?" Rhasha knew that the little girl couldn't answer her, but she could blink her eyes. "If you want me to give Jim a message for you," Rhasha whispered, "blink your eyes once."

The little girl blinked her eyes, but she looked like she wasn't sure Rhasha would know what she wanted to say to Jim.

"OK," Rhasha said. "You want to kiss Jim on the cheek and you want to tell him he has pretty eyes . . . right?"

The little girl's eyes widened in amazement. She blinked her eyes quickly.

"Oh, but I'm not finished," Rhasha said. "You also want to tell him that you love him . . . right?"

The little girl blinked her eyes again.

"You also want to hold his hand between both your hands . . . right?"

The little girl blinked her eyes again, then, as if she wanted to make sure that Rhasha saw her, she blinked her eyes yet again.

Rhasha kissed her on the cheek. "Alright, I'll go ask Jim to come over here. I'll tell him what you want to say . . . OK?"

The little girl smiled warmly. She blinked again.

Rhasha walked over to Jim, who was getting ready to go to the next bed. "Jim," she said, "the little girl in bed one wants to tell you something. Do you have a minute?"

"Can she talk?" Jim asked, surprised.

"No," Rhasha replied, "but it's something I figured out when I was sick. She can't talk, but she can blink her eyes."

"OK," Jim said, "let's go see how this works."

Jim and Rhasha went back to bed one. Rhasha sat in the chair and picked up the little girl's hand. She held it between both of hers and said, "Sweetheart, if you would like for me to give Jim a message, blink your eyes."

The little girl quickly blinked her eyes. Jim grew excited.

"Would you like for me to tell Jim what we talked about?" Rhasha asked.

The little girl blinked her eyes again. Rhasha released her hand and stood up.

"OK Jim," Rhasha said, "sit in the chair, and place your cheek next to her lips."

Jim did as Rhasha asked. The little girl couldn't move her lips, but Jim understood. "Thank you, pretty girl," he said, "that kiss made me very happy." Jim held her hand.

Rhasha pulled their hands apart and placed one of Jim's hands on the bed. She picked up both the little girl's hands and placed them on either side of Jim's hand, then held them in place with her own hands.

"Now watch her eyes, Jim," Rhasha said. "She'll blink, if this is what she wants to tell you." Rhasha drew a deep breath and said, "She wants to tell you that you have very pretty eyes."

The little girl blinked her eyes and, to make sure Jim saw her, she blinked again.

"Also Jim, she wants to tell you that she loves you."

The little girl blinked her eyes again.

Tears ran down Jim's face. "Sweetheart," he said in squeaky voice, "I love you, too."

Tears ran from the little girl's eyes, too. She looked so happy that she could tell Jim these things. Rhasha watched the little girl's eyes, to see if she had anything else to say. The little girl blinked twice. She held her eyes shut for about two seconds each time. Rhasha knew what it meant: thank you, and I love you, too.

Rhasha nodded. "You're welcome, dear," she told the girl, "and I love you, too."

Jim kissed the little girl on the cheek again. "Angel, you go to sleep now and we'll see you again this afternoon."

The little girl closed her eyes, but she didn't go to sleep.

Jim went to the third bed as Rhasha went to the second bed. They visited all twenty-one occupied beds and kissed each patient on the forehead. They tried the same communication technique on all the patients. Several of the patients blinked their eyes for Jim and Rhasha. Some were too weak. All the patients gazed lovingly at Rhasha. They already loved Jim.

It didn't take Rhasha long to figure out why Jim spent so much time with the patients. It made her feel good all over to be helping people. After Jim talked to the last patient, Rhasha pulled her chair up to the bed. She kissed the elderly woman on the cheek. Rhasha talked to her and held her hand between both of her hands.

Jim was impressed as he watched Rhasha tend to each patient and pour her heart out to them. He knew she gave them new hope. She told every patient she had been a patient, just like them, when she first came to the hospital.

Jim went to the office to talk with the doctor. Sara was filing away a folder when Jim walked in. "Sara," he asked, "are you busy?"

"Not right now," she said, "come on in."

"I've got a question for you."

"OK Jim, what is it?"

"Would it be all right if Rhasha and I sing for the patients every evening?" he asked.

Sara replied, "I think three or four songs would be good for the patients."

"Good. I'll talk to Rhasha. If she wants to, we'll start this afternoon."

"We'll be waiting for you, Jim," Sara replied, then added, "this could be exciting."

When Jim left the office, Rhasha was walking toward him. They met in the middle of the open area between the office and the beds. Rhasha jumped up and locked her legs around Jim's waist and her arms around his neck and rested her left cheek on the top of Jim's head. Jim locked his arms around her waist and spun her in a circle. Rhasha slid down Jim's body and placed her hands on his chest. She kissed him.

Jim saw the doctor from the corner of his eye, watching what Rhasha did in surprise. She was clearly amazed that they showed this kind of affection for each other. Jim didn't care. He was hopelessly in love with Rhasha. He knew she would marry someday, and his heart would break.

Jim pulled back. "Rhasha, how would you like to sing for the patients every evening?"

"I'd love it," Rhasha exclaimed. "Just you and me?"

"For two or three days," Jim replied, "and then I'll hire a drummer and a keyboard player."

Little did Jim or Rhasha know it, but singing would become their passion.

Jim and Rhasha left the hospital. As they walked down the street, Rhasha, full of energy, kept cutting up with Jim all the way home. When Jim opened the front door, Rhasha put her arms around his neck.

"Carry me across, Jim," she asked.

Jim picked Rhasha up, carried her through the door, and gently set her on the sofa. He took off his shoes and socks, then pulled his shirttail out and sat on the sofa with both bare feet on the cushions. Rhasha leaned back against Jim. She faced upward between his knees, with the back of her head on his chest. He placed his chin on the top of her head and put his arms around her neck. He began acting like a schoolboy. He gently pulled her hair back and stroked it with his hand, and kissed her on the side of her neck. Rhasha shivered with pleasure. Every time he nibbled on her ear, she turned around and acted like she was going to slap him, but when she turned back around, Jim could see her smiling, waiting for him to do it again.

After about an hour, he threw his left leg over Rhasha's head, planted both feet on the floor, and sat up straight, forcing Rhasha to sit up as well. He picked up her right hand and slipped his fingers between hers. "Rhasha," he said, "let's make a pact."

"OK, but what's a pact?"

"An agreement," Jim replied.

"Oh. OK, Rhasha said. "What kind of agreement?"

Jim extended his hand with his pinkie finger sticking out. "Put your pinkie finger next to mine." Rhasha held up her pinkie finger. "Now," Jim said, "any time one of us holds up a pinkie finger, the other has to put their pinkie finger up. We'll put our pinkie fingers next to each other and hook them together." Jim and Rhasha hooked their pinkie fingers together. "Let's do this often," Jim said, "as a reminder that you and I pledge our friendship, to last forever."

Rhasha was smiling. Jim knew she was going to tease him. Rhasha held up her second finger. "Why not this finger, Jim?"

"No," he said, knowing she was clowning around.

Rhasha held up her middle finger. "What about this finger?"

"No."

She held up her thumb.

"OK," Jim said, "we'll hook thumbs."

"I changed my mind," Rhasha said. "Let's hook pinkie fingers."

"I've got a better idea." Jim released her finger and put his hands around her throat. He gently shook her back and forth. Rhasha stuck her tongue out, acting as if he was really choking her. He let go of her neck and grabbed her hands. He didn't know what she would do next.

"I've got a better idea, Jim." Rhasha leaned over and gave Jim a sexy kiss. She turned her head to one side, then the other, and back again.

Finally he broke the kiss. "A kiss would never work, Rhasha."

"Why not?" she asked.

"Because, angel, we need a sign that wouldn't offend anyone. When you get married, your husband wouldn't like it if I kissed you."

"In that case," Rhasha said, and grinned, "you marry me. No one could be offended then."

"Sweetheart," Jim replied, "you need to fall in love with a good-looking young man and get married."

"It's not going to happen," Rhasha insisted. "I'm staying with ugly old you, but the pinkie finger idea will work anyway."

Jim laughed. He knew he was old and ugly but he also knew Rhasha was teasing.

It was late in the afternoon. Jim and Rhasha hadn't eaten all day. "Do you want to get something to eat?" Jim asked.

"Sure, Jim," she said, "whenever you do."

Jim put his socks on and slipped his feet into his shoes. He pushed his shirttail inside his trousers and worked it all the way around until his belt was completely exposed. Jim started to stand up, but Rhasha stood up first. She gently pushed down on his shoulder, as a signal for him to stay. She placed her hand on his head to steady herself as she climbed onto the sofa. She stepped behind Jim and put her left leg over his shoulder, then swung her right leg around the opposite side of his neck. As she straddled his shoulders, her feet hung down in front of his chest. Jim placed his arms around her legs. She balanced herself by putting both hands on his forehead.

"OK, sweetheart," she said, "I'm ready to go."

"Rhasha, dear," Jim replied, "do you want to go back to the hospital-as a patient?"

Rhasha hesitated, trying to figure out what Jim meant. "Not really," she finally said. "Do you want me to?"

"No, but if I stand up, your head will go through the ceiling."

The ceiling was made of bamboo strips. Rhasha giggled. She gently spurred Jim in the ribs with her heels. "Gitty up, horsy," she said. "I'll bend over until we get outside."

Jim stood up, and Rhasha leaned forward. Her face was in front of his face. Smiling, she stuck her tongue out at him, then kissed him on the forehead.

"Rhasha," Jim said, "you're a handful, but I don't know what I'd do without you."

With Rhasha sitting on his shoulders, Jim crouched low, shuffled toward the living room door, and stepped out onto the front porch. Once he was in the front yard, Rhasha sat up straight. As Jim walked toward the dining hall, Rhasha acted as if Jim was her horse, and waved at the people on either side as they passed. With one hand holding his collar, Rhasha threw her other hand up in the air, swinging it wildly. She greeted everybody within hearing with, "Howdy partner," and bounced up and down on Jim's shoulders, as though she was in a saddle. No one could resist laughing at her.

A car pulled up behind them when Jim had crossed the street. He couldn't see who was in the car-Rhasha's legs blocked his view.

"Hey Jim," a voice said, "it looks like you have a big black growth on your back."

Jim turned all the way around and saw Jackie standing behind them. "Yeah," Jim said, "but I'm getting ready to dump her."

Rhasha spurred Jim in his side with her heels. "Where's my gun?" she said, "I'm gonna shoot the varmint."

Jim and Jackie laughed as Rhasha fixed her hand in the shape of a pistol. She cocked her thumb as if it was the hammer of a gun and pretended to shoot Jackie, then blew imaginary smoke off the end of her finger.

"Who's the charming cowgirl, Jim?" Jackie asked.

"This is Rhasha," Jim said. "Isn't she beautiful?"

"I'll say," Jackie replied, "but what happened?"

"Well Jackie, do you remember how God healed your car?"

Jackie nodded.

"Strange thing, Jackie. It turns out, he can heal people, too." Jim and Rhasha smiled as Jackie chuckled.

"Oh," Jackie said. "I was talking about her mental condition."

Rhasha tried to kick him, but he was too far away. Jackie didn't seem surprised that Rhasha was healed. He knew what God could do.

"Let's go into the dining hall to eat," Jim suggested. "This bag of bones is getting heavy."

Rhasha threw her right arm up in the air as she held on with the other. "Yahoo!" she yelled. "Let's go."

Jackie walked beside Jim and Rhasha as they entered the dining hall. Rhasha was still on Jim's shoulders. Her parents and brother had finished eating and were getting ready to leave. When they saw Rhasha jumping up and down on Jim's back, they all laughed.

"Rhasha," Thamish said, "what are you doing to Jim?"

"This is my horsy," Rhasha said, "and I'm breaking him in."

Jim turned his head up so he could see Rhasha's face. "Is that right?" he said. "Well, I'm fixin' to buck you off."

She kissed him on the forehead. "Oh Jim, I was just starting to have fun."

"Angel," he reasoned, "how are you going to eat, sitting on my shoulders?"

"That's no problem, Jim. Just send me a plate of food up here. I'll set it on top of your head."

With that, Jim placed his right arm under Rhasha's right leg and pushed out, slipping her leg around his arm. Then he pushed her left leg off, and she slid down Jim's back until her feet landed on the floor.

"You wasn't a very good horse anyway," she said. "You didn't make any horsy sounds."

Jim and Rhasha's antics had amused several of the diners, who smiled as Jim and Rhasha went from table to table, saying hello to everyone. They ended their tour at the dining hall door, where Rhasha kissed her family good-bye and Jim shook their hands just before Thamish, Thasha, and Robbie left.

The dining hall served all meals in buffet style, so people could choose what they wanted to eat. The elderly and the weak were served by a generous staff of volunteers. Jim, Rhasha, and Jackie each picked up a plate and made their choices from a healthy selection then, loaded plates in hand, they looked around for an empty table. Only one table was vacant. It was located in the center of the dining hall. They made their way to the vacant table and sat down to eat.

Jim and Jackie lowered their heads to say grace. Rhasha saw what they were doing and bowed her head. Jim asked God to bless the community church. It worried him that very few people ever attended Sunday services. He asked God to do something that would cause people to be interested in the church, then concluded with "Amen," and they all raised their heads and began to eat.

Jim hadn't realized until now that this was Rhasha's first full meal since he'd met her. "Rhasha," he said, "I'm sorry that I didn't bring you to eat earlier. I don't eat much during the day and I just didn't think about it."

"It's OK, Jim. I was enjoying all that we did. I didn't think about food, either." Rhasha bit off a chunk of chicken and chewed it slowly. She swallowed and smacked her lips, then bit off another chunk. She chewed each bite as if it were the last meal she would ever get. Every now and then she mumbled comments about the food through a mouthful of chicken. "Ooh, this is sooo good."

Jim hadn't eaten anything. He enjoyed just watching her eat. "Rhasha, do you like the food?"

"Ohhh, yes. This chicken is just . . . ohhh, it's sooo . . . I could just eat all day." Rhasha winked at Jim and smiled. "I'm going to eat until I get really fat."

Everyone at the table laughed.

"Sweetheart," Jim said, "I'll still love if you get really fat, but it would cause a problem."

Rhasha knew Jim was teasing, so she played along. She stopped munching, but held her drumstick where she could get another bite. "And what would that problem be?"

Jim bit off his first chunk of chicken and chewed it slowly. Rhasha and Jackie watched him, waiting for an answer. Jim took his time. "Ohhh," he said, "this is sooo good." He washed it down with tea.

Rhasha kicked his leg under the table. "Well, Jim?"

"Well, angel," he replied, "if you get really fat, I won't be your horse anymore."

"In that case, " Rhasha said, "I'm not getting fat. You're the only horsy I ever want." She laid her drumstick on her plate. Jim and Jackie were smiling, but tears ran down her cheeks. She covered her face with her hands.

Jim placed his hand on Rhasha's shoulder. "Sweetheart," he said softly, "I was teasing. If you get really fat, I'll still be your horse. Even if it breaks my back."

Rhasha wiped the tears from her eyes. "It's not that, Jim," she whimpered. "It's just that . . . this has been the best day of my life."

Jim thought about that. He set down his fork and took his left hand off Rhasha's shoulder. Then he picked up both of Rhasha's hands. "Sweetheart, thanks to you, this has been the second best day of my life. The best day was when I accepted Jesus into my heart."

Rhasha sniffled. "I know what God did for me and I hear you talk about Jesus. I'm not trying to be stubborn, but I don't understand."

The meal lasted three hours as Jim and Jackie tried to explain to Rhasha how Jesus died on the cross for everyone's sins.

Chapter 9

New Passion

While they talked, several other people pulled chairs up to their table and listened. Some even asked questions. Neither Rhasha nor the other guests could understand. It didn't make sense to them that a dead man could be the savior of the world. Jim couldn't find the magic words to make them understand.

Suddenly Jim remembered their appointment. "Rhasha, are you ready to sing at the hospital?"

"Yes, dear," she replied, "whenever you are."

Nobody at the table had known they were planning to entertain the patients. "Can we come and listen?" Jackie asked.

"Sure Jackie, you're all welcome to come."

Everyone at the table accepted his invitation. Jim and Rhasha led the way through the dining hall and across the street. When they got inside the hospital, Jim asked the fourteen guests to sit in the waiting area. There were just enough chairs.

Jim looked around. Six beds were facing in the wrong direction. He asked the nurse to help him turn those patients toward the office so they could see the entertainment. As he walked by bed one, where the little girl lay, he asked, "Would you like to hear Rhasha and me sing tonight?"

She blinked her eyes. Jim smiled and kissed her on the cheek. The little girl smiled, happy she could answer Jim now.

Jim turned out all the lights above the beds except for the light between the office and the patients, the area Jim and Rhasha would use for a stage. He realized he'd left his guitar at Rhasha's parents' house, but Jackie volunteered to get it for him. While he was gone, Jim and Rhasha visited with patients.

Thamish let him in when Jackie knocked on the door.

"Jim needs his guitar," Jackie said. "He and Rhasha are singing for the patients tonight."

Thamish fetched Jim's guitar. "Would it be OK if Thasha and I went to the hospital to hear Jim and Rhasha sing?" he asked when he returned.

"Sure, Thamish. Thirteen other people are already there."

Thamish and Thasha walked with Jackie toward the hospital. They passed several people along the way, and Thamish told them about the singing event. Some of the people he told walked with them to the hospital. Other people he told went home to tell their families. Their families told other families. Shortly, sixty-seven more people straggled into the hospital.

Jackie gave Jim his guitar and sat down in the aisle between the beds. The sixty-seven new arrivals sat on the floor around Jackie.

Jim and Rhasha began to sing. They sang as though they were at a concert.

"Oh lord, my God, when I in awesome wonder consider all the worlds thou hands hath made . . . "

As they sang, the lightbulb above Jim and Rhasha's heads burned out. There should have been complete darkness, but a strange glow surrounded them. They didn't know the lightbulb had blown-they kept singing.

"I see the stars. I hear the rolling thunder. Thy power throughout the universe, displayed. Then sings my soul, my savior, God to thee. How great thou art. How great thou art."

A man's voice in the audience yelled, "Look, it's beautiful."

"Praise God in heaven," the nurse called.

Several voices *ooh*ed and *aah*ed.

Streaks of light shot out from Jim and Rhasha. Each streak extended anywhere from four feet to forty feet. Bright white spears seemed to bounce off the back wall. Hundreds of white rays zapped throughout the hospital. The awesome effects held everyone spellbound. Jim and Rhasha didn't know what was going on. They thought the audience was impressed with their singing.

"Then sings my soul, my savior, God to thee. How great thou art. How great thou art. When Christ shall come, with shouts of acclamation, and takes me home, what joy shall fill my heart. Then I shall bow in humble adoration, and there proclaim, my God, how great thou art."

As Jim and Rhasha sang, the streaks of light shot out in cadence with the music.

"Then sings my soul, my savior, God to thee. How great thou art. How great thou art. Then sings my soul, my savior, God to thee. How great thou art. How great thou art."

When Jim and Rhasha finished singing the first song, the streaks of light stopped. Only the blue glow around them remained. To them, it was no brighter than a light bulb. Jim and Rhasha began to sing again.

"My heavenly home is bright and fair. I feel like traveling on. No pain nor death can enter there. I feel like traveling on."

Again light streaked outward, flashing in time to the music. Lower beats in the music generated shorter streaks of light.

"Its glittering towers, the son outshines. I feel like traveling on. That heavenly mansion shall be mine. I feel like traveling on. Yes, I feel like traveling on. I feel like traveling on.

"Yes, I feel like traveling on. My heavenly home is bright and fair, and I feel like traveling on. I feel like traveling on. My heavenly home is bright and fair, and I feel like traveling on."

The light show continued as long as Jim and Rhasha sang. Sometimes the streaks changed to blue. Other times, they changed to different colors. The multicolored streaks shot from Jim and Rhasha across the hospital.

"The lord has been so good to me. I feel like traveling on. Until that blessed home I see, I feel like traveling on. Yes, I feel like traveling on. I feel like traveling on. My heavenly home is bright and fair, and I feel like traveling on."

When Jim and Rhasha finished singing the second song, the streaks of light stopped. Only the blue glow remained. Jim and Rhasha began singing the third song.

"I am weak, but thou art strong. Jesus, keep me from all wrong. I'll be satisfied, as long as I walk close to thee. Just a closer walk with thee. Grant me Jesus, this my plea. Pray the legend ever be. Just a closer walk with thee."

The audience didn't know why the streaks of light shot across the hospital. All they knew was that the lights were pretty. Several people clapped their hands with the music. Jim and Rhasha smiled at each other as they continued to sing.

"When my feeble life is o'er, time for me will be no more. Fly me to that peaceful shore, let me walk close to thee. Just a closer walk with thee. Grant me Jesus, this my plea. Pray the legend ever be. Just a closer walk with thee."

They began singing the fourth song.

"Would you be free from the burden of sin? There's power in the blood, power in the blood. Would you o'er evil a victory win? There's wonderful power in the blood. There is power, power, wonder-working power, in the precious blood of the lamb. There is power, power, wonder-working power, in the precious blood of the lamb."

By now, everyone was smiling and clapping their hands. Children were trying to catch the streaks of light. The patients smiled.

"Would you be whiter, much whiter, than snow? There's power in the blood, power in the blood. Sin's stains are lost in his life-giving flow. There's wonderful power in the blood. There is power, power, wonder-working power, in the blood of the lamb. There is power, power, wonder-working power in the precious blood of the lamb. There is power, power, wonder-working power in the blood of the lamb. There is power, power, wonder-working power in the blood of the lamb. There is power, power, wonder-working power in the precious blood of the lamb."

As Jim and Rhasha finished the fourth and final song, the streaks of light stopped shooting across the hospital, but the blue glow remained around them. They still didn't know the lightbulb above their heads had blown.

Jim and Rhasha kissed tenderly. As they kissed, miniature stars popped into being all around their faces. When their lips separated, the stars stopped popping. Jim and Rhasha both had their eyes closed and didn't see the stars. They turned and faced the audience, holding hands. They bowed to each other and then to the audience. Jim told the audience he and Rhasha had enjoyed singing for them. "You're a good audience," he said. "Thank you for coming."

Everyone began chanting, "More, more, more."

Jim held up his hand to quiet them. "We'd love to sing more," he said, "but I don't want to put too much stress on the patients."

Several of the patients murmured that they wanted them to sing more.

"We'll be singing every evening," Jim said. "You're all welcome to come and listen anytime you want." He brightened. "If it's all right with Rhasha, and with Reverend Morris, we'll also be singing at church every Sunday." He looked at Rhasha, waiting for an answer.

"I'd love to sing with you every Sunday, Jim," she said.

The audience was getting ready to leave. Jackie turned on the lights. The bright lights filled the hospital and the glow around Jim and Rhasha disappeared. Jim looked up and noticed the light above them wasn't on.

"Jackie," he said, "it's a good thing we finished singing when we did. The light above Rhasha and I burned out when you turned the other lights on."

"That light burned out right after you and Rhasha began singing," Jackie told him. "Didn't you see the streams of light shooting out and the blue glow around you and Rhasha?"

Jim thought Jackie meant that blue fire shot out of the lightbulb when it blew and caused a blue glow around him and Rhasha. "No," he said, "I guess I was too much into my music."

Rhasha knew what Jackie meant. "I didn't see it either," she exclaimed.

Rhasha went over to talk to her parents while Jim talked to the other guests. Finally everyone left the hospital except Jim, Rhasha, and Jackie.

"Jackie," Jim said, "why don't you stay at our house tonight?"

Jackie's eyes bugged out. "Did you say 'our house'? Do you and Rhasha live together?"

"Yes Jackie," Jim said, "and we sleep in the same bed, but all we do is talk and sleep."

"Jim," Jackie said, "you didn't have to say that. I know how much you care about Rhasha."

They left the hospital and walked across the street to Jim and Rhasha's house. When they got inside, Jim noticed Rhasha yawn. "Jackie, Rhasha's tired, so I think we should go to bed."

"OK, I'll see you in the morning." They all said good night and Jackie went to his bedroom.

Jim got two glasses of water for himself and Rhasha, then said, "Rhasha, wait in the living room until I return." He went into the bedroom and lifted his guitar from his shoulder, hanging it on a hook that was screwed into the wall. He put his glass of water on his night stand, took his shoes off, and went back to the living room.

Rhasha was still waiting for him. Jim scooped her into his arms. Rhasha wrapped her arm around his neck, and he carried her into the bedroom. He gently laid her on the bed and took off her shoes, then kissed her on the forehead. "I'm going to take a shower, angel. I'll hurry so you can take yours."

He left Rhasha smiling contentedly and headed for the bathroom to shower and put on his pajamas and brush his teeth. When he came out, Rhasha hurried into the bathroom and took her shower. When she came back to the bedroom, she was wearing a set of Jim's pajamas. They were too big for her and hung loosely around her waist. The legs bunched up at the ankles and slipped under her heels.

"Rhasha," Jim said, eyeing her, "tomorrow we'll get you some pajamas that fit."

"Please don't, Jim. It feels good to wear your pajamas."

"OK." Jim shrugged. "But at least let me roll the legs up." He knelt down on one knee. As he rolled Rhasha's pajama legs up, he could feel her fingers running through his hair.

When he finished, Rhasha sat down on the side of the bed and Jim retrieved a hairbrush from the dresser and sat down next to her. As he began brushing her hair, Rhasha grew pensive.

"What are you thinking?" he asked.

"I'm remembering all the times you brushed my hair when I was sick. You were always so gentle and caring."

When Jim finished brushing her hair, he knelt beside his bed, put his elbows on the mattress, and clasped his hands together to say his evening prayer. Rhasha understood what he was doing and knelt beside him. She placed her elbows on the bed and put her hands together. They both closed their eyes. As Jim prayed, Rhasha listened to every word.

When he finished praying, Jim pulled the covers back, climbed into bed, and lay on his back. Rhasha crawled in beside him and placed her arm across his chest and her left leg across both of his. Jim's arm was under Rhasha's neck and her face pressed against his shoulder. Rhasha's lips were no more than two inches away from Jim's-close enough to kiss, so he did. "Goodnight, sweetheart," he said. He rested his cheek on her head.

"Good night, Jim."

As Jim reached to turn the lamp on his night table off, Rhasha said, "Can we sing one song together before you turn the light out?"

"If you want to, sweetheart. What do you want to sing?"

Rhasha smiled. "Would it be OK if we sing 'This Little Light of Mine?"

Jim grinned. "Rhasha, I love you so much. You've been sick so long. You're like an innocent child."

Rhasha placed her hand on Jim's cheek. "You sang that song to me every night when I was sick. I don't know if I could go to sleep, if you didn't sing it now."

Jim slipped his arm out from under Rhasha's neck, got out of bed, and took his guitar off the hook. Then he sat on the edge of the bed with Rhasha, who had slipped her legs over the side of the bed and sat up.

As Jim began to sing, Rhasha joined in. *"This little light of mine, Lord, I'm gonna let it shine. This little light of mine, Lord, I'm gonna let it shine. This little light of mine, Lord, I'm gonna let it shine. Let it shine, let it shine, let it shine."*

When Rhasha and Jim finished the song, they heard Jackie knock lightly on the bedroom door. "Jim," he called, "can I come in?"

Jim and Rhasha looked toward the door. "Come on in, Jackie," Jim replied.

Jackie opened the door and looked in before walking in to sit on the opposite side of the bed. He turned sideways to look at Jim and Rhasha. "Jim, I've got an idea. If you don't like it, I'll understand."

"What is it?"

"Well," Jackie replied, "I've got a drum set at home. It includes the bass drum, snare drum, and cymbals." Jackie got up and walked around to the other side of the bed. He pulled up a chair and sat in front of Jim and Rhasha. "I'm not the best drummer in the world, but I can play fairly well. Anyway, I thought maybe I could play drums for you and Rhasha."

"That would be great, Jackie," Jim said. "I'll pay you for it. Also, I'll give you a house to live in."

"A house here would be great, Jim," Jackie said, "and I wouldn't need much pay. I plan to quit my job and spend all my time here."

Jim looked at Rhasha. "I'll pay you too, Rhasha," he said, "for singing."

Rhasha lowered her head. "Jim, I love you and you love me. We live together and I think of you as a husband. If I accepted wages from you, I would feel like an employee. Thank you, but I don't want any pay."

Jim understood, and didn't say anymore about it. He decided to secretly set up a bank account for her.

They all said good night. Jackie went to the bathroom to take a shower and brush his teeth and Jim and Rhasha returned to their comfortable position in the bed. They put their arms around each other and soon fell asleep.

The next morning, Jim woke from a sound sleep to find Rhasha awake and staring into his eyes. She kissed him on the cheek, held his right hand between both of hers, and said, "Good morning, sunshine. You have beautiful eyes."

"Good morning, sweetheart," Jim replied. He smiled and kissed her. "But *you* have the prettiest eyes."

They rose and prepared to go to breakfast. Jackie woke up before they left so Jim asked him to join them when he was ready. Jackie arrived at the dining hall about thirty minutes later. While they were eating, Jim told Jackie which house he could move into. After breakfast, Jim and Rhasha went to the hospital, and Jackie left to get a truck and trailer, so he could move.

When Jim and Rhasha entered the hospital, Jim headed toward the office to talk to the nurse, but before he moved away, Rhasha grabbed his arm. "Jim," she said, "could I use your hairbrush?"

He pulled the small brush out of his pocket and handed it to her, then walked into the office as Rhasha walked over to bed one. She placed a chair next to the little girl lying in the bed. The little girl watched her, her eyes gleaming.

Rhasha leaned over to kiss her on the cheek. "You have very pretty eyes," she said. "Did you have fun last night?"

The little girl blinked her eyes.

Rhasha began brushing the little girl's hair. "Do you want us to sing again tonight?"

The little girl blinked twice.

Rhasha put down the hairbrush. She lifted the little girl's hand and held it between both of hers as she spoke to her. When Rhasha finished talking to the little girl, she kissed her on the cheek and went to the office to find Jim. The office door was closed.

When Rhasha entered the office, she saw Jim sitting in a chair, crying. The nurse stood beside him with her hand on his shoulder. Alarmed, Rhasha immediately leaned over and put her arm around Jim's neck. She kissed him on his tear-soaked cheek.

Jim quickly stopped crying and wiped the tears away. In front of him, on the desk, lay a picture of a little girl in a hospital bed. The girl's face was sunken, and her body was twisted. Her hair was thin and her stomach was swollen from hunger. She had an open sore above her right eyebrow and another below her lip on the left side.

As Rhasha looked at the picture, tears ran down her cheeks, too. She was sure the girl in the picture was dead. Rhasha suddenly lost all strength and dropped to her knees. She lay her head on Jim's leg as she sobbed. Jim put his arm around her neck and kissed her on the back of her head.

Rhasha stopped crying, but she still blinked tears from her eyes. "Who is she?" she asked.

Jim couldn't control his expression. Tears fell from his eyes, and he covered his face with his hands.

The nurse put her hand on Rhasha's shoulder. "Rhasha," she said, "we take pictures of every patient who comes into the hospital. It helps us to determine the patient's recovery progress."

Jim stopped crying, but his hands still covered his face.

Rhasha thought something bad had happened to the little girl. "Is the little girl dead?" she asked. Before the nurse could answer, Rhasha began crying again, dreading the answer to her question.

"No, Rhasha. The first day you were in the hospital, we took this picture. This is a picture of you."

Rhasha wiped the tears from her eyes and looked at the picture again. She hadn't known what she looked like when she'd first come to the hospital. She pictured herself lying in the hospital bed. She remembered Jim holding her hand between both of his as he smiled at her and told her she had pretty eyes. She remembered how good it felt when Jim kissed her on the cheek.

Rhasha picked up the picture to take a better look. Then she looked up at the nurse, blinking back tears. "Jim loved me," she said, "even when I looked like I did in this picture."

The nurse knelt in front of Rhasha. "Yes," she replied. "You mean a lot to Jim."

As Rhasha looked at the picture again, Jim raised his head from his hands and looked into Rhasha's face. "You do mean everything to me, angel," he said, "and I love you with all my heart." He leaned over and kissed her on the forehead.

"I love you, too, sweetheart," Rhasha replied, "and I always will." She couldn't keep her eyes off her picture. "Jim, did you come into the office without me just to see this picture?" She thought her question may have sounded rude, so she rephrased it. "I mean, did you want to compare how I look now with how I looked in the picture?"

Jim started to answer Rhasha's question, but the nurse interrupted him. "I've been showing this picture to all the patients, to give them hope," she said. "When Jim came into the office, he saw it lying on the desk."

Suddenly, Rhasha understood everything. "Nurse, can I keep this picture?"

"Sure," the nurse replied. "You're healed now, so we don't need it anymore. Besides, we have other pictures of you."

Rhasha stood up and pulled on Jim's arm. When he rose, she put her arms around his neck and pressed her head against his. She didn't want to release him. Jim was very special to her, and she knew she was very special to Jim.

They left the office together, and paused at each bed to visit with the patients. As Jim prayed for each patient, Rhasha was right at his side. She couldn't look at him without feeling a surge of love. From that day forward, she was a different person. She loved life more than ever. She wanted to be just like Jim. She wanted everyone she met to feel like they were special to her.

The day passed much like the day before. Rhasha continued to show her youthful energy. Jim got permission from the preacher to sing at church every Sunday, and hired Simbatu, a friend of Jackie's and a keyboard player with band experience. He asked Jackie and Simbatu to meet with them the next day, so they could all practice together for three or four hours before playing publicly that Sunday at church.

The next morning, Jim took Rhasha to town to buy her some clothes suitable to wear to church. He also bought a shirt and a new pair of shoes for himself.

Later that afternoon, Jim, Rhasha, Jackie, and Simbatu met at the church. Each had brought their own instruments, and they set up the drums and keyboard at the back of the stage, then placed three microphones at the front of the stage-one each for Jim and Rhasha and one set lower for Jim's guitar. When they were happy with how everything looked, they began to practice. Jim and Rhasha began singing *The Old Rugged Cross*, then the instruments joined in. At first, the vocals and the instruments were out of sync, but the more they practiced, the better the music sounded. After about an hour, vocals and music blended together into a heavenly melody.

Local people passing by outside heard them practicing, and within an hour the church was almost full. Everyone, including the performers, were having a good time. Some members of the audience even clapped in time with the music. The practice session lasted two hours, then everyone went home.

Sunday morning, the church was packed. Every chair was occupied. The church walls had been pushed out, up, and braced, so the church was now open on all four sides, and people stood outside. Not only local people came, but also people from the next village and, Jim found out later, even some tribal people were present. They didn't speak English, but they came to hear the music.

The church didn't have a choir and it didn't offer Sunday school. So far all the church offered was Sunday morning services delivered by Reverend Morris, a black African preacher who had been educated in the United States. He was a young minister, fresh out of seminary, with a wife and two young children.

Reverend Morris began the services with a prayer. "Almighty God in heaven, may we feel your presence in our little church today."

His prayers were nothing like the way Jim prayed, but Jim felt sure God heard every word.

"Bring angels with fast wings, God," he prayed, "with the power to shower gifts on these people. Oh God, the first gift they need is the gift of understanding, that they may understand your holy word. Later, precious God in heaven, send them the gifts of prophecy and wisdom. Of teaching and preaching. Speak to their hearts, that they no longer be strangers to their creator. Thank you, God, for all the wonderful things you have done for them. We ask not for these gifts out of greed, but rather to glorify you. In the name of your son, our savior, Jesus Christ, we pray. Amen."

Jim knew Reverend Morris deliberately said a short prayer so the non-Christian people wouldn't lose interest. None of them knew anything about Jesus. Earlier, Reverend Morris had told Jim his theory: If they could learn that God hears short prayers as well as long prayers, maybe they would pray more often.

Most preachers rehearsed prayers before church services, but Reverend Morris never did. He thought anyone who memorized a prayer to be said publicly was not praying to God, but praying to impress the congregation. Jim felt the same way. When Jim prayed, he felt as though he was talking to God just as if he were talking to his best friend.

Reverend Morris asked Jim if he was ready to start the singing services, and Jim asked if they could sing two songs now and two songs after the sermon. Reverend Morris said he could do it in whichever way he wanted.

As Jim, Rhasha, Jackie, and Simbatu walked onto the stage, silence overtook the congregation. The instruments began first, playing a pre-selected hymn, then Jim and Rhasha joined in.

"On a hill far away stood an old rugged cross, the emblem of suffering and shame. And I love that old cross, for the dearest and blessed, for a world of lost sinners, was slain. So I'll cherish the old rugged cross, till my trophies at last I lay down. I will cling to the old rugged cross and exchange it someday for a crown."

The skies had been cloudy since early morning, but now a thunderstorm hovered in the near distance. Outside, lightning flashed and thunder rumbled. The wind picked up. It was obvious that rain would pour down at any moment.

Jim and Rhasha smiled at each other as they sang, *"To the old rugged cross, I will ever be true, its shame and reproach, gladly bear. Then he'll call me someday to my home far away, where his glory forever I'll share. So I'll cherish the old rugged cross, till my trophies at last I lay down."*

Reverend Morris was worried. The ferocious wind threatened to ruin the morning worship services. It was the first time the church had overflowed with people. As he listened to Jim and Rhasha sing, he said a short, silent prayer: *"My God in heaven, if you could just hold the wind, I think we could deal with the rain."*

Reverend Morris could see the rain falling in the distance. It hadn't reached the church yet, but it was surely coming their way. The trees in the wooded area whipped back and forth, their branches tossing in every direction. The wind blew through the open-air church. The congregation began to look worried. People shifted uncomfortably.

Suddenly they heard a humming sound that rose until it could be heard pulsating over the music. After a few seconds, it faded away. The wind stopped blowing. Not even a breeze could be felt. Reverend Morris could see lightning, but the thunder had fallen silent. Not a sound could be heard, except for Jim and Rhasha's singing. Above the church, the clouds parted and a wide beam of light bathed the building and warmed the congregation. Something that looked like a transparent wall surrounded the building. Beyond it, the rain poured straight down, but not a drop touched the little church or the ground within a twenty-foot radius. Voices could be heard singing with Jim and Rhasha. It sounded like a choir of angels, a thousand angels singing in harmony and filling the air with music.

People in the congregation stirred, looked around, trying to figure out what was going on. Jim, Rhasha, and the angels continued to sing. The soothing music calmed everyone down. People began clapping with the beat. The warmth of the Holy Spirit filled the congregation.

"I will cling to the old rugged cross and exchange it someday for a crown. So I'll cherish the old rugged cross, till my trophies at last I lay down. I will cling to the old rugged cross and exchange it someday for a crown. I'll exchange it someday for a crown."

As the first song ended, not a sound could be heard. Jim and Rhasha prepared to sing the second song. When they started singing, the angels joined in with them.

"Sowing in the morning, sowing seeds of kindness. Sowing in the noontide and the dewy eve. Waiting for the harvest and the time of reaping. We shall come rejoicing, bringing in the sheaves. Bringing in the sheaves, bringing in the sheaves. We shall come rejoicing, bringing in the sheaves. Bringing in the sheaves, bringing in the sheaves. We shall come rejoicing, bringing in the sheaves."

The sound seemed amplified; the heavenly music could be heard all over the village.

"Sowing in the sunshine, sowing in the shadows, fearing neither clouds nor winter's chilling breeze. Bidding by the harvest and the labor ended, we shall come rejoicing, bringing in the sheaves. Bringing in the sheaves, bringing in the sheaves. We shall come rejoicing, bringing in the sheaves. Going forth with weeping, sowing for the master. Though the loss sustains, our spirit often grieves. When our weeping's over, He will bid us welcome. We shall come rejoicing, bringing in the sheaves. Bringing in the sheaves, bringing in the sheaves. We shall come rejoicing, bringing in the sheaves. Bringing in the sheaves, bringing in the sheaves. We shall come rejoicing, bringing in the sheaves."

Before long, Jim and Rhasha and the angels finished singing. Jackie and Simbatu remained sitting at their instruments, but Jim and Rhasha stepped outside the church and sat on the ground. Several people inside the church offered Jim and Rhasha their seats, but Jim refused.

Reverend Morris stepped up to the pulpit and slammed his fist down on its top. The loud thump echoed through the church. He wanted to get everyone's attention, and he did. "Now I want to tell you about the greatest man that ever lived. His name is Jesus."

Not a sound could be heard in the church or outside the church as Reverend Morris told the congregation about the birth Jesus and how he had lived. He ended the sermon by explaining how Jesus was crucified. He didn't read anything from the Bible because he knew it would only confuse them. He knew the congregation respected him and his beliefs, but while they liked his stories, they didn't understand Jesus was the only savior they would ever have.

Reverend Morris said the Lord's Prayer so the congregation could get familiar with it. When he said "Amen," he stepped away from the pulpit and motioned for Jim and Rhasha to come forward.

When they began singing, the angels again sang with them.

"Whispering hope, oh how pleasant thy voice, making my heart, in its sorrow, rejoice. Soft as the voice of an angel, breathing a lesson unheard, hope with a gentle persuasion, whispers a comforting word."

As Jim, Rhasha, and the angels continued to sing, Reverend Morris studied the congregation. Many looked thoughtful, and he hoped they were thinking about what he'd said. Very few people believed his stories, because they had their own gods.

"Wait till the darkness takes over. Wait till the tempest is done. Hope for the sunshine tomorrow, after the shower is gone. Whispering hope, oh how pleasant thy voice, making my heart, in its sorrow, rejoice. Whispering hope, oh how pleasant thy voice, making my heart, in its sorrow, rejoice."

As the song ended, Jackie remained seated at the drums and Simbatu stayed with the keyboard, but Jim and Rhasha stepped to the side of the stage.

Again the humming sound could be heard. It grew louder, began to pulsate, then, after a few seconds, it faded softly away. The storm had passed and now the distant grumble of thunder could be heard from it. A light breeze blew through the church. The congregation murmured nervously and started looking around.

When Reverend Morris stepped up to the pulpit, everyone settled down. He finished the sermon by telling the congregation about heaven and hell. He explained that it was important for everyone to believe in Jesus Christ. If they didn't accept Jesus as savior, he said, they would die a second death-a death that was much worse than the first. When he finished, he stepped to the side of the stage and Jim and Rhasha walked up to their microphones to sing the benediction. This time they didn't have the angels singing with them.

"Just as I am, without one plea, but that thy blood was shed for me. And that thou bids me come to thee . . . Oh lamb of God, I come, I come."

Reverend Morris waited at the altar, searching every face in the congregation, watching for any sign of movement.

"Just as I am and waiting not, to rid my soul of one dark plot. To thee whose blood can cleanse each spot, oh lamb of God, I come, I come. Just as I am, thou wilt receive, will welcome, pardon, cleanse, relieve. Because thy promise I believe . . . Oh lamb of God, I come, I come."

No one came forward. Reverend Morris said his closing prayer. He told the congregation he was glad they'd all come and he hoped to see them again next Sunday.

The congregation began to disperse. Jim and Rhasha talked to several people as they walked across the church grounds. When they got home, they made themselves comfortable on the sofa.

Jim thought about the sermon and the stories Reverend Morris told. He thought it had been an excellent sermon. He thought about the songs he and Rhasha had sung. He knew the congregation didn't understand what the songs meant, but the music was pretty to their ears. Jim remembered a scripture in the Bible that said something about "as a very lovely song," but he couldn't remember where he'd read it.

He rose and retrieved his Strong's Concordance and started a search for the scripture by looking up the word, song. Sure enough, he found the sentence: "art unto them as a very lovely song." It was in the book of Ezekiel, chapter 33, verse 32. He opened his Bible and found what he was looking for near the end of chapter 33. He read it again, beginning from verse 30. He paid special attention when he got to verse 31: "And they come unto thee as the people cometh, and they sit before thee as my people, and they hear thy words, but they will not do them: for with their mouth they shew much love, but their heart goeth after their covetousness."

Then Jim read verse 32, the verse he had been looking for: "And, lo, thou art unto them as a very lovely song of one that hath a pleasant voice, and can play well on an instrument: for they hear thy words, but they do them not."

Jim thought about that. He remembered all the people who had been in the church that morning. They were people whose only thoughts were of survival. They didn't have much opportunity to sin against God. Jim knew people in the States who professed Jesus as savior, but committed sins on a continual basis. Supposedly, they would go to heaven. *These people,* he thought, *have very little influence from sin, but because they don't know Jesus, they could die and go to hell.* He found this ironic.

Chapter 10

Rhasha Learns How To Drive

Jim laid his Bible and Concordance on the end table. He stared into space, unable to get the events of the morning out of his head.

Rhasha could see that Jim was deep in thought. "What are you thinking about?" she asked.

"Oh, I was thinking about the people at church this morning." Jim knew Rhasha wouldn't understand so he didn't try to explain it to her. Instead he asked, "Rhasha, do you want to do something fun today?"

"Sure!" Rhasha immediately answered. "What do you want to do?"

Before he answered her question, Jim put his arm around Rhasha's neck and kissed her gently on the lips. "I thought maybe we could go to the waterfalls, to have a picnic and go swimming."

Rhasha bounced up and down in excitement. "Yes! Let's go now."

Jim smiled at her enthusiasm. "OK," he said, "let's get blankets, pillows, and towels, and you get an extra set of clothes. I'll wear my cutoff blue jeans and take some clothes with me."

Rhasha gathered the towels and blankets as Jim changed. They put everything in the jeep, but before they left, they visited the hospital.

It was eleven o'clock. Jim and Rhasha were about two hours late for their usual visit with the patients. They spent more than an hour in the hospital, then Jim told the nurse he and Rhasha were going on a picnic at the waterfalls. The nurse smiled and told them to have a good time.

Jim and Rhasha walked across the street to the dining hall, and Jim asked the cook for some picnic supplies. As she filled a box with sandwiches, potato chips, cookies, and fruit, she asked Jim where they were going for the picnic. When she went to the front of the dining area to get a pitcher of tea, she mentioned Jim's plans to several people there before returning to the kitchen to pour the tea into a gallon jar.

Jim thanked the cook and picked up the picnic box. Rhasha picked up the jar of tea, and they walked through the dining hall on their way to the jeep. Not a person was in the dining hall. Jim thought this was strange. at this time of day, the dining hall was always packed.

They put the supplies in the back of the jeep, then Jim walked to the passenger side and climbed in. Rhasha stood beside the door, her head cocked to one side in bewilderment. "OK, Jim," she said, "I can sit in your lap, but who's going to drive?"

Jim chuckled. "Rhasha, have you ever wanted to learn how to drive?"

"Sure," Rhasha said a little uncertainly, "but . . . do you mean right now?"

"Yes. What better time than when we're driving to a destination twenty miles away?"

"Are you sure?" She looked a little scared.

Jim nodded. "That is, unless you don't want to." He smiled reassurance.

Rhasha squinted her eyes and returned the smile. She ran to the driver's side and jumped in behind the wheel. "But first," she said, "before you start yelling at me, I want you to kiss me."

Jim laughed and placed a loving kiss on Rhasha's lips. "Sweetheart," he said, "I might have to grab the steering wheel a few times, but I would never yell at you."

"I knew you wouldn't," Rhasha said. "I was just teasing."

Jim grabbed her and began tickling her ribs. As Rhasha squirmed and laughed, he put his left arm around her neck and kissed her. "I was just kidding, too. I'm going to yell at you all the way to the falls."

Rhasha gently slapped him. "You'd better not!"

"OK, beautiful," Jim said, "what do you do first?"

Rhasha looked helplessly at the dashboard, then at Jim. "I don't know. You're the one teaching me, remember?"

"Oh, this is going to be fun," Jim drawled. *"Put your seat belt on,"* he yelled.

Rhasha pouted, but he saw the twinkle in her eye. She smiled as she hooked her seat belt together. "Now what?"

"Put it in gear and let's go."

She stared at Jim and shrugged her shoulders. Jim pointed to the gearshift knob. "See these numbers one, two, three, four, five, and R on the gearshift?" he asked.

"Oh," Rhasha said, grinning. "So that's the gears? I thought it was the brakes."

Jim just looked at her and shook his head. He was grinning also. "OK dear," he said, "always start out in first gear, but push in on your clutch first. After you get it in first gear, let off the clutch slowly. When you feel a little pull on the jeep, then push on this pedal." Jim pointed to the gas pedal.

"It will start to roll, so hold onto your steering wheel. After you build up speed, push on your clutch, and shift to second gear. You just keep doing that-push on the clutch, shift to the next gear, and let out on the clutch. But," he added, "at all times, *watch where you're going*."

Rhasha stuck her tongue out at him and smiled. She pushed in on the clutch and with a little difficulty, finally got it into first gear. She slowly let up on the clutch and pushed on the accelerator, but nothing happened.

"Did you forget something?" Jim asked.

Rhasha had a puzzled look on her face. "I don't think so. I did everything you told me to do."

"Would you like to start the jeep, Rhasha?"

"Well," Rhasha said huffily, "you didn't bother to tell me to do that." She kissed him to take the sting out of her words and started the motor.

When Rhasha let out on the clutch, the jeep took off perfectly and she had control of the steering wheel. She tried to shift to second gear, but the gears ground.

"Sweetheart, you need to push in on the clutch before you shift."

Rhasha pushed in on the clutch and shifted to second. She had very little problem with the other gears. She drove down the road very well, even though the jeep weaved a few times. She was only driving thirty-five miles per hour when they saw the main road ahead of them. The stop sign was about thirty-five yards in front of her.

"Jim," Rhasha said, "do I need to slow down to make that turn ahead?"

"You have to stop at the main road."

"Hurry Jim," she said, "how do I stop?"

The stop sign was getting closer and Rhasha hadn't slowed down. Jim was afraid they would go across the main road and plow into a tree. Rhasha was just as scared. She clung tightly to the steering wheel.

He quickly turned off the ignition switch and pulled the emergency brake. The jeep came to a stop about ten yards from the stop sign.

Jim's heart was pounding. He rubbed his face with his hands. Rhasha was in tears.

"I'm so sorry, Rhasha," Jim said. "That was my fault. I should have shown you where the brake was. I'm not much of a driver's education teacher."

Rhasha opened her teary eyes and looked at Jim. She tried to laugh, but it sounded more like a sob. He calmed Rhasha by giving her a big hug. Then he gave her a five minute crash course on how to stop the jeep. When he was confident Rhasha understood how to stop the jeep, he instructed her to continue driving.

By the time they arrived at the waterfalls, Rhasha's driving had really improved. She was feeling very confident, until she tried to find a place to park. When she came to a stop, she tried to put the gearshift in first gear. It slipped into third, instead. When she let out on the clutch, the motor died. She quickly started the motor and put it in first gear. With Jim's instructions, she parked the jeep and turned the key off with a sigh of relief.

In front of them, water cascaded one hundred feet down the side of a mountain into a clear pool, then flowed along a rocky riverbed that in places meandered around large boulders. The air was filled with the roar of hundreds of gallons of water crashing into the pool. Further down the river, the water turned into rapids as it continued down a rocky incline. Some distance from the shoreline, tall trees rose from a tangle of undergrowth toward the sky. Clouds were still in the sky, but the storm had long since passed. Grass carpeted the edge of the pool, kept short by grazing animals.

Jim and Rhasha laid their blankets far enough away from the falls that the noise wasn't overwhelming. The grass made a springy cushion underneath the blankets, but it was still wet from the rain and the blankets soon became soaked with water. Jim noticed that the sun was about to come out from behind the clouds, so he suggested they unload the jeep, then go for a swim.

They walked into the pool where it was shallow and didn't stop until the water was chest high. Rhasha was in a playful mood. She seemed to get a lot of pleasure from cupping her hands and splashing Jim in the face. After she splashed him several times, Jim picked her up and dumped her over his shoulder. He threw her high enough into the air that Rhasha made a big splash when she hit the water. She sank like a rock to the bottom of the pool and remained underwater for a long time.

Jim watched for her head to surface, but it didn't. She had been underwater long enough that he got worried. He dove to the bottom of the pool to pull her out, and saw her motionless body lying at the bottom of the pool. A large rock lay a few inches from her head. Her eyes were closed. She lay face up, with her arms straight out to each side and her knees bent so her feet were under her body. Frantic, Jim reached for her arm to pull her out.

As soon as he touched her, Rhasha opened her eyes and threw her arms around his neck. Even underwater, Rhasha's smile was big. Her large black eyes gleamed at him. She drew Jim close and kissed him.

Jim pulled away from Rhasha and grabbed her arm. he jerked her out of the water.

Rhasha surfaced, gasping for air. She coughed a few times and wiped the water off her face with her hands. Laughing, she put her arms around Jim's neck. "You thought I drowned, didn't you?"

Jim was so scared, he was shaking. "Rhasha," he said, "please don't ever do that again."

Rhasha's laughter died as she realized her little prank had scared Jim to the point of hysteria. "I promise you, I will never scare you like that again."

Jim calmed down, and after a few moments, relaxed. He held up his pinkie finger and Rhasha locked her pinkie finger with his. They kissed and held each other for several minutes. As they held each other, they heard a voice from the shore call, "Can anyone join this party?"

"I thought I forgot something," Jim joked when he saw Jackie. Jim and Rhasha were still holding each other tight. They released each other and Jim grabbed Rhasha's hand and escorted her through the water to where Jackie was standing on shore.

Jim looked past Jackie and saw four people getting out of Jackie's car at the top of the hill. They unloaded picnic supplies and carried them down to the water's edge. They set everything on the sand close to the falls, where the noise from the crashing water was louder.

By the time Jim and Rhasha got to the shore, five more cars had arrived. Each car was full of passengers. Jim recognized nurses, cooks, and other workers from the village. Even Reverend Morris and his family were there.

While they were unloading their cars, the ambulance showed up, also full of people. Before long, over fifty people were splashing in the water or sitting on their blankets, eating. Jim even saw people holding long sticks with strings tied on the ends over the pool. The strings dangled homemade fishhooks, crafted from sharpened bones and laden with bait, into the water.

The sun came out and the clouds began to disappear. The heat from the sun quickly dried the blankets. It grew so hot, steam rose from the ground.

For the rest of the day, people splashed, hollered, laughed, played, and fished. As the day waned, people lounged on their blankets. Some slept, while others finished eating the last of their food. Only a few children were playing in the water.

Bed of Leaves

Jim and Rhasha lay on their blankets, making faces at each other. The truth was, Rhasha was the only one making faces. All Jim did was laugh at her. "Rhasha," Jim said as Rhasha stuck her tongue out and squinted her face, "you're really pretty with your tongue hanging out."

Rhasha pulled her tongue inside her month and grinned. "Do you really think so?"

Jim smiled. "No, dear. It reminds me of a dog, panting."

Rhasha grimaced and stuck her tongue out again.

Jim pulled the sides of her eyes back, to make her look Chinese. The problem was, she looked like a Chinese black girl. He chuckled. "Now that I've seen a black girl look like that, I'll never forget it."

She laughed, then changed her face. She made circles with her thumbs and middle fingers and held the circles over her eyes, like eyeglasses. Three fingers stuck straight up on each side of her head. Again she stuck out her tongue and tried to touch it to her nose. She held her head up as she looked at the tip of her nose, and her eyes crossed.

Jim couldn't help but laugh at her. She grinned, then made a different face.

"Rhasha," Jim asked, "do you make faces to yourself in front of your mirror, like American teenage girls do?"

"Of course I do," she teased, "don't you?"

Jim suddenly felt guilty about his love for Rhasha. He knew she should fall in love with someone more her own age. Then he remembered what God's messenger had told him in his dream, that Rhasha would be an inspiration to him for the rest of his life. As Jim thought about it, he came to two conclusions. Either he would have a short life or he was going to be the happiest man alive for a long time.

Jim also remembered the vision of Rhasha in a twin engine plane, crashing into the side of a mountain, and he sobered. He knew that he must never let her ride in a twin engine plane.

Jim noticed two black boys about Rhasha's age, playing on a boulder in the water. One boy gripped a thick vine that hung from a tree tilted over the pool. Jim realized the boy intended to swing from the boulder onto another boulder. Jim stood up, about to announce his displeasure, but it was to late. The teenage boy wrapped both hands around the vine and swung from the rock to the other rock, yodeling like Tarzan.

The two boulders were about fifteen feet above the water. Between the two boulders, a rock protruded just above the surface of the pool. Jim was worried the boy would lose his grip and crash onto the lower rock. If that happened, it would cause severe injury, at best.

The boy successfully landed on the opposite boulder. His parents were watching from the grassy area, so Jim sat down and thought no more about it. Both boys continued swinging from one boulder to the other and back again. Several people watched as the boys laughed and played.

The sun was still up, but the time was getting late. Jim was getting tired and wanted to go home. He remembered he and Rhasha had to go to the hospital to sing. "Rhasha, are you ready to go sing for the patients?"

"Sure. I'll start packing."

Rhasha packed the leftovers in the box as Jim folded the blankets. When everything was loaded, Jim slid into the jeep on the passenger side and Rhasha, grinning, climbed into the driver's seat, put her seat belt, and started the motor. She put the jeep in gear, let out on the clutch, and pressed on the accelerator. The jeep took off perfectly. She had trouble shifting as she drove toward the highway, twice placing the gearshift in the wrong position and twice forgetting to push in the clutch, but Jim knew the more she drove, the better she would get at it. He told her not to worry about grinding the gears. After she got onto the pavement Rhasha accelerated to fifty, and less than thirty minutes later, she parked the jeep in front of the hospital.

Other cars were returning from the waterfalls. Jim and Rhasha waved at them as they walked into the hospital.

Shortly, Jackie and Simbatu joined them. They'd brought their instruments, and Jackie'd thought to bring Jim's guitar. The hospital filled up with people as the performers set up their equipment. Jim turned out all the lights except for the one closest to the office. Before long, music filled the room.

Jim and Rhasha sang four songs. The music pleased the guests and patients. After they finished singing, Jim turned on the remaining three lights and all four performers talked to the patients. Jim and Rhasha started with bed one. Jackie and Simbatu waited until Jim and Rhasha went to bed two, then they started with bed one. Jim and Rhasha went through their daily ritual of kissing the patients on the cheek and brushing their hair. They held the patients' hands and told them how pretty or good-looking they were.

When Jackie and Simbatu had talked to the last patient, they met Jim and Rhasha at the front of the hospital. It was well after dark. All the guests had already left. Jim said a prayer, loud enough for everyone in the hospital to hear. He asked God to be with each and every patient and to heal them all as soon as possible. When the prayer was over, Jim thanked the nurse for her hard work, said good-bye to everyone, and they walked home. Jackie and Simbatu walked behind them, on the way to their own houses. Jim's jeep remained parked in front of the hospital.

Jim knelt beside his bed to say his nightly prayer. Rhasha knelt beside him to listen. Then they showered and changed into their pajamas. Within minutes, they began to sing, *"This little light of mine, I'm gonna let it shine. This little light of mine, I'm gonna let it shine. This little light of mine, I'm gonna let it shine. Let it shine, let it shine, let it shine."*

Local people had heard them singing on other nights. Tonight villagers, mostly children, started gathering outside their bedroom window to watch Jim and Rhasha. They stared. They'd never seen the pair singing in their pajamas before.

Jim and Rhasha didn't know the children were watching them. When they finished the first song, Jim kissed Rhasha on the lips for a long time. As he kissed her, the children started giggling and cutting up.

Jim and Rhasha looked wide-eyed toward the window and saw a young black girl outside the window screen, covering her eyes and laughing. Jim and Rhasha looked at each other and began laughing also.

"Would you night owls like to hear another song?" Jim asked.

All the children yelled, "Yes papa, sing some more."

All they could see of the children in the darkness were a few faces pressed against the screen, but Jim guessed there were more than twenty people standing outside the window, four of whom were adults. He winked at Rhasha and smiled. He cued her when he was ready to sing the second song.

"My mommy told me something that every kid should know. It's all about the devil and I dislike him so. He only causes trouble when you let him in your room. He'll never, ever leave you when your heart is filled with gloom. So let the sunshine in. Face it with a grin. Smilers never lose and frowners never win. So let the sunshine in, face it with a grin. Open up your heart and let the sunshine in.

When you are unhappy, the devil wears a grin, but oh he's much too lonely when the light comes crawling in. I know he'll be unhappy cause I'll never wear a frown. Maybe if we keep on smiling, he'll get tired of hanging around. If I forget to say my prayers, the devil jumps with glee, but he feels so awful, awful, when he see's me on my knees. So if your full of trouble and you never seem to win. Just open up your heart and let the sunshine in. So let the sunshine in. Face it with a grin. Open up your heart and let the sunshine in."

Jim and Rhasha sang two more songs as the children listened quietly. At the end of the fourth song, Jim made an announcement. "OK, children, Rhasha and I are getting sleepy. It's time to go to bed."

A flurry of voices called through the darkness, "Good night, Papa. Good night Rhasha."

"Good night, everyone," Jim and Rhasha yelled back.

"You can come back tomorrow night," Jim added. "We'll sing for you every night, if you want us to."

The children left Jim's yard and scampered home. Jim and Rhasha snuggled into their bed and went to sleep.

Chapter 11

Jim Takes Rasha Flying

Bed of Leaves

The next morning Jim woke up and again Rhasha was wide awake, staring into his eyes.

"Good morning, sunshine," she said, and held his hand and kissed him on the cheek.

"Good morning to *you,* sunshine," Jim said kissing her. "Are you going to do this every morning?"

"As long as we both live," Rhasha replied solemnly.

Jim hugged her and climbed out of bed. He knelt and said his morning prayer.

In the dining hall, they both chose eggs and bacon, washed down with orange juice. Every meal Rhasha ate was like a new experience for Jim. She chewed every bite over and over. When they finished eating, Jim and Rhasha headed for the hospital to visit the patients.

As they crossed the street, Jim heard the distant sound of airplane engines. He knew it was Charlie, coming in with medical supplies. He and Rhasha stopped and watched the plane draw nearer and nearer. The plane roared over them, circled around the village, then dropped out of sight as Charlie landed on the runway and taxied to the hangar.

"Jim," Rhasha said, "I've never flown in a plane before. I think it would be fun."

"No!" Jim blurted, remembering the vision he'd had of Rhasha crashing into the side of a mountain. He strove for a reasonable tone as he added, "Rhasha, planes can be dangerous. Promise me you will never go flying. Ever."

Rhasha studied his face, remembering the night God healed her. Jim had promised he would be with her every night until she asked him to go. She knew a promise was binding, and that Jim was living up to his promise. She knew if she made this promise, she could never fly in a plane as long as she lived.

"I love you, Jim," Rhasha said, "but I can't make that promise."

"Why not?" Jim asked.

"Because someday you'll go back to America, and I want to go with you."

Jim hadn't thought about that. He realized Rhasha would have to fly in planes. Jim recalled his dream again. No one had been with her in the plane. He sighed. "OK, then make me a different promise. Promise me you will never fly in a twin engine plane by yourself."

Rhasha didn't understand. Why was Jim pushing her so hard to stay out of planes? She didn't want Jim to be upset with her, so she constructed a new promise. If he needed a promise, she knew one she could keep. "OK Jim," she said, "I promise you, *as long as we both live,* I will never fly in a plane by myself."

Jim didn't like the way Rhasha worded her promise, but at least she'd made him a promise she would keep. "If that's the best you can promise me, I'll accept that."

"Good," Rhasha replied. "So can we get Charlie to take us flying in the hospital plane?"

Jim laughed. "Let me get this straight. First, you thought it would be fun to go flying."

Rhasha smiled and nodded.

"Then you refused to promise never to fly in a plane because, you said, you want to go with me to America."

Rhasha, still smiling, nodded again.

"Next you promised never to go flying by yourself, as long as we both live."

Still smiling, Rhasha bit her bottom lip and lowered her head. She teased Jim with her big black eyes. Wiggling back and forth with her hands locked together in front of her, she nodded vigorously.

"And now," Jim laughed, "it's back to 'let's go flying.' "

Rhasha put her arms around Jim's neck and kissed him lightly on the lips. She assumed an exaggerated, cocky attitude and answered, "Great, Jim-you understand it perfectly."

Jim laughed and shook his head. "You're just like a wife, Rhasha. You've already figured out how to get your way with me."

"Well," and Rhasha grinned, "not in everything, but I'm working on it. I'll have my way when I become your wife." She stepped back and held up her pinkie finger. Jim locked his pinkie finger around hers.

Jim knew that Rhasha wasn't being manipulative. She was just being her sweet, beautiful self. He loved her youthful innocence. *How can I turn down such an angelic face?* he thought. *She's doing nothing but beaming love at me.*

Aloud he said, "Let's go visit the patients, and then we'll go flying."

Rhasha bounced up and down in excitement. They released pinkie fingers, and Rhasha held onto Jim's arm with both hands as they walked into the hospital.

Jim and Rhasha again started with bed one. The little girl's face lit up when she saw them. Jim said a prayer for her as he held her hand between both of his.

"Sweetheart," he said, "you have such pretty eyes."

Smiling, both he and Rhasha kissed the little girl on the cheek. The little girl blinked her eyes.

"Jim," Rhasha said, "she blinked her eyes to tell you that your eyes are pretty, too. Is that what you told Jim?" she asked the little girl as she began brushing her hair.

The little girl blinked her eyes. She waited a second and blinked two more times.

"Thank you," Rhasha said, "you're very sweet." She turned to Jim. "She blinked two more times to tell me that I have pretty eyes, too."

Another little girl waited for them in bed two. She was just as excited to see Jim and Rhasha as the girl in bed one. They repeated the ritual of prayer, kisses, and hair-brushing, but just as Jim started to tell her how pretty she was, he heard a commotion at the hospital entrance. He turned and saw Charlie carrying a box of medical supplies. Jim continued to talk to the girl as he held her hand. Charlie proceeded to the doctor's office to wait while Jim and Rhasha finished talking to all the patients. All the hospital beds were occupied, so it took a little longer than usual.

At last they joined Charlie in the office. The doctor was out taking care of patients, so they had the office to themselves. Jim shook Charlie's hand. "Good morning, Charlie."

"Good morning, Jim; Rhasha," Charlie replied, nodding at Rhasha. She returned the greeting.

Charlie wore a long face. "Is everything all right?" Jim asked.

"Jim," Charlie replied, "I had a job offer this morning." He hesitated for a second. "I've decided to accept it."

"OK Charlie," Jim said, "but you're a good man and I'm sorry to lose you."

"I don't want to go, Jim," Charlie replied, "but I don't have anything to do here and this new job will keep me flying, routinely."

Since Jim had hired a permanent doctor, he didn't really need a pilot, but he did regret losing Charlie. "So when do you start your new job?"

Charlie hung his head and spoke in a low voice. "That's something else I need to talk to you about."

Jim realized what Charlie was saying. "Do they need you to start immediately?"

"Yes. But I told them I would have to talk to you before I accept the job."

"Charlie," Jim said, "you do what you need to do. I'll understand. I just hope you'll come back to visit."

"I will, Jim," Charlie said, looking relieved. "Would it be all right if I use your landing strip when I do?"

"You can use the landing strip anytime you want to."

They said their good-byes and Charlie walked out of the hospital, never to be heard from again.

When Jim looked at Rhasha, he could tell she was disappointed. She tried not to show it, but it was obvious. "What's the matter?" Jim asked. "You look sad."

"I'm just sorry Charlie quit his job," Rhasha replied.

Jim put his arms around her waist and Rhasha circled his neck with her arms. They put their foreheads together.

"Ahhh . . . Rhasha. And you wanted to go flying today, didn't you?" He was teasing her, but Rhasha didn't know it.

"Yes, but I understand why we can't."

"We could go and sit in the plane if you want."

Rhasha's sadness turned into excitement. She kissed him. "Could we? I've never even been close to a plane before."

Jim led her from the hospital to the jeep, still parked in front of the hospital from the day before, and he drove to the hangar. He opened the hangar door and backed the jeep close to the nose of the airplane, then hooked a bar on the front of the plane and hand pulled the plane to the jeep's bumper so he could hook the bar over the trailer hitch and close the latch. He towed the plane into the open area in front of the hangar, unhooked the bar, and parked the jeep in front of the hangar office.

By this time, Rhasha was already standing beside the plane. "Go ahead, Rhasha," Jim said. "Get inside."

He climbed onto the wing and opened the door. Rhasha climbed into the plane and slid to the far seat. Jim slid into the seat next to her, fastened his seat belt and instructed Rhasha to fasten hers.

Rhasha didn't understand what Jim was doing. When he started both engines on the plane she exclaimed, "Jim, what are you doing!"

He winked at her and smiled. "I know how to fly a plane, Rhasha. Do you still want to go flying?"

Rhasha giggled nervously. "Yes," she said slowly, and quickly added, "but I'm really, really, really scared."

Jim laughed at her, which seemed to make her more comfortable. She could see he wasn't scared at all. "Don't be afraid. God will take care of us."

Jim taxied onto the dirt road. He spun the tail of the plane so it was lined up with the runway. The plane's engines roared. When he spoke to Rhasha, he had to shout. "Did you know I was a paratrooper in the army?"

"What's a paratrooper?" she yelled back.

"Well, if you don't know what a paratrooper is, then you wouldn't understand if I told you."

Rhasha looked puzzled. "Understand what?"

Jim winked at her. "That I jumped out of airplanes, way up in the sky." Before Rhasha could say anything, he revved the engines to a scream. The plane shot down the runway to begin Rhasha's first flight.

Rhasha was now more scared than ever, but she kept her eyes open. She wanted to see everything. As the plane left the runway, she gasped. "My stomach just turned upside down!"

Jim flew low over the village so Rhasha could spot their house, but she was too disoriented to look down. It took all she had to maintain her sanity. At first she felt like screaming, but she controlled the urge.

Jim saw Charlie driving down the highway, so he tipped his wing. Charlie waved back. Jim climbed to five hundred feet and leveled off. He flew straight so Rhasha could get comfortable. She looked down and all fear left her face, replaced by wonder.

The engines were quieter now, but she still had to speak loudly. "Ohhh Jim, it's so beautiful. Everything looks so different up here."

"I love flying. Up here I feel closer to God than any other place on earth." He could see Rhasha wasn't afraid anymore so he dropped the wing on her side. He wanted her to get a better view of the ground. "Look," Jim said, "I tilted the plane your way so you can see better."

Jim continued to fly low. "So what do you think, Rhasha?" he asked.

She was holding her stomach, but she looked in every direction, as though afraid she might miss something. "My stomach feels funny," she replied, "but I've never seen anything like this in my life."

Jim leaned over and kissed her. "Rhasha," he said, "I believe this is just a flickering glimpse of what heaven is like."

"Look, Jim," Rhasha said. "The trees and houses look so small. The sky looks much bigger now."

Jim flew Rhasha around for over an hour. She took in all the sights, absorbing as much as she possibly could. He didn't want her to be in the air too long on her first flight, so finally he suggested, "Sweetheart, why don't we go back to airport and land the plane? We can fly again tomorrow."

With all the excitement, Rhasha looked tired. "OK," she replied, but added, "so are we going flying every day?"

"Do you want to?"

"I'd love to-if you want to."

As the small twin engine plane headed back to the runway, it was clear Rhasha had something else on her mind. "Jim," she finally asked, "is it hard to learn how to fly an airplane?"

Jim misunderstood, thinking she thought he was extra-intelligent because he knew how to fly. "It's not hard. Anybody who can drive a car can learn to fly a plane." When he looked at her, he could actually see the gears turning in her head. He realized he'd been mistaken.

"Jim," Rhasha said slowly, "you're teaching me how to drive the jeep, so do you think I'm smart enough to learn how to fly?"

Now he understood. Jim didn't know how to answer her. If he said yes, he knew Rhasha would ask him to teach her. If he said no, he would be lying. "Rhasha," Jim said, already knowing what his answer would lead to, "you're smart enough to do anything you want to do."

"Do you really think I'm smart?"

"Yes, I do. You're as smart as anyone I know." Jim waited for the inevitable.

"Jim, could you teach me how to fly?"

The one thing he didn't want to do was the very thing Rhasha had asked of him. Not wanting to hurt her feelings, he answered her the only way he could. "I can teach you how to fly, but don't you think you should get more experience at driving first?"

Rhasha didn't have a problem with that. "OK," she said, "after we land, could you finish teaching me how to drive the jeep? I can learn how to fly tomorrow."

Rhasha had a goofy smile on her face. Jim laughed as he kissed her. He knew she was just teasing. Or was she? "Sweetheart," he said, "you can't learn to do everything in a day. It's going to take forty hours of lessons before you can solo a plane." Jim thought about what he'd said, and added hastily, "I can never let you solo a plane by yourself. You promised me you would never fly alone as long as we both live."

"And I don't want to, Jim," Rhasha said. "I can't think of one reason why I would ever want to go flying without you at my side."

"I'll make a deal with you, Rhasha," Jim said. "If you can drive for one hour without making any mistakes, I'll start teaching you how to fly tomorrow." He knew she couldn't do it, so he felt safe making that deal.

"I'll do it. You'll see. I won't make even one mistake."

The village came into view, with its thatched roofs and bamboo frameworks, the hospital and dining hall, the swimming pool and the church.

"Look, Jim!" she yelled, "There's our house! Look! It's right over there! See?" Rhasha waved her arm and pointed toward the ground.

Jim didn't have the heart to tell her he'd seen it long before she did. "Yes," he said, acting excited. "I see it! It's right there!"

Ahead of them was the dirt runway with the hangar at its end. Jim circled around the village until the runway was lined up straight ahead of them. He lowered the nose of the plane ready for landing, and Rhasha braced herself and started to shut her eyes, then quickly realized she needed to watch Jim land. She opened them with a determined look on her face. The closer they got to the ground, the bigger everything looked. Rhasha looked ready to panic as the tires touched the ground. When Jim slowed almost to a stop, she began to relax.

He taxied to the hangar and spun the tail around, revving the engines to a deafening pitch. He wanted to line up with the door so he could back the plane straight into the hangar with the jeep.

Satisfied, Jim turned the engines off. Rhasha unbuckled her seat belt and climbed out of the plane. She climbed into the jeep and started the motor, then backed the jeep until it was lined up in front of the plane. By this time Jim was out of the plane and had the bar hooked to the front wheel of the aircraft. Rhasha backed the jeep to the bar and Jim hooked the bar over the hitch and latched it, then she backed the plane into the hangar.

Rhasha parked the jeep in front of the open hangar doors, got out, and walked around to the passenger side to wait for Jim as he closed the hangar doors. Rhasha beamed at him when he walked to the passenger side of the jeep.

"Do you want me to drive, Jim?" she asked.

Jim put one hand on the back of Rhasha's seat and the other hand at the top of the door and leaned toward her. "Rhasha," he said, "you're going to be doing all the driving. From now on, when we get in the jeep, you get in on the driver's side."

Rhasha slid around to face Jim and dropped her feet to the ground. When she stood up, her body was against Jim's, forcing him to stand up straight. She gave him a big kiss and immediately stepped around him.

Rhasha was wearing her blue denim shorts with a long scarf run through the belt loops and tied in a knot on her right side. Her oversized, button-up shirt was draped over her small frame and gathered into a knot above her belly button. Jim thought of her beautiful body, as being delightfully sexy. Her angelic face always supported an innocent smile.

Rhasha was full of energy. She ran toward the runway, yelling all the way, "Yes, yes, yes! Jim's going to teach me how to fly." When she reached the center of the runway, she stopped running and jumped as high as she could into the air, flinging her arms above her head with her fingers locked together. When she landed, she twirled in a circle, then wrapped her arms around her waist and hugged herself.

Rhasha suddenly lowered her head. Her happiness turned to tears. The strength in her legs gave way and her body dropped to the ground. Rhasha sat in the middle of the runway and held her face in her hands. She began to sob.

Jim had been watching Rhasha's excitement. Her fall to the ground alarmed him. He ran as fast as he could and dropped down beside her. "Rhasha, what's wrong? Are you OK?"

She looked up at him. Tears were running down her cheeks. "Jim," she said, "I'm just so happy. Nobody should be this happy. I just know something bad is going to happen."

Jim couldn't keep his secret any longer. It was time to tell her about his vision. "Rhasha," Jim said, "I love you more than anyone on earth. I never want you to be sad, but I have to tell you something."

He put his arms around Rhasha and kissed her. Her tears dried up and she regarded him with a serious look on her face. "What is it? Is something wrong? Is it your health?"

"My health is fine. This isn't about me, it's about you."

Rhasha frowned in puzzlement. "It's about me? Am I in bad health?"

Jim grinned. Rhasha would know if she was in poor health. Then he sobered and said, "When I was on the plane coming to Africa, I had a dream."

Rhasha's expression shifted to one of curiosity. "Was it a bad dream?"

"It was actually a vision, Rhasha," Jim replied, "and I'm afraid it showed me something that will happen. In the vision, you were flying alone in a twin engine plane. You were by yourself." He paused. "You crashed into the side of a mountain."

Rhasha thought a moment, then brightened. "OK Jim," she said, "if I never fly a plane by myself, then your vision can never happen."

"Well, what if I . . . somehow fell out of the plane? You would be alone."

Rhasha laughed and put her hand on Jim's knee. "What if, what if." She giggled. "Why don't we just make sure you keep your seat belt on?"

Jim had remained serious, but now he realized how ridiculous he sounded. He chuckled. "OK, Rhasha. We'll make sure I keep my seat belt on."

They helped each other up and walked toward the jeep.

"One more thing, Jim," Rhasha said. When he looked at her, she yelled, *"What did you mean, you jumped out of airplanes? Were you crazy?"*

Laughing, Rhasha took off running. Jim chased her. He caught up with her at the jeep and pretended he was going to choke her, but kissed her instead.

Jim got in on the passenger side and Rhasha jumped in behind the steering wheel and started the jeep. She put it in first gear and slowly pulled onto the dirt road. She never shifted to another gear. She was determined not to make any mistakes. Every now and then, she looked over at Jim and smiled. She drove all the way to town at five miles per hour.

When they got to town, Jim asked her to park in front of the dining hall. "That was very interesting, Rhasha," Jim said, smiling, when she complied.

"I thought so, too." She was grinning from ear to ear. "But sweetheart, I didn't make any mistakes, did I?"

Jim shook his head, still smiling. "No, you didn't. But are we always going to drive that slow?"

"Yes!" she said emphatically as she climbed out of the jeep.

Jim met her in front of the jeep and they walked arm in arm into the dining hall. They talked to several of the guests before they ate lunch. Rhasha proudly told everyone that Jim was teaching her how to fly. No one had known Jim was a pilot.

When they finished talking to their friends, they headed for the buffet table and loaded two plates with roast beef, mashed potatoes, and vegetables, then found an empty table and sat down. Rhasha listened as Jim gave thanks to God, then they began to eat. The conversation throughout the whole meal was about flying. Rhasha couldn't stop talking about her new experience.

Chapter 12

The Village Goes To Work

Bed of Leaves

After lunch, Jim had Rhasha practice driving. Rhasha drove slowly to the main road and turned left at the stop sign to drive thirty miles one way, then thirty miles back. She'd chosen the main road because she wouldn't have much shifting to do. Mindful of the fact that she made mistakes only when she needed to shift, Rhasha shifted slowly and carefully into each gear as she accelerated to forty miles per hour. Rhasha didn't make one mistake during the whole hour and fifteen minutes she drove. Jim was impressed, mostly because she'd used her head and figured out how to drive for over an hour and rarely work the clutch.

"Very good job, Rhasha," Jim said as she turned the motor off in front of their house and handed him the keys. "In a year or so, you should be ready to learn how to fly."

She punched him on the shoulder. "I'll be ready first thing in the morning, dear," she said confidently.

Jim smiled. "You got it, angel. And I'm sure you'll do just fine."

Rhasha winked at him. "I think everything will be OK, as long as your paratrooper instincts don't come back to you."

Jim returned the wink. "You'll never know until it's too late, will you, dear?"

The remainder of the day went as it usually did. Jim and Rhasha spent most of their time at the hospital, talking and singing to all the patients.

That night, after Jim's prayer and their showers, Jim took his guitar off the hook and began to sing. Rhasha joined in. *"This little light of mine, I'm going to let it shine. This little light of mine, I'm going to let it shine. This little light of mine, I'm going to let it shine. Let it shine, let it shine, let it shine."*

The children stood silently at the window again, watching Jim and Rhasha singing in their pajamas. After two more songs, Jim told them it was time to go to bed, and the children disappeared into the night. He and Rhasha snuggled into bed together and drifted into a sound sleep.

When Rhasha woke up, Jim had his right leg across both her legs, and his right arm across her waist. She watched his face as she waited for him to wake up. Finally she saw two big blue eyes looking back at her. "Good morning, sunshine," she said, and kissed him on the cheek. She began brushing his hair.

"Good morning, sweetheart," Jim replied. "I love you." It was the first time Jim had said "I love you" in private, like her lover.

Rhasha was all over him with kisses. Then she said, sincerely and lovingly, "I love you so much, Jim." Tears welled up in her eyes. They held each other tight.

Jim pulled away. "I think it's time for me to take a cold shower."

As Jim threw his legs over the side of the bed, Rhasha teased, "I agree. Let's both take a shower."

Jim knew she was teasing. "You first, sweetheart," he said. "You're the one that stinks."

Rhasha sat up in bed and laughingly threatened, "Take it back, or you'll be sorry."

"I'm going to be sorry? Ooh, I'm so scared, Rhasha."

She snatched the full glass of water Jim had left on her night stand the night before and threw it in Jim's face. He gasped and wiped the water off his face with his hands. Laughing, Rhasha ran to the bathroom. She returned with a towel and wiped the water off his face.

Jim was still in shock, but he was smiling. "I'm sorry, Jim," Rhasha said, "I just did it without thinking." Before she got the last word out, she noticed Jim had a glass of water in his hand. "Jim!" she yelled. Before she could throw her hands up, a full glass of cold water hit her in the face. Rhasha sputtered and swiped at her face. It was Rhasha's turn to be shocked.

"I'm sorry, Rhasha," Jim mimicked, "I just did it without thinking." As she had done, he dried her face with the towel. They were both soaked from their heads to their waists. Surprisingly, not much water had hit the bed.

Suddenly there was a knock at the door. "That's Jackie," Jim said, heading for the door. Before he reached it, Rhasha ran up behind him and jumped on his back. She locked her legs around his waist and her arms around his neck. Jim opened the door with Rhasha hanging on his back.

Jackie was smiling, but his smile turned sour when he saw how wet Jim and Rhasha were. "What happened?" Jackie said, staring at their wet clothes. Then he must have realized Jim and Rhasha were having a water fight, because he smiled again and said, "Good morning Jim, Rhasha. I came over to see if you two were ready for breakfast, but I see you're still taking your showers."

"Good morning, Jackie," Jim and Rhasha said in unison.

Rhasha slid off Jim's back and stepped up beside him. "Come on in, Jackie," she said. "We can find another glass of water, if you care to join us."

Jackie stepped back from the door and held his hands up in front of him. "No thank you, Rhasha! I've already had my shower. I think I'll just go have breakfast by myself."

"We'll be there in about an hour, Jackie," Jim said. "That is, if I can get stinky here to take a shower."

"Jim," Jackie said, "I have a feeling that's how you got wet in the first place."

Rhasha nodded, grinning.

By the time Jim and Rhasha reached the dining hall, Jackie had eaten his breakfast and left. The hall was almost full. Jim and Rhasha filled their bowls with boiled oatmeal. As they made their way to the last empty table, a family eating breakfast stopped Jim and thanked him for all he had done for them.

"Is there anything we can do to repay you for the food, home, and clothes we've received?" one of them asked.

Other people in the dining hall had overheard. The hall grew quiet as everyone waited for Jim's answer.

"I don't ask for any kind of payment from anyone," Jim said. "I require nothing from you, but I would ask each of you do one thing for me."

Several voices rose, all asking the same question: "What do you want us to do, Jim?" Those in the hall leaned forward, eager to hear Jim's answer.

"Share what you have with others," he said.

One woman sitting some distance behind Jim said, "I would like to share with others, but I don't have anything to share."

Jim turned to face the woman. He could tell she was sincere. "Are you busy every minute of every day?" he asked.

The woman looked confused. "No," she said. "I don't have a job. I get bored because I don't have anything to do."

Jim smiled at her. "Then you have plenty to share."

The woman looked thoughtful. "All I have is what you gave me. What could I possibly share with other people?"

Jim answered her in a gentle voice. "Your time."

Everyone listened intently to the conversation.

"I would like to share my time, but what could I do?" she asked.

Jim walked over to the woman and knelt down beside her. He looked into her warm black eyes. She was a young woman and appeared to be in good health. "Sweetheart," he said, "the patients in the hospital love to have people come talk to them. They feel all alone in the world and helpless."

Jim stood up and walked to another table where six people sat. "The cooks need help," he said. "There are dishes to wash and tables to clean." He walked to another table occupied by three black men. "The grass needs to be mowed and buildings need repair." He walked to a table where four children sat watching, and placed a hand on two of the children's shoulders. "We have an orphanage now," Jim said, "and these children need special attention. They need people to care about them."

Jim walked back to the table where Rhasha waited, but remained standing. "We have a community," he said, his voice intense, "and it's growing bigger every day. For a community to survive, everyone needs to pitch in and work together."

Jim paused. He hadn't meant to get so fired up. He looked around. Everyone was quiet, but he could tell they wanted to hear what he had to say. "Soon I'm going to have a hundred more houses built. I'm going to expand the hospital and dining hall." Jim had big plans for the village. Now was the time to expose his future plans. "I'm not going to live on earth forever. Someday, heaven will be my eternal home." He paused. "I had a will drawn up. When I die, my money and company profits will go to this village." Rhasha was sitting in a chair beside him, and he rested a hand on her shoulder. "The will is in Rhasha's name. I trust her to take care of everyone."

Rhasha looked surprised. Even Rhasha hadn't known about this.

"In the event something should happen to Rhasha," he added, "the money will go to a trust fund for the village."

Jim looked around the dining hall. Everyone was quiet. He knew he had taken a simple answer and turned it into a speech. "We need to set up a village government, with a mayor and city council. These officials will be elected by you, the people. I'm going to have a school built. Our children need an education."

People were still coming in but no one was leaving. The new arrivals were filling plates and sitting on the floor to eat.

"What I'm most concerned about," Jim said, "is taking care of the sick and feeding the hungry. I want to teach people about God and Jesus Christ." Jim thought about Rhasha, and how sick she'd been. He remembered her swollen stomach and the sores on her face. He broke down. Tears forced their way under his eyelids and his body felt suddenly weak. When he spoke again, his voice was shaky. "I don't ever want another person to die of hunger because I was too selfish to share what I have with them."

Rhasha stood up put her arms around him. They held each other tight for a moment, then released their hold on each other and Jim stuck his hand in his trouser pocket. Rhasha put her arm through the crook of his arm. Jim decided this was a good stopping point. "I want to thank everyone for your attention," he said.

Bed of Leaves

No one said a word as Jim and Rhasha left the dining hall. Neither one of them had eaten their oatmeal. They walked to the middle of the street, where Rhasha stopped Jim. They faced each other, and from the corner of his eye, Jim saw all the people in the dining hall standing at the windows, watching his and Rhasha's every move. Rhasha put her arms around Jim's neck and Jim slipped his arms around her waist. They didn't kiss. They just stood in the middle of the road and gazed into each other's eyes. Finally Rhasha pulled Jim tight against her body and Jim tightened his embrace. They held their foreheads together. A light breeze ruffled their hair. Jim thought only of Rhasha, and wished this moment would never pass.

The dining hall windows were open. After a few minutes Jim heard giggling. Their audience began clapping and cheering. Voices yelled, "Kiss her, Jim." Others were telling Rhasha to kiss Jim.

They both turned their heads so they were cheek to cheek and smiled at the people inside the dining hall. The people inside the dining hall cheered even louder as Jim and Rhasha kissed passionately. Then they turned and, within seconds, they disappeared through the hospital door.

Unknown to Jim, the people inside the dining hall were deeply touched by what he'd said. They held an unscheduled village meeting and talked about Jim's plans for expanding the village. Rhasha's parents and brother were among the people in the dining hall. Thamish was a big voice in the discussion. In the end, everyone present agreed that it was time to help Jim expand with the village.

While Jim and Rhasha were talking to patients, they heard the hospital door open. Eight people walked in and immediately started talking to the patients. Jim watched in growing excitement. When he and Rhasha had talked to all the patients, they approached the volunteers, and Jim thanked them for their help. When they said good-bye to everyone and walked through the hospital door, they stopped dead on the porch.

Something unusual was going on-people were working all around the village. Several men were mowing grass in several locations. Other people were making repairs on buildings. Jim even saw four women sweeping the street in front of the hospital and dining hall. He saw people walking in and out of the orphanage. Across the street, people carried garbage out of the dining hall. He looked down the street and saw women walking with elderly people, helping them with each step.

Jim knelt on the hospital porch and put his hands together. A humming sound could be heard. It grew progressively louder and began to pulsate. After a few seconds, it faded, then ceased. Suddenly clouds appeared in the east. They spread across the sky like water running off a mountain. Bolts of lightning streaked toward the ground and thunder rumbled far and wide. Then the sky cleared, and a window into heaven appeared. Jim, eyes still closed, raised his head toward the window. Rhasha knelt beside him.

A pale blue glow surrounded Jim and Rhasha. The soft humming sound rose again. It pulsed for a few seconds, then faded and stopped. Not a sound could be heard. Everything moved as if in slow motion. The breeze became calm.

Everyone stopped what they were doing. The men who'd been mowing grass turned off their mowers. All the workers looked toward the hospital. They saw Jim and Rhasha bathed in the blue glow. They knelt on the ground and put their hands together.

Rhasha glanced up and saw all the workers kneeling with their faces turned toward heaven and their hands clasped together. She could see a light blue glow surrounding everyone who was kneeling. Those who weren't yet kneeling also saw the blue glow around them and fell to the ground and put their hands together as well. Rhasha closed her eyes and began to pray.

A nurse opened the hospital door and looked across the village. She saw all the people kneeling and the blue glow surrounding them as they prayed. A thin beam of light shot from every worker's head toward heaven. She looked up, and saw four angels in the sky, holding a window open. The beams of light went through the window and into the throne room of God. She dropped to her knees and began to pray. Soon a beam of light shot toward heaven from her blue-limned body.

His eyes still closed, Jim didn't see the beams of light. As he prayed, he formed a mental picture of God, sitting on his throne. Jesus sat at his right hand side. "Father," Jim said, "please forgive me for my sins and have mercy on my soul. Thank you for the friends you gave me and thank you for sending me to Africa. Please bless these people and speak to their hearts. In the name of Jesus, I pray. Amen."

Jim saw all the people praying when he opened his eyes. One by one, they opened their eyes and the blue glow surrounding them faded. Clouds rolled in like waves across the ocean, spreading across the sky. Lightning flashed and the thunder roared. The humming sound rose, pulsated, faded away. Then the wind began to blow again and the sky cleared-everything returned to normal. The vision was over.

Jim and Rhasha rose and stepped out into the hospital yard to meet the crowd of people that gathered around them. Everyone talked about the blue glow and the beams of light. The nurse exclaimed about the window to heaven. After a while, everyone drifted away and returned to work.

Rhasha knew all the people in the village respected Jim, but until now, she had no idea how much. She was very touched by the peoples' response.

Chapter 13

Tunnel Vision

Jim and Rhasha got into the jeep and Rhasha slowly drove to the airstrip for her first flying lesson. At the hangar, after they'd pulled the plane out, Jim showed Rhasha how to do a walk-around inspection. He pointed to the cables that operated the wing flaps and told her to always check for frayed or broken wires. He told her to check the fabric covering the plane for tears, and to always check the propellers for any signs of damage, because dirt and rocks got whipped up into the propellers, causing them to become pitted and worn. "When the propellers start looking ragged, they need to be replaced," he told her.

Everything looked good. They climbed aboard and Jim started the engines, then did a thorough inspection of the gauges and maneuvering controls. Satisfied, he taxied over to the fuel pump and filled the tank with fuel.

"Rhasha," Jim said when he'd clambered back into the plane and they'd both put their seat belts on, "no matter what you do, always know how much fuel you have." He pointed to a gauge on the dash. "You'll never find a gas station in the sky. Never fly when you're low on fuel."

He started the engines and taxied onto the runway. The propellers stirred up dust all around the plane.

"For the next month, I'm going to do all the taking off and landing," Jim shouted over the roar of the engines. "I want you to get the feel of steering the plane."

"OK," Rhasha replied, "but I just have one thing to do before we take off." She leaned over and kissed him on the lips. She held up her pinkie finger. Jim locked his pinkie finger around hers.

He knew Rhasha was nervous. "Angel," Jim said to reassure her, "I think you're going to be my favorite student." Rhasha returned his smile. He released her pinkie finger.

"Do all your students kiss you?"

“So far they do, sweetheart,” Jim replied loudly. The engine noise was deafening. “You’re my first student.”

The plane shot down the runway and quickly became airborne. Rhasha felt queasy as they flew over the village. Jim ascended to fifteen hundred feet and leveled off. He let Rhasha have the controls and told her to simply fly straight. He allowed her to fly for thirty minutes, then told her how to turn around. She completed the maneuver and steered the plane back toward the airstrip. Jim landed the plane and they hangared the aircraft, then drove back to the village.

When they arrived at the dining hall, Rhasha excitedly told everyone that Jim had let her fly the plane. Everyone she talked to became as excited as her. They’d seen the plane when it took off and when it came in for a landing.

Days turned into weeks. Jim and Rhasha’s love grew stronger and stronger. Rhasha had become a good driver, and Jim now let her do all the driving. She’d learned how to take off and land Jim’s plane, and did all the flying, too. She could fly well enough to solo, but Jim wouldn’t allow her to be alone in the plane.

Jim hired Buju Construction Company to build additions to the hospital and dining hall, doubling the size of both buildings. The community now had a school and four teachers, all born and educated in Africa. Every child above the age of five was asked to go to school, and anyone who wanted an education was allowed to attend classes. Many adults found pleasure in learning and those in the village who had already been educated were always ready to assist.

Jim was planning to go to the United States and wanted Rhasha, Jackie, and Simbatu to go with him. He needed someone to watch over the village while they were gone, so he decided to set up a village government. Jim announced there would be an election and encouraged people who displayed leadership qualities to have their names added to the ballot. He launched a campaign to educate those in the village about elections, so people would know how to become candidates and how to vote. He patterned the government after the American political system and so the ballot listed candidates for mayor and city council, for school board members, and for treasurer. Several people signed up for each position, because Jim pledged to pay a small wage to each office holder. Even Rhasha's dad Thamish was on the ballot for mayor.

The elections would be held in one month, allowing candidates time to sway voters to their side. After the election, Jim would have one month to train the elected officials in their new jobs. In the meantime, Jim and Rhasha went to an overcrowded church every Sunday and sang to a dedicated congregation. Every Sunday, Jim prayed for God to speak to the hearts of the village people. Every Sunday the congregation went home without professing Jesus as savior. Reverend Morris, Jim, and Jackie spoke to listeners daily, but it was as if a wall stood between the church pews and the altar. Several people told Reverend Morris they believed in Jesus, but no one was willing to be the first one to walk down the aisle.

Jim prayed for Rhasha every day, that she might understand. Rhasha wanted to understand, but Jesus just didn't make sense to her. She told Jim she would believe in Jesus if he wanted her to. He told her to wait until Jesus was in her heart. Rhasha sang Christian music as beautifully as any Christian Jim had ever known, but she would not come forward to profess Jesus as savior.

Bed of Leaves

Every Sunday the congregation met at the waterfalls after church, and this Sunday was no exception. Jim and Rhasha already had prepared everything they needed for the picnic, so they only had to load the jeep and stop by the hospital to talk to the patients for an hour and a half before meeting everyone else at the falls.

As Rhasha parked the jeep, Jim watched the water flow over the edge of the cliff and crash into the clear pool. Mist hung in the air around the pool. People sat all around the waterfalls on blankets, eating sandwiches and drinking tea. Two men were fishing with their homemade fishing poles and several children played in the water. Jim could hear laughter over the noise from the falls.

Jim and Rhasha unloaded the jeep and laid everything neatly on their blankets. Then they went swimming, keeping mostly to themselves, but occasionally returning the greetings of passing swimmers. Jim and Rhasha played in the water until Jim got tired, then they swam toward the shore. They waded onto the bank, dripping water onto the ground.

Jim threw two sandwiches together as Rhasha set out paper plates and plastic forks. He placed the sandwiches on the plates and dished out some potato salad. Rhasha poured two glasses of iced tea and handed one to Jim.

When they finished eating, Jim lay back on his pillow with his hands behind his head. Rhasha lay on her side facing him, with her elbow on her pillow and her cheek resting on the palm of her hand. Her hair fell around her wrist. Jim moved his right hand to cover his face and block the sun.

"Are you going to sleep?" Rhasha asked.

"You could easily talk me into it, Rhasha," Jim murmured.

"You know, Jim, you really need to do more exercises. You're really out of shape."

Jim opened one eye. Rhasha was smiling. Jim played along. He sat up and crossed his legs in front of him. "You young whipper snapper," he snapped, "I can do anything you can do, only better."

"OK, grandpa, can you do this?" Rhasha threw her leg up in front of her body and wrapped it around the back of her neck. Jim and Rhasha both knew he could never do that.

"You think you're elastic girl, do you?" Jim could hide a smile.

"Let's see you do it, grumpy," Rhasha challenged.

"Well, if I was wearing anything but these denim cutoffs, I could throw both my legs behind my head and walk to the water on my fingers."

"Jim," Rhasha replied seriously, "the only way you could ever do that is if we broke both your legs." They both laughed.

"Well, I guess we'll never know, will we?" Jim replied as Rhasha used her hands to lift her leg from behind her head. Jim thought that would end the discussion, but not Rhasha. She found a way to keep it going.

"You're wearing briefs," she said. "Just slip your shorts off and show me that you can put both legs behind your head."

Jim reached down and unbuttoned his denim shorts. He acted as if he was going to pull the zipper down. Rhasha looked surprised, obviously wondering if he would really do it.

"Oh, I forgot," Jim said. "I don't wear briefs when I go swimming." They both knew he had briefs under his cutoffs. Jim buttoned them and lay back on the pillow.

Rhasha reached inside the cutoffs, grabbed the elastic waistband on his briefs, and yanked. "And what do you call this, Jim?" Rhasha asked, laughing.

"That's not briefs. That's my undergarments."

"It looks like briefs to me," Rhasha said.

"It doesn't matter," he replied, "I'm still not taking my pants off."

They heard snickering and looked around. People sitting on both sides of them had heard every word. While Jim was looking around to see how large their audience was, he caught sight of two boys swinging on a vine-the same teenage boys who swung on the vine at every picnic.

As Jim watched, one teenager grasped the vine and jumped off the fifteen-foot-high boulder, aiming for another boulder a short distance away that was about the same height. As he swung over the water, the vine snapped. The boy plummeted to a flat rock that lay at water level, fifteen feet below. When he hit, the impact was the same as if he'd been hit by a car going thirty miles per hour.

Jim jumped up and ran as far as he could along the shore. Rhasha was right behind Jim, crying as she ran. Several other people had already reached the boy before Jim could dive into the pool. The lower boulder lay in about thirty feet of water. The teenage boy had bounced off the rock and slid into the water. Several people, including the boy's parents, pulled him back onto the rock and laid him on his back.

As Jim and Rhasha swam to the crowd around the boy, Jim could see both his parents crying. The boy's face was crushed. It looked as though it had been run through a meat grinder. Blood covered the boy's face and chest. He looked dead. A nurse had climbed onto the rock and was checking his vital signs.

"Nurse?" asked Jim, still in the water, gripping the rock to keep his head above water.

The nurse turned to look at Jim. Tears were in her eyes. All she could do was shake her head. Jim burst into tears and fell back into the water. The water was too deep for Jim to stand, so he clung to the rock with one finger. He closed his eyes and said a silent prayer.

Jim's resolve grew. Stern faced, he climbed onto the rock. When Rhasha made to join him, he asked her to stay in the water. Not a tear was in his eyes. He demanded that everyone, including the boy's parents, go to shore.

No one moved.

Jim squatted next to the boy and lifted his upper body in his arms, holding him tight against his chest. The boy's face and chest were covered in blood. A stream of blood ran across the rock. Jim's left cheek was smeared with blood, and his shirt dripped red. He laid the boy's lifeless body on the rock and stood up. Jim was numb. It was as if his heart had turned cold. He scowled. He demanded again in a loud voice, "Everyone go to shore. Now!"

They stared in shock, unable to understand his zombie-like appearance. No one did as he demanded.

Suddenly Jim's body began to transform. He became transparent, as if he were clear glass. The village people watched in terror. Jim looked monstrous. Anger suffused his face.

Everyone, including the boy's parents, fled to shore. Only Rhasha remained in the water next to the rock.

Once the people were on the shore, Jim's monstrous appearance subsided, but he remained transparent. He knelt beside the boy. His transparent body gleamed in the sunlight. Jim raised his face toward heaven and placed his hands together. He began to pray. His voice didn't sound like his own, but like his spirit's voice, coming from deep within his body and sounding as though it was being amplified through speakers.

"Father in heaven," his voice boomed, "please forgive me for my sins and have mercy on my soul."

A pale blue glow appeared as a dome over the boy and Jim. It covered the rock and Rhasha and extended twenty feet over the water.

"Father," Jim said, "since you sent me to Africa, you have not let one of these people die, until today. It's my fault, Father, that the boy is dead. I should have stopped him from swinging on the vine. Father, if there is even an ounce of life left in the boy's body, could I beg you to heal him?

Clouds began to form in the sky, gathering in the east. Suddenly, the clouds let loose with the force of an explosion. They rushed toward the west like a tsunami across the ocean. Lightning streaked across the sky and thunder rumbled through the clouds. The clouds seemed to simmer for a few seconds, then rolled back to the east. The humming sound rose, then faded. The breeze stilled; everything fell silent. A large portion of the sky opened up like a large window, held open by angels at its four corners, and heaven became visible to all the villagers. They dropped to their knees and began to pray. They prayed the way Reverend Morris prayed.

Jim, in his glass form, continued to pray. "Father, I love you with all my heart and I want to be in heaven. Please take my life instead of the young boy's."

Rhasha heard. "Noooo!" she screamed. He voice echoed across the pool. Tears coursed down her cheeks. "If you take Jim's life, Father," she sobbed, "then I pray you take my life."

The humming sound rose to a high pitch, then ceased. It sounded like it was gearing up again. A beam of blindingly bright light, twenty feet wide, shot from the throne room in heaven and descended at an angle toward the rock where the young boy lay. The village people had to turn their backs to the brilliance and cover their eyes.

"Father," Jim said, "your power is awesome and I have no more strength in me." He slowly sank to his knees. He continued to hold his face toward heaven, but opened his eyes. Inside the bright beam of light was a tunnel, ten feet wide, that reached all the way to heaven. Inside the tunnel it was bright, but pleasant to Jim's eyes. It sparkled like diamonds.

Rhasha was also inside the tunnel. She thought the bright beam of light had come for her and Jim. "Jim," she whispered, "are we going to heaven now, through the tunnel?"

Jim heard what she said, but before he could answer, a blue glow flowed from heaven. As the glow descended quickly toward the rock, Jim could see that it encompassed two angels.

"Father," Jim said, "I don't understand what's happening." At this point, Jim's body began to transform again. His transparent body resumed its normal appearance.

When the angels' feet touched the ground, they leaned over the motionless boy. Jim couldn't see what was going on, and he was too confused to pray. He reached down to help Rhasha out of the water. The angels knelt beside the boy and covered him with their white gowns. Jim and Rhasha held each other tight.

The angels stood up and said words in a language Jim and Rhasha had never heard before.

While the angels were speaking in the unknown tongue, the boy opened his eyes. Jim stared in wonder. The boy's face was healed and he appeared very content. Jim could see no blood on the boy or the rock. He felt his own face and his hand came away clean of blood. He looked down at his clothes. The bloodstains were completely gone.

As the angels ascended toward heaven, the boy stood up. When the angels arrived at the throne room, the humming sound grew louder. Suddenly the beam of light disappeared, as did the blue glow. A beam of light shot out of heaven again, but this time it shot toward the village hospital. The light was too bright to watch. Even Jim and Rhasha had to turn around and cover their eyes. A moment later the light disappeared and the breeze began to blow. The window to heaven closed.

The humming rose, pulsed, faded away. Again clouds formed; lightning streaked and thunder rumbled through the simmering clouds as though a storm was building. Then they rolled back to the east.

Jim and Rhasha grabbed the young boy and all three hugged each other tight. At the water's edge, people dashed into the pool and swam as fast as they could toward the rock where Jim, Rhasha, and the boy stood.

Before they reached the rock, something strange happened. Everyone stopped swimming and began treading water, looking around as though trying to figure out what they were doing in the water. Jim, Rhasha, and the boy stepped away from each other and watched the swimmers.

"What are we doing, Rhasha?" Jim asked. "Why are we standing on this rock?"

"I don't know," Rhasha replied.

They both looked at the young boy. He shrugged, indicating that he didn't know what was going on either. "The last thing I remember," the boy said, "I was swinging on that vine." He pointed to the vine that was now secured to the tree.

Everyone swam to shore, still curious about why they were in the water, but unable to remember what had happened. No one recalled that the vine had snapped with the boy swinging on it. No one realized it had been mended. When Jim and Rhasha returned to their blankets, they were still trying to figure out how they'd ended up on the rock.

"Rhasha," Jim said, "Would it be OK if we go back to the village?"

Rhasha nodded. "I'm ready to go, too."

They loaded the picnic supplies and blankets into the jeep. As Rhasha pulled the jeep onto the highway, Jim noticed something different about the air. It felt like the calm after a storm. Normally, at this speed, he could feel a breeze blowing through his hair.

"Have you noticed how calm it is?" he asked Rhasha.

"Yes. The sun is shining-it should be steaming hot." Rhasha paused and looked at Jim. "Are you hot?"

"No," Jim said, "the temperature is just right." Jim looked at Rhasha. He could tell something was on her mind.

After a moment she said, "Do you feel something sort of . . . magical in the air?"

"Yes," Jim replied, "I do. It feels so calm and peaceful. I think something happened at the falls today, but what was it? I can't remember."

"I don't know, but I have the same feeling."

"Rhasha, I think something happened to us on that boulder, but I feel like it was something good."

"I think so, too." Rhasha looked puzzled. "But if it was something good, then why did we all block it out of our minds?"

Jim didn't have an answer for her, because he was asking himself the same question.

Rhasha turned off the main road onto the road that led to the village. The hospital could be seen in the distance.

"Let's stop at the hospital," Jim suggested.

"OK."

Rhasha shifted into second gear. As she shifted into third gear, something down the road caught Jim's attention. "Look," he said, "do you see all the people in front of the hospital?"

"Yes. What's going on?"

"I don't know. Let's pull over and find out."

Rhasha eased toward the curb and pushed on the brake. Jim realized that all the people gathered in the hospital yard were strangers. The only person he recognized was the nurse. Jim couldn't understand why they were all wearing hospital gowns.

Jim and Rhasha got out of the jeep. They held hands as they walked toward the crowd. Everyone was laughing and dancing.

A young boy saw Jim and Rhasha walking toward them. "There they are!" he yelled excitedly. "There's Papa and Mama!"

Everyone stopped singing and dancing and flocked around Jim and Rhasha. Some of the people tried to kiss Jim, others tried to kiss Rhasha. They were all telling Jim and Rhasha they loved them. Confusion reigned. People tried to jump over each other to talk to Jim and Rhasha. The nurse was trying to get to Jim to tell him what was going on. Several times, she tried to squeeze through the crowd, but kept getting pushed back. Finally she gave up and stepped back.

A high-pitched scream pierced the noise of the crowd. Everyone stopped yelling and turned to see what was wrong.

A little girl stood by herself, no more than twenty feet away. Her hands wiped floods of tears away from her cheeks. "I want to tell Papa something," the little girl cried.

The crowd opened up just enough to allow Jim and Rhasha to walk to the little girl. They knelt down in front of her, and Jim kissed the little girl on the forehead. Rhasha held the little girl's hand. She threw her arms around their necks and began to weep. Her knees buckled.

"Sweetheart, are you OK?" Jim asked.

The little girl stopped crying and wiped her eyes. She stepped back and waited until both of them were looking into her eyes. Then she deliberately blinked her eyes. To make sure Jim and Rhasha saw her, she blinked her eyes again. Tears began to trickle down her cheeks. In a shaky but certain voice, she said, "That means 'I love you both.' "

Jim and Rhasha both gasped, suddenly recognizing the little girl who had lain in bed one, nearly crippled by starvation. She shouldn't have been standing. She shouldn't have been able to talk. Yet this little girl stood before them, pretty and healthy, and spoke to them in the voice of an angel.

They threw their arms around her and hugged her.

A woman with two little girls, all healthy, walked up to Jim and Rhasha. The woman knelt beside them, while her two daughters remained standing. The little girl who had previously occupied bed one released Jim and Rhasha and Jim looked at the woman and her two children. They had tears in their eyes, obviously overwhelmed by the situation. The mother looked at Jim and Rhasha, speechless. One of the daughters took Rhasha's hand in both of hers.

The other daughter brushed Jim's hair with her hand. "Papa," she said, "do you know who we are?"

Jim hadn't known until that moment, but now he remembered two girls in the hospital, and that one of the girls had been smaller than the other. He kissed the smaller girl on the cheek and put his arm around her waist. "You're the pretty girl in bed two," he said. He looked at the taller girl. He kissed her on the cheek and wrapped one arm around her waist. "And you're the pretty girl in bed three."

Jim, Rhasha and the young mother rose and Jim kissed the mother on her cheek. "You're the pretty woman in bed four."

Tears rolled down Jim and Rhasha's cheeks. They knew God must have healed the patients in the first four beds. They'd figured out who four of the people in front of the hospital were, but who were all the other people?

As Jim and Rhasha hugged the mother and her two daughters, the other people gathered around. Suddenly, Jim had a crazy thought. He knew it couldn't be true, but he just had to find out. He looked at Rhasha. She raised her eyebrows-she'd had the same thought at the same time.

They both ran toward the hospital door, stopping on the porch to clasp each other's hand. Jim slowly opened the door. They both peeked around the door frame. All the beds were empty. Not a patient was in sight. Sheets and blankets were scattered everywhere.

Jim and Rhasha looked at each other in disbelief. They couldn't remember the beam of light that had shot from heaven toward the hospital, but they knew God must have healed all the patients.

They both turned to look at the crowd gathered around the hospital porch. The people began laughing at the looks on Jim and Rhasha's faces.

"We're all healed, Papa," several people yelled.

One older man said loudly, "I was in bed ten, Papa. Do you remember me?"

A young boy's voice called above all the others, "I was in bed eighteen, Papa and Rhasha. You both told me I would get well. Look at me now."

Jim took Rhasha's hand and pulled her into the crowd of people. They hugged every patient. The women kissed them.

When everyone began to settle down, Jim asked them to go to the dining hall to eat. Inside the dining hall, however, most of the patients said they were too excited to eat. They sat down at the tables and began talking to Jim and Rhasha. As they talked, people returning to the village from the waterfalls wandered in.

For over two hours, the ex-patients told the village people what Jim and Rhasha had done for them. Everyone laughed at the funny things they heard and cried about the sad things. There was a strong sense of family, and everyone thought of Jim as head of the household and Rhasha as his wife.

It was getting late when Jim realized the cured patients needed places to live. Luckily, several new houses had been completed. "I'm going to give you all houses tonight," Jim said, "and tomorrow, you can go over to The Factory to get new clothes."

Jim and Rhasha walked everyone to their new houses. Most of the families were mothers with only one child. Members of each family he assigned a house to thanked Jim for all his kindness, then rushed to check out their new homes.

When the families had been assigned, six people still didn't have houses. Three people said they could share a house, as did two others. Jim escorted them to the last two homes on the street. They thanked Jim and disappeared through their doors.

Chapter 14

A Home For Shanha

One child remained-Shanha, the little girl in bed one. She had no family.

Rhasha leaned over and cupped Shanha's face in her hands. She kissed her on the forehead and winked. Then she straightened and stepped in front of Jim. She put her arms around him and kissed him on the lips. "Sweetheart," she said, "could Shanha live with us?"

Shanha squealed in glee. "Can I Papa, can I? I'll be real good for you and Mama."

Jim watched Rhasha's face. He could tell being called "Mama" melted Rhasha's heart. Jim loved Shanha, and didn't want her to live in the orphanage. "OK, you two angels," he said, "let's go home."

Rhasha and Shanha both squealed in excitement.

They walked two streets over. At the end of the block, across from the hospital, Jim pointed to his house. "Shanha, this is where you'll be living now."

"Ooh, Papa," she replied, "we have a real home."

Jim thought about all of them living together. He smiled. "We make quite a trio," he said. "A forty-five-year-old white man, an eighteen-year-old black girl, and a seven-year-old black girl."

Rhasha smiled as she put icing on the cake. "Yes, now we can be a real family."

Tears ran down Shanha's cheeks. Jim thought she was sad. "Shanha, are you missing your Papa and Mama?"

Jim and Rhasha knelt down in front of her. Shanha put her arms around both their necks. "You and Mama *are* my papa and mama," she replied. "I don't know why I'm crying. It's just that . . . I'm so happy."

Rhasha understood. Tears trickled down her own cheeks.

Jim picked Shanha up and carried her into the house. Rhasha hung onto his other arm. Inside, Jim carried Shanha through every room, showing her first where the living room was and then the kitchen. He showed her where his and Rhasha's bedroom was, and finally took her through the bathroom into another bedroom. "This will be your bedroom," he told her as he set her down on the bed.

Shanha didn't stay there. She jumped up and stood beside Jim and Rhasha.

"Shanha," Rhasha asked, "would you like to take a shower now?"

Shanha was acting fidgety. She locked her hands together and rocked back and forth. It was obvious she was acting bashful. "Would you help me, Mama?" she asked.

Rhasha knelt down in front of Shanha and put her arms around her. "Sweetheart, anytime you need help, all you have to do is ask."

Jim went back to his bedroom as Rhasha and Shanha took showers. When they came out of the bathroom, Rhasha was wearing a pair of Jim's pajamas with the legs rolled up. Shanha was wearing one of his pajama tops as a gown. The shirt sleeves hung well past her fingertips. Jim smiled as they stood together in front of him, wearing sheepish grins on their faces. He knew something was going on.

They walked toward Jim, but stopped when they were about three feet away from the bed. They raised their arms straight above their heads and turned around in a full circle, standing on the tips of their toes. Shanha's sleeves folded over the tips of her fingers. They finished facing Jim. He knew they'd planned this modeling event while they were in the bathroom.

Rhasha and Shanha were both smiling as they gave each other the high five. After they slapped each other's hands, they hugged each other tight.

"Shanha," Jim said, "tomorrow we'll get you some pajamas that fit."

"Papa," she said, "can I just wear your pajama shirt every night?"

Rhasha remembered the first night she'd worn Jim's pajamas, and how happy it had made her feel. "Jim, you'll never know how important this is to her."

Jim looked at the sleeves hanging past Shanha's fingertips. "OK, but let's cut those sleeves off." He found a pair of scissors and cut both sleeves to a length that wouldn't hang past the palms of her hands.

He went to the bathroom and took a shower, put on his last pair of pajamas, combed his hair and brushed his teeth, then returned to the bedroom.

Jim walked close to the bed and lifted his arms above his head. He had a sheepish grin on his face. Rhasha watched him knowingly, then whispered in Shanha's ear. Jim stood on the tips of his toes and started to turn all the way around. Before he could complete his slow pirouette, Rhasha and Shanha jumped up and pushed him onto the bed. They began tickling his ribs and blowing in his hair. Jim kicked and squirmed.

As they bounced around on the bed, they heard children laughing. They looked toward the window and saw two children's faces peeking through the screen.

Jim got up and took his guitar off the hook. When he got back to the bed, Rhasha and Shanha were sitting up. "Rhasha, are you ready to sing."

"Yes."

Jim sat on the bed between Rhasha and Shanha. He began strumming his guitar. Music filled the room.

Jim and Rhasha began to sing. *"This little light of mine, Lord, I'm gonna let it shine. This little light of mine, Lord, I'm gonna let it shine."*

A third voice joined Jim and Rhasha's. Shanha had a beautiful voice.

"This little light of mine, Lord, I'm gonna let it shine. Let it shine, let it shine, let it shine."

It sounded heavenly as all three sang together. Jim didn't know it, but there were over thirty people standing outside his window. As Jim, Rhasha, and Shanha sang, everyone in Jim's yard joined in the singing.

"Jesus gave me light, now I'm gonna let it shine. Jesus gave me light, now I'm gonna let it shine. Jesus gave me light, now I'm gonna let it shine. Let it shine, let it shine, let it shine."

When they finished the song, Jim, Rhasha, and Shanha walked out onto the porch. With the porch light on, Jim could see all the people in his yard; he saw several more approaching. "It's no wonder my grass won't grow," he said.

They all laughed, then Jim, Rhasha, and Shanha sang *Whispering Hope*. Again, the children joined in. They sang two more songs, then Jim announced it was his bedtime. Everyone said good-bye and all the children left Jim's yard. Jim, Rhasha, and Shanha went back to the bedroom.

Jim hung his guitar on the hook and knelt down by his bed to pray. Rhasha and Shanha knelt down beside him, one on each side. When Jim finished saying his evening prayer, he told Shanha it was time for bed and carried her to her bedroom and laid her gently on the bed. He pulled the sheet up to her waist and he and Rhasha kissed her good night. They stayed with her until she fell asleep, then sneaked back to their bedroom.

Jim poured two glasses of water. He placed one glass on Rhasha's night stand and one glass on his. Rhasha got into bed. Jim turned out the lights and crawled into bed beside her and kissed her good night, but though he closed his eyes, he couldn't sleep. He tossed and turned. *What happened at the waterfalls?* he thought over and over. Why were he and Rhasha on the lower rock? It didn't make any sense. They had never been on that rock before. Jim couldn't understand. Why couldn't anyone remember what happened before that?

Jim heard a noise at the bathroom door. It sounded like someone had come into the room. The noise was loud enough to wake Rhasha. "Shanha," Jim said, "is that you?"

After a short pause, Jim heard a timid voice. "Papa, I couldn't sleep. Could I sleep in here with you and Mama?"

Jim couldn't see Rhasha in the darkness, but he could feel her hand press against his cheek.

"Please, Jim," Rhasha whispered.

The bed was small, but Jim didn't want Shanha to be alone if she couldn't sleep. He reached over and turned on the lamp. "Sure, sweetheart, come on to bed."

Shanha climbed over Rhasha so she could sleep between the two people she loved the most.

Rhasha always slept snuggled up to Jim so she had to find a way to deal with this new arrangement. She squeezed Shanha tight against Jim and put her leg across Shanha's and Jim's legs. She stretched her arm across Shanha and rested her hand on Jim's chest. Shanha didn't mind this arrangement, because it was exactly how she wanted to sleep. A few minutes later, Rhasha and Shanha were asleep.

Finally Jim fell into a restless sleep. As he slept, a dim light grew in his mind. A fuzzy picture came into focus, in the way of dreams. As Jim studied the fuzzy picture, it became clearer and clearer. The picture began to roll as if it were passing through an old movie projector. Jim viewed the scene of a teenage boy swinging on a vine at a waterfall. The vine broke and the boy went crashing onto a rock at water level. In his dream, Jim recognized the boy and the waterfalls.

He could see all the people, including an image of himself, running to the boy's aid. He watched himself rudely telling all the people to go to shore. He could see all the blood on the boy's face, and on his own face and clothes. He saw the blood running across the rock. He watched himself transforming into a transparent, glass-like figure as all the people fled in fear. His dream image prayed to God, and he could hear the booming of his voice. He saw the window open up into heaven, and the bright beam of light that descended from the throne room to the rock.

Then the boy stood up. All the blood was gone. The beam of light disappeared, then reappeared to shoot toward the hospital. The beam of light disappeared and the window to heaven closed. He watched all the people swimming toward the teenage boy. Jim knew, before they got to the rock, that everyone had become confused.

A loud voice entered Jim's dream. It sounded like it was amplified through speakers. *"Jim, we didn't want you to dwell too much on what happened at the waterfalls. This vision was given to you so you will understand. The boy fell to the rock, but his life was spared."*

Jim felt weak, but he heard himself asking, "Are you God's messenger, sir?"

"I am God's messenger."

Jim began to relax. The vision he saw now was in the throne room of God. "Was the boy dead?" Jim asked.

God's messenger didn't hesitate to answer. *"It is appointed unto man only once to die, Jim. The boy had a spark of life left in him."*

As the messenger spoke, Jim could see bright lights flash in heaven with each word the voice uttered.

"That's why it was important to transform you into glass. We needed to get all the people out of the way."

"Could I ask, sir, why you erased everyone's memories?"

"Jim," the voice said, *"if the people could remember you turning to glass, then they would believe that you're God. If they could remember the beam of light that came from heaven, then they would believe you brought the boy back to life. God could have healed the boy without sending angels, but then it would have appeared that you healed him. The people would worship you and not the true God in heaven. After the boy was healed, God considered the vision too powerful for the African people, so he erased everyone's memory."*

"God's messenger, if I could ask just one more question, I would be content."

"So be it," the voice boomed, *"if I'm permitted to answer it."*

Jim thought about how to ask the question. "God has performed many miracles around me," he said at last, "and I just wanted to know if you could tell me why."

"Jim, soon all things on earth will come to an end. Don't be alarmed, It will not happen in your lifetime."

"Sir, I'm not concerned about me if it did, but what about the people in the village?"

"God will take care of his children. You're living in an area where people have never heard of Jesus. God is using miracles to help speed up the acceptance process."

"But sir," Jim argued, "the people hear the word of God in our church, yet they refuse to come forward."

"Be patient, Jim. Their hearts will open up one day and they will flood to the altar."

With that, the voice was gone and the dream was over. Jim slept contentedly throughout the night.

The next morning, Shanha was still lying between her and Jim when Rhasha opened her eyes. Shanha was awake and staring into Rhasha's eyes.

"Good morning, Mama," Shanha whispered. "You have such pretty eyes."

Rhasha smiled. "Good morning, sweetheart," Rhasha whispered back, not wanting to wake Jim.

Shanha kissed Rhasha on the forehead and quietly placed both her hands around Rhasha's hand. "You're a very pretty lady, Mama." Shanha said.

"You're a very pretty little girl," Rhasha whispered. "You're also very precious and I love you very much."

"I love you too, Mama," Shanha whispered.

Rhasha could feel Jim moving and knew he was about to wake up. "Shanha," Rhasha whispered, "when Papa wakes up, let's both say those things to him at the same time."

"OK, Mama," Shanha said. "He will like that."

"He'll love it," Rhasha said.

When Jim slowly opened his eyes a while later, Rhasha winked at Shanha. "Good morning, sunshine," they said in unison.

"It's going to be a beautiful day, Papa," Shanha said as she brushed Jim's hair in the usual morning ritual.

Jim slipped his feet over the side of the bed and stood up. "I knew Rhasha was going to be a handful," he said, "but put you two together and it spells double trouble."

Rhasha and Shanha both put their hands over their mouths and giggled. Jim kissed them both on the forehead and went to the bathroom to take a shower. Rhasha and Shanha were right. Jim loved what they did for him.

"Isn't Mama pretty, Papa?" Shanha said when they'd all had their showers. She gestured at Rhasha, who wore her usual outfit of cutoff denim sorts, scarf belt, and shirt. Shanha was still wearing Jim's pajama top.

"She sure is, sweetheart," Jim replied, "and after we eat breakfast, we're going to go to The Factory and get you some pretty clothes, too."

"Thank you, Papa. I want to be pretty, like Mama."

"Shanha," Jim said, "you have a beautiful face, but the important thing is . . . you're a very sweet girl. That makes you beautiful on the inside, as well." She giggled as Jim kissed her on the forehead. "No matter what happens in life, always stay pretty on the inside, and you will always be pretty on the outside."

"I will, Papa," Shanha replied. "I want you to be proud of me."

Rhasha added, "Papa's a good example of being pretty on the inside." Jim could tell that Rhasha was getting ready to tease him again. "You see, Shanha," Rhasha continued, "because Papa is so pretty on the inside, it makes him not quite so ugly on the outside." She winked at Shanha.

Shanha played along. "Yes, Mama. It sure is lucky for Papa that he's pretty on the inside."

Jim stuck out his lip and acted hurt. Rhasha kissed him on the forehead, so Shanha did the same. They were interrupted by a knock on the living room door. Jackie had come to walk with them to the dining hall for breakfast.

It was seven o'clock in the morning and villagers were busy all over town. Everyone had heard what happened at the hospital the day before. They were all trying to make their new neighbors feel comfortable. Jim saw some people, still clad in their hospital gowns, walking to The Factory to get new clothes. When they entered the dining hall, Jim saw people helping the cook. Others cleaned tables and washed dishes.

As Jim, Rhasha, and Shanha filled their plates with biscuits and gravy, Jackie went to talk to Simbatu. Jim took the opportunity to tell Rhasha about his dream. He didn't want anyone but Rhasha and Shanha to hear, so as they ate, Jim said in a low voice, "Rhasha, I found out why we were on that rock at the falls yesterday."

"OK," Rhasha joked, "tell me we went swimming and we both bumped our heads on that rock. That's how we developed amnesia, right?" She was being goofy and she knew it, so she smiled.

Jim remained serious. "I had a dream last night, and God's messenger showed me what happened." He spoke so low that Rhasha and Shanha had to lean forward to hear him. Jim wasn't sure Rhasha would understand what he had to say, but he knew she was also upset about her memory loss. "In my dream, we were at the waterfalls. The vine the boys swing on every week broke, and one of boys almost died. God sent a beam of light and healed the boy. The beam of light went back into heaven, then it came down again and healed all the people in the hospital."

"OK Jim," Rhasha whispered, "I can understand that, but why did God block our memories?"

"Because of the situation," Jim replied. "God knew that the village people would mistakenly worship me for healing the boy, so to prevent that he wiped what happened from everyone's memory."

Rhasha nodded. All her questions had been answered. “So now that all the patients are healed, what are we going to do with our time?”

“I haven’t thought about it,” Jim admitted, “but I suppose we could go flying early today.”

Jim and his new family finished eating breakfast and before long they were in the double engine plane, flying at fifteen hundred feet. Shanha was too excited to be scared as the plane slipped through the sky at a hundred and forty miles per hour. When they passed over the village to land, Rhasha showed Shanha their house.

Shanha was thrilled. “Look Papa, look at our house! It looks so small.”

Jim looked down, just to please Shanha. He smiled and asked, “How do you know that’s our house? They all look the same.”

Shanha looked at Rhasha. “Yeah Mama, how do you know which house is ours?”

“Because, sweetheart,” Rhasha replied, “it’s right across the street from the hospital.”

“Papa, you knew that,” Shanha scolded.

Jim and Rhasha giggled.

“Papa, could you teach me how to fly a plane, like Mama?”

“You need to learn how to drive a car first,” Jim told her.

“OK, can you teach me how to drive a car . . . tomorrow?”

Jim was impressed by how similar in temperament Rhasha and Shanha were. “Sweetheart,” he said, “you have to go to school tomorrow. Besides, you can’t learn to drive until you’re sixteen.”

“Is that a long time, Papa?”

“When you’re sixteen, you’ll be almost as big as Rhasha,” he said.

Shanha hung her head and pouted. "Do I *have* to be sixteen before I can drive, Papa?"

"Yes, sweetheart."

Shanha leaned over Rhasha's shoulder and acted like she was sad. She whispered in Rhasha's ear, knowing Jim was close enough to hear what she was saying. "Mama, Papa's a mean papa."

Rhasha and Shanha giggled. Jim put his arm around Shanha's neck and scrubbed her noggin with his knuckles. Shanha tried to wrestle free of Jim's hold, but couldn't.

"But I love you, Papa," she said. She quit struggling and smiled.

Jim quit scrubbing her head. "I love you too." He winked at Rhasha, then released Shanha and told her to lean back and fasten her seat belt. Rhasha lowered the landing gear so she could land. Within moments the twin engine plane touched down on the runway. Rhasha coasted to a stop, and taxied to the hangar.

Jim and Rhasha parked the plane in the hangar, then they all climbed into the jeep and drove to The Factory. Several other ex-patients were inside, still in their pajamas. Jim went to talk to the manager about ordering more clothes while Rhasha assisted Shanha in picking out her own clothes. Shanha knew how much Jim liked the clothes Rhasha wore and she was sure he would like the clothes she picked out, too.

By the time Rhasha and Shanha came out of the dressing room, Jim was eagerly waiting. He looked at Shanha, then he looked at Rhasha. Jim chuckled, then rubbed his chin with his fingers. He tried to act serious, but it was obvious he wanted to laugh. "Hmm," he said, "this is very interesting."

Other people in The Factory did laugh. Rhasha and Shanha were both wearing blue jeans shorts with a scarf run through the belt loops. The scarves were tied in a knot on the side and hung down along beautiful black legs. They both wore oversize, button-up shirts of the same color, with the shirttails knotted above their waists. Shanha looked like a much shorter version of Rhasha. Smiling, they both rushed over to Jim and gave him a hug and a kiss. Everyone in the factory started clapping their hands.

Tears welled up in Jim's eyes. "I don't know what I'm going to do with you two."

They gathered Shanha's new clothes and left The Factory. When Jim, Rhasha, and Shanha entered the dining hall for lunch, everyone looked up. When they saw Rhasha and Shanha dressed alike, they stood and clapped. While they were eating, several people complimented Shanha on her pretty clothes.

Shanha entered school the next day.

Jim and Rhasha went flying every day. Shanha went with them on weekends. Whenever Shanha wasn't in school, she was always with Jim and Rhasha. Jim knew Shanha would be OK when she came home from school one day and asked if she could go play with friends.

In the next four weeks, twelve new patients were admitted to the hospital. All the houses were occupied; thirty new houses were almost completed. The dining hall was twice as big as before and the village now had a city hall.

Chapter 15

The Village Has A Name

On election day, Jim set the ballot box near the entrance to the dining hall, where a good voter turnout would be guaranteed. By the end of the day, ninety-five per cent of those eligible to vote had filled out a ballot. The votes were counted, and the village had a new mayor-Rhasha's dad, Thamish.

The mayor thanked everyone who had voted for him and vowed to do the best job he could. "The first thing I want to do as mayor," he said, "is to find a name for our village." He opened the floor to discussion. Several names were suggested, but dismissed for one reason or another. Thamish prepared to table the discussion until a later date. "Can anyone else think of a good name?" he asked one last time.

Jackie Short was sitting with Jim, Rhasha, and Shanha. He raised his hand to be recognized.

"Mr. Short," the mayor said, "what is your suggestion?"

Jackie stood up. "Mr. Mayor, in the United States, there's a large and beautiful city that has a pretty name."

"OK Mr. Short, tell us the name of the city, and we'll consider it."

Jackie watched Jim's face for an expression as he said the name. "Los Angeles."

Jim showed no expression.

Before Thamish went any further, he wanted to know one thing. "Mr. Short, most every name has a meaning, so what does Los Angeles mean?"

"I don't know, Mr. Mayor," Jackie replied, "but I'll find out."

As Jackie sat down, Jim raised his hand.

"Yes, Mr. Brown," Thamish said.

Jim stood. "No suggestion, Mr. Mayor," Jim said, "but I know what Los Angeles means. It means 'The Angels.' "

Thamish thanked him, then said, "Would everyone like to vote for Los Angeles as the village name?"

Several people said yes. Jim could tell people liked the name and was sure they would vote for it. As Thamish was about to ask for a show of hands, Jim raised his hand again.

"Mr. Brown," Thamish said, "did you have something, you wanted to say?"

Jim rose. "Mr. Mayor, there is an alternative."

"What is your suggestion?"

"Los Angeles is often referred to as the city of angels. It's a big city, with a lot of crime and corruption. Instead of naming our village Los Angeles, we could just name it 'Angel Town.' "

"Thank you, Mr. Brown," Thamish said. He looked around the hall. "Does anyone else have anything to say?" No one raised their hand. After a pause, Thamish said, "Jim built this village, and I, for one, think it would be proper to let him choose a name for it."

Jim wished now that he hadn't said anything. He wanted the voters to choose a name. He raised his hand again. "Mr. Mayor, there could be better names. Why don't we postpone voting on a name for one week? Everyone could think of names for our village and submit them to your office. We could get everyone, including the children in school, to submit their favorite village name." Jim sat down to let the discussion continue.

"Thank you, Mr. Brown," Thamish said. "Does anyone object to what Jim said?" No one raised their hand. "OK, we'll leave the ballot box here in the dining hall. We ask that everyone put the name of their choice in the box."

Blank paper and pens were placed by the ballot box so everyone could easily suggest a name. The mayor thanked everyone for voting and closed the meeting. The villagers filed out of the dining hall. Some paused to write their choice for the name of a town on a sheet of paper they then dropped into the ballot box. Those who couldn't write were assisted by people who could.

The mayor posted a notice announcing a town meeting on Saturday at three o'clock for the purpose of selecting a village name. During the next week every student put a suggestion for a town name on a sheet of paper. On Friday, the teachers put all the suggestions in one box and one of the teachers, Julia, carried them to the dining hall and put them in the ballot box.

On the afternoon of the meeting, the dining hall was filled to overflowing. Everyone wanted to know the village's new name. Talk, laughter, and shouts filled the air.

The mayor tapped his gavel on the table. "Quiet, please. Would everyone be seated?" The crowd began to settle. The mayor rapped his gavel again. "Could I have your attention, please?"

Everyone took a seat and stopped talking. A large number of people waited outside the building. Every window had faces peering inside. When everyone was quiet, Thamish called the meeting to order.

"The only purpose for this meeting is to select a town name. Most everyone of school age and up has submitted a name for the village. All suggestions have been placed in the ballot box." Thamish placed a notebook and a pen on the table in front of an empty chair next to his. "Could I get someone who can write to assist me while I'm checking each sheet of paper, please?"

The teacher Julia came forward and sat down.

"Thank you, Miss Julia," Thamish said. "As I call out the names, would you write them by number on a sheet of paper?"

As the temporary secretary picked up the pen and prepared to write, Thamish reached into the ballot box and pulled out the first slip of paper. "The first name I've drawn is . . . " The Mayor looked at the audience. "Angel Town."

The audience immediately began clapping. Everyone in the village knew what Jim wanted to name the village. As Julia wrote "Angel Town" in the notebook, Thamish drew the second sheet of paper from the ballot box. "The second name is . . . Angel Town."

Again he reached into the box, and again he announced, "Angel Town." And again. And again. Finally, amidst continued clapping, Thamish picked up the ballot box and dumped the contents onto the table. He pushed all the sheets of paper together and squared the corners. The mayor held the stack of papers in his hand. He read aloud all 247 sheets. Every sheet suggested Angel Town.

Knowing ninety-five percent of the voters couldn't write and that those people had someone else write their suggestion down for them, Thamish called out, "OK, before I declare Angel Town to be the new village name, I would like everyone who voted for Angel Town to raise their hands."

Everyone raised their hands. As the people clapped and cheered, the mayor rapped his gavel on the table. The audience settled down. Thamish waited until the last voice fell silent before he continued. "Did anyone not vote for Angel Town?"

Nobody raised their hand.

"From this day forward," Thamish announced, "our village will be known as Angel Town." Before everyone started clapping and cheering again, he added, "This meeting is adjourned."

One week later, a large sign was erected at the entrance to the village:

Angel Town
We want the hungry and the homeless.
We welcome the sick and the lame.
We love the elderly and the orphan.
We seek the unloved and the unwanted.

In time, every man, woman, and child grew to love the words on that sign.

During the next four weeks, Jim, Rhasha, Shanha, Jackie, and Simbatu prepared for their trip to the United States. Jim arranged for Shanha's education to continue through correspondence with her teacher. He enrolled Rhasha for a correspondence course as well. He also planned to be Rhasha and Shanha's teacher for the next two months.

Rhasha and Shanha applied for expedited passports. Rhasha had very little trouble acquiring hers, but Shanha was denied a passport because neither Jim nor Rhasha was her legal guardian. Jim knew one important thing about African officials: Money talks. He bought Shanha a passport at a substantial cost.

Jim, Rhasha, and Shanha continued to visit the patients at the hospital. They sang for them every day, and Jim prayed for them. All three followed what was now an established ritual: kiss each patient on the cheek, hold every patient's hand between theirs, brush each patient's hair, and tell every patient they have pretty eyes. The new patients loved Jim, Rhasha, and Shanha, but they loved many other people as well. Every day, scores of caring volunteers visited every patient during visitation hours.

Jim knew the patients would miss them when they went to the States. It was some consolation to Jim that the patients had other people to love and care for them now. He felt a little better about being away from the hospital for two months. He told every patient they would be gone for two months but always added, "But God willing, we will return." The patients were assured that when they got well, they would have a home, food, and clothes.

Bed of Leaves

Angel Town residents planned a big party in honor of Jim, Rhasha, Shanha, Jackie, and Simbatu for the day of their departure. The event was held at large public meeting building in the park. The building was nothing more than a concrete floor with slender tree trunks holding up a pole-constructed, straw-thatched roof, but it had a large wooden stage. Picnic tables had been placed evenly throughout the building and bolted to the floor. The mayor stepped onto the stage. Almost everyone in Angel Town was present for the event, and they gathered around the stage. Many people had to stand outside the public meeting area. As Thamish picked up the microphone, everyone began clapping and cheering. "Speech, speech," they yelled.

He held the microphone up to his mouth and started to speak, but the crowd was so noisy, he lowered the microphone and waved. He let the people cheer a few moments longer, then lifted the microphone to his mouth again. "Thank you, friends and neighbors, thank you."

The crowd began to settle down. Thamish looked at his wife. "Is this my birthday?" he joked. The crowd laughed. He looked back toward the crowd and became more serious. "I want to thank everyone for coming out today. You all seem to be in such high spirits."

The crowd began to clap again, but soon stopped. They wanted to hear what more the mayor had to say.

"I thank you for the applause," Thamish said, "and I know your enthusiasm is directed at Jim, Rhasha, Shanha, Jackie, and Simbatu." Everyone clapped and whistled again. The mayor looked at the five guests of honor who stood together on the ground in front of the stage. Thamish noticed Jim had his guitar on his shoulder. He looked back toward the crowd and smiled. "But . . . let's don't act like we're happy to see them go."

Everyone started clapping again. “I, for one, love all five of them with all my heart, and I know all of you do too.” Thamish wasn’t finished, but everyone began clapping so he yelled into the microphone, “They will be missed for the next two months.”

Rhasha’s mother began crying. Seeing this, several people became subdued. Tears ran down their cheeks. A hush fell over the crowd. Everyone began to cry. Jim looked up at Thamish and saw tears in his eyes before he covered his face with his hands.

Jim rushed onto the stage. Rhasha and Shanha were close behind. Rhasha stopped on her way up the stairs to hug her mother and kiss her on the forehead, then rushed to catch up with Jim and Shanha. Rhasha hugged her dad and told him everything would be OK.

Jim slipped the microphone from Thamish’s hand. He looked across the crowd. He couldn’t see one person who wasn’t crying. The mood overtook Jim and tears flowed from his eyes too. He knew he would miss these people. He quickly composed himself and looked at Rhasha and Shanha. They were both crying. Jim leaned over and whispered in Rhasha’s ear. She stopped crying and whispered the same words in Shanha’s ear.

Jim took his guitar off his shoulder and asked Rhasha to hold it. Two more microphones were brought out. Jim placed the microphone he held in its stand and arranged all three microphones at the front of the stage. He slid one microphone down to Shanha’s height. Then he took his guitar from Rhasha and stood in front of the first microphone. Shanha and Rhasha stepped up to the other microphones.

Thamish figured out what they were doing and left the stage. Jim began playing his guitar. He, Rhasha, and Shanha began to sing.

"This little light of mine, Lord, I'm gonna let it shine. This little light of mine, Lord, I'm gonna let it shine."

All the people slowly stopped crying and listened. Jackie was still in front of the stage, on the ground. He joined in the singing.

"This little light of mine, Lord, I'm gonna let it shine."

Simbatu joined in also.

"Let it shine, let it shine, let it shine."

Everyone in the crowd had heard Jim and Rhasha sing *This Little Light of Mine* so many times, they knew every word by heart. Almost every man, woman, and child joined in the singing.

"Jesus gave me light, now I'm gonna let it shine. Jesus gave me light, now I'm gonna let it shine. Jesus gave me light, now I'm gonna let it shine. Let it shine, let it shine, let it shine."

Everyone stopped singing at this point so Jim could do his instrumental part. At the proper time, they joined in again.

"Everywhere I go now, I'm gonna let it shine. Everywhere I go now, I'm gonna let it shine. Everywhere I go now, I gonna let it shine. Let it shine, let it shine, let it shine. This little light of mine, Lord, I'm gonna let it shine. This little light of mine, Lord, I'm gonna let it shine. This little light of mine, Lord, I'm gonna let it shine. Let it shine, let it shine, let it shine. Let it shine, let it shine, let it shine."

When everyone finished singing, Jim, Rhasha, and Shanha bowed. The crowd burst into applause. They whistled and cheered. A man's voice was heard urging, "Speech, speech, speech." One by one, other voices joined in, calling "Speech, speech, speech" in unison.

Jim slid the microphone holder up on the stand so it would be closer to his mouth. "It's so nice to be among people who love you," he said. They smiled as the crowd cheered and whistled.

"And," Jim said as the crowd calmed, "I want you to know Rhasha, Shanha, and I love each and everyone of you with all our hearts." Jim didn't tell them a thing they didn't already know. The crowd cheered wildly.

As the crowd began to settle, Rhasha felt compelled to add to what Jim said. "I want you to hear the same words from me. I love each and everyone of you."

Shanha put her mouth up to the microphone. "Me too," she yelled. The microphone made a loud, electronic squealing sound. It scared Shanha and she jumped back.

Rhasha and Shanha looked at each other. They both put a hand up to their lips and giggled. The crowd cheered loudly and laughed at the expression on Shanha's face. Rhasha raised both her pinkie fingers up to head level. Jim and Shanha did the same. They locked their fingers together. They released pinkie fingers and bowed to the crowd. As the people cheered, Jim hugged, then kissed Rhasha and Shanha on the lips. Rhasha in turn kissed Shanha. They put their hands to their lips and threw kisses to the crowd. The people went wild and threw kisses back.

Jim, Rhasha, and Shanha held hands as they walked off the stage. They met Jackie and Simbatu at the front of the stage and embraced them. The crowd gathered around all five of them, giving them hugs and kisses.

The crowd followed the five as they left the park and went to the hospital to visit with the patients. Afterward, almost everyone in Angel Town gathered around the jeep as Rhasha got in on the driver side and Jim climbed into the passenger seat. Shanha sat between Jackie and Simbatu in the back seat. It turned into a tearful departure. Everyone pushed and shoved, trying to say good-bye.

Rhasha started the jeep and eased it through the crowd, which parted to let them pass. They all waved to the crowd.

"I love you-bye!" everyone yelled. The crowd whistled and cheered until the jeep was out of sight. The Angel Town ambulance followed behind the jeep, loaded with all the luggage and band equipment. Rhasha's parents also rode in the ambulance.

As Rhasha pulled onto the main road, heading toward Nairobi, Shanha began thinking about America. She'd seen pictures of beautiful American cities in school. She leaned forward in her seat and asked Jim, "Papa, what are people like in the United States?"

Rhasha, Jackie, and Simbatu were just as anxious to hear Jim's answer. Jim turned his head toward Shanha and kissed her on the forehead. "Sweetheart," he said, "I wish I could say Americans are a race of angels, and would never do anyone harm."

Jim looked around. Suddenly everyone looked worried about what America was like. "Just like every country," he continued, "America has good people and it has bad people. I'll do my best to keep you away from the bad people."

The gears began to turn in Shanha's head. "Papa, does everyone in America believe in God?"

Jim replied, "Most people in America believe in God and over half the people claim to believe in Jesus Christ. Most of the people want to do good, but only a fraction of the people live the way God wants us to live."

Shanha considered what Jim had said. "Papa, how does God want me to live?"

Jim searched his memory for the right answer. "He wants you to love your neighbor as you love yourself."

Shanha looked confused. Jim tried again. "Do unto others as you would have them do unto you."

"If I do those things," Shanha asked, "will I go to heaven someday?"

"Sweetheart, those things are important, but there's only one way for you to get to heaven."

"What way is that, Papa?"

"You have to believe that Jesus is your savior," Jim said, "and that he died on the cross for your sins." He decided to quote a scripture, hoping to give her better understanding. " 'For God so loved the world, that he gave his only begotten son so that whosoever believeth in him shall not perish, but have everlasting life.' John 3:16."

Shanha frowned. "I don't know what that means."

Jim realized that she was only seven years old. He would have to explain it in a way that a child could understand. "It means, if you believe Jesus is God's son and he died on the cross for the bad things you do, then you are a Christian."

"So all I have to do is believe in Jesus?"

"Yes," Jim replied, "but if you really believe in Jesus, then you become a different person."

Rhasha, Jackie, and Simbatu strained to hear every word Jim said.

"Sweetheart," Jim said to Shanha, "when Christians do something bad, they feel sad, because they disobeyed God. True Christians always pray to God and ask him for forgiveness. They tell him they will try really hard not to ever do that bad thing again." Jim didn't know if Shanha could understand his explanation, but he didn't know any other way to explain it.

"I think I understand," Shanha said. "If I don't do anything bad, then I won't feel sad." She winked at Jim and smiled. "But if I do something bad, then I need to get down on my knees, like you do, and tell God I'm sorry."

"You've got it, Shanha," Jim replied, "but always remember this: Everyone does something bad sometimes. Just never forget to tell God you're sorry. Also, when you finish telling God you're sorry, then tell him that you're praying to him in the name of Jesus."

"OK, Papa. I promise you that I will always try to be good and I will always pray to God, even when I don't do something bad."

"Sweetheart, if you always do those things, then I will always be the happiest papa in the world." Jim looked at Rhasha, hoping that something he said had helped her to understand.

Rhasha felt Jim's eyes on her. Tears began to run down her cheeks and she couldn't see where she was going. Rhasha pulled the jeep off to the side of the road. The ambulance pulled off the road behind the jeep. "Jim," Rhasha sobbed, "I promise to do those things too, but I still don't understand how Jesus, who died, can cause people to live forever."

Jim smiled confidently at her. "Someday you will feel the presence of Jesus in your heart. He may or may not speak words to you, but you will know he is speaking to you. Then you will understand."

Shanha leaned forward and thrust her face between Jim and Rhasha. She rested one arm around Rhasha's neck and her other arm around Jim's neck. As Rhasha cried, Shanha pulled Jim and Rhasha toward her until all their heads touched. They all kissed each other at the same time.

Attempting to change the mood, Shanha began cutting up with Rhasha. "Mama, did Papa make you sad?"

Rhasha smiled back with tears in her eyes. She winked at Jim. "Yes sweetheart, Papa's a mean papa."

Rhasha and Shanha each put a hand to their lips and giggled. Rhasha reached over and gently slapped Jim. She put the jeep in gear and pulled back onto the roadway with the ambulance behind. Within minutes, they arrived at the airport.

Jim's company jet was parked in front of a rented hangar, already fueled and ready to go. Mario and Chuck had been at the hotel for over a day and were well rested. The jeep and ambulance both came to a stop next to the jet.

When Rhasha saw the company jet, her expression turned to astonishment. "Jim, do you own that plane?"

Everyone stared at the large aircraft.

"My company owns it, Rhasha," Jim replied. "It's used to transport company employees from one city to another in the States."

"But you own the company, don't you?" she exclaimed.

"Yes, that's how I make a living."

"So you own that plane, if you own the company, right?" Rhasha asked.

Jim couldn't understand why Rhasha was so hung up about who owned the plane. He knew she didn't admire money and she certainly wasn't a gold-digger. "Yes, I own the plane."

Rhasha's eyes opened wide. She threw her arms around Jim's neck and kissed him wildly. "Please, please, please, can I please fly that plane, Jim?"

Jim had to laugh, now that he knew what she was up to. "Rhasha, even I don't know how to fly that plane. It's different from our little propeller-driven plane."

Rhasha's excitement turned to disappointment. She hung her head, but Jim knew how to cheer her up. "Sweetheart, when we get inside the plane, I'll get the pilot to show you the instruments. After you see the instruments, then you'll understand why you can't fly a jet."

"OK, Jim. I'd love to see the controls."

They all climbed out of the jeep and walked toward the ambulance, where the ambulance driver and Rhasha's family were also climbing out. The driver opened the back door and Jim, Jackie, Simbatu, and Thamish unloaded the luggage and band equipment. They carried everything to the steps of the plane.

Mario and Chuck walked down the steps to greet everyone. They were happy to see Jim. Jim introduced everyone, then asked Mario if they'd got enough rest. Mario assured Jim they had, and informed him that the jet was ready to go.

Everyone carried baggage and instruments onto the plane. Rhasha and her family said an emotional good-bye. The ambulance driver, Thamish, and his family got back in the ambulance and headed back to Angel Town.

Jim, Rhasha, Shanha, Jackie, and Simbatu boarded the plane. While the others were getting settled, Jim took Rhasha to the cockpit. Mario was glad to show Rhasha the instrument panels and controls, but when Rhasha excitedly threw her arms around Jim's neck and kissed him, and Jim put his arms around her waist, Mario and Chuck looked at each other in disbelief.

"Am I in the twilight zone?" Chuck asked. "Or could it be my eyes are deceiving me?"

"Why's that, Chuck?" Jim asked.

"You, Jim. You had every woman in Dallas chasing you, but you had to come to Africa to find the woman you wanted."

"Chuck," Jim said, "I'm not a foolish man. Those women didn't want to marry me, they wanted to marry my bank account."

"If you're happy, then I'm happy for you."

"I am happy, Chuck," Jim said, "but the fact is, I'm just keeping an eye on Rhasha until her future husband comes along."

Mario laughed. “From what I could see, you *are* her future husband.”

Rhasha piped up. “Thank you, Mario. I agree with you.”

Jim decided to change the subject. “Now that we’re through with that, shall we get this box of nuts and bolts in the air?”

Chapter 16

Flying To America

Mario began preparing for takeoff as Jim and Rhasha walked back to the passenger compartment. Chuck pulled the stairs up and latched the door. After they got seated, Jim asked everyone to buckle their seat belts. He helped Shanha with hers.

Mario warmed the engines and eased the jet to the taxiway. He finally got the go ahead from the tower, and moments later the jet was speeding down the runway. Jackie and Simbatu had never been on a plane before and appeared very nervous as the jet left the ground. The jet ascended to thirty-three thousand feet and leveled off. At the speed of 550 miles per hour, Jim and his guests were on their way to the USA.

Everyone except Simbatu continued to look out the windows. He had a tight grip on his armrests. Jackie still looked nervous, too. Noticing this, Rhasha unbuckled her seat belt and walked to the front of the plane. Jim watched her fold a sheet of paper into the shape of a hat and put it on her head, then walk over to the kitchenette area. He didn't know what she was doing, but he knew she was planning to do something cute. She filled four plastic cups with water and placed them on a serving tray, which she balanced on the palm of her hand. She placed her other hand on her hip.

The paper cap cocked to one side, her beautiful body, the oversize shirt that covered her well-formed breasts, her beautiful black legs and her small, feminine feet-Jim looked at the girl he loved and saw a picture of pure innocence.

With a cute but phony smile on her face, Rhasha pranced down the aisle and stopped beside Jackie. "Would you like something to drink, sir?" she asked.

Jackie could see that all she had on the tray was water. "Yes dear," he said. "I think I'll have a cup of coffee."

“I’m sorry, sir,” stewardess Rhasha said. “We’re all out of coffee at this time, could I offer you something else?”

“That’s OK, I’ll just have a coke, then,” Jackie said.

Rhasha shook her head and bit her lip. “I’m sorry, si-”

“Do you have orange juice?” Jackie snapped in mock anger.

Rhasha shook her head again and bit her lip. “I’m sorry-”

“What *do* you have on this fly-by-night operation?” Jackie yelled.

Rhasha put an irritated look on her face. “We have water, sir.” Then she shouted, “Would you like a cup of water?”

“No! Thank you!” Jackie yelled.

Everyone laughed.

Jim decided to get in on the fun. “Oh, stewardess.” He snapped his fingers.

Rhasha rushed over to Jim. “Could I offer you something to drink, sir?”

“No thank you, dear,” he said. “I just wanted to let you know that there are colas and orange juice in the fridge. There’s also a coffeemaker on the counter. That is,” he added, “if you care to make a pot of coffee?”

Now Rhasha pretended to get angry at Jim. “The problem is . . . sir . . . *I don’t know how to make coffee!* But since you’re so smart, you make it.” With that, Rhasha sat down and scowled theatrically.

Jim unbuckled his seat belt and rose. He took Rhasha’s hat off her head and put it on his head. “Where’s your name tag, young lady?” he asked. “You’re going to lose your job over this.”

“My name is Kathy,” Rhasha said, “and I’ll have you to know, the captain and I are very, very good friends.” Rhasha almost cracked up when she said that.

He took the tray out of her hand and went to the kitchenette area. Chuck had already made coffee. Jim filled a cup with the black brew. He pulled two colas and two cartons of orange juice out of the refrigerator and placed everything on the tray, then placed the tray flat on the palm of his hand. He placed his other hand on his waist.

Rhasha couldn't help but smile at the man she loved. Anyone else would have seen an older man with thinning hair, wearing a suit and tie, acting silly. What Rhasha saw was the most wonderful man she'd ever known.

Jim minced down the aisle and stopped beside Jackie. "Would you like something to drink, sir?"

"Yes ma'am." Jackie smiled. "Could I get a cup of coffee, please?"

"You certainly can, sir." Jim grinned as he handed the cup of coffee to Jackie. "And thank you, sir, for flying the skies with Jim's Airlines."

Jim looked at Simbatu. "Would you like something to drink, sir?"

Simbatu was still too nervous to play around. "No thanks, Jim. I'm not thirsty right now."

Jim walked over to Shanha and knelt to the floor. "And how about you, sweet little girl? Would you like something to drink?"

Shanha had never seen a stewardess before so she didn't know what Jim was doing. "Oh Papa," she said, "you're being silly. But can I have that?" She pointed at a carton of orange juice. She had never had Coke before and didn't know what it was.

"You sure can, sweetheart." Jim set the tray on an empty seat and opened a carton of orange juice. He handed it to Shanha.

"Thank you, Papa."

Jim kissed her on the forehead and stood. He picked up the serving tray and walked toward Rhasha, stopping beside her seat.

Rhasha looked up at Jim and smiled. "Now, aren't you just the prettiest little thing?" she cooed.

Jim knew some airlines had stewards, but he knew Rhasha didn't know that. "Thank you, dear," he replied. "Would you like some orange juice?"

Rhasha again acted as if she was upset. "No. Thank you." She pouted.

"How about a Coke?" he said. "We have some good, yummy Coke."

"No, thank you." Rhasha maintained her hard-to-please role.

"Well, is there anything I can get you?"

"Yes there is," Rhasha snapped.

"You name it, dear," Jim said. "If we have it, I'll get it for you."

Rhasha didn't hesitate. "Could I please . . . *just have a cup of water?"*

Jim took off his hat and went to get Rhasha a cup of water. Rhasha met him at the kitchenette and they embraced.

"Have I ever mentioned that I love you?" Rhasha said.

Jim looked at his watch while he pondered the question. "No, I don't think you ever have."

"Oh," Rhasha said, "it must have slipped my mind."

Jim smiled and kissed her on the lips. "Have I ever told you that I love you?"

Rhasha decided to be serious. "Sweetheart, even if you never told me you love me, I would know it anyway."

Seeing Jim and Rhasha kissing, Shanha unbuckled her seat belt and rushed over to squeeze between them. "Papa, Mama, don't forget about me."

Jim and Rhasha knelt and Jim kissed her.

“We’ll never forget about you,” Rhasha said, and kissed her too.

Jim picked Shanha up and carried her back to her seat. Rhasha followed. He gently placed Shanha in her seat, then he and Rhasha returned to their seats.

As they sat down, Jim said, “Rhasha, I just want to ask you one thing.”

“No, I don’t want to change my name to Kathy,” she quipped.

They both smiled, then Jim got serious. “You’ve never been on an airliner. How did you know what a stewardess says and does?”

“Some of it was guesswork and some of it, I overheard.”

“I know there’s got to be more to this story,” Jim said.

“Not really. I overheard two girls talking at the Nairobi airport.”

“And I guess these two girls were stewardesses?” Jim suggested.

“I don’t know what they call themselves.”

“So what did they say?” Jim asked.

“One of the girls was telling the other girl what she would like to do to one of the passengers on her flight. She said she would like to put a glass of water on her tray, walk up to the passenger, and say, ‘Sir, would you like something to drink?’ ”

By this time, Jim was smiling. Rhasha continued her story. “Then she said, ‘When he says, “Bring me some coffee”-’ ”

“I get the message, Rhasha,” Jim interrupted. “You took someone else’s fantasy and turned it into reality.”

“You got it.” Rhasha smiled and pinched Jim’s cheek. “I’m so proud of you.”

By this time, Jackie had fallen asleep. Before too long, sleep overcame Rhasha and Shanha. Simbatu was still too nervous to shut his eyes. Jim tried to sleep, but he began thinking about the dream he had on the night Shanha moved in with him and Rhasha. God's messenger had said in his dream that soon all things would come to an end on earth. The messenger also said that it would not happen in his lifetime, but what about Rhasha and Shanha? Would it happen in their lifetime?

Jim knew what the book of Revelations said about the end times. Would God take care of the residents of Angel Town, he wondered, or would they suffer the same agony as the rest of the world?

Finally Jim shut his eyes, but he still couldn't sleep. He noticed that the sound of the engines was getting quieter. He could hear a humming sound. It grew louder. The humming sound began to pulsate then, after a few seconds, it faded away. Jim opened his eyes, but all he could see was a soft blue glow. He tried to close his eyes and open them again, but still all he could see was the blueness.

Jim didn't know if he was asleep or awake. He heard himself speak, but his lips didn't move. *"Father,"* he yelled, *"is this a vision or is it just a dream?"*

Suddenly a huge image of the earth materialized, fifty feet tall and fifty feet wide. As the earth turned, he could see an outline of each country. As Jim tried to figure out what this meant, he saw ten beams of light shoot out toward him. The beams were like brilliant white rays from a ray gun, and each came from a different point around the world. The rays hit Jim and pulled him to each of the ten places. He could see ten images of himself leave his body at the same time, each drawn to the country from which the beam originated. Each beam set their image of Jim on the ground and disappeared.

Jim discovered he could choose the image whose eyes he used to view the earth. He chose to view his surroundings through the image of himself in the United States.

The world image vanished; now Jim could see trees, roads, and buildings. The ground began to shudder and move under his feet, and he knew the movement could only be an earthquake. He realized all ten versions of himself felt the earth shake, in all ten countries where they stood. Large crevasses split the ground all around them.

Through the eyes of his United States image, he saw skyscrapers falling like rocks in Los Angeles. Cars were being thrown in every direction. Fires burned out of control.

Jim switched his view of the earth to his image in China. Again, the ground shook and buildings toppled. He knew the earth was expanding with the pressure from within, then collapsing and contracting as it found release. The earth would be egg shaped until pressure pushed the sides out, causing the poles to draw in.

Jim viewed the earth from other images of himself. He could see molten lava rolling across parts of Russia. Tsunamis hammered every shore of Japan. England, France, and Germany were engulfed in flames.

Jim could see people dying horribly in his vision-being ripped apart or burned to death. Fear was on every face. He saw hundreds of cars crashing into each other and people running insanely in every direction, fleeing from a wall of water that rolled over the tops of the buildings behind them. Shouts and screams filled the air. The ground shook and the pavement split in front of them. The ground rose up on one side of the split and a large crevasse opened on the lower side. Several people fell into the deep gap; others were pushed into it by those running into them from behind. Two people clung to the edge of the crevasse, their fingers locked onto the edge of the jagged pavement all that prevented them from falling into the hole. Above them, the survivors looked for a way around the gap, to no avail. The wall of water crashed down on top of them. Cars, people, and debris were washed into the crevasse.

Meteorites struck the earth in many places. One hit the ocean, and Jim saw multitudes of dead sea creatures floating on the surface. Tidal waves hit every shore on earth. Volcanoes erupted in several countries, including the United States. Somehow Jim knew that the catastrophes had killed a third of the population of earth.

His multiple images disappeared, replaced by a new vision. The United States was crippled by spreading famine; Russia and China were also crippled, but managed to join forces. Their armies swept across the oil soaked deserts of the Arab countries. Many nuclear missiles were launched, and some found targets in the United States.

Time flashed before Jim's eyes. He knew three and a half years had passed.

He saw a million soldiers from Russia and China, in league with the Arabs, converging on Israel. Death and destruction were everywhere. A nuclear explosion leveled an area between Gebo and Ramon, northwest of Jerusalem.

People all over earth were dying, many from lack of food and water. Law and order broke down; murderers, thieves, and rapists flourished. Jim saw people with numbers stamped on their foreheads or on the backs of their hands. Those without numbers couldn't buy or sell goods. Anyone caught not wearing the number was tortured and killed. He looked at the number, and knew it was evil: 666.

Finally something made sense to him. He saw new Jerusalem descending from heaven. It came to rest where the old Jerusalem had stood. Almost immediately, healing waters flowed from new Jerusalem. Trees on the banks of a river each produced twelve different kinds of fruit. Of all the people on earth, only God's people had survived.

Jim was drained of energy; he didn't want to see any more death.

A booming voice in his vision said, *"Jim, be not fearful. The things you saw will occur some time from now. Destruction of the earth will begin soon after your death."*

Jim heard himself speak, but his lips didn't move. *"Messenger of God,"* he said, *"what will become of Angel Town?"*

The voice replied, *"You need not be concerned. Angel Town is special to God."*

The voice spoke no more. Jim heard a now familiar humming sound that gradually grew louder. The humming throbbed for a moment, then faded away. The vision was over.

Jim opened his eyes. He knew that what he'd seen was a vision, not a dream. He remembered reading in the Bible about some of the events he'd seen, but those were written by the prophets in the Old Testament. The things the prophets wrote about had been revealed to them through dreams and visions.

Am I a prophet? Jim wondered. *Why did the messenger of God show me these things? What am I expected to do? Does God want me to write a book? Should I tell the world?*

Jim considered what he'd seen. *No,* he thought, *these things have already been written. The messenger of God wanted me to know Angel Town would be protected.*

As Jim continued to think, he recalled that the book of Revelations described many of the same things he'd seen in his vision, but what happened after new Jerusalem came down to earth? According to the Bible, life on earth would continue for another thousand years. This, Jim thought, would not be the end of the world. It would be the end of the world as it was now known. Many people would die, then the world would become godly.

Jim felt confident now-God would take care of Angel Town. He rested his head on the back of his seat and fell asleep.

When Jim awoke, Rhasha and Jackie were already awake. Simbatu had come to terms with his fear and was now sound asleep. Shanha was sleeping across two seats.

When Rhasha saw that Jim was awake, she clasped his left hand between both of hers and kissed him on the forehead. "Good morning, sunshine," she said, grinning at the ritual, "you have beautiful eyes."

Shanha woke up and saw what Rhasha was doing. "Mama," she said indignantly, "you didn't wait for me."

Rhasha hugged Shanha and kissed her on the forehead. "I'm sorry, sweetheart. You were asleep and I didn't want to wake you."

Determined not to be left out, Shanha gripped Jim's hand with both of hers and kissed him on the forehead. "Good morning, sunshine," she said, "you have beautiful eyes." Then she released Jim's hand and picked up one of Rhasha's hands. "Good morning, sunshine," she said, "you have beautiful eyes, too."

Rhasha started to say something to Shanha, but Jim spoke first. "You're both crazy, but you both have beautiful eyes." He winked and smiled at both of them.

Rhasha and Shanha each put a finger to her cheek and twisted the finger one way, then the other. They giggled and hugged each other. Jim gathered both of them into his arms for a hug and told them how much he loved them.

The aircraft hit a series of air pockets, bumping along like a car hitting a pot hole. The turbulence was so rough it woke up Simbatu, who held onto his armrests with both hands and looked around fearfully, not knowing what was going on. Rhasha, Shanha and Jackie held onto their seats too.

"Everything's okay," Jim said, "we just hit some turbulence."

"But Jim," Rhasha exclaimed, "it feels like the wings are going to break off."

"I promise you, sweetheart, it's normal. Planes hit air pockets all the time."

Rhasha and Shanha's faces had paled-they looked like they had seen a ghost. Jim would have laughed, but he knew how scared they were, and kept a straight face.

Mario slowed the plane as they flew through the turbulence, then brought it back to five hundred and fifty miles per hour a few minutes later. The sound of the engines was no more than a low-keyed hum coming through the pressurized jet. The crew and passengers began to relax. Jim, Rhasha, and Shanha stood to stretch their legs, pacing up and down the aisle just to work the kinks out of their muscles. Jackie and Simbatu saw what they were doing and did the same.

After a while, everyone became bored. They began to feel like prisoners on the plane, and they were relieved when Mario landed the plane at an airport outside of Dallas a few hours later. He taxied the plane to the company hangar and parked it. Raymond was waiting by the hangar with the company limousine.

Rhasha, looking out her window, caught sight of the car. It fascinated her. "Look Jim," she said, "isn't that the most beautiful car you ever saw?" She pointed out the window at the limo.

"It is pretty, Rhasha," Jim replied, "but there are prettier cars."

Rhasha shook her head firmly. "I don't think so. That car is almost as long as this plane."

The limousine was parked on the side opposite the door of the plane. Suddenly remembering the prank Rhasha had played on him at the waterfalls in Africa, when she'd pretended she'd hit her head on a rock and drowned, Jim said to Rhasha, "When Mario turns off the engines, Chuck will open the door. Jackie, Simbatu, and I will be getting the luggage together. When Chuck opens the door, stairs will extend out from the plane."

Rhasha had been listening attentively to everything Jim said. "Okay," she interrupted, "what do you want me to do?"

"I want you to take Shanha down the stairs and around the back of the plane."

"Okay, and then what?"

"Then," Jim replied, "walk over to the man at the car and say hello."

"Then what?"

"Ask him if you, your boyfriend, and Shanha can have a ride in his pretty car."

Rhasha looked puzzled. "Do you think he will let us, Jim?"

"I think so," Jim replied, maintaining a serious expression. "He looks like a friendly man."

Mario turned off the engines and Chuck opened the door. Rhasha and Shanha walked down the stairs and ran around the back of the plane. They slowly walked up to the limousine. Raymond was leaning against the outside of the car door. When Rhasha and Shanha approached him, he stood up straight.

"Hello sir," Rhasha said.

"Hello miss," Raymond replied, "what can I do for you?"

"I was wondering if Shanha, my boyfriend, and I could have a ride in your pretty car."

Raymond peered at the plane and scanned the area around the car. "Where is your boyfriend, miss?" he inquired.

"Well," Rhasha said, "he's busy right now, but he'll be here soon."

"Miss," Raymond said firmly but kindly, "I'm sorry, but I can't give you a ride. This is a company car, and I'm here to pick up my boss." Seeing the disappointment on Rhasha's face, he added, "Miss, if you really want to ride in this car, you can ask my boss about it. He's a real nice man."

Rhasha thanked Raymond and started to walk away. Suddenly she turned around. "Sir," she said, "you said this is a company car. Could you tell me who your boss is?"

"Sure," Raymond replied, "it's Jim Brown."

"I thought so," Rhasha said, realizing Jim had played a trick on her.

Jim, Jackie, and Simbatu were walking toward the limousine, carrying the luggage. Jim had a cocky smile on his face, and he was watching Rhasha. She whirled around and ran to meet him. She jumped up and threw her arms around his neck and locked her legs around his waist, kicking the luggage out of his hands. Jim reflexively wrapped his arms around her waist. Rhasha kissed him, then dropped her feet to the ground. She kept her arms around his neck. Raymond gaped.

"Please, please, please Jim," Rhasha pleaded, "can I drive that car?"

Jim smiled, remembering how Rhasha had wanted to fly the company jet in Africa. "Sweetheart," he said, "there's to many people here right now. In a few days, I'll let you take me for a drive."

That wasn't the answer Rhasha was looking for, but at least now she had something to look forward to. "Thank you, thank you, sweetheart," Rhasha said. "I'll drive it really carefully. You'll see."

Jim knew she had never driven a vehicle with an automatic transmission. He decided to wait until she tried to drive the limousine, to spring that surprise on her.

Raymond helped Jackie and Simbatu pack their luggage in the trunk and picked up the luggage Jim had dropped, loading that in the trunk as well. When Mario and Chuck joined them, Jackie and Simbatu helped them with their luggage.

Jim walked over to Raymond and shook his hand. "Raymond," he said, "how's everything with you and the family?"

"My family and I are doing well, Jim." Raymond grinned.

As the others joined them, Raymond glanced at Rhasha, who was hanging onto Jim's arm. Shanha was hanging onto Jim's other arm. "It looks like you're doing pretty good yourself, Jim," he observed.

"Raymond," Jim replied, "I've never been happier in my life."

As Jim introduced everyone to the chauffeur and gave him some literature on Africa, Jackie watched with a puzzled look on his face. "Jim," he finally asked, "is it common in America for the boss to introduce his guests to the chauffeur?"

"No Jackie," Jim chuckled, "but Raymond is my friend as well as my driver." Raymond beamed.

They bid good-bye to Mario and Chuck and slid into the limousine. Soon the limo was pulling away from the hangar. As the company car joined traffic on a busy Dallas highway, Jim's guests watched everything excitedly. Rhasha and Shanha had never seen so many cars. Traffic was stop and go. After a while, the limousine merged with traffic on Interstate 20, and Raymond was able to drive the speed limit. Less than thirty minutes later, the limousine pulled up in front of Jim's apartment.

His apartment was large enough to accommodate everyone. It had three bedrooms, two bathrooms, a generous kitchen, and a spacious living room. As everyone carried their luggage into the apartment, Jim assigned them to their bedrooms. He gave the two smaller bedrooms to Jackie and Simbatu; Rhasha and Shanha would share the master bedroom with him.

Both girls *ooh*ed and *ahh*ed over the master bedroom furnishings. The dresser, chest of drawers, bed tables, and bed frame were elegant in design and workmanship and constructed from Jim's favorite material, solid wood. A plush comforter covered a firm mattress, and each pillow seem to be three times as big as their pillows in Angel Town.

Rhasha and Shanha had never seen a king-size bed before. They were accustomed to sharing a smaller bed, where they could sleep close together. "Papa," Shanha said, "that bed is too big for us."

"That's a king-size bed," Jim said. "I think you'll find it very comfortable."

Shanha shook her head. "I don't think so, Papa. I like being able to touch you and Mama at the same time, while I'm asleep."

Jim could tell Rhasha didn't care much for it either. He smiled and kissed each of them on the forehead. "We can still sleep close together, girls," he said as he ushered Rhasha and Shanha out of the bedroom and into the living room.

It was getting late in the afternoon, so Jim decided to wait until the next day to go to the office. "It's after five, Raymond," he told the chauffeur. "You can go home now, but pick us up at eight o'clock in the morning." Raymond left amidst a flurry of good-byes.

Rhasha and Shanha sat on the sofa. Jackie and Simbatu plopped down in recliners. Jim went to the bathroom to wash his face and brush his teeth. When he came back, Shanha was standing in front of the entertainment center. The door that covered the front of the television was open.

"What is that big box?" Shanha asked. "I opened the door and it had a window behind it."

"That's a television," Jim told her. "Do you want to see what it does?" He picked up the remote control and turned the television on. As the picture began to focus, he adjusted the volume.

Rhasha and Shanha had never seen television before and didn't know what to expect. Suddenly they heard an explosion, and the television screen displayed an image of running people. Jim had turned the volume up to loud. With surround sound, it sounded like the explosion was in his living room.

Shanha screamed and ran for Rhasha's arms. Rhasha was just as terrified. Jim recognized an action-packed thriller on television, but to Rhasha and Shanha, it was as real as life. Jim turned the volume down.

"Papa," Shanha screamed, "Papa!"

Jim turned off the television and rushed to comfort Rhasha and Shanha. "It's only a movie," he said. "It's not real. It's just make-believe." They both clutched Jim, crying. Fear had control of them. They shook uncontrollably.

Jackie and Simbatu knew what television was, but they understood why Rhasha and Shanha were scared. After a few moments, Jim was able to calm both girls. He left the television turned off.

"I don't know why anyone would want that thing in their house," Rhasha said. Shanha agreed.

Jim released Rhasha and Shanha. "The only reason I have it," he admitted, "is so I can watch the news."

"Papa," Shanha asked, "does everyone in America have a box like that?"

"Yes. Most people have three or four televisions."

"Well, I don't ever want one, Papa," Shanha stated.

"That makes two of us," Rhasha agreed.

Jim and his guests sat around for a couple of hours, looking at the walls. Jim could tell everyone was getting bored. In Angel Town, Jim and his guests would be at the hospital now, singing for the patients. That thought gave Jim an idea.

"Would anyone like to hear some music?" he asked. The only kind of music Jim listened to was religious, but he did have some "oldies" rock and roll.

"I would, Papa," Shanha said.

Rhasha and Shanha watched Jim closely as he went to his entertainment center and opened the door, hoping he wouldn't turn the television on again. He pulled out several CDs and checked to see what songs were on each one. Finally he found the CD he was looking for-a collection of twenty uplifting songs, all pleasant to the ear and featuring male and female artists who had been popular when he was younger. He'd compiled his favorite songs on one high-quality CD through his computer, so he didn't have to listen to a lot of music he didn't like. Jim slipped the CD into the player, making sure the volume was turned down. As it began to play, he turned the volume up.

The first song was an immediate success with his guests. It just happened to be one of Jim's all-time favorites, an upbeat song by Donna Fargo, titled "Happiest Girl in the Whole USA." As the song began to play, Jim knew his friends were being introduced to an old style of music, but it was new to them.

Rhasha and Shanha fell in love with one verse in the song: *"I thank you, lord, for making him for me. And thank you for letting life turn out the way that I always thought it could be. Now, I once was a child and I could not imagine how it would feel to say, I'm the happiest girl in the whole USA."*

Jim looked at Rhasha and saw tears well up in her eyes. He knew this song reminded her of when she'd been sick, and how happy she was now. Jim went to her and put his arms around her. The minute he put his arms around her, Rhasha lost control and burst into tears. With her hands covering her face, Rhasha sank against Jim's chest, her black hair falling over his shirt like strands of silk. Tears dripped from her face onto his shirt.

"I'll turn it off, if you want me to," he said.

Rhasha raised her head. "Please don't, Jim. I want to hear it again."

"But it makes you so sad."

"I'm not sad," Rhasha said. "I'm crying because I am the happiest girl in the whole USA."

Jim smiled. "Sweetheart, happy people are supposed to laugh, not cry."

The song ended. Jim quickly pushed the repeat button so Rhasha could hear it again.

As the song began to play, Rhasha said, "I want to learn the words to this song." She listened to it three times before she let the CD player continue to play the rest of the songs.

Jim called in an order for pizza. After they ate, Jim, Rhasha, and Shanha went to the bedroom for their nightly ritual. Jim said his evening prayer as Rhasha and Shanha listened. They sang three songs together, then climbed into bed.

Chapter 17

Trouble In Chicago

The next morning, Raymond was waiting in front of Jim's apartment. As they all got in the car, Jim asked Raymond to stop someplace for breakfast. Moments later, the limousine stopped in front of a high class restaurant, and everyone, including the chauffeur, went inside to eat. They found an unoccupied table large enough to seat six, and sat down. A waitress brought six glasses of water and six menus. She looked at Shanha and smiled. "You're a pretty young lady," she said.

"Thank you," Shanha replied, "and you're a pretty old lady."

The waitress stared at Shanha in disbelief. Everyone else was smiling. They knew Shanha didn't mean to be rude. Shanha suddenly realized what she'd said. "Lady," Shanha gasped, "I didn't mean it like that."

A smile spread across the waitress's face.

Jim decided to have some fun with the situation. "Shanha," he said, "what did you mean?"

Shanha appeared nervous. "I *meant,"* she replied, "she's a pretty old la-" She realized she was about to say the same thing again. Everyone, including the waitress, was snickering. The waitress placed her hands on her hips, waiting to hear what Shanha would say next. "You're not an old lady," Shanha said. "Old people have wrinkled skin."

"But Shanha," Jim teased, "you said 'old lady.' If she's not an old lady, what is she?"

Shanha knew Jim was trying to trick her now. "Papa, she's not as old as you are."

Rhasha and Shanha looked at each other. They held their fingers to their lips and giggled, then gave each other a high-five as everyone laughed.

The waitress said, "You're a very sweet young lady."

“Thank you,” Shanha replied, “and you’re a very sweet . . . ” She hesitated, knowing she was about to make the same mistake again. “ . . . lady.”

Everyone laughed. The waitress put her order pad in her apron and went to get their drinks.

“Is everyone ready to order?” she asked when she returned. Jim, Jackie, Simbatu, and Raymond were still looking at menus. Rhasha and Shanha didn’t have their menus open. “Honey,” the waitress said as she looked at Rhasha, “did you already look through the menu and decide what you want?”

“No ma’am,” Rhasha replied, “Shanha and I don’t know how to read.”

The waitress looked incredulously at Rhasha.

“Kathy,” Jim said, “they come from an area in Africa where very few people ever get an education.”

Rhasha and Shanha both looked surprised. “Sweetheart,” Rhasha whispered, “did you know you called her Kathy?”

“Yes I did, angel,” Jim replied. “That’s her name. It’s on her name tag.”

Everyone at the table snickered; Kathy smiled uncertainly.

“I’m sorry, Kathy,” Jim said. “Your name was part of a joke we had on the plane coming from Africa.”

“Lady,” Shanha said, “I go to school and I’m learning how to read.” She paused. “Papa’s teaching Mama how to read. He reads the Bible to us all the time.”

Suddenly realizing these people had an interesting story to tell, the waitress put her hand on Rhasha’s shoulder. “You have a beautiful daughter. I’m sure you’re very proud of her.”

“I love Shanha with all my heart,” Rhasha replied, “but I’m not her real mother. Jim, Shanha, and I live together, and I think of her as being our daughter.”

"Yes," Shanha added, "Mama and I almost died and Papa saved us."

Kathy looked very curious now. "How did you almost die?"

"I didn't have any food," she replied. "Papa built a hospital and he helps lots of people. He gives everyone food and clothes and houses."

Kathy looked at Jim in admiration.

"Shanha," Jim said, "let's don't tell everyone about Angel Town while we're in America, okay?"

"Okay, Papa," Shanha replied, "but she did ask."

"I'm so happy he did save you, sweetheart," the waitress said, "and I can see why Mama loves you so much." She kissed Shanha on the forehead.

She had an order book and pen in her hand. Jim knew she was waiting for them to order. "I'll have two eggs, over easy, bacon, and hash browns, please," he said.

Rhasha and Shanha said they wanted eggs, bacon, and hash browns also. Jackie, Simbatu, and Raymond made their selections and Kathy went to the kitchen to turn in their orders.

While they waited for their food, Jim and Jackie talked about things to do and see around Dallas. Jackie and Simbatu decided they wanted to go to the Dallas zoo. Jim wanted to go to his office. Rhasha and Shanha wanted to stay with Jim. Jim told Rhasha and Shanha he would take them to the zoo later.

"Raymond," Jim said, "why don't you take us back to the apartment and drop Rhasha, Shanha, and me off? Then you can take Jackie and Simbatu to the zoo. Rhasha, Shanha, and I will get my car out of the garage and go to my office." Jim gave Jackie a spare apartment key that he kept in his wallet. "If you and Simbatu get back to the apartment before we do, this key will let you in."

After they ate, Raymond drove back to the apartment and let Jim, Rhasha, and Shanha out. Jim punched some numbers into the automatic garage door opener and was soon backing the car out of the small, two-car garage.

Jim had one stop to make on the way to the office-A. Teague and Sons Accounting Service. It was a large accounting firm, but Jim's account was handled by only one person: Molly Parks. When they walked into the lobby, Molly spotted Jim from her office and rushed out to meet him with a smile.

"Jim," she said, "you're really looking good."

"Thank you, Molly," Jim replied, "and you're as charming as ever."

Molly looked at Rhasha and Shanha. "And who are these lovely ladies?"

"This is Rhasha, and this is Shanha." Jim placed his hand on Shanha's head. Molly had wanted to go out with Jim ever since his divorce. She looked uncomfortable as she eyed him and Rhasha holding hands.

They all walked into Molly's office. Molly only had one chair in front of her desk for clients, so Jim pulled up another chair for Rhasha, and held Shanha in his lap.

"Molly," Jim said, "how bad is my financial situation now?" He knew he'd spent several million dollars in Africa and had no idea how much money was left in his account.

"Jim," Molly replied, "there's something very strange going on." She typed Jim's name into the computer and brought up his file. "Look." She pointed at some numbers. "You spent over a hundred million dollars."

She indicated other numbers. "Your original account shows a balance of 841 million dollars." Molly typed something else into the computer. "See this? This is all the checks you wrote until the twenty-first of last month."

Molly was wearing half-glasses that had a chain attached to their arms. When Molly wasn't wearing her reading glasses, they hung on the chain from around her neck. Now she peered over their tops at Jim. "Your company is showing a higher profit, but not enough to do this." She pointed to the ending balance.

Jim looked at the amount and couldn't believe his eyes. "Is this right?" he sputtered. "I still have 841 million dollars left in my account?"

Until now, Rhasha had never known how much money Jim had. She heard the dollar amount, but she still didn't understand how much it was. She just looked back and forth between Molly and Jim.

"I can't explain it, Jim," Molly replied. "I've done the figures over and over. I've had other people do the figures. They come up with the same balance." Molly looked at Jim to see his reaction. "I checked with the bank," she added, "and they show you have a balance of 841 million dollars."

As Jim studied the figures, Molly continued watching his face. "Let me show you something else, Jim."

Molly set the computer up to print a statement. She clicked on "print" and the printer went into action. When it finished printing, Molly handed Jim a soft blue sheet of paper with his statement printed on it. "Every time I try to print out your statement, it comes out in soft blue. I can print anything else and it comes out on white paper."

Jim now knew why his account still had 841 million dollars in it. "It all makes sense to me now."

"Okay Jim," she said, leaning back and taking off her half-glasses, "explain it to me so I'll understand."

"Molly," he said, "God took over my account. The soft blue paper is a sign, so I would know."

Molly didn't say so, but she looked like she didn't believe God had anything to do with it. Even though Molly was a Christian, she always dealt with facts and figures. "Well, I guess that's one explanation for it."

Jim was satisfied with his explanation. He stood to leave, still holding Shanha in his left arm. Rhasha rose too and held Jim's right arm. "Molly," Jim said, "thanks for the good work you've done. I'll see you again before we go back to Africa." Shanha was getting heavy so he set her on the floor.

"Jim," Molly asked bluntly as she pointed to Rhasha, "are you two married?"

"No Molly," Jim replied, "but only because of our age difference."

"I can understand that," Molly said. "She looks so young."

Jim could tell Rhasha and Shanha didn't like Molly much. She wasn't very friendly toward them. Jim liked her as a friend, but knew she would marry him in a heartbeat, for his money. He suspected she was jealous.

He drove them all to his company and they spent two hours in the office building. Jim introduced Rhasha and Shanha to all his employees. When he talked to Mary, he found out they had a problem in shipping and receiving. Rhasha and Shanha accompanied him when he went to investigate. As they entered the warehouse, Jim looked around for the shipping manager, Bill. They found him sitting at his desk in his office.

Bill rose and shook Jim's hand. "Hi Jim, long time, no see. It's nice to meet you," he said when Jim introduced Rhasha and Shanha. He shook their hands.

"Thank you," Rhasha said, "it's nice to meet you, too." Shanha, holding onto Rhasha's arm, just smiled.

Jim wanted to get right down to business. "Bill, I understand there's a problem with the truck drivers."

"Yes. The drivers that are available all refuse to deliver to a hostile company."

"Who is the hostile company?" Jim asked.

"It's Randell Tool Distributors, out of Chicago."

"Okay," Jim said, "we've had complaints about them before. I told Jim Randell that if we had any more problems, we would discontinue further shipments."

"But Jim," Bill protested, "they're one of our biggest accounts."

"If we chop that tree down, other trees will take its place," Jim said.

"I'm sure you're right," Bill said, "but we've delivered to Randell for several years."

Jim wanted to know more before he made a decision. "What are the drivers complaining about?" he asked. "Are they being reasonable?"

Bill reached into a filing cabinet and pulled out a folder labeled *Randell Tool Distributors*. "We've had many complaints about Randell Tools," Bill said. "Enough to create a complaint folder. They're the only company that gets any complaints." Bill slipped the complaint forms out of the folder and silently read one after the other. After he'd read through five complaints, he pushed them all together and placed them back in the folder. "They all complain about the same three problems: They have to wait in their trucks for ten to twelve hours before they get unloaded."

"Okay" Jim asked, "what's the second complaint?" Bill pulled one of the complaint forms out of the folder and glanced at it. "And they're not able to back up to the unloading dock-the company now allows employees to park in front of the dock. The drivers have difficulty lining their trailers up to back them in."

"Okay," Jim said, "what's the third complaint?"

Bill glanced down at the complaint form again. "The forklift drivers give them a lot of verbal abuse. They yell at the drivers and threaten to get them fired."

Jim picked up the folder and took out all the complaints. As he laid them on the desk, he counted twelve forms. The company only had twelve drivers, which indicated to Jim that every driver had lodged complaints.

"Bill," he said, "do you have any trucks that aren't being used for a few days?"

"We have a driver on vacation," Bill replied. "His truck's in the parking lot."

"How long has he been on vacation?" Jim asked.

"He's been gone a week. He should be back next week."

Jim looked at Rhasha and Shanha. "Would you girls like to ride in a truck for four or five days?" They nodded excitedly.

Jim picked up the phone and punched in a series of numbers. "Raymond," he said when someone answered, "is that you?" He could hear monkeys chattering in the background.

"Yes, this is Raymond," the chauffeur said. "Who am I speaking to?"

"This is Jim, Raymond. Can I speak to Jackie or Simbatu?"

"Jackie's gone to get some peanuts for the monkeys, but here's Simbatu." There was a pause. Jim could hear Raymond mumbling to Simbatu. He could still hear the monkeys chattering in the background.

"Hello Jim," Simbatu said.

"Hello Simbatu. I've got a question for you."

"What is it?"

"I need to drive a truck to Chicago," Jim said. "Could you and Jackie find enough to keep you busy around here while we're gone?"

"Sure Jim," Simbatu quickly answered. "If nothing else, we can watch television or listen to music."

"Thanks, Simbatu. I'm sorry for doing this to you and Jackie, but we have a situation here at the plant. We should be back in five days."

"It's no problem, Jim. But do be careful and have a good trip."

"We will. If you or Jackie need any money, tell Raymond. He can get it for you." Jim hung up the phone and turned his attention to the shipping manager. "Bill, we're going home to get everything we need for the trip." Jim paused, thinking about what they would need. "Did the driver leave his CB radio in the truck?"

"I think so. They usually do when they go on vacation."

"Okay, while we go home, get someone to back the rig up to the dock. I'd like to have it loaded when we get back."

They drove to Jim's apartment and loaded the car with traveling gear. Jim loaded sheets, blankets, and pillows while Rhasha loaded extra clothes for everyone. They drove back to the factory and unloaded the contents of the car into the truck, a new Freightliner Classic with a fifty-three foot, dry box trailer. *South and West Tools* was painted in big letters on both sides of the trailer.

Jim started the engine and, while the motor was warming up, he began his pretrip inspection, checking his gauges and the windshield and mirrors. Everything looked fine on the inside of the truck so he turned the motor off. He turned on his headlights and flashers and got out of the truck to do a walk-around inspection. Rhasha and Shanha joined him. As Jim checked to make sure all the lights were working, he noticed Rhasha was acting strange. She was watching everything Jim did. When he finished checking the tires and walked around the back of the trailer to check the tail and brake lights, Rhasha stuck to him like glue.

"Sweetheart," Jim asked, "what's wrong?"

Rhasha hung her head and fidgeted with the trailer door latch. "Nothing," she said.

Jim knew she was nervous about something. The loaders had already closed and latched the trailer doors. Jim walked around to the front of the truck. Rhasha followed him closely, with Shanha right behind her.

Jim unhooked the rubber straps on both sides of the hood. Rhasha was being very quiet and kept getting up close to him. "Rhasha, I can't stand the suspense. Please tell me what's wrong."

Rhasha hung her head again. "I can't tell you," she said. "I already know what you'll say."

Jim walked to the front of the truck and checked the headlights. After he checked the directional lights, he reached to a holder at the top of the hood, put his foot in a hole in the bumper, and leaned back as he jerked the hood open. He checked the water in the radiator, and the fan belts.

"Rhasha," Jim said, "there should be a rag in the compartment on the side of the truck. Could you get it for me, please?" Rhasha left to find a rag. Jim checked around the motor for oil or water leaks.

Moments later, Rhasha returned with the rag in her hand. Jim grabbed her and put his arms around her waist. She instinctively put her arms around his neck. The rag hung down his back. "Sweetheart," Jim said, "I'm not going to turn you loose until you tell me what's wrong."

Rhasha's eyes looked straight into Jim's. "It doesn't matter. I know you can't do what I want you to."

"Angel," Jim replied, "I can't if you don't ask me."

Rhasha smiled as she turned on her teenage charm. She kissed him and hugged him tight. "Jim, you're an intelligent man. I'm sure you can see the sense in what I'm going to ask you."

"Okay," Jim replied, *"so what is it?"* He smiled, waiting for an answer. He'd already figured out what she was going to say.

Rhasha hesitated, then said, "Could you please teach me how to drive that truck?"

Jim shook his head, still smiling. "Being an intelligent man, how is that supposed to make sense to me?"

"If you teach me how to drive, we could keep the truck on the road," she explained. "When you got tired or sleepy, I could drive." Smiling, Rhasha dropped her arms and locked her hands together. She swayed back and forth, and wet her lips with her tongue.

"Angel, I don't have time to teach you how to drive right now."

"I know," Rhasha replied, "but if I could learn to drive a big truck like that, I could drive anything."

Jim gave in. "When we get unloaded, I'll take you to a big parking lot and turn you loose with it."

Satisfied, she kissed him.

"What about me, Papa?" Shanha asked. "Are you going to teach me how to drive a truck?"

Jim placed the back of his hand against Shanha's cheek and smiled. "No, sweetheart," he replied. "I'm going to teach you how to ride a bicycle."

Shanha smiled back. "That's okay, I'll get Mama to teach me after she learns how."

Jim knew both his girls wanted to learn too much, too fast, but he loved their enthusiasm. He pulled the dipstick out of the motor and wiped it clean, then checked the oil. When he'd closed and latched the hood, they climbed into the truck; Shanha sat on the bottom bunk in the sleeper. Jim started the truck and opened his window; the diesel engine clattered as he filled out his log book.

Shanha discovered the Velcro that held the curtains on the sleeper closed. She had never seen Velcro before and couldn't figure out how the two pieces of material stayed together. She kept ripping it apart and pushing it back together. Rhasha, looking in a compartment above her head, found a Rand McNally laminated atlas and thumbed through the pages, trying to figure out what all the lines were.

Finally Jim was ready to go. He looked around and saw that both girls were preoccupied. He reached up to a strap that hung down from the top of the truck and pulled on it, holding it for several seconds. The noise of the air horn was deafening. When he released the strap, both girls had their ears covered.

"What was that, Papa?" Shanha asked loudly. Rhasha was sitting on the edge of her seat, her eyes fixed on the strap Jim had pulled.

"That's called an air horn," Jim replied.

Shanha stood in the space between Jim and Rhasha's seats. "Do it again, Papa!"

Jim pulled on the strap again. The air horn blared. Rhasha and Shanha giggled and held their ears. It was time to hit the road. Jim slowly pulled away from the loading dock. Within minutes, the semi was trucking down Interstate 20. Rhasha and Shanha watched excitedly as Jim maneuvered in and out of traffic.

Rhasha was watching all the cars as they passed. "Riding in a truck is almost like flying. We sit way up here and look down on all the cars below us."

"Yes," Jim replied, "but there's one major difference."

"What's that?"

Jim looked at Rhasha and smiled. "There's a lot more traffic down here than there is up there." He pointed toward the sky.

“Yes Papa,” Shanha said, “but I’m sure cars get out of the way when a truck comes through.”

“Angel,” Jim replied, “you’d be surprised by how many foolish people drive cars. And trucks, too,” he added. “Many truck drivers are tired and sleepy. They don’t mean to be careless, but sometimes, they are.”

Rhasha didn’t understand what Jim meant. “If they get sleepy, why don’t they stop and rest?”

The only time Jim had ever driven a truck was when he first started his company, so he didn’t know all their problems. He did know some of them, though. “Most drivers have deadlines to meet and dispatchers pushing them. Many drivers get paid by the mile, and try to drive too many miles. It’s a hard life, but driving is all they know how to do. Many drivers get trapped, driving down the road, day after day. They see their families only once or twice a month.”

“But Papa,” Shanha said, “if it’s so hard, why do people live like that?”

Jim replied, “For many drivers, driving is a way to get away from their problems. To others, it’s a way to solve their problems. Most drivers don’t know what else they can do, so they keep driving.”

Shanha yawned. The hum of the diesel engine was soothing. After a few minutes, she laid back down in the bunk and fell asleep.

Jim veered off Interstate 20 and onto Interstate 635. As they passed a car on Rhasha’s side of the truck, two young white boys in the back seat looked up at Rhasha, sitting high up in the truck. They smiled and waved vigorously. Rhasha smiled and waved back. “Jim,” she said, “there are good things about truck driving, aren’t there?”

Jim realized he had painted a gloomy picture of truck drivers. “Yes, truck driving can be an honorable profession. It mostly depends on the individual driver.”

Just past the Oklahoma state line, Jim saw a sign: *Weigh Station 1 mile.* He pulled onto the scales and waited until he received the signal to go. When he left the scale house, he didn't stop the truck again until they arrived at a truck stop in Big Cabin, Oklahoma, where they ate at the truck stop restaurant. Rhasha was surprised by how much the countryside of Oklahoma reminded her of Africa.

Jim was making good time, but had to slow down after he crossed the Missouri state line. It was well after dark when they arrived at Cuba, Missouri. He had driven over nine and a half hours. He pulled into the truck stop and found a parking place. They trashed around the truck stop for a while, and Jim explained to Rhasha and Shanha that "trashing around" was a truckers' term for being in a truck stop and not spending money.

When they finally returned to the truck to go to sleep, they discovered Rhasha had forgotten to pack their pajamas-they would have to sleep in their clothes. Jim said his evening prayer as Rhasha and Shanha listened. They all wanted to sleep in the same bunk together, but the bunk was only big enough for one person, two at the most. He climbed into the bunk first and lay with his back against the wall of the sleeper. Shanha climbed in next and pressed her back against Jim. This arrangement would have worked better if Rhasha had lain with her back against Shanha, but she didn't. She always slept facing the other two and that's how she wanted to sleep tonight. She fell off the bunk during the night, but climbed right back in and fell asleep facing the same way as the other two.

When Jim woke, Rhasha and Shanha were waiting for him. After their Good Morning Sunshine ritual, Jim told Rhasha and Shanha, "The next three nights, we're staying in motels."

He crawled out of the bunk and said his morning prayer. Rhasha and Shanha bowed their heads and listened. All three went into the truck stop and took showers, then stopped by the restaurant to have breakfast.

Once they were on the road again, Jim appreciated the new day. The sun was shining and the dew sparkled in the grass. Jim set the cruise control and settled back in his seat for the drive to the "Gateway City," St. Louis, Missouri.

The highway crossed the bridge built high over the Mississippi River that separated Missouri from Illinois. From the bridge, Rhasha and Shanha could look down on St. Louis. Jim poked Shanha in the ribs and pointed to something on the left side of the truck. She almost had to climb in front of Jim to see it.

"Look, Mama! Look!" she yelled.

Rhasha pushed to the driver's side of the truck and squeezed between Shanha and Jim, pushing Jim's head against the driver side window. "Jim," Rhasha gasped, "it's a silver rainbow."

"No it's not, Angel," Jim replied, "but if you don't move back, we're all going to be swimming in the Mississippi River." Rhasha shifted and continued gazing at the structure.

"What is it, Papa?" Shanha asked.

"It's called The Archway," Jim said. "It's a symbolic gate from the east to the west."

"It sure is big," Rhasha observed.

"And it's pretty," Shanha added.

Jim crossed over the bridge and the silver archway dropped out of Rhasha and Shanha's view. Rhasha sat back in her seat, and Shanha crawled onto the bunk.

Jim continued driving on Interstate 55. It was late when they arrived in Chicago. Jim parked the truck at a truck stop and called a taxi. He didn't want to deliver his load until the next morning-he wanted to make sure Jim Randell would be in his office.

A taxi took them to a car rental company, where Jim rented a car and took the girls shopping. Rhasha and Shanha had never seen so many nice-looking things in their lives. Rhasha didn't want to buy anything, but Shanha found a teddy bear she just loved. Jim bought nightgowns for the girls and pajamas for himself.

They had no problem finding a motel room. They'd brought their luggage with them in the car, and once they'd unloaded it, they took showers and proceeded with their nightly ritual. The motel room was furnished with two beds, but Jim, Rhasha, and Shanha all slept in one bed.

The next morning, Jim parked the car at the truck stop and started the truck. He didn't want to turn the car back in yet, because he planned to take Rhasha and Shanha to the zoo after he made his delivery.

Within thirty minutes, the Freightliner was parked beside the Randell Tool Distributors warehouse. Jim got his shipping invoice out of the cubby hole above his head and headed toward the unloading dock area. Rhasha and Shanha walked with him.

As they walked across the unloading dock looking for the receiving office, a forklift driver pulled up beside Jim. "What do you think you're doing, driver?" the large man yelled in a gruff voice.

"I'm looking for the receiving office," Jim replied.

The man looked angry. "You drivers think you know everything," he said, "but you don't. You have to stop me from doing my job, because you're not smart enough to find the receiving office."

"I didn't stop you, mister," Jim replied. "You came to me. If you had signs up, telling drivers where to go, it would be a big help."

The driver got off his forklift and snatched the invoice out of Jim's hand. "We're not here to baby-sit you truck drivers," the man said. He looked at Rhasha and Shanha. "What are those niggers doing on my dock?"

Jim became fighting angry. He grabbed the front of the man's shirt and pushed him up against the forklift. When he realized he was getting violent, he let go of the man's shirt, but stayed in his face. "Don't you ever call my girls names again."

The man held up his hands, showing that he didn't want to push the issue. He climbed back on the forklift. "Get 'em out of my warehouse," the man snapped.

Jim backed away from the forklift and put one arm around Rhasha's waist and the other across Shanha's shoulders. "I'll do better than that, mister," Jim replied. "I'll get my truck off 'your' property. I'll take this load back to Dallas."

The forklift driver looked at the invoice. "We've been waiting for that load," he said. "You move that truck one inch and you won't have a job when you get back to Dallas."

Jim scowled at the man. "When I get back to Dallas," Jim said, "I'll see to it that no driver ever delivers to this company again."

"You drivers are all alike," the man replied. "This is your first delivery to this company and you think you can stop your company from delivering here."

Jim wordlessly turned to leave.

"Driver," the man said, "you best not leave with that load on your truck."

Jim, Rhasha, and Shanha walked out of the warehouse and climbed into the truck. Jim took a moment to update his log book. Rhasha fidgeted with the gearshift knob. Shanha was being very quiet.

"Sweetheart," Rhasha finally asked, "what does nigger mean?"

"Yeah, Papa," Shanha added, "it sure made you mad, when that man called us niggers."

"I've never seen you mad before," Rhasha said. "I hope you never get mad at me like that."

Shanha placed her hand on Jim's cheek. "Me too."

Jim smiled. He wondered how to explain racism to them.

He glimpsed a forklift driving through the warehouse door, and watched it drive around to the back of his truck, where it parked. Another forklift pulled out of the warehouse and parked in front of his truck. Jim's truck was pinned between the two forklifts. Jim knew what the forklift drivers were up to, but decided to answer Rhasha's question. "Girls," he said, "prejudiced white people, those who still live in the stone age, call black people that name. It's not a nice name. It makes them feel superior, to put black people down. There are also prejudiced black people, who call white people honkies."

A man got off the front forklift and walked over to Jim's window. Jim recognized the gruff-voiced man he'd had the altercation with in the warehouse. "That truck's not leaving this yard until I get it unloaded," the man said, looking cocky. "That will be at least ten hours from now."

Jim hesitated as he thought about what to do. Then he said, "Mister, get that forklift out of my way immediately, or I'll call your boss."

The man laughed. "This just isn't your lucky day, driver," he said. "I *am* the boss."

The man started to turn away, but noticed Jim punching numbers into his cell phone. The receiving department phone number was on Jim's shipping invoice, but that wasn't the number he called.

"You're wasting your time, driver," the man said. "I'm not in my office to answer the phone."

A voice on his cell phone said, "Jim Randell's office, how can I help you?"

Jim didn't want the forklift driver to know who he was talking to, so he was careful how he communicated with the secretary. "Hello, could I speak to your boss, please?"

"Could I ask who's calling?" the secretary asked.

Jim spoke in a low voice. "This is Jim Brown."

"Yes sir, Mr. Brown. I'll put you right through to him."

While Jim waited for an answer, the forklift driver continued to gloat, thinking he had everything figured out. "I don't know who you think you're bluffing. My number is the only number you could possibly have."

Jim didn't say anything. A new voice on the phone said, "Hello Jim, how's everything going?"

"Not so well," Jim replied. "I need you down here at your receiving office immediately."

"I'll be right there, Jim."

Jim turned his phone off and put it away.

The forklift driver wasn't worried at all. "You're a real nut case, driver," he said as he turned to walk away. "Talking to yourself on the phone."

Moments later, Jim got out of his truck and walked back to the receiving dock. Rhasha and Shanha went with him. He looked around and spotted a little office he thought might be the receiving office. When the three of them entered the office, the gruff-voiced man screamed, "Get out of my office, *now!*"

"We're not going anywhere until your boss gets here," Jim told him.

The forklift driver-the receiving manager-jumped up, rushed to the door, and jerked it open. "I said, get out."

About that time, a well-dressed businessman walked through the door. "What's going on here, Clyde?" he asked.

The manager's voice became deferential. "Nothing, Mr. Randell. This driver is here with a shipment and I was just getting ready to unload his truck." Clyde looked at Jim and said in a friendly voice, "Sir, if you'll back your truck into the dock, I'll get you unloaded."

Jim shook his head. "How am I supposed to do that, Clyde? You parked a forklift in front of my truck, and another behind it."

"Oh, I forgot," Clyde said hastily. "I was so busy, I didn't notice you were parked there."

"Hello, Jim." Randell reached out to shake Jim's hand. "Were you having a problem here?"

Clyde stared from one to the other, dumbfounded. "Do you two know each other?" he sputtered, worried now.

"Yes," Randell said, his voice tinged with anger. "We've been doing business together since long before you ever came to work here. What did you do to make Jim so mad?"

"I didn't know you two knew each other," Clyde almost whined. "I might have been a little rude to him. I get so busy around here that I don't have time to be real friendly with the drivers."

Jim reached into his pocket and pulled out the tape recorder he'd carried there ever since they'd arrived. He placed it on the desk. Clyde's face went blank as he tried to remember everything he'd said. Jim pushed the stop button and then pressed rewind. He could hear the tape inside the recorder racing backwards. Finally it clicked to a stop and Jim pushed the play button.

The recording was of low quality, but the voice was legible: "What do you think you're doing, driver?"

Randell recognized Clyde's voice. He listened, appalled, as the tape played through to the end. Then Jim took the tape out of the recorder and handed it to Randell along with the twelve complaint forms, saying, "We stress to each of our employees that they are representatives of our company. What they do or say is a reflection of our company. In that respect," he looked at Clyde, "I hold you responsible for what I and my girls endured, as heard on that tape."

Clyde hung his head. He knew he was in serious trouble.

"Jim," Randell said, "I apologize for what Clyde said to you, but I'm a busy man. I don't have time to baby-sit my employees."

Jim was saddened by what he'd just heard. "Jim," he said to Randell, "If that's your attitude, I regretfully inform you that my company will no longer do business with Randell Tool Distributors. I will not allow my drivers to be treated the way I and my girls were treated today."

"We've done business for many years," Randell protested. "Won't you reconsider cutting all ties?"

"Mr. Randell," Jim replied, "I told you over a year ago, if we had any more problems with your company, we would cancel your account. Gentlemen, we have nothing more to discuss. My girls and I are going to the zoo. Have a nice day."

Jim, Rhasha, and Shanha walked through the open door. As they headed for the dock area, Jim overheard Clyde saying, "Sir, I didn't know who he was."

"You're fired, Clyde," Randell yelled. "Get off my property."

When they got to the truck, Rhasha and Shanha climbed into the truck while Jim climbed onto the front forklift and drove it out of the way. Then he pulled himself into the truck and started the engine. "Girls," he said, "I'm sorry I acted the way I did in front of you."

Rhasha replied, "I thought you handled yourself very admirably."

"I did too, Papa," Shanha said, then added, "Mama, what does admur-bab-ly mean?"

Jim and Rhasha laughed. While Rhasha tried to explain the word to Shanha, Jim slowly let out on the clutch, but something caught his attention. He quickly pushed the clutch down to the floor. Clyde was walking in front of the truck toward his car, carrying a small box of personal items. Clyde got into his car and peeled rubber as he left the parking lot. Jim pulled out of the parking lot behind Clyde.

He drove back to the truck stop, where they ate lunch, then drove the rental car to the zoo. Rhasha and Shanha had never been to a zoo before so this was going to be a new experience for them. It was a weekday, so the zoo wasn't very busy.

"Would you girls like to see some snakes?" Jim asked, leading them toward the Reptile House.

Rhasha and Shanha were reluctant. "If you want to, Papa." Shanha replied.

They entered the building and began looking through the glass windows. As they moved through the building, Jim noticed Shanha hiding behind Rhasha as she held onto her arm.

"Shanha," he said, "the snakes are behind glass. They can't hurt you."

Shanha stuck her head out from behind Rhasha, between her arm and her waist. She clutched her teddy bear in front of her. "I don't like snakes."

"I don't either," Rhasha said. Jim noticed she was also keeping back from the glass.

"Girls," Jim said, "did you know a snake was the first creature mentioned in the Bible, after God created Adam and Eve?"

Shanha became inquisitive. "Did the snake bite anyone?"

"No, sweetheart. What he did was worse."

Rhasha was now curious about the first snake, too. "What did the snake do?"

Jim had read most of the Bible to them, including the story about Adam and Eve. He said, "Do you remember the story of how God created the heavens and the earth?" When both girls nodded, he continued. "Several days later, God made man from the dust of the ground. He took a rib from the man and made him a wife. They were called Adam and Eve."

Rhasha and Shanha liked the story about Adam and Eve. They listened to every word as Jim told the story. "God told Adam and Eve they could eat the fruit of every tree in the garden, except the fruit of one tree. God commanded them not to eat the fruit of the tree in the midst of the garden, or they would die."

"What kind of fruit was it?"

"The Bible doesn't say, Shanha," Jim replied, "so nobody knows."

"So what about the snake?" Rhasha asked.

"The snake-and, I assume, all the animals at that time-could talk to Adam and Eve."

Shanha opened her eyes wide at that. "All the animals could talk to people?"

"The Bible doesn't say all the animals could talk. The snake could talk to Eve, so I would think all the animals could." Not wanting them to get hung up about talking animals, he said, "I do know that the snake could talk. The Bible said the snake was the most subtle of all the creatures of the field."

Rhasha and Shanha looked thoughtfully at the snakes inside the glass cages. Jim turned around to look at the poisonous vipers too, but continued to tell his story. "The snake tempted Eve to eat the fruit that God said not to eat. The snake told Eve that if she ate of the fruit, she would not die. He said she would be like God, and know good and evil."

Jim looked back at Rhasha and Shanha. Shanha was still looking at the snakes, but Rhasha looked at Jim and asked, "Did she eat the fruit?" A snake began slithering around a large rock inside the cage. She moved further away from the glass, dragging Shanha with her.

Jim laughed, then answered, "Yes, sweetheart. Adam and Eve both ate the fruit."

"Did it make them like God?" Rhasha asked.

"No, angel," Jim said, "but they did know the difference between good and evil. When they ate the fruit, Adam and Eve realized they were naked. They sewed leaves together for clothes, and hid themselves from God."

"Did God find Adam and Eve?"

"Yes, dear. God walked on earth in those days, and on that day he walked through the Garden of Eden. He called for Adam and Eve, but they wouldn't answer him. When he found them, he knew what they had done."

"What did he do then?" Shanha piped up.

"He put them out of the Garden of Eden, and caused Adam to have to work for a living. He also caused Eve to have children."

Rhasha frowned in thought. "Did God punish everyone on earth because of what Adam and Eve did?"

"No, sweetheart. God punished everyone on earth because everyone ate of the fruit he commanded them not to eat. Everyone, that is, except for Jesus. He always obeyed God."

"I don't understand," Rhasha said. "You always say Jesus died on the cross, so was he punished by God too?"

"No, Jesus was God in the flesh and was sent to earth to do what he did."

Rhasha was still confused. "That doesn't make sense to me. If Jesus was God in the flesh, then how could he also be God's son?"

Jim knew he was only confusing Rhasha more. "Sweetheart, it would be hard for me to explain how God, Jesus, and The Holy Spirit are all separate beings, but of the same person. In time you will understand these things."

Shanha said, "It's not fair. The snake got Adam and Eve into trouble and nothing happened to him."

"Not true, Angel," Jim replied. "In those days, snakes walked on feet, like other creatures. God took away the snake's feet and caused him to crawl on his belly. He also caused man to fear snakes. Man and snakes couldn't talk to each other anymore."

"I think we should get away from these snakes," Shanha said, "before they get us into trouble."

Jim smiled at Shanha. He knelt in front of her and touched her cheek. "Okay sweetheart, what would you like to see next?"

Jim could see the gears turning in Shanha's head as she thought. "Do they have any monkeys here?"

"It wouldn't be a zoo, if they didn't have monkeys."

It didn't take Jim, Rhasha, and Shanha long to find the monkeys. When they did, Shanha had another question. "Do you have any stories about monkeys?"

Jim knelt down and kissed her on the forehead. "Yes, I sure do." Jim assumed a serious expression as he began his story. "Once upon a time, there was an older white man, a teenage black girl, and a little black girl, who went to the zoo."

Shanha grinned, already liking this story. She listened attentively. The monkeys chattered and ran all around the cages.

"The little black girl kept asking a lot of questions . . . " Rhasha smiled as she figured out who Jim was talking about. " . . . so the older white man threw the little black girl in the cage with the monkeys and left her there."

Jim grinned as Shanha figured out that Jim was talking about her, and jumped behind Rhasha. She poked her head between Rhasha's arm and her waist. "Mama," she yelled, eyes twinkling-she knew Jim was teasing, "don't let Papa throw me in the cage with the monkeys!"

As people nearby laughed, Jim snatched Shanha from behind Rhasha and picked her up. She squealed in mock horror. He kissed her, then set her back on the ground.

Jim was having fun just being with Rhasha and Shanha, but as they walked around the zoo, he grew uncomfortable. He felt as if someone was watching them. He kept looking behind him to see if anyone was there. He saw ordinary people; no one seemed suspicious.

Rhasha and Shanha both noticed that Jim was acting strange. Rhasha asked, "What's wrong?"

Shanha watched Jim as he glanced behind them again and said, "Mama, I think Papa sees ghosts." They both snickered.

Jim couldn't shake the strange feeling. "I don't know, girls. I just have a feeling something's about to happen." Jim shrugged, not wanting to alarm them, and ignored his feelings. They continued looking at the animals.

Jim spotted a bench beside the sidewalk, nestled beside some bushes, with two tall trees towering over both bushes and bench. He realized how tired of walking he was and suggested, "Girls, let's go over to that bench and rest a while."

Shanha and Rhasha were ready to take a break as well. As they approached the bench, Jim heard twigs snapping and branches rustling in the bushes. As Jim looked toward the sound, he saw a man emerging from his hiding place in the bushes. He clutched a gun in one hand.

Shanha saw Jim peering at the bushes, but she didn't see the man with the gun. "Papa, are you seeing ghosts again?"

Jim had stopped. He stared at the man, who was pointing the gun at them. "Driver," Clyde said, "this just isn't your lucky day."

Jim pushed Shanha behind him and tried to get in front of Rhasha. "Clyde," he said, "you're taking this too far. Put that gun away and let's talk about it."

A few people in the area saw what was going on, and fled immediately.

"Jimbo," Clyde said, "I wanna see the look on your face when I pull the trigger."

"Clyde," Jim begged, "let the girls move out of the way first."

Clyde chuckled. "What a man," he mocked. "A real hero." Clyde leveled his gun at Jim.

Jim saw his finger tightening on the trigger. He tensed.

Clyde's finger paused. Jim lifted his eyes from the gun to Clyde's face. He was staring at the sky.

Jim looked up too. There was something strange about the weather. Clouds rolled across the sky like waves rolling across the ocean. They moved from the east to the west, then back again. Lightning flashed and thunder groaned. A humming sound grew louder and louder, then began to pulsate. After a few seconds, it faded to soft and ceased. Everything seemed to go into slow motion. Not a sound could be heard. Not a leaf fluttered on the trees.

Clyde spoke, but his words came out slow and sounded bass-deep, as though dragging from a record player playing at low speed. "Your . . . tricks . . . aren't . . . going . . . to . . . save . . . you . . . driver. What . . . are . . . you, some . . . kind . . . of . . . freak?"

Clyde looked scared, confused by what was happening. A large blue bubble had surrounded Jim, Rhasha, and Shanha and lifted them two feet off the ground. Angry that Jim might escape, Clyde pulled the trigger, but nothing seemed to happen. He pulled the trigger several more times, as fast as he could while moving in slow motion, but there was a two-second interval between each discharge.

Jim, Rhasha, and Shanha could see the bullets coming toward them, moving so slowly that they looked like they would fall to the ground. As each bullet hit the blue glowing bubble, sparks radiated in every direction. Jim could see the head of each bullet flatten out on impact with the blue bubble. It sounded like the bullets hit a steel plate. The loud sound vibrated the air in slow motion: *Pang . . . pang . . . pang*. Then each bullet fell slowly to the ground.

"What's . . . going . . . on . . . here?" Clyde screamed, frustrated. He threw the pistol at Jim. The gun tumbled slowly through the air. The gun hit the blue bubble with a long, drawn-out *thunk*.

Jim could see fear in Clyde's face. He was trying to run, but something held him in place. Slowly Clyde's body began to change. He appeared to be diced into small cubes. Dissected, he was still trying to move, but in slow motion. A spark ignited at the top of Clyde's head and burned like a fuse, burning its way toward his feet. Above the burning fuse, it was as if his body was being erased. When the fire reached his feet, Clyde had vanished. The gun and bullets were also gone.

Somehow Jim knew that everyone who had ever known Clyde had no memory of him; all records of him had disappeared. Only Jim, Rhasha, and Shanha knew he'd ever existed. It was as if the incident with the gun had never happened.

Jim, Rhasha, and Shanha heard the humming again, growing louder. Everything went back to normal motion. After a few flashes of lightning and grumbles of thunder, the clouds rolled back where they'd come from, and the sky brightened. The soft blue bubble set Jim, Rhasha, and Shanha on the ground and disappeared. They could hear sounds and feel the breeze. Jim looked at the people walking by and realized that nobody in the zoo remembered anything unusual happening.

Everything was back to normal, except for Clyde.

Jim looked at the space where Clyde had been standing. The ground wasn't even scorched. People walking around them were laughing and having a good time. Jim, Rhasha, and Shanha gradually regained their composure.

Shanha was the first to speak. "He was a bad man, Papa."

"Yes he was, sweetheart."

Rhasha was still in shock. She continued to stare at the bushes. "Jim, did God kill Clyde?"

Jim wasn't sure what happened to Clyde, but he didn't want Rhasha to think he was dead. "I don't think so."

Shanha asked, "If Clyde's not dead, then what did God do with him?"

"I don't know," Jim replied again, helplessly. "Maybe God turned him into a baby and sent him home."

Rhasha and Shanha chuckled. Their ordeal over, Jim, Rhasha, and Shanha began to relax.

"Girls," Jim said, "it's been a strange day. Do you think we should go back to the truck stop?"

Rhasha was disappointed, but tried to hide it. "If you want to," she said in a subdued voice. "Things *have* gotten very strange."

Shanha hung her head. "Papa, are we going to let that bad man mess up our happy, fun day?"

Jim realized that Rhasha and Shanha didn't want to leave. "No," he said firmly, "we're not. We're going to see everything we came to see."

Rhasha and Shanha hugged Jim, giggling with excitement. They continued looking at the animals as if nothing had happened.

"Papa," Shanha asked, pointing to an animal that moped around its enclosure, head hanging down, "what kind of animal is that?"

Jim looked. "That's a donkey."

Shanha tried to get the donkey's attention, but it ignored her. Jim noticed zoo personnel feeding livestock across the yard. They stopped what they were doing and started walking toward the donkey.

"Look at him," Shanha said, "he looks so sad."

For the first time, the donkey looked up and saw Shanha. He emitted a loud *hee haw* and began jumping up and down and kicking his back legs out behind him. The donkey backed away from the fence and stared at the people approaching on the opposite side.

Rhasha became alarmed. "Jim, do you think that could be . . . ?"

Jim laughed. "No, it's not Clyde."

When the donkey heard "Clyde," he responded with another *hee haw*.

Rhasha agreed it couldn't be Clyde and they began to walk away. Jim had to look back again, just to reassure himself. By this time, the zoo personnel had reached the donkey. One of them scratched his head and looked at the other zoo worker. "Where'd this donkey come from?" Jim overheard him say.

Jim and Rhasha smirked at each other. They looked at Shanha. It took her a second or two, but she figured out the donkey was Clyde. They all began laughing, and took off running. They didn't stop running until they were out of the donkey's sight. As they were catching their breath, Shanha had only one comment: "Papa, I think I'm ready to go now."

"Me too," Rhasha agreed.

They left the zoo, returned the rental car to the rental company, and took a taxi back to the truck. Soon the truck was back on the highway. The diesel engine hummed as Jim drove toward Texas.

Chapter 18

The Pirate Ship

They arrived in Troy, Illinois, late that night, and rented a motel room. By eleven o'clock the next morning, they were back in the truck and on the road again. Thirty minutes later, the Freightliner approached the Mississippi River. As they crossed the bridge into Missouri, they had a clear view of the St. Louis Archway.

Rhasha noticed some boats on the Mississippi river and commented, "Aren't those boats pretty? I think it would be fun to ride in a boat."

Jim remembered that Rhasha had been sick most of her life and never got to do many of the things that most people did. "Have you never been on a boat?" he asked her.

"I've seen lots of boats," she replied, "but I've never been on one."

"I've never been on a boat either," Shanha said.

Jim continued to drive, but the gears in his head began to turn. He realized he was having fun exposing Rhasha and Shanha to new adventures. "Girls," he said, "did you know I own a small sea cruiser?" He looked at Rhasha, but she didn't say anything. She just looked back at him, waiting for him to say something else. Shanha didn't say anything at first. Jim was beginning to wonder if they'd heard him.

Finally, Shanha broke the silence. "Papa, what's a sea cruiser?"

"Yeah," Rhasha said, "I don't know what a sea cruiser is, either."

Jim smiled, realizing why they hadn't answered him. "It's just a boat."

"Oh!" Shanha said. "You have a boat? Where is it?"

Before he could answer, Rhasha interrupted. "Could you take us for a ride on your boat?"

"It's a long ways from here," Jim told them. "It's in Pensacola, Florida."

Shanha observed, "You have everything, don't you."

Jim stroked her face. "I do now, sweetheart-now that I have you." He smiled. He had never seen a seven-year-old black girl blush before.

"You're being silly, Papa," she said, "but I love you."

"I love you too, angel. If you and Mama want to go to Florida, I'll take you for a boat ride."

"Yes!" Rhasha said. "Let's go to Florida." Shanha agreed.

He picked up his cell phone and dialed the number of a man in Florida. Jim instructed the man to have his boat seaworthy by the next day, then hung up and thought about what route to take. He'd already merged onto Interstate 44 so now he would have to get back to Interstate 55.

"Okay girls," he said, "we're on our way to Florida."

Rhasha and Shanha were all smiles. They knew Jim was going out of his way just for them, but they also knew he didn't mind. It pleased Jim to show Rhasha and Shanha new and exciting things. He felt like he was living life all over again. As the truck traveled down Interstate 44 toward Interstate 270, Jim calculated the miles to Pensacola, then from Pensacola to Dallas. Almost eight hundred miles out of the normal route.

Less than an hour later, Jim turned south on Interstate 55. He would stay on Interstate 55 until he got to Interstate 12 near Hammond, Louisiana. Jim didn't like to drive in Louisiana; there was a lot corruption in the state's law enforcement. Officers were often accused of planting narcotics in victims' vehicles. The arresting officer then confiscated the vehicle and, in time, the vehicle would be placed on the auction block. A nationwide television show had exposed the corruption, but not before the practice had ruined the lives of an untold number of innocent travelers.

As Jim continued down I-55, he thought of a way to entertain Rhasha and Shanha. "Rhasha, have you ever heard of pirates?"

“No,” she replied. “What are pirates?”

Shanha knew Jim was going to tell another story. “Papa,” she said, “could pirates talk like other animals?”

Jim chuckled. “Pirates aren’t animals, they’re people.”

“Oh.” Shanha looked confused. The two stories Jim had told her at the zoo were about animals.

“Well, a lot of people did think they were animals, because they were so mean.”

Shanha giggled. “At the zoo you told us about animals that could talk, and now you’re telling us about people that were animals.”

Jim smiled. “Pirates lived a hard life,” he said. “Most of them had broken or missing teeth. Some of them had an eye shot out or punctured by knives. They covered the damaged eye with a patch. They ran a strap through the patch and secured it over their eye by tying it at the back of their head. A lot of pirates were missing a leg, and tied a piece of wood to their stump so they could walk.”

Rhasha became inquisitive. “How did they lose their legs?”

“Well,” Jim said, “I guess their legs were hacked off with swords or blown off in some way. Swords are like real long knives,” he added, stretching his arms out to demonstrate how long swords were.

Shanha was puzzled. “Who hacked off their legs?”

Jim realized he’d missed a portion of his story. “Shanha, pirates were people who killed other people and stole from them. They pulled their ships up next to other ships and jumped onto those ships with knives between their teeth and guns in their hands. They killed everyone on the other ship and stole their gold or whatever they could find that was worth anything. Also, they talked mean.” Jim began to talk in a gruff voice. “They said things like ‘Arrr mate, you’re nothing but a landlubber’-that’s what they call people who don’t know how to sail.”

"Oh Jim," Rhasha said, " I don't ever want to see any pirates. Where do they live?"

Jim smiled. "There aren't any pirates anymore. They lived many years ago."

Rhasha and Shanha's had grown eyes large as Jim talked about pirates. He decided to have some fun with them. "Girls, when we get on the boat, we'll be just like any other sailors. I'll be the captain and you two will be my crew."

Rhasha and Shanha knew he was teasing. "Is the captain the boss of the crew?" Rhasha asked.

As Jim prepared to answer her question, he painted a serious look on his face. He continued to talk in a gruff voice. "Yes," he said, "and when I yell 'all hands on deck,' both of you have to run to me and stand in front of me with your arms straight down at your sides and your feet together. You have to stand stiff as a board. Also," he added, "you have to salute me." He raised his right hand to his forehead and snapped it down to his side.

Rhasha and Shanha mimicked him, and of course Rhasha stuck her tongue out at him, then smiled.

Shanha said, "You're being silly again, aren't you."

"Yes," Jim confessed. "I just couldn't resist."

Jim drove until midnight and then slept for five hours. The next day he drove past Gulfport and Biloxi, Mississippi. After they passed Mobile, Alabama, they were only about seventy miles from Pensacola, Florida. They arrived in Pensacola at one o'clock in the afternoon and quickly parked the Freightliner at a local truck stop.

Jim called a taxi to take them to the marina. On the way, he had the taxi stop at a grocery store and picked up a few supplies. When they got to the marina, they walked up to a railing that separated a restaurant from the boat docks and hung over the rail, Rhasha and Shanha babbling excitedly about all the huge and beautiful boats.

"Which boat is yours?" Rhasha asked.

Jim stared at a small dinghy moored to the dock. The dinghy was used by marina personnel to move around in the marina. "I said it was just a small sea cruiser."

Jim hid a smile and watched Rhasha and Shanha as they looked down at the dinghy. The dinghy couldn't have been eight feet long.

"Papa," Shanha said, "if all three of us get in that boat, it's going to sink."

Rhasha tried a smile. "It's a beautiful boat, Jim. Let's go for a ride."

Jim smiled as they walked down the steps toward the dinghy. Rhasha and Shanha were walking in front of him. When they got to the dinghy, Rhasha stepped down into the small boat. Shanha waited behind her.

"Angel," Jim asked, "are you going to steal that boat?"

Rhasha looked confused. "I thought you said this was your boat."

"No." Jim snickered. "I said I own a small sea cruiser. This is a dinghy."

Shanha hadn't gotten into the boat yet. Rhasha hurriedly stepped from the dinghy back onto the dock. They looked around for another small boat. Rhasha said, "There aren't anymore small boats."

Jim winked at them and started walking down the boardwalk. Rhasha and Shanha followed close behind.

They passed several beautiful sea cruisers on their way to the last slip. Parked in the last slip was the prettiest boat Rhasha and Shanha had ever seen. Jim pointed to the boat and smiled. "That's my boat," he said.

Rhasha and Shanha were dazzled by its sparkling beauty and overwhelmed by its enormous size. "Jim," Rhasha exclaimed, "that's not a boat, that's a ship!"

Shanha was just as excited. "I don't think three of us can sink that boat," she said seriously. Jim and Rhasha laughed.

Jim escorted Rhasha and Shanha onto the boat and clambered belowdecks to unload his groceries. While there, he cut the legs off his last pair of blue jeans and changed clothes. He heard Rhasha and Shanha running all over the boat, exploring every nook and every cranny. Whenever they saw a hole, they wanted to know what was in it or what it was used for. Finally, just for fun, Jim put on his captain's hat and went back on deck.

"All hands on deck," he yelled. Rhasha and Shanha had gone to their cabin to get dressed for the occasion. When they heard Jim yelling, they both ran to stand at attention in front of him, side by side. They both touched their hands to their foreheads, palms down, and saluted Jim. He saluted back, then cracked up laughing.

Rhasha and Shanha both wore a head scarf tied around their forehead and a paper patch covering one eye. The patches were cut square, and way too big. Shanha held a cardboard sword. They were both wearing their blue jean shorts with a scarf run through the belt loops and tied on the right side. Their oversize shirts were tied in a knot above their belly buttons.

"Mates," Jim laughed, "you're the funniest looking pirates I've ever seen."

Rhasha pulled her face tight and spoke with a harsh voice. "Take that back, landlubber." She scowled. "Or I'm gonna hack off your leg."

"Yeah," Shanha added in a gruff voice, "and I'll give you a wooden leg."

They all laughed. Jim got down on one knee and kissed Shanha on the cheek. Rhasha got down on one knee too, and Jim put his arms around both his girls and hugged them tightly.

"Wait, Papa," Shanha said. She ran down the stairs. Seconds later she came back on deck and returned to Jim and Rhasha. She took off Jim's hat and placed a paper patch over his left eye. She handed Rhasha a head scarf and asked her to tie it around Jim's head. Rhasha and Shanha were giggling as Rhasha did as Shanha asked. The patch slipped down on Jim's face, so Shanha readjusted it. "Now, Papa," Shanha said, "we can all be pirates." She smiled, proud of herself.

Jim smiled too. He left everything as it was.

He walked to the steering wheel and started the motor. He waved to the people in the boat next to them, who were laughing, and eased the cruiser backwards away from the dock. No other boats were moving in the area, so Jim pushed the throttle forward and slowly maneuvered the pirate ship out to sea. He headed south for about an hour. Rhasha and Shanha entertained themselves by making pirate faces and talking in gruff voices. Jim's patch blew off his head, and the wind had loosened his scarf, which slipped down close to his eyes. Jim throttled down, slowing the cruiser. He let go of the wheel to tighten the scarf around his head.

Rhasha had made herself a cardboard sword; she and Shanha were engaged in a mock sword fight. Jim laughed as he watched both his angels try to cut each other's throat. His eighteen-year-old pirate thrust her sword against his seven-year-old pirate's stomach. The flimsy cardboard sword curled on the end, but Shanha acted as if she were dying. She fell back against the seat with one hand holding the imaginary wound, the other hand holding the cardboard sword flung outward, hanging over the side of the boat. She pretended to lose consciousness and her cardboard sword slipped out of her hand and fell into the water.

"My sword!" she yelled as she jumped to retrieve it. She jumped too far. "Papa!" she screamed as she tumbled over the edge of the boat and fell to the water below. Shanha couldn't swim.

Without thinking, both Jim and Rhasha dived into the water. Jim forgot until he hit the water that the boat was still moving. Rhasha was crying. Jim was frantic. They thrashed around in the water, heads turning, looking for Shanha. They both spotted her at once, just a short distance away from them.

"Papa! Mama!" she yelled. "Help me."

"Shanha," Jim called, "hold your breath."

As Rhasha began swimming toward Shanha as fast as she could, Jim realized the boat was getting away. He had a hard decision to make. Should he go after Shanha, or try to get the boat? If he went after the boat, Shanha could drown; if he didn't get the boat, they could all drown.

Jim called to Rhasha, who was still swimming hard toward Shanha, "Get Shanha. I'll try to get the boat."

"Okay," she yelled, "hurry."

Jim swam toward the boat as fast as he could. He reached it and swept his hands all over the side of it, trying frantically to find something to hang onto. The cruiser slid on past him. Jim tried to catch up with the cruiser.

Rhasha had gotten to Shanha in time and was holding her out of the water. Jim gave up trying to catch the boat and swam back to Rhasha and Shanha. They were both crying. During their ordeal, Jim cut his arm; blood swirled all around him in the water. He held his fingers over the cut, trying to stop the bleeding.

"Shanha," he asked, "are you okay?"

Shanha could see the cruiser getting farther away. "I'm sorry, Papa," she said, "I'm so sorry."

Jim knew it wasn't Shanha's fault, and didn't want her to feel guilty about falling off the boat. "Angel," he said as he tread water, "you didn't do anything wrong." Unaccustomed to having a seven-year-old in the boat, he'd never thought about putting a life vest on her. "It's all my fault, sweetheart," he continued. "I should have put a life jacket on you."

Jim closed his eyes to pray. "Heavenly Father," he said, "please forgive me for my sins and have mercy on my soul."

Shanha moaned. She'd seen something in the water through her tears. She threw her arm around Jim's neck. "Papa, Papa!" she yelled. "What is that?"

Jim opened his eyes and tried to see what Shanha was pointing at, but salt water blurred his vision.

Rhasha could now see it, though. "Jim," she whispered, "what is it?"

As his eyes began to focus, fear gripped Jim's soul. Still distant but coming toward them, three fins sliced through the water. Jim knew below those fins were three man-eating sharks. "Rhasha," he said, "pray like you've never prayed before."

He took his own advice and closed his eyes. "Father," he said, "you know my heart, and you know I want to live. But what's more important to me, Father, is that no harm comes to Rhasha and Shanha."

As Jim prayed, he remembered that he was bleeding. He realized the sharks had picked up the scent of his blood. Jim opened his eyes and looked at his arm. Blood still flowed into the water. "Rhasha," Jim said, "take Shanha and swim far away from me."

Rhasha knew what Jim was doing. "No. I want to be with yo-"

"Do it *now,* Rhasha," Jim snapped. "For Shanha's sake."

Rhasha began to cry. She pulled on Shanha and swam away from Jim. The sharks were about thirty yards away, swimming cautiously toward him.

"Rhasha," Jim said, "after you get far enough away, I want both of you to lay on your backs and hold your breath. The salt water will help you float. Don't make any movements and maybe they will leave you alone." He wanted to give her more advice, but it was to late. The sharks were within a few feet of him and ready to attack.

"Rhasha, Shanha," he said as the first shark moved in, ready to sink its teeth into Jim's arm, "I love you both."

"I love you too, Papa," Shanha cried.

"I love you, Jim," Rhasha called. Tears flowed down her cheeks. "Please tell me everything will be okay."

Suddenly clouds rolled across the sky. Lightning flashed; thunder roared.

"Everything will be okay, girls," Jim replied, staring at the sky.

The sky grew dim. Not a sound could be heard. The waves on the ocean became as calm as water in a bottle. A soft blue glow formed over Jim, Rhasha, and Shanha and pulled them together. All three sharks bumped into the soft blue glow, but couldn't penetrate it.

Instantly, Jim, Rhasha, and Shanha found themselves lying on the deck of the sea cruiser. The soft blue glow continued to hug them. Jim looked up to heaven and saw four angels at the four corners of a window. Inside the window was a bright glow, and Jim could see what looked like a throne room.

A loud voice boomed in Jim's head, as if amplified through speakers, *"Jim, we need you back in Africa."*

Jim lost what strength he had left, but he managed to speak. "Sir," he said, "are you a messenger?"

"I am a messenger."

"Sir," Jim asked, "could you tell me why I'm needed in Africa?"

"Jim," the messenger said, *"you will see a vision on the plane ride back to Africa. Everything will be explained to you then."*

The voice fell silent and the window into heaven closed.

They heard the humming sound rise, pulsate, then fall. The blue glow disappeared and the waves rolled across the ocean again. The wind began to blow, and water slapped against the sides of the boat.

The clouds rolled from east to west across the sky, then rushed back to the east. They could see lightning flash and heard thunder. Then the skies cleared and the sunshine burst through.

As they continued to look toward heaven, Jim, Rhasha, and Shanha slowly pulled themselves off the deck and stood up. They all looked at each other. Jim's arm wasn't bleeding anymore, and there was no sign of a cut.

Shanha looked dazed, but she was the first to speak. "Papa," she said, "I don't want to be a pirate anymore."

"I don't either," Rhasha agreed.

Jim hugged both his girls and smiled. "That's good," he said, "because you're both angels."

He gave Rhasha and Shanha life vests and put one on himself. Now that the danger was over, Rhasha and Shanha began to get comfortable. "Jim," Rhasha said, "I've figured something out about God."

"What would that be?"

Rhasha wiggled back and forth in her innocent teenage way. She gently nipped on her fingernail. "It seems to me," she said, "that God has a full-time job just taking care of us."

Jim smiled. "You're probably right," he said, "but I'm sure he doesn't mind, as long as we love him."

Jim walked to the wheel and throttled forward. He quickly turned the boat around and headed back to the marina. He docked the boat and they took a taxi back to the truck stop. As they put the groceries in the truck, Jim thought, *If God needs me in Africa, then I'd better hurry up and get there.* He started the truck and shortly they were rolling west.

Within fifteen minutes, Jim crossed into Alabama. An hour after that, they passed through Mobile. The Freightliner continued down Interstate 10, and in less than an hour, they were in Mississippi. Jim was making good time as he crossed the Louisiana state line. He took Interstate 12 and proceeded toward Baton Rouge. Jim stopped in Hammond, Louisiana, to get fuel. They slept in the truck and ate breakfast at the truck stop restaurant. At nine o'clock the next morning they were back on the road again.

Chapter 19

Louisiana Law

Bed of Leaves

Jim had driven some distance past Baton Rouge when he saw a cop in his side mirror. He hadn't broken any laws that he knew of, but the cop stayed right on his tail. Jim was worried, remembering the Louisiana vehicle confiscation laws. He just knew the cop was going to stop him for no reason at all.

He slowed down to five miles below the posted speed limit. He hated driving in Louisiana. A sick feeling churned in his stomach as the cop turned on his overhead lights. Jim hadn't done anything wrong so he knew this was going to be a bad experience. He pulled onto the shoulder of the road and set his brakes and flashers. The officer pulled up behind him and parked.

Shanha was asleep in the bunk; Rhasha was riding in the passenger seat. She could tell that Jim was worried. "Sweetheart," she said, "is something wrong?"

"Yes," he replied tersely, "a cop just stopped me."

Shanha was awake now. She sat up.

"Rhasha," Jim said, "I'll go and talk to the cop. You and Shanha stay in the truck."

"Okay," Rhasha said. She unbuckled her seat belt and slid the seat back.

Jim took his truck folder with him as he climbed out of the truck. As he stepped down to the ground, the officer was waiting for him beside the truck. He held the leash of a police dog. Jim saw a second patrol car pull in behind the first patrol car.

"Driver," the officer said, "I noticed your trailer was weaving. Have you had anything to drink?"

Jim knew the cop was lying, but he was courteous. "No sir. I don't drink."

"I need to see your driver's license, registration, and insurance papers." The police dog remained almost motionless as Jim pulled his license, the truck registration, and the Louisiana state permit out of his truck folder.

The officer glanced at the documents and handed them back to Jim. "Is there anyone else in the truck?" the officer asked.

"Yes," Jim replied. "I have a teenage girl and a seven-year-old girl with me."

"Get 'em out of the truck," the officer commanded.

Jim saw two more police cars pull up behind the second police car. All their lights were flashing. The dog never moved a muscle. "Officer," Jim asked, "what's with all the patrol cars? What's going on here?"

The officer stuck the driver's license under Jim's chin and flipped it upwards. "I said to get those girls out of the truck."

Jim looked at the officer with cold eyes. "Sir," he said, "you don't have any reason to harass me or my girls."

The officer grabbed Jim's arm, twisted it behind his back, and shoved him against the truck. Jim's truck folder was knocked out of his hand. "Put your hands up on the side of the truck," the officer demanded.

Jim placed his hands on the side of the truck as the officer spread Jim's legs apart with his foot. "What you're doing is illegal," Jim said.

The officer ran his hands up and down Jim's body. "We'll see who goes to jail," he said, grinning.

When he finished the body search, the officer slapped handcuffs on Jim's left wrist and twisted his arm behind his back. He grabbed Jim's right arm and twisted it behind him also. The other officers rushed up to assist the arresting officer, but he had already latched the cuffs on Jim's wrist.

Rhasha had watched what was going on through the truck mirror. She jumped into the driver's seat and kicked the door open, then jumped down to the ground. Shanha was close behind her.

"What are you doing to him?" Rhasha screamed. "Leave him alone." She hurried to check on Jim, but the arresting officer grabbed her, spun her around, and shoved her against the side of the truck.

Shanha ran toward Jim. "Papa, Papa!" she cried. Tears ran down her face. "Is that bad man hurting you?"

The officer was putting handcuffs on Rhasha.

"Girls," Jim said, "everything will be all right, you'll see."

One of the officers grabbed Shanha and pulled her to the side. Rhasha and Shanha were both crying. Shanha clutched her teddy bear.

"I know everything will be okay." Rhasha sniffled. "They think they're tough, wearing those badges, but they don't know God will protect you."

All the officers began to laugh. The arresting officer laughed the loudest. "With this black girl," he said, "I thought you were a pimp. Now I'm wondering if you're a preacher. It doesn't matter, though," he added. "Where you're going, you're going to need all the God you can get."

"What do you mean, where I'm going?" Jim yelled. "What are you doing to us?"

The officer slapped Jim callously on the back. "Partner," he said, mocking Jim's Texan accent, "I'm arresting you for transporting an illegal substance into the great state of Louisiana."

"That's crazy," Jim replied, "I don't have any drugs, and you know it."

All the cops laughed again. "If I say you have drugs," the officer said, "then you have drugs. See how petrified my dog is? He could smell drugs all the way back to my car." The three assisting officers snickered.

Jim couldn't believe what was happening. Rhasha and Shanha had stopped crying and were looking at the sky, waiting for God to turn the four cops into donkeys.

"Does the great state of Louisiana arrest a man for transporting drugs without even searching his truck?" Jim asked, trying to reason with the officer.

"Oh, so you want us to search your truck?" the officer sneered. He looked at one of the assisting officers and pointed to the Freightliner. "Mark, get in the truck and get that four pounds of marijuana out of this driver's glove box."

Jim knew this wasn't right. "What about a search warrant?"

The arresting officer was getting irritated. "Don't you worry about a search warrant," he said, "I'll take care of that when we get to the station. Mark," he yelled, "I said to get that marijuana out of the glove box."

Mark, a young, slender man with an arrogant smile on his face, slipped past the police dog. The dog barked and began sniffing urgently at his clothes. The officer pushed the dog away and climbed into Jim's truck. He fumbled around with something inside his jacket, finally pulling it out. He didn't even open the glove box. He climbed back out of the truck, holding a package of marijuana in his hands.

"Looks like we caught a real criminal," he said. "I found four pounds of marijuana in the glove compartment." He handed the package to the arresting officer. Jim stared at it in disbelief, absently noting that the package couldn't weigh more than a pound.

"Looks like about four pounds to me," the arresting officer said.

Rhasha and Shanha kept glancing at the sky.

The arresting officer took hold of Jim's arm to escort him to the police cruiser. "Mark," he said. He pointed to Rhasha. "Put her in your car and follow me." He pointed to Shanha. "Jerry, take the young miss to Children's Division. Hank, get someone down here to get this truck."

Rhasha and Shanha began crying again as they were led to the police cars. They thought for sure God would turn the four officers into donkeys, but he didn't. Jim, seated in the first police car, watched bleakly as Rhasha climbed into the second car. Shanha was in the third car. All four police cars took off, one after the other, lights flashing and sirens blaring.

At the police station, Jim and Rhasha were led inside, still wearing handcuffs. They had their mug shots taken and they were fingerprinted. "Jim, what's happening?" Rhasha whispered as they were wiping the ink off their fingers.

Before Jim could answer, they were handcuffed again and led to separate interrogation rooms. Shanha was nowhere to be seen. Jim saw Rhasha seated in her interrogation room through the open door as three officers led him into his interrogation room and closed the door.

Inside the room was a desk with a confession form and a pen laying on top of it. A tape recorder was placed in the center of the desk and the "on" button was depressed. The arresting officer sat on the corner of the desk, facing the other officers. Jim was still handcuffed. One of the assisting officers held Jim's arm, pushing him forward.

Suddenly the third officer sucker punched Jim in the stomach. The force behind the blow lifted him into the air. He bounced off the wall and sprawled on the floor. "That was just to get your attention," the officer said. All three officers laughed.

Jim tried to stand up. With his hands cuffed behind him, it was awkward for him to get to his feet. A strange blue glow had formed around him.

“What’s that blue around you?” the arresting officer asked, frowning.

Jim didn’t answer. When he regained his feet, he walked over to the officer who had punched him, thrust his face within inches of the officer’s face, and, gritting his teeth, stared into the officer’s eyes. “Is that the best you can do?” he snarled. “Shanha can hit harder than that.”

The officer looked at Jim in disbelief. His eyes kept sliding to the blue glow around him.

God had surrounded Jim with his protective shield. He hadn’t even felt the blow.

The officer’s face turned red, then anger overtook his shock. He hauled off and hit Jim with everything he had, smashing his fist into Jim’s face. This time God held Jim solid. Not a hair moved on his head. The officer howled, then clutched his right hand in his left hand, groaning. The force behind the blow had broken two of the officer’s fingers.

Another officer rushed toward Jim, yelling, “You’re going to sign that confession form if I have to break every bone in your body.” He pulled his pistol out of its holster and held it in the palm of his hand as he slapped Jim on the side of his head so hard, the gun flew out of his hand. Jim never felt a thing.

Silence filled the room. All three officers stared at Jim. Finally one of the officers broke the silence. He looked at the arresting officer. “Sarge, what do we do now?”

The arresting officer put his hand over his mouth, rubbing his chin with his fingers as he studied Jim.” “Well,” he said, “we don’t need a confession. With the evidence we have and a confession from the girl, we’ll get a conviction.”

Jim felt confident God would protect Rhasha. “Officers,” he said, “God didn’t let you harm a hair on my head. Do you really believe he’s going to let you hurt Rhasha? If I were you, I’d get down on my knees and beg God to forgive me.”

The arresting officer was walking toward the door. “I’m not you, freak,” he threw over his shoulder. At the door he turned around. “Mark,” he said to the officer with the broken fingers, “you stay with the prisoner while Gary and I talk to superman’s girlfriend.”

Jim smiled as the other two officers walked through the door. “I feel sorry for you two,” he said. “You will never get a confession from Rhasha.”

The officers walked confidently into Rhasha’s room. Her heart was pounding and she was shaking all over. Rhasha knew they had done something to Jim, but she didn’t know what. She began to cry as they shut the door. “Did you hurt Jim?” she sobbed.

There were now three officers in the room. The two interrogating officers smiled as they watched Rhasha cry. She would be easy to crack.

“Little girl,” the arresting officer said, “your pimp’s on the way to the hospital as we speak.”

Anger and hatred transformed her face. That was the wrong thing to say. Her head was hanging low, but her eyes glared at the officers, sizing them up.

Suddenly a blue glow surrounded her. Rhasha felt strength flow into her body from an unknown source. Her wrists were cuffed together behind her back, but Rhasha pulled her wrists apart and the cuffs snapped. She held her arms in front of her, the cuff bracelets still on each wrist, with the two halves of the severed chain dangling from them. God had given Rhasha the strength of ten men. The three officers stumbled back in awe.

The door was locked. No one could get in. Inside the interrogation room, people were screaming. Those outside rammed the door and twisted the knob, trying to get in. They could hear bodies being slammed against the walls, and moans of pain.

Finally, everything became quiet. Even the officers outside the room settled down. A click of the latch. Their eyes fell to watch the doorknob as it turned. The door flew open with such force that it came loose from its hinges. It struck the opposite wall. The young black girl ran out, through the crowd of officers, knocking four of them to the floor as she rushed to the room where Jim was.

Behind her, officers rushed into the interrogation room and found three injured officers lying on the floor. Their shirts were ripped, their faces blood-streaked. One officer's shirt was completely torn off, but his shirtsleeve cuffs were still around each wrist. The desk and chairs were overturned and the desk drawers were lying in the center of the room. Papers from the desk drawers and trash can were scattered all over the floor. The room looked like a tornado had hit it.

Jim's interrogation room door was shut and latched. Rhasha twisted the knob, but it was locked and wouldn't open. She jerked on the knob so hard, it pulled the door and the door frame out of the wall. When she released the knob, the door fell to the floor.

Rhasha rushed to Jim, who was sitting in a chair. When she saw he was unharmed, she began to cry openly. The officer left to guard Jim ran to apprehend Rhasha. He ran into a fist that knocked him out cold. Rhasha reached behind Jim and pulled his handcuffs apart.

Jim rose and they hugged each other tight. Miniature stars popped all around their heads as Jim and Rhasha kissed passionately. Rhasha held up her pinkie finger, then Jim held up his. They locked their pinkie fingers together and kissed again.

No one dared to come into the room.

Jim turned toward the door and put his left arm around Rhasha's waist. She slid her right arm around his waist, and they walked together to the open door. Outside the room, twenty-two officers waited with their guns aimed at Jim and Rhasha.

"God's not going to let you hurt us," Jim said. "You might as well put your guns away."

No one complied with Jim's suggestion. Every officer in the department wanted a reason to shoot. As Jim and Rhasha walked over to the desk where the police report was, all the officers followed them with their guns still trained on their backs.

Two folders lay open on top of the desk, with a form lying at an angle on top of each-one containing Jim's fingerprints with his mug shots paper-clipped to the top, the other, Rhasha's.

The arresting officer and his assistants had regained consciousness and staggered into the central receiving area. The officer from Jim's interrogation room arrived at the same time. The arresting officer saw all the guns pointed at Jim and Rhasha and yelled, "Shoot them! Can't you see they're escaping?"

All the officers looked down their gun barrels. The prisoners stood motionless. No one fired. They didn't want to be accused of murder.

"Never mind," the arresting officer growled, "I'll do it myself." Hatred for Jim and Rhasha made him irrational-he didn't care if he was arrested for murder. He pulled his gun out of its holster and pointed it at Jim's head. His finger slowly squeezed the trigger. Jim closed his eyes and began praying out loud, asking God to spare Rhasha's life. The sergeant had a sinister smile on his face-a smile of triumph.

All the officers suddenly jerked their heads around, trying to locate the source of a humming sound that got louder and louder until the air throbbed with its power. After a few seconds, it faded away. The officers, including the arresting officer, lowered their weapons and looked around in confusion. The room grew dim and totally silent.

Jim stopped praying. All the officers had moved away from him and Rhasha. Suddenly there was a flicker, like a warp in time. When the flicker died, Shanha was standing between them, holding her teddy bear.

Jim and Rhasha put their hands on Shanha's shoulders and waited to see what else would happen. Shanha was calm, having already figured out what was going on. Rhasha and Shanha waited for God to turn all the officers into donkeys.

The humming sound returned, sounding as if it was gearing up for more action. Suddenly everything went into high-speed motion. One by one, each object in the room winked out of existence. Finally nothing was left but the people. Even the guns were gone. Confused, the officers stood with their jaws hanging open, their faces sagging in disbelief. They stood with their arms out before them, as though they were still holding weapons.

There was another flash and everyone in the room, except Jim, Rhasha, and Shanha, froze. They looked like wax statues with confused looks etched onto their faces. Their arms were still pointing outward. Jim, Rhasha, and Shanha stared. Suddenly the officers disappeared, one by one. They were there, then *poof,* they were gone. Finally nothing remained in the room except Jim, Rhasha, and Shanha. Jim knew the event wasn't over; he remained motionless. Rhasha and Shanha wondered if there was a new herd of donkeys at the zoo.

The humming sound started up again, but quickly faded away. Inanimate objects began to reappear. First desks popped in, one after another, and then chairs. The desks were bare, then *poof,* computers reappeared, one by one. Pens, coffee mugs, papers-everything-popped instantly into being, one at a time. Everything that is, except people. When the room looked as it had before, silence reigned.

Suddenly there was a loud *click* and a flash.

The humming sound geared up again, then ceased. Now there were officers walking around the room, performing various tasks. Everything moved normally, and the room was bright and noisy again. The light blue glow around Jim, Rhasha, and Shanha was gone.

The officer at the desk where Jim, Rhasha, and Shanha stood was talking on the telephone. "Yes dear," he was saying, "I'll remember. Don't worry. I'll see you tonight. I love you, too. Bye."

Jim looked around the room. No one was paying any attention to them. The officer at the desk hung up the phone and addressed Jim. "Sir, I'm sorry about the interruption. My wife wants me to stop and get some bread on my way home tonight." He smiled as if to say "you know how it is."

Jim stared at the officer, trying to adjust to his changed attitude. "It's not a problem," he managed.

The officer opened some folders on his desk. "Anyway," he said, "we do look for missing persons, but not for friends you haven't seen in five days."

Jim and Rhasha tried not to laugh.

"My advice," the officer continued, "is to start your search in Dallas. You said Dallas was the last place you saw Jackie Short."

Jim and Rhasha couldn't hold it any longer. They burst out laughing. The officer laughed as well, though he didn't understand why.

Jim glanced up and saw four men being led out of the police station, all handcuffed and wearing prison coveralls. They were crying. One man kept repeating, "I don't know what happened. We're police officers. Don't any of you remember us?"

When the men saw Jim, Rhasha, and Shanha, their eyes widened in recognition, and they hung their heads and never said another word. They knew they were getting a just punishment.

"What did those guys do?" Jim asked the officer at the desk as the four were escorted out the door and shoved into a waiting patrol car.

The officer looked out the glass door at the men Jim was pointing at. "Oh, those guys," he said. "They're four construction workers convicted of murder. They're being transferred to the big house. I've got their files right here." The officer pointed to four folders lying open on his desk. The officer had been fastening additional forms to them.

Jim could see the ex-cops' fingerprints on the bottoms of the forms, and their mug shots, attached with paper clips. No evidence of Jim's and Rhasha's folders could be seen.

"Thank you, sir," Jim said, preparing to leave.

The officer was closing the folders and slipping them inside a manila envelope. "I'm sorry I couldn't be of more help," he replied, "but if you check in Dallas, I'm sure you'll find your friend there."

Jim, Rhasha, and Shanha smiled as they walked out the front door. They stood on the front steps, holding hands.

Shanha was the first to speak. "Papa, how are we going to get home?"

Jim's truck was no where to be seen. As Jim and Rhasha knelt down and kissed Shanha on the forehead, he could see she really was worried. "I'm so glad we're all together again," Jim said. "Let's not worry about how we're going to get home. Let's give God praise and count our blessings."

"We've had a lot of blessings lately, Papa," Shanha said as she cradled her teddy bear in her arms. Jim and Rhasha smiled and nodded their agreement.

The prisoners, still waiting in the patrol cars, heard every word Jim and Shanha said. One officer waited with them, watching for a second officer to return to the patrol car with the manila envelope. As the four ex-cops looked on, a light blue glow surrounded Jim, Rhasha, and Shanha. *Poof!* In a flash, they were gone. No one but the four prisoners saw them disappear. Speechless, the ex-cops could only stare at the spot where Jim, Rhasha, and Shanha had stood as the patrol car sped away from the police station.

A few seconds later Jim, Rhasha, and Shanha found themselves sitting in the truck, which was parked beside a large building. Jim was sitting in the driver's seat, and Rhasha was sitting in the passenger seat. Shanha was sitting on the bunk in the back.

They looked around in disbelief. Jim tried to determine where they were. "I don't believe it," he said. He climbed out of the truck and turned all the way around in a circle, holding his hands in the air, as if he were dancing.

Rhasha and Shanha climbed out of the truck and ran to Jim. "What's the matter, Jim?" Rhasha asked.

"Look around you, angel," Jim replied. "Where do you think we are?"

Rhasha and Shanha looked around. Excitement filled their faces. "We're home!" Shanha said. "We're back in Dallas."

Jim raised his face toward heaven. He could feel the sun on his face and a cool breeze in his hair. Creating a mental picture of God sitting on his throne with Jesus at his right side, Jim began to pray. Rhasha and Shanha bowed their heads.

"Father," he said, "please forgive me of my sins and have mercy on my soul. Thank you, Father, for all the things you have done for us. I know a day will come when you will call us to heaven, and death will no longer be our enemy. That will be a great day and a great blessing.

"Father, I pray for the four officers who did us wrong. Please speak to their hearts and show them the right way. I love you, Father, and I pray these things in the name of Jesus. Amen."

Rhasha and Shanha raised their heads and opened their eyes. Jim continued to view a mental image of God sitting on his throne. Jesus sat on his right-hand side. A few seconds later he opened his eyes and raised his head.

As they rose and walked to the truck, Rhasha was thinking about Jesus. She wished with all her heart that she could understand the things Jim taught her about God's son.

They climbed back into the truck to get their clothes. Jim reached up to the cubby hole above his head to get his log book. He knew the last place he'd filled it out was in Hammond, Louisiana. He snickered as he read the daily entry.

Rhasha, gathering clothes, noticed Jim chuckling to himself. "What's funny, sweetheart?" she asked.

Jim decided not to log his trip, but a strange thought occurred to him. "It's not anything that's funny, angel," he said, "it's more a 'what if' situation."

By this time Shanha was helping Rhasha fold blankets. "'What if' what, Papa?"

Jim now had two curious people waiting for an explanation. "I was just thinking, what if an officer pulled up right now and asked to see my log book? He would see that we were in Hammond, Louisiana, at nine o'clock this morning."

"I don't understand," Rhasha said. "Why would it matter?"

"Well," Jim replied, "how could I explain being in Dallas, Texas, four hours later?"

"I'd just tell him the truth," Rhasha said.

"Sure, Rhasha," Jim said, then started acting goofy. "All I'd have to say is, 'Officer, God zapped us to Dallas.'" He snickered again. "He'd lock me up for being stupid."

Shanha had a serious look on her face as she swayed back and forth in the bunk. "I'm sure people have told osafers that before."

Jim and Rhasha laughed.

The warehouse door was open. Jim could see his car parked in the warehouse, no more than a hundred feet from where they were. Rhasha and Shanha were tidying up the truck, so Jim walked to his car and pushed the key into the ignition switch. With a turn of the wrist, the engine hummed to life. He pulled the sedan up next to the Freightliner and parked it. They loaded everything from the truck into the car, Jim locked the truck, and they were soon on the road, going east toward his apartment.

Chapter 20

Shanha's Faith

At two o'clock, Jim pulled into his two-car garage. When they entered the apartment, he discovered Jackie and Simbatu were gone. Jim thought something might be wrong-they hadn't answered the phone and the apartment didn't appear to be used much.

He picked up the phone and called the police station. When a Sargent Snider answered the phone, Jim asked if he had any information about Jackie and Simbatu's whereabouts. Sargeant Snider put Jim on hold and checked his records. A moment later the sergeant told Jim there was nothing in their files about Jackie Short or Simbatu Hilundas. Jim thanked him and hung up the phone.

He decided to check Jackie and Simbatu's rooms for any evidence that might help locate his friends. Everything was as it should be in Jackie's room. He walked across the hall to Simbatu's room and found it clean, except for a shirt lying on the bed and the apartment key lying on the night stand. His wallet and passport were in the shirt pocket.

Jim was really worried now. Jackie and Simbatu had no way to get back into the apartment and Simbatu was without any identification. Rhasha was worried too. As far as Shanha was concerned, God would fix everything. Jim and Rhasha knew God took care of all their problems, but they weren't sure he always would, so they continued to worry.

Jim called several hospitals, but nobody had any knowledge of Jackie or Simbatu. He talked to neighbors, but nobody had even known Jackie and Simbatu were staying in Jim's apartment. They searched for two hours, driving up and down every street and alley in the area. Jim checked with local restaurants and grocery stores. No one had seen Jackie or Simbatu.

Rhasha knew Dallas was a big city. Fearing she might never see Jackie and Simbatu again, she started to cry. Tears ran down her cheeks.

Shanha couldn't understand what all the fuss was about. "Papa," she said, "why don't you just ask God where they are?"

Rhasha stopped crying. She and Jim looked at one another, then at Shanha. "Out of the mouths of babes," Jim said. "I am so proud of you, angel. Your faith is pure."

Jim raised his face toward heaven and closed his eyes. Rhasha and Shanha bowed their heads; their eyes were shut tight. Shanha held her teddy bear as if he were praying too. Jim asked God to direct them to Jackie and Simbatu. His prayer was short and to the point. He ended the prayer by giving God praise and glory for all he had done for them.

They all opened their eyes and looked around. Rhasha and Shanha thought maybe God would deliver Jackie and Simbatu right to the spot where they were standing. Rhasha finally wondered out loud if God was going to do anything at all.

"Jim," she said, "why is it that God sometimes zaps us from one place to another to get us out of trouble, and other times he doesn't?"

"Let's not always expect God to come to our rescue," Jim told her. "If we take God for granted, he'll quit helping us." Jim hoped God would show him where Jackie and Simbatu were. He continued to look around for a sign, still praying in his heart.

Rhasha looked toward heaven. Tears pooled in her eyes. "Father," she said, "please forgive me of my sins and have mercy on my soul." Rhasha had heard Jim pray that way many times, and she knew God heard his prayers. "Father, I will always appreciate everything you do for me, and I pray that you will help me understand what Jim taught me about Jesus." Even though Rhasha didn't understand how Jesus could be her savior, she ended the prayer the way Jim had taught her. "In Jesus' name, amen."

When Rhasha ended her prayer, she opened her eyes and looked at Jim. Tears ran down his cheeks. He quickly put his arms around her waist and pulled her toward him. Rhasha put her arms around Jim's neck, and they held each other tight.

"Papa, Mama," Shanha said, "don't forget about me."

Jim and Rhasha knelt down beside Shanha and hugged her. "Sweetheart," Rhasha replied, "we will never forget about you."

Jim heard a familiar sound and looked toward heaven. A few seconds later, Rhasha and Shanha heard it as well, and they looked upward too. The soft white clouds scattered across the sky began to pull toward the east, leaving the sky cloudless above them.

They could hear the humming sound getting louder until it pulsated with power. After a few seconds, it faded and ceased. Jim, Rhasha, and Shanha sensed they were the only people in Dallas who could see what the clouds were doing. Life went on as usual for everyone else. A heavy, dark cloud had formed in the east. The wind began to blow. Suddenly dark clouds rolled in above them like foam on a raging river. Lightning cracked across the sky. Thunder roared like an earthquake. The clouds rolled back toward the east.

Four angels appeared above them, off toward the east. The four angels pulled the sky back in four different directions, exposing a window into heaven. What happened next came in rapid succession. Two beams of light shot from the throne room toward the northern part of Dallas. Each beam was thin, like a bright white laser, and pinpointed a different location in the distance. Both beams remained fixed across the sky. Jim knew the beams pointed toward Jackie and Simbatu, but he didn't know why there were two beams of light.

They got in the car and Jim sped toward the spot where the nearest beam touched the earth. As their car approached it, the beam began to expand. When he turned away from the beam, it became thinner.

Shanha was sitting in the back seat, but leaned forward. She'd remembered something Jim had read to her from the Bible. "Papa, when God showed the three wise men where the baby Jesus was, all he did was put a star above him."

Jim made a turn, heading toward the beam. The beam of light again began to expand. "Yes Shanha," he replied, "and they found the baby Jesus."

"Yes," Shanha said. She hugged her teddy bear. "But how did they know they found the right baby?"

Jim smiled, pleased that she remembered the stories he read to her. "God told the three wise men they would find the baby Jesus lying in a manger," he said, "so that was what they were looking for." Realizing Shanha was still confused, he added, "I'm sure God helped to guide their footsteps."

Jim stopped the car at a red light. He glanced at Rhasha and could tell she was thinking about Jim and Shanha's conversation.

Finally she said, "I think it would be impossible to find someone in a city by following a star. Why didn't God point to the baby Jesus with a beam of light?"

The traffic light changed to green and Jim continued driving toward the expanding beam of light. The closer they got, the wider it grew. "In those times," he told her, "if people saw a beam of light coming from heaven, they would think the world was cracking. People would have panicked."

He looked at both his girls and knew they still weren't convinced. "Girls," he added, "Christianity is based on faith, as are all beliefs. I know someday Jesus will reveal himself to you-he did to me." Jim noticed the beam of light was directly in front of him, now about five feet wide. He knew they didn't have much farther to go.

Rhasha was still thinking about what Jim said, but something else caught her attention. "Jim! There's Jackie, standing beneath the beam of light."

The beam of light disappeared as Jim pulled up to the curb. Everyone babbled excitedly as Jackie climbed into the car. Jim looked at his surroundings as Jackie hugged Rhasha and Shanha. They were parked in front of the bus station.

"Jackie," Jim asked, "where is Simbatu?"

Jackie was now looking at the beam of light in the distance. "I don't know, Jim. We got separated in a heavy crowd of people."

Jim looked at the other beam of light. "I think I know where Simbatu is," he said. Jim put the gearshift in drive and headed toward the second beam.

Moments later, they were parked in front of the Dallas zoo. Jim spotted Simbatu sitting under a shade tree, praying. Jim honked the horn and Simbatu looked up, then grinned-his prayers had been answered. Simbatu rushed to the car and climbed into the back seat. They were all happy to be united again.

The beam of light disappeared and the window to heaven closed. Clouds rolled across the sky like waves across the ocean. Lightning flashed and thunder roared. The clouds rushed toward the west, then quickly returned to their former place.

Jim drove back to his apartment and spent an hour talking on the telephone, making arrangements for the company pilot to take them back to Africa. They would meet Mario at the airport at eleven o'clock the next morning.

When he finished talking to Mario, Jim made several more calls, then called Bill, his shipping manager, and let Bill know that no more shipments were to be made to Randell Tool Distributors. Last of all, Jim called Raymond, the company chauffeur, and asked him to be at the apartment by ten o'clock the next morning.

Chapter 21

Shanha Lost In The Woods

Bed of Leaves

The following morning, Jim and his guest climbed aboard the company jet and took off for Africa. Everyone was comfortable, but anxious to get home. Shanha was bouncing the teddy bear she'd named Honeycup back and forth on her knees. She often pretended Honeycup was her little brother.

Rhasha was listening to music through a set of headphones. Jackie and Simbatu were talking about their adventure of the previous day. Everyone had their minds on different things as the jet flew 33,000 feet above the ground.

The sun was shining, but white, puffy clouds filled the sky below the plane. The sound of the engines was nothing more than a constant hum as the jet slipped though the sky. Jim looked out his window and saw an angel riding on a white horse as it galloped alongside the company jet. At times, the white-robed rider was lost from view as he passed through clouds, then burst through on the other side. Jim saw the white horse spread its wings, gliding along with the plane as gracefully as a bird. Sometimes the horse flapped its wings and flew faster than the jet.

Jim looked across the sky and saw other angels sitting on the clouds, strumming on harps and singing. In the distance he could see two angels tossing a ball back and forth. The angels playing with the ball drew closer and closer to the plane. As they got closer, the ball got bigger and bigger. Finally Jim saw that it wasn't a ball they were throwing to each other, but a planet, with oceans and mountains, swirled green and blue. It was earth.

In the far distance, a bright light shone across space. Jim heard hearty laughter. It was the first time Jim had ever heard God laugh. Tears ran down his cheeks as he listened to the heavenly sound. Jim knew God was amused as he watched his children play. He thought about how wonderful heaven would be. Life would go on forever and ever.

God's laughter caused the whole universe to sing. Not only did the angels sing, but the clouds sang. Every rock, on every planet, sang. The whole universe sang in harmony to the most heavenly song Jim had ever heard. He could see musical notes dancing across the sky. As the musical notes got farther away, they disappeared. Planets filled the solar system, swaying back and forth with the music.

Ahead, just below the plane, Jim could see black clouds forming. They seemed to come in from everywhere, gathering like a ferocious storm. The angel on the white horse turned back and wouldn't go any farther. God's laughter could no longer be heard. The bright light from heaven disappeared and the singing stopped. Jim couldn't see any angels anywhere.

Darkness and horror seem to emanate from the black clouds. Jim smelled a nauseating stench. As the plane flew farther over the clouds, the sky became dark. Jim looked down into a deep, dark abyss that seemed to call for him. Violent flashes of lightning crackled down the sides of the hole. Thunder roared from it. As the plane flew over the center of the swirling anomaly, Jim heard the sounds of torment. Feelings of shame and fear rose with screams of pain from the glowing red bottom of the hole. Jim felt as if he was being pulled into the crater. He screamed. Satan had won his soul, he thought, and he would spend eternity in hell.

He felt hands pulling and tugging at him. Jim fought against the forces as if his life depended on it. He could hear voices that sounded like they were miles away. He could hear himself screaming. He continued to push and squirm.

Finally he could make out what the voices were saying.

“Papa, Papa!” Shanha cried as she pulled on his arm. He opened his eyes and saw tears running down her cheeks.

Rhasha was crying and pulling on his other arm. “Jim,” she pleaded, “please wake up.”

Jackie and Simbatu were behind Jim, shaking him as well. As Jim calmed down, tears streamed from his eyes. He realized he had been dreaming. He hugged Rhasha and Shanha. He was still shaking from the horrors of his dream.

Simbatu went back to his seat. Jackie saw that Jim was okay, so he sat down also. Jim still had his arms around Rhasha and Shanha. “Girls,” he said, “I’m sorry I scared you.”

Rhasha laid her head on Jim’s shoulder, content. Shanha laid her head against Jim’s arm. “Papa,” Shanha said, “did you dream about a big scary monster, trying to eat you?”

Jim raised her head with his fingers and kissed her on the cheek. “No.” He smiled. “It was much worse than that.”

Shanha looked into Jim’s eyes. “If it was worse than a monster trying to eat you, then I don’t want to hear about it.”

“Then I won’t tell you that the monster was trying to eat you, too.” Jim smiled as Shanha’s eyes grew big. She knew Jim was teasing her. Jim winked, then looked at Rhasha and kissed her tenderly.

The jet continued its flight toward Africa. One by one, they each fell asleep. Rhasha, holding one of Jim’s hands between both of hers, slept with her head on Jim’s shoulder. He rested his head on hers. Shanha’s head still lay on Jim’s arm. She held his other hand.

As Jim slept, a foggy picture began to focus into a vision. The picture began to roll like an old movie projector. Many images began to come together. Jim felt as though he were watching a movie in a theater.

An old, worn out locomotive was parked at a railway station. Jim recognized the scenery of Africa. Black African people were gathered all around the train. Most of them carried bags; others carried small children. Smoke billowed from the engine, and it released a hiss of built-up pressure. The train whistle sounded, announcing the train's impending departure.

People were climbing onto the train. A conductor checked their tickets. Everyone was in a hurry. The train was getting ready to leave. The conductor had a problem with one of the passenger's tickets, and people waiting to get on the train began to panic. Jim could see the wheels on the train slowly start to turn, but several people still hadn't boarded.

A young girl clung to her mother's dress. The girl wore nice clothes and a hat was pinned to her hair. She looked familiar, but all Jim could see was her back. The crowd began to push and shove, and people at the back of the line yelled at the people at the front of the line, "The train's leaving. Hurry up and get on."

The young mother climbed onto the train with her bags, but the young girl's hat got knocked off her head, and she reached down to get it. Passengers pushing past the young girl's mother shoved her out of the doorway, back into the train. The young girl didn't know her mother had left without her. She picked up her hat, but saw something moving in the bushes-a rabbit. The train continued to build up speed. The young girl forgot about the train and ran toward the bushes, and the rabbit bolted into the trees. The young girl chased after it, but the rabbit ran deeper and deeper into the woods.

The young girl's mother knew her daughter hadn't boarded the train. She began to panic, but the other passengers continued to push her forward. They didn't stop until the last person found a seat. The train didn't have compartments or sleepers, just seats down both sides of an aisle. The young mother ran through the train, looking for her daughter. She was nowhere to be found. The mother looked out the train window, but the train station was well out of sight.

The scene of the young girl chasing the rabbit reappeared, but this time Jim saw the young girl's face as she looked back to find the train. The young girl was Shanha. Jim shifted anxiously.

Shanha had ended up so far in the woods, she could no longer see the train. To make matters worse, she'd gotten turned around, and didn't know which direction to go. She looked for the train station, but kept getting deeper and deeper into the woods. Fear overtook her and she began to cry.

Tears ran down Jim's cheeks as he watched.

Darkness fell in the woods and all Shanha could do was cry. She hid herself in some bushes for the night.

A voice thundered through the vision as if amplified through speakers. *"Jim,"* the voice boomed, *"what you just saw happened over a year ago. It's how Shanha became a patient at the Angel Town Hospital."*

As the voice spoke, Jim looked up. A window had opened into heaven and he could see a bright glow illuminating a throne room. Jim knew the voice was coming from there.

The voice thundered, *"Shanha found a village, but no one could keep her. She wandered for almost a year, eating anything she could find."* A rainbow formed over the brilliant light that emanated from the throne. *"Shanha was only six years old. She eventually became to weak to look for food. She survived only on scraps that were given to her."*

Jim thought, *Why didn't anyone take care of Shanha?*

"People gave her all they could," the messenger continued, reading his thought, *"but they were too poor even to feed themselves."*

Jim remembered what Shanha had looked like when she was in the hospital. "Messenger, is there a reason you're showing me these things?"

After a short pause, the voice spoke again. *"Jim, Shanha was the reason it was urgent for you to go back to Africa."*

When Jim heard what the messenger said, he knew something was wrong. *"Messenger, can you tell me what's going to happen to Shanha in Africa?"*

The messenger replied, *"Shanha's mother has been searching for her in every town. She searched for over a year and just recently discovered Shanha had been in Angel Town. She knows Shanha went to America and is waiting in Angel Town for her to come home."*

Jim was saddened by the news. He knew he was about to lose one of the people he loved most in the world. But he also knew it was only proper and righteous for Shanha to be with her mother. "Sir," he said, "this news is going to break Rhasha's heart. Could God erase her memory of Shanha?"

"Don't worry, Jim," the voice boomed. *"When you get to Africa, you're going to take Shanha and her mother on a boat trip. Rhasha, Jackie, and Simbatu will be with you."*

There was a moment of silence as Jim tried to sort out his thoughts. "Sir," he said, "where are we going on a boat?"

Jim could hear a low humming sound coming from heaven. *"Jim,"* the voice said, *"Reverend Morris will be asked to go across the river and preach to a small village. A few of the people in the village go to his church. Reverend Morris will invite you, Rhasha, Jackie, Simbatu, Shanha, and her mother to go along. The boat ride back to Angel Town will draw Shanha and her mother closer together. Shanha will begin to remember more and she will want to stay with her mother. God will draw you and Rhasha closer together and take away your pain of loosing Shanha."*

Jim didn't know what else to say. The window into heaven closed. The vision was over. Jim opened his eyes, but he continued to sleep. He didn't know if he was dreaming or if this was a vision. He saw an image of Rhasha at the waterfalls. He was kneeling on one knee in front of her, saying, "Rhasha, will you make me the happiest man on earth? Will you be my wife?" He was holding a crown of flowers in his right hand. Rhasha burst into tears. Jim watched himself stand and lean forward to kiss her.

The vision faded out and another vision faded in. He saw a man dressed in a white robe standing in front of Rhasha. A heavenly rainbow hung above the man's head. Standing beside Rhasha was an image of himself, looking much younger than he really was. He and Rhasha wore white robes and crowns, and smiled as they held hands. The people in the congregation all sat on pillows made from clouds. The man in white was reciting wedding vows. Jim heard Rhasha say, "I do." The man in white turned to Jim and recited wedding vows. Jim heard himself say, "I do."

The man in white put a ring on Rhasha's finger and kissed her on the forehead. He then put a ring on Jim's finger and kissed him on the forehead. Jim watched himself put a ring on the man's finger and speak some vows to him. The man said, "I do." Jim didn't understand what the vision meant, or if it meant anything. It seemed as if all three were getting married. He watched himself and Rhasha kiss. Jim was sure this was just a dream. It wasn't like a regular wedding.

The dream ended. Jim continued to sleep.

When he woke up, Rhasha and Shanha were already awake. Shanha was sitting on Rhasha's lap, and they were whispering to each other. When they saw Jim open his eyes, they both kissed him on the cheek. "Good morning, sunshine," they said in harmony, "you have such beautiful eyes."

Shanha held Jim's right hand between both of hers. Honeycup lay in her lap. Rhasha held Jim's left hand and continued to balance Shanha on her legs. "Good morning, girls," he replied, "you both have pretty eyes." Jim smiled at them but suddenly remembered his dream.

"Sweetheart," he said to Shanha, "always remember, Mama and I love very much."

"I love you too, Papa," she replied, "but why do you look so sad?"

Jim looked at Rhasha, then back to Shanha. "Angel," he said, "while we were asleep, I had a vision about you." Jim didn't want to worry Rhasha, but he thought she and Shanha should know what to expect when they arrived at Angel Town. "He showed me that you were getting on a train with your mother. You were wearing pretty clothes."

Shanha's expression changed as she began to remember the train. "Was I wearing a dress?" Shanha's beautiful black eyes held Jim's.

"Yes," he replied, "and you had a pretty hat pinned to your hair. Do you remember?"

"I haven't thought about it in a long time, but I can remember being at a train station. I remember a baby rabbit ran into the woods."

Jim knew Shanha's memory wasn't completely accurate. The rabbit in his dream was full grown. "You chased the rabbit into the woods and got lost."

"Yes," Shanha exclaimed, "and I was crying. I couldn't find my mama and I was all by myself."

"Angel," Jim continued, "your mama was pushed onto the train by other people. You ran after the rabbit and the train left without you." Jim could tell Shanha was deep in thought. "Shanha, your mama has been crying ever since. She never stopped looking for you."

Shanha said, "Do you know where my mama is?"

Jim looked at Rhasha and back to Shanha. "Angel," he said, "your mama is waiting for you in Angel Town."

Rhasha burst into tears. She knew she was about to lose Shanha. She threw her arms around Shanha and held her tightly. "No Jim," Rhasha cried, "I can't give her up. Let's go back to Dallas."

Jim placed his arms around Rhasha and Shanha and gently shushed them. Jackie and Simbatu were still asleep. "God showed me everything would be okay."

Shanha didn't like the idea of losing Rhasha either. "Mama," she said, "maybe she could live with us." Shanha looked eagerly at Jim. "Would that be okay, Papa?"

God hadn't shown Jim that Shanha's mother would be living with them. He knew it would make it easier for Rhasha and Shanha if she did. "Yes," Jim replied, "if she wants to, she can live with us."

Rhasha held Shanha tight. Jim clasped Shanha's hand between both of his. "Shanha," he said, "when we get back to Angel town, we're all going on a boat ride. A messenger of God told me your mama would be with us."

Rhasha remained silent. She appeared very distraught. She reminded Jim of a whipped puppy dog. Shanha was deep in thought, probably wondering what her mother was like. She must have forgotten almost everything about her, and had only a vague memory of her mother's appearance.

"Papa," she said, "could you see what my mama looks like, in your dream?"

Jim smiled as he pictured Shanha's mother in his head. "Your mama is very pretty, just like you. She has curly black hair. Your mama loves you very much. You'll be very happy when you see her."

Jackie and Simbatu woke up and began looked out the window, trying to see where they were. They couldn't see anything but clouds. When the two men heard the news about Shanha's mother, they looked sad too.

Hoping to cheer everyone up, Jim walked to where the instruments were stowed and found his guitar. He sat down facing Rhasha and Shanha and began strumming on the guitar. The girls' faces lit up.

"This little light of mine, Lord, I'm gonna let it shine." Jim propped his foot on the seat and laid the guitar across his leg as he sang. *"This little light of mine, Lord, I'm gonna let it shine. This little light of mine, Lord, I'm gonna let it shine. Let it shine, let it shine, let it shine."*

Rhasha and Shanha joined in on the second verse. *"Jesus gave me light, now I'm gonna let it shine. Jesus gave me light, now I'm gonna let it shine."*

The company jet slipped through the high blue sky as the sweet melody ascended to heaven. They sang until the wheels touched down on the runway in Africa, and Mario slowed the silver plane almost to a stop.

Minutes later, the passengers disembarked and loaded the luggage and instruments into Jim's jeep. Jim climbed into the front passenger seat and Jackie, Shanha, and Simbatu sat in the back seat. Rhasha reclaimed her position as driver. As Rhasha drove toward Angel Town, dodging pot holes and slowing for curves, everyone began singing. Rhasha sang along with the others.

"Jesus loves me, this I know, for the Bible tells me so. Little ones to him belong, they are weak, but he is strong. Yes, Jesus loves me, yes, Jesus loves me. Yes, Jesus loves me, the Bible tells me so."

The singing eased Rhasha's pain, but when she turned off the main road onto the Angel Town road, Jim could see tears slowly running down her cheeks. He squeezed her hand gently to let her know everything would be okay.

When they neared the hospital, people ran from every direction to welcome them back. Rhasha finally had to stop in the middle of the road because a crowd had formed around the jeep. Jim, Rhasha, Shanha, Jackie, and Simbatu climbed out of the jeep and everyone began hugging each other. Jim picked Shanha up in his arms so people wouldn't have to bend over to kiss her.

As everyone kissed and hugged, Jim saw a familiar figure walking toward them-Shanha's mother. Her hands clasped her cheeks; tears glittered in her eyes. When they noticed her approaching, everyone moved out of her path.

Shanha recognized her mother and started to cry. "Mama," she whimpered as Jim set her on the ground. Shanha and her mother ran to each other and embraced. Shanha's mother lost control of her emotions as she kissed Shanha, and started crying too. Tears filled the eyes of those watching the joyful reunion. Time seemed to stand still. A hush fell over the crowd.

Jim and Rhasha, tears running down their cheeks, held onto each other for strength. Jim was happy that Shanha and her mother were reunited, but at the same time, he felt like something precious had been taken from him. Rhasha didn't cope with the loss very well; she buried her head in Jim's chest and soaked the front of his shirt with her tears. Jim wanted so much to ease Rhasha's pain, but felt helpless to do so.

As Jim and Rhasha held each other, Jim felt someone touch his arm, and looked up to find Shanha and her mother standing beside them. Jim released Rhasha, who covered her face with her hands. Tears spilled between her fingers. After a moment Rhasha dropped to her knees and threw her arms around Shanha. Shanha's mother didn't hesitate; she put her arms around Jim's neck and kissed him. She had been in Angel Town long enough to hear about all the love Jim and Rhasha gave her daughter. She didn't say anything, just hugged Jim.

When Reverend Morris walked up to introduce them to each other, Shanha's mother interrupted. "I know who Jim and Rhasha are. God showed them to me in a dream. I know how much they love Shanha." She didn't take her eyes off Jim's face as she spoke. "God showed me how you built a village to take care of sick and hungry people." Tears welled up in her eyes again, but she was able to maintain her composure. "He showed me how Shanha almost died and how she was taken to your hospital."

Jim looked down and noticed Shanha was still holding her teddy bear. He started to kneel down to hug her, but Shanha's mother continued to talk. "God showed me in a vision how you and Rhasha went to the hospital every day. I saw how you prayed for Shanha, and how you showered her with your affection. I saw you and Rhasha kissing her and holding her hand and brushing her hair."

Shanha's mother couldn't control herself any longer. She began to cry. As she sobbed, she continued to speak, wanting to show Jim and Rhasha her appreciation. Jim kept his arms around her as she talked. "I could see Shanha's sunken face and her swollen stomach, her twisted legs and her discolored skin. I heard you tell Shanha how pretty her eyes were as you smiled at her. I saw how you read the Bible to her and talked to her about Jesus. I saw how she loves you and Rhasha, and I know it will be hard for her to go home with me. I know it will be hard for you and Rhasha, too."

Shanha's mother pulled her arms from around Jim's neck and buried her face in her hands. Jim leaned over to pick Shanha up. Rhasha rose and put her arm through Jim's arm. "Sweetheart," Jim said to Shanha's mother as tears seeped between her fingers, "what is your name?"

She stopped crying, but kept her hands over her face. "Francis," she whimpered, "But everyone calls me Fran."

Jim was still holding Shanha, but Francis was standing close enough for Shanha to put her arms around her mother's neck. She'd heard everything her mother said. "Mama," she said, "I love you too."

Francis uncovered her face and kissed her daughter on the cheek, beaming with pleasure.

Jim kissed Shanha on the other cheek. "Francis, Rhasha and I love Shanha very much, but we know it's right for her to be with her mother." When Jim said that, tears began to run down Rhasha's face again.

"Mama," Shanha said to Rhasha, "everything will be okay, you'll see." She looked confident. "We can all live together."

Jim, Rhasha, and Shanha looked at Francis, waiting for an answer. "Please, Francis," Rhasha asked, "could you come live with us?"

Sadness filled Fran's face, revealing the answer before she spoke the words. "Rhasha, we can't live with you and Jim. All of our relatives live in Zimbabwe, and they're anxious for us to come home."

Rhasha sobbed. Jim tried to comfort her. He was saying a silent prayer himself. Rhasha's knees suddenly went weak, and she almost collapsed. A blue glow surrounded her, supporting her. The glow expanded slowly to include Jim and Shanha, then continued to grow until it also enclosed Francis, Jackie, and Simbatu. Jim knew God sent the blue glow to heal everyone's pain and to ease the tension. The blue glow expanded, until it formed an oval dome covering every man, woman, and child who stood next to the jeep. It continued to expand, until the dome covered the entire village. It hung over Angel Town for several minutes, then disappeared.

A hush fell over the people. All sadness had been eliminated, all tears had dried.

Rhasha had received understanding, strength, and hope from God. She kissed Shanha on the forehead and gave Francis a hug. "Francis," she said, "I love Shanha with all my heart. I can only imagine how much you love her. I'll miss her every single day, but my life is richer, having known her."

Francis smiled, showing she understood how Rhasha felt, and loved her for it. She knew Shanha had a childish magic about her.

"Mama," Shanha said, looking at Rhasha, "I'm not dead. You can come see me whenever you wish." She looked at Francis. "Is that okay, Mama?"

Francis placed her palm against Shanha's cheek. "Yes, sweetheart. And we'll come back to see Rhasha and Jim, too."

Chapter 22

Shanha Talks To Jesus

Jim remembered what God's messenger had said in his last vision. "Reverend Morris, I was told you've been invited to preach at a neighboring village. Is that right?"

Reverend Morris moved closer. "Yes, Jim. I'll be preaching across the river this afternoon. Would you and Rhasha like to come?"

Jim didn't hesitate. "Yes. And could Shanha, Fran, Jackie, and Simbatu come too?"

Reverend Morris looked at each of them. "I'd be pleased if you all came along."

Rhasha and Jim climbed into the front seat of the jeep. Shanha, Fran, Jackie, and Simbatu climbed into the back seat, and within minutes, the jeep was headed toward the river, with Reverend Morris and his family following in his car. A large wooden boat was waiting for them when they arrived at the river. It was old, and had to be steered with a hand-operated rudder. When they boarded, the captain started a small motor and eased the boat away from shore, his hand on the rudder.

Even at full speed, the boat couldn't go fast enough to leave a wake behind it. The wooden boat slipped slowly through the calm water, but remained close to shore. At times, the captain had to steer around rotten stumps and dead trees to avoid damage. A scenic jungle landscape passed them. Green foliage lined the shore. Monkeys jumped from tree to tree.

Everyone seemed to be in good spirits. There were no life jackets on the boat so Jim watched Shanha to make sure she didn't get too close to the side. He had his guitar strapped across his shoulder and Simbatu supported his keyboard. Jackie had left his drum set in the jeep, but had brought along a set of bongo drums.

Jim had an idea, and relayed it to Jackie and Simbatu. He moved away from Rhasha to join Jackie and Simbatu at the front of the boat. Jim motioned for Rhasha and Shanha to remain seated across from them.

Jackie began beating on his bongo drums with his hands. The long, drawn-out drum roll echoed across the water. Rhasha, Shanha, and Francis listened intently, trying to figure out what the men were going to sing. Finally Jim's voice joined the drum roll: *"Dayo . . . Dayyy-o. Daylight come and we wanta go home . . . "*

All the girls' faces lit up as they recognized the song. Jim sang solo again, then Jackie and Simbatu joined in. Shanha stood and began dancing. Jim sang solo again. *"Come, Mr. Tally man, tally me banana . . . "*

As the boat continued toward the village, people could be seen along the shoreline. All the natives were familiar with Jim and Rhasha, and smiled and waved as the boat passed. The closer the boat got to its destination, the more people could be seen on shore. Some could be heard singing along with the people in the boat, who were all smiling and clapping to the music. Even the birds in the trees seemed to be cheerful.

When the song ended, everyone laughed and clapped, but the singers weren't silent for long. Simbatu began playing the keyboard. Jim started strumming on his guitar, and began singing "Brother Love's Traveling Salvation Show" as if he were Neil Diamond himself: "*Ahhh, an august night and the leaves hanging down and the grass on the ground smelling sweet . . . "*

Soon Rhasha, Shanha, Jackie, and Simbatu joined in. Everyone clapped to the beat. *"Halle, halle. Pack up the babies and grab your sweet ladies and everyone goes, cause everyone knows, it's Brother Love's show . . . "*

They finished the song just as the captain pulled his boat up to the village pier. Several people stood on the shore, waiting for the gospel group to unload. The boatman tied up to the pier and assisted everyone off the boat to be greeted by the villagers, who led them to a treed area not far from where they docked. There was no church in the village, but a section of land had been cordoned off and designated a public meeting place. Logs laid lengthwise on the ground served as pews, with an aisle of hard-packed dirt down the center. It was obvious the aisle was used frequently. A makeshift podium stood at the front. Tree branches hung out over the log pews to form a jungle roof.

Several people filed into the public meeting area. Reverend Morris walked to the podium and opened his Bible to a premarked page. He looked around at the few people sitting on the logs. "I see people are still coming," he said as four more people walked down the aisle, "so let's wait to start the sermon. Let's give everyone a chance to get here."

Jim thought that, since everyone was waiting, they might as well have some music. "Reverend Morris, would it be all right if we sing a few hymns while we wait?"

"Sure Jim, singing might help draw people."

Jim, Rhasha, Shanha, Jackie, and Simbatu walked up to the front of the clearing, Jim with his guitar and Simbatu with his keyboard. Soon heavenly music filled the air around the village. It seemed to pull on the natives, coaxing them to follow it to its source.

Rhasha sang lead like she was an angel: *"I am weak but thou art strong. Jesus keep me from all wrong. I'll be satisfied as long as I walk close to thee."*

Shanha kept glancing at her mother to see if she was watching her sing. Francis watched her daughter proudly, never taking her eyes off her.

"Just a closer walk with thee. Grant it Jesus, this my plea. Pray thee, let it ever be, just a closer walk with thee."

As the group sang, Africans began arriving in numbers.

"When my feeble life is o'er, time for me will be no more. Fly me to that peaceful shore. Let me walk, close to thee. Just a closer walk with thee."

Jim noticed Francis and Shanha looking at each other. He could see how happy they were.

"Grant it Jesus, this my plea. Pray thee let it ever be. Just a closer walk with thee."

When the song was over, Francis clasped her hands as if she were praying. As she smiled at Shanha, tears ran down her cheeks.

Jim whispered an idea to Shanha. She nodded excitedly. Jim whispered the same message to Rhasha, Jackie, and Simbatu, then he and Simbatu began playing. A hush fell over the congregation as Shanha began to sing.

"My mommy told me something that every kid should know. It's all about the devil and I learned to hate him so."

Shanha smiled at her mother. Francis was so excited, she looked like she wanted to leap up and dance. All eyes were on Shanha as she sang.

"She said he causes trouble when you let him in your room. He'll never ever leave you, if your heart is filled with gloom. So let the sunshine in. Face it with a grin.

"Smilers never lose and frowners never win, so let the sunshine in. Face it with a grin. Open up your heart and let the sunshine in.

"When you are unhappy, the devil wears a grin, but he's oh-so gloomy when the light comes pouring in. I know he'll be unhappy, cause I'll never wear a frown. Maybe if we keep on smiling, he'll get tired of hanging around.

"If I forget to say my prayers, the devil jumps with glee, but he feels so awful, awful when he sees me on my knees. So if you're full of trouble and he never seems to leave, just open up your heart and let the sunshine in. So let the sunshine in, face it with a grin. Smilers never lose and frowners never win . . . "

The meeting area continued to fill with new arrivals as Shanha sang. When Shanha finished, she stood smiling at her mother. Fran's face glowed with happiness, but tears still eased down her cheeks. Jim and Rhasha knelt down to kiss and hug Shanha.

By this time, every seat in the meeting area was occupied. Some of the children sat on the ground in front of their parents. Other people stood outside the meeting area, and a few sat on the log borders that cordoned off the church area. Reverend Morris opened with a prayer. Most of the local people didn't know what he was doing and simply sat, watching him. When he finished, Jim, Rhasha, Shanha, Jackie, and Simbatu walked to one side of the meeting area. All the seats had been taken so they sat on the ground. Francis rose and walked over to join Shanha.

Reverend Morris began his sermon by telling the village people about the life of Jesus. He explained how Jesus was born in a manger to a virgin mother. "Jesus was God's son," Reverend Morris said, "and he died on earth so you and I could live forever." He talked about the miracles Jesus performed and the people he healed.

Most of the congregation was attentive, but considered Reverend Morris an entertainer, telling pretty stories. The village people didn't understand he was trying to teach them about Christianity. One older man sitting at the back of the congregation came to understand clearly what Reverend Morris was trying to do, and he didn't like what he heard. He sat with his hands covering his face. He tried to control himself, but his mumbling could be heard throughout the church. Finally he blurted out, "What you're saying is all lies. We don't want to hear anymore."

It was obvious the old man was of high standing in the community. Reverend Morris would have to reason with the man in order to continue the sermon. "Sir," he said, "if I'm telling the truth, would you not let your people hear it?"

"No," the man replied. He stood to leave. "We will hear no more." As he left the meeting area, most of the congregation rose and followed him.

"Please listen to what God wants you to hear," Reverend Morris said. "I didn't come here to deceive you."

Everyone continued to leave, even though most of them looked like they wanted to stay and hear more stories about Jesus. Reverend Morris closed his eyes to pray. Jim began to pray silently. They asked God to speak to the people's hearts.

As the congregation walked out of the meeting area, clouds began to move rapidly across the sky. The clouds seemed to line up like soldiers preparing for battle. Suddenly the sky grew dark and the wind began to picked up. The clouds rolled in waves across the sky above their heads. The village people cringed in fear as lightning struck the ground in front of them. Thunder roared. Everyone ran back to the public meeting area. When the last person sat down, the lightning and thunder stopped and the clouds rolled away. The wind stopped blowing. A hush fell over the church as the sky brightened again.

Everyone waited, prepared to listen to what the preacher had to say, but God sealed his mouth shut. He tried to speak, but not a word could be heard. The congregation heard a humming sound. The congregation looked around, seeking its source. One of the children tipped his head back and looked upward.

"Look!" he yelled. He pointed toward the sky. Everyone looked up.

High above the village was a window into a throne room in heaven, held open by four angels pulling the corners of the window in four different directions. The village people saw a bright light emanating from heaven down to earth. A rainbow hovered above the source of the bright light.

A voice boomed, as if coming through a loud waterfall. "Be not afraid," the thunderous voice said. "No harm will come to you."

Everyone, including, Jim, Rhasha, and Shanha, fell to the ground. Fear was etched on every face. No one had their eyes open.

"Sit up," the voice roared, "and see what comes forth from heaven."

Everyone slowly sat up. As the people in the congregation raised their heads, strange things began to happen. A blinding beam of bright light shot out from the throne room in heaven toward the village. The bright light flashed as it hit the ground, blinding everyone in the congregation. In their mind's eyes, a vision began to evolve. An ancient city stood before them. People lined the street, yelling and cheering. They were dressed in strange clothes and talked in a foreign language, but God caused the village people to understand what the ancient people were saying.

"Crucify Jesus," they yelled. "He claims to be the king of the Jews."

A man bathed in glowing light walked down the street carrying a wooden cross on his back. Blood ran down his face from a crown of thorns. Bystanders and mockers called him Jesus. Two other men walked behind him, dragging crosses as well. Roman soldiers walked on both sides of Jesus as he dragged the cross behind him.

The cross was heavy and the walk was long. Jesus staggered and fell, weakened by the wounds inflicted upon him. He didn't have the strength to get up. A young black man watched from the side of the road. He looked strong, so the soldiers ordered him to carry the cross for Jesus.

The village people continued to watch the events unfolding in the vision, as if they were watching a movie at the theater. It seemed vividly real. Jesus was escorted to a small hill at the edge of the ancient town. The place was called Calvary. The black man laid the cross on the ground and was allowed to leave.

Reverend Morris and Jim knew what was happening and prayed as the events unfolded.

Spectators watched as soldiers drove spikes through Jesus' hands and into the cross. When Francis saw the first nail go into Jesus' hand, she told Shanha not to watch anymore. Fran turned her head away and held Shanha close to her. Reverend Morris, Jim, and Jackie also refused to watch the crucifixion. Tears ran down their cheeks as they prayed. The village people could see agony and pain on the Lord's face as the large spikes broke through his bones and pinned his ankles to the wood of the cross. They felt uncomfortable, watching what was happening to Jesus and the two thieves.

After the cross of Jesus was shoved into a hole, it stood tall between the other two crosses. Jesus was secured to the standing cross only by the nails through his hands and ankles. His body sagged helplessly from the cross. A sign was nailed at the top of the cross, containing words that mocked Jesus: *This is Jesus, King of the Jews.*

The village people didn't know how powerful Jesus was. If he had asked, ten thousand angels would have come to his rescue. "Father," Jesus said instead, "forgive them, for they know not what they do."

Soldiers behind the cross were gambling for Jesus' clothes. People around the cross mocked him. "He saved others," they yelled, "let him save himself, if he be Christ, the chosen of God."

The congregation heard Jesus saying, "My God, my God. Why hast thou forsaken me?"

The ancient people in the vision thought Jesus was calling to Elias. They yelled, "Let be, let's see if Elias will come to save him."

A man secured a sponge to a reed and filled the sponge with vinegar. He raised the sponge with vinegar to Jesus' lips, for him to drink.

Jesus cried out, "It is finished." He died, and the earth shook. The veil of the temple tore, and large rocks broke in half.

Jesus had hung on the cross for nine hours before he died, but God revealed his crucifixion to the congregation within minutes.

The village people feared for their lives as a black cloud hovered over the ancient city. Lightning flashed and thunder rumbled continuously. It was getting late, so a soldier broke the legs of the two thieves who hung beside Jesus. He could see that Jesus was already dead, so he rammed a sword through his side. Blood ran down Jesus' leg, onto the ground. A bright light flashed in the ancient village and a white beam shot to heaven. Jim knew the beam of light was Jesus Christ.

The vision faded, followed by the humming, the darkness, the rolling clouds-all the strange phenomena that signaled that the vision was over. The African village came back into focus. Most of the village people were in tears. They realized the man in the vision must truly be the son of God. They were aware the vision would not have been shown to them, if he wasn't. No one spoke a word. Everyone sat and thought about what they'd seen. Even the old man now believed Jesus was the son of God.

Reverend Morris slowly walked up to the pulpit. He observed the emotions that held the congregation captive. "The miracle you just witnessed," he announced, "is how our Lord and savior died. After Jesus was crucified, he was resurrected and now sits on the right-hand side of God."

Everyone sat quietly as Reverend Morris prayed, "Lord God Almighty, thank you for showing us how Jesus died. Please forgive us for the part we played in his crucifixion." He began to weep. "Lord God, I know everyone here believes in Jesus now, and I pray you will guide us in the paths you want us to walk."

Jim had a mental picture of God sitting on his throne. He could see Jesus sitting on his right-hand side. Jim asked God to speak to Rhasha's heart, whispering his prayer softly at first, but as he prayed, his voice rose until he was talking normally. Rhasha could hear every word he said. "Father," Jim pleaded, "I pray everyone here loves you as much as I do, and will serve you from this day on. You know how much I love Rhasha. I only love you and Jesus more."

When Rhasha heard what Jim said, she opened her eyes and looked at his face. She knew he couldn't possibly know how much she loved him. Rhasha could see tears in his eyes, and knew Jim was speaking to God from his heart.

"Father," he said, "Rhasha and Shanha are the most important people on earth to me, and it would break my heart if I went to heaven and they didn't."

Reverend Morris was still praying, but at this point, neither Jim nor Rhasha heard a word he said.

"Father," Jim continued, "I had a dream that Rhasha and I would get married. I don't want to be with her just until death parts us. I pray that we can be together through eternity."

This was the first time Rhasha had ever heard Jim say anything about getting married. Tears trickled down her cheeks. Reverend Morris was still praying and Jim was still talking to God, but now Rhasha couldn't hear either of their prayers. She was saying a prayer of her own. She prayed the way Jim had taught her-she conjured a mental picture of God sitting on his throne.

"Father," she said silently, *"please forgive me of my sins and have mercy on my soul. Please help me to understand how Jesus was given the power to cause me to go to heaven just by believing in him. I love you, Father, and I know you're real. I've seen the miracles you've done for us and I know you do them because you love us."*

Jackie had also learned from Jim to form a mental picture of God sitting on his throne. He did that now, and thanked God for all he had done and gave him praise for all creation. Simbatu was also deep in prayer. He thought about all his wrongdoing. He promised God he would devote the rest of his life to teaching Christianity. Everyone who knew how to pray was praying. Everyone else was thinking about the vision of Jesus being crucified.

When Reverend Morris said "amen," everyone raised their heads. He asked Jim and Rhasha if they would sing a closing song, and Jim, Rhasha, Shanha, Jackie, and Simbatu walked to the front of the congregation. Jim picked up his guitar and Jackie sat on a log with his bongo drums. Simbatu sat behind the keyboard. Jim, Rhasha, and Shanha stood next to each other and began to hum. As the instruments joined in, Rhasha sang the invitation. The sound of her voice filled the village.

"Just as I am without one plea, but that your blood was shed for me, and that thou bid me come to thee. Oh lamb of God, I come, I come."

Reverend Morris held his arms out, palms upward. "Come as you are," he pleaded, "Jesus is calling. The lamb of God wants to give you eternal life."

Jim and Shanha's voices joined in with Rhasha. *"Just as I am, thou tossed about with many a conflict, many a doubt. Fighting and feelings within, without. Oh lamb of God, I come. I come."*

Village people began to rise and walk toward Reverend Morris. The old man was the first to stand. Tears ran down his cheeks as he walked toward the altar. Seventeen other people followed close behind. Each person walked to Reverend Morris and professed Jesus as lord and savior.

Shanha looked at Jim. "Papa," she said, "Jesus held his arms out to me and told me he loves me. I told him I love him, too. I want to go tell Reverend Morris."

Tears welled up in Jim's eyes. He kissed Shanha on the forehead. Shanha stepped into the aisle and began her walk to profess Jesus as her savior. Francis already knew the Lord, but wanted to be with Shanha. They held hands as they walked down the aisle together.

Jim and Rhasha looked at each other. Rhasha knew what Jim wanted her to do. She believed in God and she knew Jesus must be God's son, but to her, a dead man couldn't save anyone.

Jim and Rhasha began to sing the last verse. *Just as I am, I will receive. Will welcome, pardon, please, relieve. Because your promise, I believe. Oh lamb of God, I come, I come. Because your promise I believe, oh lamb of God, I come, I come."*

All the chosen told Reverend Morris that Jesus came to them in a vision. Jesus told them he was the way to everlasting life. They all said Jesus told them he would always be with them. Shanha was very sad about what happened to Jesus and promised him, in a silent prayer, that she would always love him.

Reverend Morris prayed with the new children of God. He told them he would be back to preach every Saturday morning, and invited the congregation to attend the Angel Town services every Sunday. He explained to the new Christians that people who believe in Jesus must be baptized. He asked them if they wanted to be baptized today, or wait until next Saturday. Eager for the new experience, all the new Christians asked to be baptized as soon as possible.

A parade of Africans escorted God's new children to the river, using the same path women used every day to wash their families' laundry. Voices could be heard, humming a heavenly tune. The music came from an unknown source; it sounded like the music was coming from above. Unseen by anyone, angels hovered above the river. Even though Jim couldn't see them, he knew they were there.

Large rocks protruded from the water and lined the shore. They provided seating for several elderly people. Everyone else lined up along the shore. Reverend Morris walked straight into the water until it reached his waist. The river was calm and the skies were clear. It was late in the evening by now, and the sun left a reflection across the water. Tall trees rustled along the river and the sound of music filled the air. Candidates for baptism walked single file into the river toward Reverend Morris. The angels stopped humming as they waded through the water. Reverend Morris baptized each one in the name of the Father and the Son and the Holy Ghost.

After Reverend Morris baptized the old man, Jim, Rhasha, Shanha, Jackie, and Simbatu began to sing. *"When the trumpet of the Lord shall sound and time shall be no more, and the morning breaks eternal, bright and fair; when the saved of earth shall gather over on the other shore, and the roll is called up yonder, I'll be there. When the roll is called up yonder, when the roll is called up yonder, when the roll is called up yonder, when the roll is called up yonder, I'll be there.*

"On the bright and cloudy morning when the dead in Christ shall rise, and the glory of his resurrection share; when his chosen ones shall gather to their homes beyond the skies and the roll is called up yonder, I'll be there. When the roll is called up yonder, when the roll is called up yonder, when the roll is called up yonder, when the roll is called up yonder, I'll be there. When the roll is called up yonder, I'll be there.

"Let us labor for the master from the dawn to setting sun., Let us talk of all his wondrous love and care, when all of life is over and the work on earth is done. When the roll is called up yonder, I'll be there. When the roll is called up yonder, when the roll is called up yonder, when the roll is called up yonder, When the roll is called up yonder, I'll be there. When the roll is called up yonder, I'll be there. When the roll is called up yonder, when the roll is called up yonder, when the roll is called up yonder, when the roll is called up yonder, when the roll is called up yonder, I'll be there."

By the time they finished singing, Reverend Morris and all the new Christians were back on shore. Water dripped off their clothes onto the ground. Several people who hadn't been baptized spoke with Reverend Morris. When they told him Jesus spoke to them also, he asked if they would like to be baptized. They all declined. It was a new experience for the village people and they weren't ready to make the commitment.

Jim and Rhasha hugged Shanha, and Jim told her he was very proud of her. Shanha's face glowed, and her smile warmed Jim's heart. Shanha's mother was already a Christian, and was happy that her daughter believed in Jesus.

Reverend Morris, Jim, Rhasha, Shanha, Francis, Jackie, and Simbatu walked among the people, hugging them and shaking their hands. Finally the village people escorted the traveling salvation group to the boat. The Angel Town residents climbed aboard and waved good-bye to all their new friends. Reverend Morris called a reminder to everyone about the services in Angel Town at ten o'clock the next morning, and everyone said they would be there.

The captain unhooked the rope from the pier. He started the motor and the boat slipped away from the dock. As it slowly made its way to Angel Town, Francis and Shanha talked about relatives that Shanha hadn't seen in over a year. So much had happened to Shanha that she'd forgotten about them. Shanha laughed as her mother told her stories about the crazy things her Uncle Jhami did. She showed Shanha pictures of her family. It wasn't long before Shanha realized how much she loved her mother.

Jim and Rhasha watched Francis and Shanha hold each other. Jim remembered what God's messenger had said to him in his vision: Shanha and her mother would grow closer to each other on the boat ride back to Angel Town. He'd also said that Jim and Rhasha would get closer. Jim looked at Rhasha and smiled. She shyly smiled back. He kissed her on the lips and held his pinkie finger up in front of him, and Rhasha locked her pinkie through his.

Shanha saw what they were doing and ran over to Jim and Rhasha. She hooked her pinkie finger with Jim and Rhasha's fingers and said, "Papa, Mama, I will always love both of you." Tears slipped from Jim's and Rhasha's eyes as Shanha unhooked her finger and returned to her mother.

The boat slowly moved through the water. Soon Jim could see his jeep and the Reverend's car as they eased closer to shore and pulled up to the wooden pier. Soon everyone had returned to Angel Town, and the travelers finally unloaded their luggage.

Shanha's bag remained packed because she and Francis planned to leave the next day after church. Francis had been staying in one of the Angel Town houses, but Jim asked her if she and Shanha could spend the night with them. Rhasha and Shanha were excited when Francis said they would.

They talked a while, then went to the dining hall to eat. While they were eating, Shanha told her mother how excited she was to be a Christian. Francis smiled, proud of her daughter. She said, "You have really grown since the last time I saw you."

Shanha looked puzzled. "I'm seven years old," she said, as if to say, "I'm a big girl now."

"I know you are," Francis said, "and you're so pretty."

Shanha's confused look turned into a smile.

Francis had great respect for Rhasha, and wanted to talk with her, but didn't really know what to say. "Rhasha," Francis finally said, "how long have you been a Christian?" The way Rhasha sang Christian music, Francis had assumed Rhasha believed in Jesus.

Rhasha hung her head. "I love God with all my heart," she replied, "but I don't understand how Jesus can be the savior of the whole world."

"Oh, I'm sorry," Francis replied. "You sing religious music so beautifully. I thought you were a Christian."

Rhasha's face fell. Everyone at the table knew Jesus except her. "I want to believe in Jesus," she said, "and I believe he was a real person, but it just doesn't make sense to me."

Jim thought he knew why Jesus hadn't revealed himself to Rhasha. "Francis, I don't think Jesus has spoken to Rhasha's heart yet. I believe he's waiting, so when he does speak to her, Rhasha will influence many more people to walk down the aisle with her." Jim paused as an idea occurred to him. "I pray for Rhasha every day. If you and Shanha would pray for her too, maybe God will help her to understand."

Shanha smiled and locked her fingers together. She stood beside her chair and wiggled back and forth. "Papa, I pray for you and Mama every time I pray."

"I know you do, angel," Jim replied, "and I pray for you and Mama every day."

Shanha rested her hand on top of Francis's hand. "Mama, from now on, I'll pray for you every day, too."

Francis exploded into tears. Shanha quickly threw her arms around her mother's neck, dropping Honeycup on the floor. "What's the matter, Mama? Did I say something wrong?"

Francis wiped the tears from her eyes and pulled Shanha into her lap. "No, I just thought about all the times I was worried sick about you. I prayed continually that God would take good care of you." She hugged Shanha and smiled.

Shanha kissed her mother and reached down to pick up Honeycup. She cradled her teddy bear in her arm and tickled his tummy. "Honeycup," she said, "I'm going to pray for you, too."

Jim could see the love Francis had for Shanha. She watched Shanha's every move.

Everyone finished eating, and Rhasha cleared the table, then returned to her seat and listened to Jim and Francis talking about how far it was to Zimbabwe. Finally Rhasha rubbed her eyes and yawned. Shanha yawned at the same time. Jim laughed as they both stretched, then covered their open mouths with their hands, elbows akimbo.

"Angel," Jim said to Shanha, "if you want, tomorrow we'll go to The Factory and you can get some new dresses to take home with you." She still wore clothes that matched Rhasha's-cut-off shorts and an oversized shirt knotted at the waist. Francis wore a dress.

Shanha was still playing with Honeycup. "No thank you, Papa, "she said, "I like my clothes." She never even looked up when she spoke.

Jim looked at Francis. Even Francis had started calling Jim "Papa." She said, "It's okay, Papa. I'll take it slow and let her adjust as time goes on."

Jim winked at Francis. "She does have a dress," he said. "She wears it to church every Sunday."

Jim was getting sleepy too. He rose and went to the kitchen to check on the cook before they all left the dining hall and walked across the street to Jim and Rhasha's house. When they got inside, Shanha wanted to show her mother a bamboo whistle, and the pair went to Shanha's bedroom. Rhasha went to the bathroom to take a shower and when she came out, she was wearing a set of Jim's pajamas.

When Jim emerged from his shower, Rhasha was sitting on the bed with his guitar. Jim glanced at the window and saw smiling faces looking back at him from the opposite side. He smiled and kissed Rhasha on the lips as he took the guitar from Rhasha and put the strap around his neck. He picked a few notes, then he and Rhasha began to sing.

"This little light of mine, Lord, I'm gonna let it shine." Before the first sentence was completed, Shanha burst into the room and began to sing. Francis followed Shanha into the room and watched as they continued to sing. *"This little light of mine, Lord, I'm gonna let it shine. This little light of mine, Lord, I'm gonna let it shine. Let it shine, let it shine, let it shine."*

Francis began clapping her hands to the beat of the music. All the children outside Jim's window clapped as they sang along.

"Jesus gave me light, now I'm gonna let it shine. Jesus gave me light, now I'm gonna let it shine. Jesus gave me light, now I'm gonna let it shine. Let it shine, let it shine, let it shine."

Jim had left his porch light on. They saw people coming from every direction to listen to them sing, and to sing along. The sound of music could be heard all through Angel Town. When they finished singing *This Little Light Of Mine,* they launched into another song.

When they finished the second song, Jim saw Shanha yawning again. Knowing she had a big day ahead of her, he stepped out onto the front porch and, when everyone gathered around, announced, "I'm happy you all came tonight, but we're tired, and it's time for us to go to sleep."

The crowd was disappointed, but slowly began to leave the yard as Jim, Rhasha, Francis, and Shanha, waved and said good-bye. They went back into the house, and everyone made their final preparations for bed. After a few seconds, Rhasha walked over to Jim's guitar, hanging on its hook on the wall, and lifted it off the hook. and Placing the strap around her neck, Rhasha began picking the guitar strings with her fingers. She didn't know how to play the guitar, but it was clear that she had something on her mind.

Jim knew what Rhasha was thinking about, but didn't say anything. It didn't take long before she did. "Jim, could you teach me how to play the guitar?"

Jim smiled and put his arm around Rhasha's shoulders. "Sure. I'll teach you, but not tonight."

Rhasha smiled. She looked down at the guitar strings, then she looked up at Jim. "Great, then you and I can both play guitars when we sing."

When Francis and Shanha came in to say good night, Francis was wearing a set of Jim's pajamas and Shanha was wearing one of his pajama tops. Jim smiled when he saw what Francis was wearing.

"Shanha told me you wouldn't mind if I wore your pajamas," Francis said.

"Sure," he said, "I don't mind. You all look beautiful wearing my pajamas."

Shanha eased over toward Jim and put her arms around his neck. "Papa," she said, "can I take my gown home with me?

"It's your gown," Jim replied, "so you can do whatever you want with it."

"I'll wear it every night," Shanha whispered.

Jim kissed her on the cheek and knelt beside the bed to pray. Rhasha and Shanha quickly knelt down beside him. Francis remained standing, but closed her eyes.

“Heavenly Father,” Jim prayed, “please forgive me of my sins and have mercy on my soul.” Jim thought about Shanha as she knelt beside him. “I’m grateful Jesus came to Shanha in a vision today. I’m sure she will serve you for the rest of her life. I pray, Father, that you will guide her in the paths of righteousness. And Father, I love Rhasha with all my heart. I love you too, Father, and I pray you will cause Rhasha to understand how Jesus is the way to eternal life. Jim now turned his thoughts to Francis. “I ask that you keep Francis and Shanha safe as they journey home. Bless them, I pray, and use them to spread the name of Jesus throughout Africa.” Rhasha, came to Jim’s mind once again. “Father,” Jim pleaded, “please speak to Rhasha and show her how Jesus became our savior. In Jesus’ holy name, we pray these things. Amen.”

Jim raised his head and looked at Rhasha, hoping God had answered his prayer. Rhasha knew what Jim was thinking, but her feelings hadn’t changed. Jim rose and sat on the side of the bed. Rhasha sat next to him. As Francis and Shanha said good night and started to leave the bedroom, Shanha walked over and put her arms around Jim’s neck. Honeycup dangled down Jim’s back. Francis paused at the door and turned to see what Shanha was doing.

“Papa,” Shanha said, “don’t worry. Jesus will speak to Mama.” She kissed him.

“I know, sweetheart,” Jim replied, “and I know he will look out for you and your Mama.”

Shanha set Honeycup on the bed beside Jim and placed both her hands on his cheeks. “Good night, Papa. I love you.”

“I love you too, angel. Sweet dreams.”

Shanha said good night to Rhasha, and she and Francis left through the bathroom door. Jim and Rhasha climbed into bed. Without Shanha between them, Rhasha could snuggle next to Jim. In no time, they were fast asleep.

Chapter 23

Fields of Flowers

When Jim woke up, daylight streamed through the window. He could hear whispering, but didn't know what was going on. When Jim turned over, he could see Rhasha was already awake and facing away from him. Francis and Shanha sat on the bed next to Rhasha, and Shanha was holding Rhasha's hand and telling her that she had pretty eyes. When Shanha saw Jim turn over, she kissed Rhasha on the forehead and jumped over Rhasha to sit on Jim's stomach. Francis looked confused; she didn't understand what Shanha was doing.

Rhasha and Shanha smiled and looked into Jim's eyes. "Good morning, sunshine," they said in unison. Jim smiled back, knowing what they were going to say next: "You have very pretty eyes."

Jim winked at Francis as she clapped her hands together and laughed. "All three of you girls have pretty eyes, too," he replied. "Good morning, angels." Jim hugged both girls.

Francis knelt on the side of the bed and leaned over Rhasha. She looked at Jim and smiled. "Yes," she said, "you do have pretty eyes."

"Thank you," Jim said, "but your eyes are prettier."

They all walked to the dining hall together to eat. When they finished breakfast, Jim and Rhasha decided to go to the hospital, and Francis and Shanha joined them. The hospital now had eighty beds, and all but one was occupied. Eight new patients had been admitted since they went to America. The new patients didn't know Jim, Rhasha, or Shanha, but all the previous patients were thrilled when the trio entered the hospital and Jim and Rhasha began talking to the patient in bed one. Francis got to see firsthand how Jim and Rhasha behaved toward each patient, and she remembered her vision, and how Jim and Rhasha had cared for Shanha, and she loved them for it.

At that moment, Francis knew she wanted to live the rest of her life taking care of people. She and Shanha went to each bed and talked to each patient, too. They said and did all the things Jim and Rhasha said and did.

When they finished, they walked across the road to the church. Jim and Rhasha had their arms around each other's waist as they walked, and they looked at each other and talked about Shanha's time in the hospital. Even though it was too early for church services, the sound of music could be heard all the way to the hospital. Angel Town residents knew all the songs Jim and Rhasha sang. Every Sunday, the early congregation liked to sing until church started.

The church was already filling up with people. The walls of the church had been pushed out and up and braced open with poles. Jim, Rhasha, Francis, and Shanha entered and found a place to sit near the back of the church, amidst warm greetings. Jim and Rhasha joined in the singing. Seconds later, Jackie and Simbatu arrived and sat behind Jim and Rhasha.

This would be the first Sunday that Jim, Rhasha, and Shanha wouldn't be singing for the congregation. Reverend Morris had already made arrangements with a gospel group from Nairobi to provide the music services. The three gospel singers arrived at the church with Reverend Morris and his family.

Reverend Morris said the opening prayer. Everyone remained silent as he asked God to send angels to minister to the people. Then Reverend Morris introduced the singing trio to the congregation. When he finished the introductions, he stepped away from the pulpit, and the singers began to sing.

The roof went off the house as the sweet melody filled the air. Jim knew these singers were sent by God. The congregation was clapping along with the music, and everyone was happy.

"On a hill far away stood an old rugged cross, the emblem of suffering and shame. And I love that old cross, where the dearest and blessed, for a world of lost sinners, was slain. So I'll cherish the old rugged cross, till my trophies at last I lay down. I will cling to the old rugged cross and exchange it someday for a crown.

"To the old rugged cross, I will ever be true. Its shame and reproach, gladly bear. Then he'll call me someday to my home far away, where his glory forever I'll share. So I'll cherish the old rugged cross, till my trophies at last I lay down. I will cling to the old rugged cross and exchange it someday for a crown. So I'll cherish the old rugged cross, till my trophies at last I lay down. I will cling to the old rugged cross and exchange it someday for a crown. I'll exchange it someday for a crown."

The gospel singers finished singing the first song and immediately began singing a second song. Jim began to pray silently that Jesus would speak to Rhasha. The skies remained clear, but something strange penetrated the air.

"Rock of ages, cleft for me. Let me hide myself in thee."

Everyone could hear a soft humming sound that rose in volume, then faded. The congregation was looking around, trying to see where the sound was coming from. The singing trio continued to sing.

"Let the water and the blood from thy wounded side which flowed, free of sin, the double cure, save from wrath and made me pure."

Moisture descended from high above the church and began to collect until it formed small clouds. People inside the church couldn't see the clouds, but they sensed something was happening. Millions of small clouds expanded rapidly into one massive cloud. The more they grew, the darker they became. When the sky was full of clouds, they began to push downward, toward the church. Music continued to fill the air.

"Good-bye tears, forever flow. Could my zeal, sustain and hold. These for sin could not atone. Thou must save and thou alone."

The sky rippled. It was as if a wave had rolled from the east and rushed across the clouds. Everything became still, as if Angel Town were in a time warp. Lightning flashed through the sky and thunder rumbled far and wide. A ferocious storm evolved. The congregation shifted uncomfortably.

The sound of the music was now mixed with the sound of the pounding rain. *"In my hand, the price I bring, simply to your cross I'll cling."*

Suddenly everything went silent. Not even the singers could be heard. Jim looked across the congregation. He could see the singers singing, but he couldn't hear the music. The singers were standing on a white, puffy cloud that was as big as the platform. They each wore a crown on their head. Everyone in the congregation was sitting on fluffy clouds too, wearing golden crowns and white robes and holding palm branches in their hands.

The singers' mouths were moving and Jim assumed everyone else could hear them singing, but he was wrong. Every person in the congregation shared his vision.

A booming voice invaded Jim's thoughts. *"Jim,"* the voice said, *"this is a special day for Angel Town."*

"Sir," Jim said, "I don't understand this vision. Is God trying to show me something?"

The messenger replied, *"The vision you see is just to occupy your mind. You think everyone is listening to the singers, but the gospel group isn't even singing. Those in the church are having different visions. God's children are having the same kind of vision you are, but Jesus is speaking to all the nonbelievers."*

"Is Jesus speaking to Rhasha?"

The voice paused for a second. *"Jesus is speaking to* all *the nonbelievers. This day, Rhasha's name will be added to the lamb's book of life."*

The voice ceased, but Jim continued seeing visions. He saw things in heaven that nobody had ever seen before. Everything he saw was beautiful and everlasting.

Rhasha could hear the now-familiar humming sound. When it ceased, she could see a hole through the straw roof of the church. Four angels in the sky held a window into heaven open. Inside the opening was a bright white glow that reflected off the sides of the window. Rhasha could see something that looked like a large chair in the middle of a beautiful room, and she knew it was the throne of God. Sitting on the throne was the figure of a man, limned in a bright light different from any light Rhasha had ever seen, a light of pure white. Above the bright light was a rainbow of many colors that Rhasha didn't recognize. In front of the light, a multitude of white-robed people sang its praises.

A lamb sat on the right-hand side of the bright light. A wooden sign hung over the lamb's head. Rhasha didn't know how to read, but she was made aware of what the sign said: *This is Jesus, King of the Jews.*

The lamb began to transform. It stood on its hind legs and began to grow. Its back legs took on the shape of a man's legs; its front legs became arms with hands and fingers. A white robe draped its body, flowing to its ankles, and sandals encased human feet. Its face became a man's face. A bright light glowed behind the man, radiating from him in every direction. As the man descended from heaven toward the church, angels sang a heavenly song.

Rhasha knew it was Jesus.

Bed of Leaves

As Jesus descended from heaven, things around Rhasha began to change. The straw-thatched church and all the people faded away. Everything became dark. When it grew light again, Rhasha had been moved. She now stood all alone in a field of colorful flowers that extended as far as she could see.

She could still see Jesus descending from heaven. As he drew closer and closer, Rhasha started to shake. She knew Jesus was coming to her, but she didn't feel worthy to be in his presence. Seconds later, he hovered in the air directly in front of her, about two feet off the ground. Rhasha began to cry. She fell to her knees and kissed his feet.

"Stand up, child, so I can see your face," Jesus said in a voice of pure innocence.

Rhasha slowly stood, but didn't open her eyes.

"Look at me, Rhasha," Jesus said, "for I have something to say."

Rhasha opened her tear-filled eyes. "Jesus," she whimpered, "I love you with all my heart. I know you must be the son of God." She covered her face with her hands, still weeping.

Jesus didn't say anything; Rhasha thought he'd left. She raised her face. He was still there, holding his hands out toward her. The bright light was still behind him; Rhasha couldn't see his features clearly.

"Rhasha," Jesus said, "I love you too, and I want you to be with me in paradise. Repent of your sins and ask me to come into your heart. I will never forsake you."

Rhasha broke down in sobs. "I beg you, Jesus," she whimpered, "will you come into my heart?"

"Yes Rhasha," Jesus said, "and when I ascend back to heaven, I'll send the Holy Spirit to guide you from this day on."

Rhasha felt loving warmth flow through her body. She stopped crying. The warm sensation felt good. She smiled at Jesus as he rose heavenward. The four angels closed the window into heaven and disappeared, leaving Rhasha standing in the field of flowers. She heard the humming sound. When it faded away, the field of flowers faded too, and everything went dark. Rhasha felt as though she had gone through a tunnel and then emerged into the light again-she was back in church.

The congregation saw a ripple move through the clouds as lightning flashed and thunder roared. The clouds rolled to the east, and the sky cleared, letting the sunlight through.

Rhasha remembered Jesus' crucifixion and her tears flowed. She covered her face.

Rhasha felt arms slide around her and knew Jim was holding her. She rested her head against his cheek. When she looked at his face, she saw tears streaming from his eyes. She knew they were tears of happiness. She looked around the church. Aside from the gospel trio standing outside the church and Reverend Morris standing at the pulpit, she and Jim were the only ones standing; everyone had experienced a vision, but they were still seated, now watching Rhasha.

Rhasha looked up at Jim and whispered his name. She wept.

"What is it, angel?"

"Jim," she repeated, whimpering. "All I can think about is how they drove nails into Jesus' hands and feet."

Everyone remained quiet. Jim held Rhasha tight. Reverend Morris nodded; he knew Jesus had spoken to Rhasha. "Rhasha, dear," he said, "would you like to come to the altar and profess Jesus as your Lord and savior?"

Jim waited for her answer. Rhasha looked lovingly into Jim's eyes and placed her hand over his. She glanced at Francis and Shanha.

Francis whispered to her daughter, then looked at Rhasha and said "Shanha and I love you very much" as Shanha ran to Rhasha and wrapped her arms around Rhasha's waist. Shanha beamed at Rhasha. She knew Jesus had talked to her.

Rhasha stepped around Jim, into the aisle. Shanha let go of Rhasha and sat back down. Rhasha pulled on Jim's hand, inviting him to go with her.

"Sweetheart," Jim said, "this is your time to be with Jesus."

Tears filled Rhasha's eyes and she released Jim's hand to hide her face again. She slowly turned and walked toward the altar, still covering her face with her hands. Tears ran through her fingers. Rhasha took two short steps, then looked back at Jim. She turned and started walking hesitantly toward the altar again. Again she stopped.

Behind her, Jim began to sing. The keyboard operator quickly joined in. *"Amazing Grace, how sweet the sound, that saved a wretch like me."*

With lowered head, Rhasha turned to gaze at Jim as the congregation joined him in song: *" I once was lost, but now I'm found, was blind, but now I see."* Rhasha resumed her walk toward the altar. Tears of happiness filled her eyes. *"Was grace that taught my heart to fear, and grace, my fears relieved."*

Jim didn't realize it, but as he sang, he began walking rapidly toward Rhasha. Everyone in the congregation rose. Tears glistened on every face.

"How precious does that grace appear, the hour I first believed."

Rhasha saw Jim walking toward her and waited for him. The congregation stopped singing as Jim clasped Rhasha's hand, and they gazed into each other's eyes. Rhasha, caught up in the words to the song, began to sing. Jim stopped singing. Now Rhasha's voice was the only voice heard.

"Through many dangers, tolls and snares, I have already come. It's grace that brought me safe thus far, and grace will lead me home."

Rhasha fell silent when she saw that Jim had stopped singing. Jim began singing again. "*When we've been there ten thousand years, bright, shining as the sun.*" He continued to gaze into her eyes as he sang. *"We've no less days to sing God's praise, than when we first began."*

Rhasha hung her head as Jim kissed her on the forehead. The congregation began singing again as Jim walked with Rhasha to the altar. *"Amazing grace, how sweet the sound, that saved a wretch like me."*

Shanha ran up the aisle to be with Jim and Rhasha. Francis followed. Every person in the congregation, still singing, stepped one by one into the aisle to follow Jim and Rhasha to the altar. *"I once was lost, but now I'm found, was blind, but now I see."*

Reverend Morris stepped in front of the altar to meet Rhasha, reaching out to take her hand. Rhasha looked up at Reverend Morris, but something behind him caught her attention-a ten-foot tall white cross. Rhasha remembered that the soldiers nailed Jesus to the cross.

The congregation still sang: " *I once was lost, but now I'm found, was blind, but now I see."*

The song ended, and a hush fell over the congregation. Rhasha knelt in front of the altar and, as she began to pray, everyone in the church sank to their knees. *"My Father in heaven, I beg you to forgive me of my sins and have mercy on my soul."*

Rhasha envisioned God sitting on his throne, with Jesus sitting on his right-hand side. *"Father, I repent of my sins and I promise to serve you as long as I live. I love you, Father, and I love Jesus."* She could feel the warmth of the Holy Spirit hugging her. Again she wept.

"Father," she whimpered, *"I'm so sorry for my part in Jesus' crucifixion. I know he died on the cross for my sins. Use me, Father, to show others the way to salvation. In Jesus' holy name, I pray. Amen."*

Everyone, including Rhasha, stood, feeling comforted by the Holy Spirit-their tears had dried. Reverend Morris shook Rhasha's hand and held her hand between both of his as he said, "Rhasha, I'm so happy about your choice today. I know you will make God very proud of you."

A hundred and eighteen people gathered around the altar, or as close to it as they could get. They all professed Jesus as their Lord and Savior, making every person in the church who was at the age of understanding a child of God.

Jim kissed Rhasha's hand and pressed it hard against his cheek. He sensed something different about her-a blue aura surrounded her body. He looked at the people gathered around the altar. They all had blue auras around them, too. Jim looked across the church. Every pew was empty. He was excited to see all God's children gathered around the altar.

As Jim looked toward the back of the church, he saw four people kneeling together in prayer. Beside them was a camera mounted on a tripod. When they finished praying, they stood up and walked to the altar. A blue aura surrounded their bodies, as well. Jim realized the four people were television news reporters.

He remembered the vision he'd had on his first journey to Africa, when a messenger of God told him of future events. *"Many people will find Jesus,"* the messenger said, *"directly because of the food they receive. Many more will have their eyes opened because of the influence of news media and word of mouth."*

Suddenly Jim heard the humming sound that heralded a vision. Blackness filled the church, as if night had fallen. Not a person could be seen and not a sound could be heard. Jim didn't know if other people shared his vision, or if God had a message for him alone.

A glow formed around the television equipment, like a spotlight from heaven. Jim heard a click, and heard the film rewinding in the camera. When the film finished rewinding, he heard another click. A television screen appeared in the darkness, floating suspended in air. A blue glow filled the inside of the screen. Jim heard another click and the camera began to project images onto the television screen.

On the television, a female journalist holding a microphone said, "This is Sharon Simanally, and I'm in Angel Town, Africa." Jim could see the church behind her as she talked. "Everywhere you find people," she continued, "you find news. Here in Angel Town is a story about one man's desire to help the African people."

The scene behind the reporter changed and a full view of the hospital filled the screen. "Angel Town was built by millionaire and Christian convertee, Jim Brown. Sources inform SORTA News that Jim Brown was sent to Africa by God on a mission to feed the hungry and house the homeless, to care for the sick and clothe the poor." The reporter pointed to the surrounding buildings. "I personally have seen good things in Angel Town."

A picture of the dining hall flashed on the screen behind the reporter. "The dining facilities are located across the street from the hospital. They feed hundreds of people every day." She pointed to the area behind the dining hall. "The residents of Angel Town have a beautiful park and recreational area with a swimming pool and flower garden."

The reporter pointed to an area across the street from where she stood. "Angel Town has over three hundred houses with paved roads and sidewalks." A picture of the residential area popped up in front of the reporter to fill the screen. "At night, the bright glow from a generous supply of streetlights illuminates the small community. Houses, food, and hospital facilities are eagerly furnished to anyone who needs them."

The reporter pointed toward the Angel Town church. "Every Sunday, residents from Angel Town and surrounding communities worship at this small church." The camera continued to roll but momentarily went blank. When the news report continued, the reporter was standing in front of the church. "Most people around the world believe in God, but in Angel Town, residents believe God performs miracles for them. Are these miracles real?" The reporter paused. "By the time I finish this report," she said, "I hope to show the world that God does in fact do miracles in Angel Town."

The television screen went blank. After a short pause, images began to appear again. This time the camera was placed at the back of the church. The reporter was facing the camera. The backs of members of the congregation could be seen behind her.

"Every Sunday," the reporter announced, "Angel Town residents meet in this simply-constructed, nondenominational building to worship God. Today, our television crew will sit in on one of these meetings."

She started to speak again but suddenly stopped. "What's that sound?" she asked. She looked around, then looked back at her cameraman. "Where is that humming sound coming from?"

He was just as confused as she was. "I don't know."

Jim knew everything he was watching on television had been recorded earlier. The humming progressed from soft to loud. It began to pulsate. After a few seconds, the humming sound faded away, then ceased. The vision continued, but the television was gone. Silence filled the room. Darkness slowly gave way to light. The interior of the church was visible again. Jim could see the backs of the congregation. He heard singing, so low it sounded as if it were a loud whisper.

The roof of the church began to ripple as though it were turning to water. Within seconds, the rippling effect stopped and the roof of the church became transparent, as if a large hole had been burned through it to reveal the sky. High above the church, Jim saw four angels, each holding back a portion of the sky, revealing a window into heaven. Within, angels stood in military formation in front of the throne. The throne room was bathed in light so brilliant, it was like the sun. Streaks of light shot out like spears, piercing the sky.

Jim continued to watch as the formation of angels descended from heaven toward Angel Town. They drew closer and closer to earth, as if they were descending down the side of a tall mountain.

He could still hear singing as the angels came down to the congregation. The church began to expand. It didn't stop growing until it was three times its original size. Each pew also expanded, creating a gap between each person large enough to seat two extra people, and room on the end of each pew for one more person. The angels descended from the sky directly into the church and slipped undetected into each gap. Every person in the congregation had an angel sitting on either side. Jim could see himself sitting in the congregation with an angel on each side of him. Between him and Rhasha were two angels-one for him and one for Rhasha.

The singing stopped and the room fell silent. Ghostly white clouds poured from both sides of the ten-foot tall white cross. The clouds swirled all through the church, flying as if they were alive. After the clouds passed over, in between, and through the congregation several times, they came to a stop and hovered above the people. They turned into a warm mist that rained down on the congregation, so gently as to be unfelt. As Jim watched the mist rain down on the congregation, he sensed that the mist was sent to the people from the Holy Spirit as a way to soften their hearts and to give them understanding.

A voice boomed in his vision, *"Jim, behold the work of the Lord."*

Jim fell to his knees and clasped his hands together as if to pray. "Sir," he said, "I don't understand. What does the vision mean?"

Everything and everyone became motionless, as if time had stopped. Jim was the only person who could move.

"Jim," the voice thundered, *"the television crew recorded the vision you saw. No one in the congregation saw it. These miracles will be shown throughout the world. Everyone who sees these miracles on television will see Jesus with his hands reaching out to them. He will ask them to invite him into their hearts. God will put understanding in their souls and over a million people will accept Jesus as their savior."*

Jim was excited by what the messenger said. He bowed his head to praise God. When he finished praying, he looked to the sky for a glimpse of the throne room, but the window to heaven was closed, and black clouds gathered in the west. The black cluster rolled across the sky. Lightning illuminated the heavens as thunder rumbled far and wide. The clouds vanished and the sun shone brightly again. The roof of the church reappeared. The vision was over.

The congregation was now gathered around the altar. Reverend Morris prayed with the new Christians. When he finished, he passed out literature and asked everyone to meet at the river for baptismal services instead of the church the following Sunday. The congregation began to disperse. Within minutes, the small church was vacant.

Knowing Francis and Shanha would soon be leaving, Angel Town residents gathered at Jim and Rhasha's house, waiting outside until Francis and Shanha finished packing. Jim and Rhasha helped Francis load her belongings into the car, and Jim gave Francis some food to take on the trip. Shanha placed Honeycup in the back seat and fastened the seat belt over the teddy bear.

All their friends gathered around Francis and Shanha. Everyone kissed Shanha and told her that they loved her. The mood was cheerful, until Rhasha burst into tears. She knelt on the ground and put her arms around Shanha and held her tight for several minutes.

Jim felt sad too. He knelt down and kissed Shanha on the forehead. He took her right hand and placed it between both of his. "Sweetheart," he said, "have I ever told you that you have pretty eyes?"

Shanha pulled away from Rhasha and threw her arms around Jim's neck. As he put his arms around her waist, she said, "Oh Papa, I love you so much."

A tear ran down Jim's cheek. "I love you too, angel."

Shanha hugged Rhasha. "I love you too, Mama."

Rhasha hugged her tight. She cried openly. "I love you too." She didn't want to let go of Shanha, but she knew she must. She stood and opened the passenger door, then picked Shanha up in her arms. As Francis slid in behind the steering wheel and started the motor, Rhasha set Shanha down on the seat and fastened her seat belt, then bent over and kissed her one last time.

The car pulled away from the crowd. Several people ran behind the car, calling farewells until the car was out of sight. The crowd began to disperse. Jim placed his arms around Rhasha and held her as she sobbed. They stood together in the middle of the road.

Chapter 24

Jim's Big Surprise

Bed of Leaves

Two weeks passed and the church continued to grow. Fifteen more people became Christians. Others were thinking about it. Reverend Morris was trying to get a choir together to sing at the Sunday morning services. Several people signed up, but hadn't practiced together yet. Reverend Morris told them if they practiced, they could start singing in two weeks. Jim was happy the church now had a choir.

Jim and Rhasha spent all their time together. Their love grew even stronger.

Three weeks after Shanha and her mother left Angel Town, after the Sunday morning church service, Jim and Rhasha loaded the jeep with picnic supplies and headed for the waterfalls. As Rhasha drove, Jim hung his arm out his window. A warm breeze stroked his face. They were quiet on the way to the falls, both deep in thought, both thinking about the other. It so happened, they were thinking about the same thing-marriage. The problem was, they were thinking of different ramifications.

Thinking how much he loved Rhasha, Jim remembered what God's messenger told him on the plane when he was coming to Africa for the first time: Rhasha would be a blessing and an inspiration to Jim for the rest of his life. Jim knew Rhasha should marry a younger man, but now he didn't want that. He knew, if he lost Rhasha, his life would be dull and boring. He didn't know what to do-he was too old to marry her, but he wanted her to be his wife.

Rhasha was thinking about how happy they would be *when* they got married. She noticed Jim was being extra quiet, and winked at him and smiled. "What are you thinking about?" she asked.

Jim winked back. "I'm thinking about you, angel," he said. "I think you should fall in love with someone your own age."

Rhasha wrinkled her nose. "Nah," she said, "I'm already in love, and someday, I'm going to be your wife. People will call me Mrs. Rhasha Brown."

Jim was flattered, but he still felt it was wrong. "You're nuts. There are so many good-looking young men who would love to marry you. Why do you want to waste your life with a broken-down old man like me?"

Rhasha had a serious look on her face as she caught his eye. "Love," she said.

"Rhasha, I love you the most."

Rhasha smiled. She had no doubt about Jim's love, or hers.

Rhasha turned right onto the road that led to the waterfalls. She drove slowly to their favorite parking place, at the top of a gradual incline that sloped down to the water's edge. Jim and Rhasha watched the water falling off the top of the mountain to collect in the mist-shrouded pool below. The roar from the crashing water was muted by distance, where Jim and Rhasha were. Beyond the beach area was a damp, green wall of large trees and grass. Birds flew from tree to tree.

Some of the Angel Town residents were already at the falls. They had blankets spread on the ground with picnic boxes resting on top. Other people were unloading vehicles and carrying their picnic paraphernalia down to the pool's edge. Three more cars were driving down the road, looking for a parking place.

Rhasha and Jim climbed out of the jeep and carried their picnic supplies down to their favorite picnic spot. Jim spread two blankets on the ground and Rhasha arranged the contents of the picnic box on top of the blankets. She began making sandwiches as Jim poured two glasses of tea.

When Rhasha parked the jeep, she forgot to set the emergency brake. As Jim and Rhasha began eating their sandwiches, they didn't see the jeep roll a few inches forward and stop. Jim heard a long wavering sound coming from the top of the hill. He and Rhasha looked around, trying to determine what it was.

The wheels rolled a few more inches, but the gravel stopped the jeep from going farther. The eerie, wavering sound continued. Jim didn't know God was trying to warn him of the danger.

The wheels rolled again, but this time the jeep didn't stop. It gathered speed as it plummeted down the hill.

There were very few trees between the area where the jeep had been parked and the pool. Those that were present were small and only served to slow the jeep down. No one saw the jeep careening down the hill toward the pool of water. And toward a family of four eating their lunch, oblivious to the jeep hurtling toward them.

Rhasha glanced up and saw the jeep. She yelled, leaped to her feet, and ran toward it. Her shout was lost in the crash of the waterfalls; few people heard her. Jim heard her yell, and took off running behind her. He didn't see the jeep until he started running.

Rhasha was well ahead of him. She was yelling and waving her arms at the family of four, but they couldn't hear her. Rhasha changed direction, running at an angle upward, hoping to reach the jeep before it plowed into the family.

Jim could see that Rhasha wasn't going to make it in time. He ran toward the family, yelling. They were talking to each other and didn't notice him.

Rhasha got to the jeep and managed to open the door. She jumped inside, but it was too late. The jeep was almost on top of the four people in its path.

The family finally heard Jim yelling. They looked up and saw the jeep coming toward them, but it was too late for them to run.

The loud, eerie sound had stopped, but now a new sound took its place-the humming sound. The sound rose, briefly pulsated, then faded away.

Rhasha jammed on the brake, but it didn't matter. A blue bubble surrounded the jeep and lifted it above the family of four. By this time, all the picnicking people could see the bubble that was now carrying the jeep above the water of the pool. The bubble circled back and passed over Jim at an angle, fifty feet in the air. He could see Rhasha sitting in the front seat, crying, as the bubble passed over him. The bubble deposited the jeep at the top of the hill, where it had originally been parked, about a hundred feet from where Jim stood. The bubble gently set the jeep on the ground, but horizontal with the pool this time. Immediately, the blue bubble disappeared.

The humming sound rose, throbbed, faded.

Jim ran to the jeep as Rhasha set the hand brake and climbed shakily out of the jeep. When Jim arrived, Rhasha was leaning against the door, crying. Breathing hard, with sweat running down his face, Jim bent over and rested his hands above his knees, trying to catch his breath. Rhasha stopped crying to check on him. She put her arm around his back and rested her left hand on his arm and bent over as if trying to help him up.

"Jim," Rhasha said, are you okay?"

"I'm okay," Jim said between huffs and puffs. "Are you?"

Rhasha began to cry again. "I'm sorry, Jim. I can't believe I did that."

Jim straightened, pulling Rhasha up with him. His breathing was returning to normal. He put his arms around her and held her tight. "Sweetheart," he said, "everyone makes mistakes. I just thank God no one was hurt."

Relieved that Jim wasn't upset with her, but still angry with herself, Rhasha hung her head.

Jim released his hold on her and pushed her head high with his fingers. He kissed her gently on the lips. "Do you want to have some fun?" he asked, hoping to cheer her.

Rhasha forced a smile. "Yes, but what do you want to do?"

Jim smiled. "It's a secret. I can't tell you right now."

Rhasha smiled again, but this time it wasn't forced. "Ohhh Jim, that sounds like so much fun. We're going to play 'I have a secret.'" She sounded as if she was the first person who had ever used that term.

Jim knew Rhasha was teasing him. He laughed. "No, we're going to play *I* have a secret."

He took her hand and pulled, indicating that he wanted her to follow him. She did. Jim led Rhasha down the hill to their picnic site. When they got there, he asked her to sit in the center of the blankets.

"Rhasha," he said, "I'm going to leave for a few minutes. While I'm gone, would you put all the picnic stuff back in the box?"

Rhasha smiled. "Sure Jim," she teased, "that sounds like *so much fun.*"

Jim grinned. "Maybe for you, angel."

Rhasha watched Jim walk to every picnic site around the pool of water, speaking to everyone he passed. Every time Jim stopped to talk to someone, he pointed at her.

Finally her curiosity got the best of her, and she yelled to the picnickers closest to her, who happened to be Reverend Morris and his family, "What did Jim tell you?"

By now Jim was well out of hearing range. Reverend Morris was surprised Rhasha didn't know what he'd said-Jim never kept any secrets from her. "Jim is asking everyone to gather around you when we see him walking this direction down the beach."

Rhasha didn't understand why he would ask that, but didn't ask any more questions. "Thanks, Reverend Morris. I guess I'll find out why when he returns."

After Jim talked to the people at the last picnic site, he began climbing up the hill. Rhasha watched him as he climbed toward the jeep. At the top of the hill, he walked to a patch of wild flowers. There were flowers of several different colors, but he picked only the white flowers until he'd gathered a large bundle. With the bouquet of flowers clutched in his hand, he walked down the hill, but away from where Rhasha waited.

Rhasha realized she really *was* having fun, trying to figure out what Jim was doing. She could see that Jim had something in his hand, but couldn't make out what it was.

A clump of reeds grew at the water's edge, the stalks swaying in the wind. He set the flowers on the ground, and waded ankle-deep into the pool to the reeds. He pulled a pocket knife out of his pocket and, finding a stalk about an inch in diameter, cut it down and waded back to shore with it. He laid the reed on the ground next to the bouquet of flowers, then knelt and cut off a short length of the green stalk.

Jim unraveled the thread from the hem in his T-shirt and tied the two ends of the reed together to form a circle with a diameter of about seven inches. He cut all but three inches of the stems off the flowers, then separated the flowers into twenty-four bundles of seven flowers-seven is considered to be a heavenly number. He tied each bundle of flowers to the bamboo ring with thread, until the ring was covered completely by white flowers.

Laying the flower-covered ring on the ground, he cut a half-inch ring off the bottom of the reed. He stood, stuck the point of his knife through the center of the half-inch piece, and hollowed it out. When he finished, he put the knife in his pocket, picked up the flower-covered ring, and walked toward Rhasha, holding the ring of flowers behind his back and the half-inch ring he'd hollowed out cupped in his left hand. As Jim walked down the beach, a crowd of people gathered around Rhasha. So far, his plan was working perfectly.

As he approached, the waiting crowd parted so he could get to Rhasha. He stopped in front of Rhasha his right hand still behind his back.

She was smiling. "Are we having fun yet?" she asked.

Jim returned the smile. "I am," he said. "Are you?"

"Oh yes," she teased. "I like being left all alone." Rhasha didn't have a clue what Jim was doing. She was standing to one side of the blankets.

"Sweetheart," Jim said, "could you stand in the center of the blankets?"

Everyone watched as Rhasha did as Jim asked. Jim knelt on the ground in front of her. When Rhasha saw Jim kneel, she dropped to her knees in front of him.

Jim pulled the crown of flowers from behind his back and placed it snugly on top of her head. Then he said, "Could you stand up please?"

This was all strange to Rhasha, but it was fun. She did as Jim asked.

Jim concealed the bamboo ring in the pocket of his blue jeans and clasped both Rhasha's hands in his. Jim had a question to ask Rhasha, but even though he knew what her answer would be, he was still nervous.

Rhasha waited. She thought Jim was playing a game with her.

Jim started to speak, but a lump formed in his throat. He swallowed and tried again. “Rhasha,” he said, “I love you with all my heart, and I know you love me.”

Tears began to ease through Rhasha’s eyelids as she realized Jim was going to ask her to marry him. She licked her lips nervously. “Sweetheart, I love you more than anyone on earth.”

Jim’s eyes teared up and his hands felt sweaty. Tears began to flow down her cheeks. He squeezed her hands.

The crowd around Jim and Rhasha moved in closer to hear what Jim was going to say. Several people grinned, already knowing what he was doing.

“Angel,” he said, “would you marry me and make me the happiest man alive?”

Rhasha dropped to her knees and pulled her hands free to cover her face as she started to cry. All the people around Jim and Rhasha began clapping. Many of the women had tears in their eyes. Everyone was smiling. Jim put his arms around Rhasha and held her.

After a few seconds, Rhasha regained control of her emotions. “Jim, are you sure you want to marry me?”

Jim smiled. “More than anything on earth.”

Rhasha wiped her eyes and gazed into Jim’s eyes. “Yes, Jim. I want to be your wife and the mother of your children.”

Jim held Rhasha tight, but only one thought ran through his head. Children. He hadn’t thought about the fact that Rhasha would want to have children. As Jim thought about raising children at his age, he remembered Shanha. “Yes, sweetheart,” he said, “I want children too.”

The crowd began to shout and cheer.

Jim pulled the bamboo ring out of his pocket and slipped it on Rhasha’s finger. It fit loosely and felt bulky, but Rhasha held her hand up to admire it. The ring looked so cheap to Jim.

“Sweetheart, tomorrow I’ll buy you a diamond ring.”

She looked into Jim’s eyes again and whispered, “I’ll cherish this ring as long as I live.”

“Kiss her, Jim,” people in the crowd yelled.

He placed a loving kiss on her lips. Rhasha smiled with contentment. Jim pulled on Rhasha’s hand to help her up, and the crowd gathered around them, offering congratulations.

When everyone had gone and Jim and Rhasha were alone, Jim held Rhasha’s hands in his and said, “Sweetheart, I want to ask you one more question.”

Rhasha pulled her hands free and draped them around his neck. Jim put his arms around her waist as she kissed him.

“You can ask me anything you want,” she said.

“Okay . . . ” Jim grinned. “Are we having fun yet?”

Rhasha giggled and batted her eyes at him. “I am. Are you?”

Jim and Rhasha held each other tight and lost themselves in each other’s love.

That night, they slept snuggled together through the night.

Chapter 25

Jim And Rhasha's Big Event

Bed of Leaves

Almost two weeks later, on Saturday night, Jim lay on his back in bed with Rhasha next to him. Her leg was draped across both of his legs and her arm was across his chest. The light was still on, but Rhasha was asleep. Jim could feel Rhasha's hair on his chest.

Jim thought about all the things he and Rhasha had done together. He remembered the first day he met Rhasha, then a girl twisted and crippled from hunger, with swollen stomach and sunken face and hair that was matted and dirty. He recalled the tear that ran down her cheek and fell on the mat of leaves on which she lay. He knew that was the moment he first fell in love with her. When God healed Rhasha, he remembered the first words she said. The words echoed over and over in his head: "I love you."

Love warmed him as Rhasha snuggled her head against his chest. Her hair tickled his chin. Sweet contentment covered her face. She moved her head to Jim's shoulder and Jim saw her contented smile as she opened her eyes to find him looking at her face as she slept.

Still half asleep, she whispered, "I love you." Then she closed her eyes and went back to sleep.

Jim smiled and kissed her forehead. "I love you too, angel." He turned off the lamp and went to sleep.

When Jim woke up, sunlight streamed through the window. Rhasha was already awake, staring into his eyes. "Good morning sunshine," she said. "You have beautiful eyes."

"Good morning to you too, sunshine. You have prettier eyes."

The morning started out like every Sunday morning. Jim and Rhasha ate breakfast, then went to the hospital, where they spent two hours talking to the patients before rushing to get to church on time. Reverend Morris said the opening prayer, then asked Jim and Rhasha to sing a couple of songs. As they joined Jackie and Simbatu onstage, they couldn't keep their eyes off each other. In less than a week, they would be husband and wife.

"I was sinking deep in sin, far from that peaceful shore," Jim and Rhasha sang. "*Very deeply stained within, sinking to rise no more. But the master of the sea heard my despairing cry, and from the waters lifted me, now safe am I . . . "*

The congregation had heard all Jim's songs so often, everyone knew the words by heart. The congregation joined in, and their singing could be heard all over Angel Town: "*Love lifted me. Love lifted me. When nothing else could help, love lifted me . . . "*

As they sang, Jim remembered what Jesus told him, the day he was saved. The words came to Jim as if they had just been spoken: *"I am the way, Jim. Let me come into your heart and you will never be alone again."*

Jim had had no way of knowing at the time that his life would change drastically. Who would have thought that he would fall in love with a beautiful young black girl? A girl who made him the happiest man on earth.

Rhasha had thoughts of her own, but of a different nature. She remembered all the times Jim had prayed for her. *Any man who really loved a woman,* she thought, *would want her to go to heaven.* Rhasha felt proud that Jim loved her that much.

When they'd finished singing a couple of songs, Jim suddenly didn't feel well. He reached for Rhasha. The blood drained from his face, and his skin felt clammy. Pain shot through Jim's chest. His left arm went numb. "Rhasha," he mumbled.

Rhasha saw the look on his face and knew something was wrong. "Jim, nooo!" she screamed.

Suddenly dizzy, Jim lost his balance and fell to the floor. Rhasha still clung to his hand. She dropped to the floor beside him, crying as she watched Jim losing consciousness.

Most of the congregation was standing. Concern dragged at every face.

As the doctor rushed to Jim's side, he mumbled in Rhasha's ear, "I love you, sunshine."

"I love you too, Jim," she cried. "Please, tell me everything will be okay."

Jim heard the humming sound. It got louder and louder until the air seemed to pulsate. After a few seconds, it faded, then ceased.

"Sweetheart," Jim said, "everything will be okay."

He looked up at the ceiling of the church. He could see a hole-a perfect circle-burning through the roof. Jim saw the window into heaven in the sky above and knew he was having a vision. A bright light shot from heaven, through the window, and down to where Jim lay. It formed a bright tunnel of light up to the throne room of God. Inside the tunnel, the walls sparkled like diamonds in the brilliant white light.

Three angels descended toward him through the tunnel. Jim could feel himself ascending toward the angels. They met halfway through the tunnel.

Jim realized his chest wasn't hurting anymore. He couldn't feel Rhasha holding his hand.

The doctor got to Jim just as his eyes shut. Sara checked his pulse, but there was none.

Jim's spirit hovered before the angels in the tunnel. The angels wore long flowing white gowns and sandals on their feet. He didn't know what to do. "Am I dead?" he asked.

"Jim," one angel replied, *"you will live for eternity . . . in heaven. Your flawed body on earth has expired."*

Jim's spirit thought about Rhasha, and how she must be feeling. "Am I going to heaven, now?" he asked.

The angel replied, *"We're here to escort you to paradise."*

Jim was anxious to go to heaven, but he was worried about Rhasha. "Sir," he said, "is there any way I can comfort Rhasha during her time of grief?"

"You will be allowed to go back to earth, but only in spirit form. You can speak to her and you can touch her, but she will not be able to see you or hear you. She will not feel your touch."

"How long will I have?" Jim asked.

"Your presence will be required in heaven at the time Jesus chooses."

Suddenly Jim was back in his body. The tunnel to heaven and the window disappeared. Jim could hear the humming sound rise, pulse, then fade.

The congregation pushed up around Jim's body, crowding the doctor. Knowing Jim was dead, Rhasha wept over his body. Thamish and Thasha eased their way in next to Rhasha and put their arms around her. Her parents helped her to stand. Rhasha covered her face with her hands.

Jim's spirit stood up to comfort her, but his lifeless body remained on the floor. He could see the tears running down Rhasha's cheeks. He could hear her sobbing. He put his arms around her. He knew she couldn't feel his arms, but he just wanted to hold her.

Rhasha immediately stopped crying. "Who touched me?" she asked.

Several people were gathered around Rhasha. They all had their hands on her. One woman looked bewildered. "Rhasha, we're all touching you."

Rhasha looked at her friends' hands. "No." She shook her head. "It was different. It was Jim."

Everyone looked at Jim's motionless body laying on the floor. One man looked sympathetically at Rhasha. "I'm sorry," he said, "but it couldn't have been Jim. I wish it was."

"No," Rhasha insisted, "Jim's spirit is here with us. I felt him touch me." She started to cry again.

Jim's spirit leaned his head against Rhasha's head. Rhasha couldn't feel it. Jim kissed her, but she couldn't feel his lips touching hers. Jim whispered in her ear, but she couldn't hear him. "I love you, sunshine," he said.

Thamish and Thasha pulled Rhasha through the crowd and walked her to their house.

Rhasha wanted to be alone, but people kept coming by to check on her. In a strange way, Rhasha felt content. She knew Jim's spirit was there. Finally she told Thamish she needed to be by herself, said good night to everyone, and went to her bedroom. She took a shower and climbed quickly into bed, somehow knowing that Jim's spirit would be lying beside her.

She was right. Jim's spirit lay next to her, on his back.

Rhasha looked at the spot where Jim normally slept. She couldn't see him, but she knew he was there. She placed her right leg across the spot where Jim's legs usually were, and stretched her hand out, as she had when she'd rested it on his chest every night. Then she closed her eyes and pretended Jim was alive and sleeping next to her. She forced a smile.

She couldn't feel Jim's legs under hers and she couldn't feel his chest under her hand. Rhasha burst into tears. She knew Jim's body wasn't there. She wasn't even sure his spirit was.

In the next room, Rhasha's parents heard her crying. It hurt them to hear their daughter suffering. They tried to go into her room, but the door was locked. Thasha was worried. "Rhasha," she yelled, "are you okay?"

Rhasha wiped her eyes. "Yes, Mama," she called, "but I need to be alone."

Thamish and Thasha knew Rhasha would have to deal with Jim's death in her own way. They said good night and returned to their bedroom.

Rhasha continued to lay in her usual position. Intuition told her Jim's spirit was lying next to her. She didn't sleep at all, sensing Jim's spirit was talking to her and loath to miss hearing even one chance word. Jim *was* speaking to her, except for the times she talked to him, but she didn't hear.

Several times through the night, Rhasha prayed to God. She told him she loved him and asked him to take her to heaven.

The next morning, as the sun poured through Rhasha's bedroom window, she took Jim's imaginary hand in both of hers. She didn't know Jim's spirit covered both her hands with his hands. She pretended she was kissing his forehead. She didn't know Jim's spirit kissed her on the forehead, or that he met her eyes when she pretended to look into Jim's eyes. "Good morning, sunshine," she whispered. "You have very pretty eyes."

Jim's spirit returned the morning greeting, as Jim had every morning, but she couldn't hear him.

Bed of Leaves

Everyone had heard about Jim's death. Silence hung over Angel Town. As the day went on, people gathered at the funeral home until it was full and people had to wait outside.

"Swing low, sweet chariot," the people sang. *"Coming for to carry me home. Swing low, sweet chariot. Coming for to carry me home . . . "*

Inside the small chapel, a casket rested before ten rows of chairs. Rhasha sat in the center of the front row. Simbatu and Jackie sat on her left and Thasha and Thamish sat on her right side. Her brother Robbie sat on the floor in front of Rhasha and Thasha.

Everyone except Rhasha and her family sang, *"Swing low, sweet chariot, coming for to carry me home . . . Swing low, sweet chariot, coming for to carry me home."*

A strange feeling came over Rhasha that compelled her to look up. "Look, Mama!" she exclaimed.

Thasha looked where Rhasha was pointing. "I don't see anything."

"Look, Mama!" Rhasha blubbered, trying to talk and cry at the same time. "Don't you see it?"

"Rhasha, what do you see?" Thamish asked.

"Papa," she said excitedly, "don't you see the angels?"

Everything behind the casket was gone. The village was visible. The top of the chapel was gone. Rhasha could see the sky. No one could see the vision except Rhasha. The people continued to sing.

"I don't see it, Rhasha," Thamish replied.

Tears were running down Rhasha's cheeks. "Papa," she whimpered, "don't you see the angels coming down from heaven to get Jim? Look," she said, unable to control her tears, "they're putting a white robe on Jim!"

Oblivious to what Rhasha was seeing, the people continued to sing. *"Swing low, sweet chariot, coming for to carry me home . . . "*

“Mama,” she cried, “they’re taking him up into the sky to meet Jesus. He’s kissing Jesus’ feet, Papa. Can’t you see it?”

Finally Rhasha fell quiet, but tears continued to run down her cheeks. She watched the window into heaven close, and once again she could see the back of the chapel. The roof reappeared, blocking her view of the sky.

“Mama,” she said, “Jim’s not here now. He’s in heaven.” Rhasha was content, now that she had seen him with Jesus. Thasha cried and held Rhasha. She knew that what Rhasha had seen was real.

After a few seconds, Rhasha gently pulled away from her mother. “Simbatu,” she said, her voice quavering and weak, “I need to be alone now. I have no strength. Could you help me to the Jeep?”

“Sure, Rhasha,” Simbatu replied, “but can we go with you?”

Before Rhasha could answer, Thamish interrupted. “Why don’t you come home with us? You shouldn’t be alone right now.”

“Thank you Papa, but right now, I want to be with Jim and I need to speak with God.”

“Are you sure you’ll be okay?” Jackie asked her.

“I’ll be fine,” Rhasha replied, fighting tears. “I’ve seen Jim, and I know where he is.” Her expression grew stern and she insisted, “If you could help me to the jeep . . . I need to be alone.”

Thamish and Thasha and Jackie and Simbatu were all eager to help Rhasha through her time of despair. They all had fond memories of Jim and knew only time could heal her pain. Her parents stepped aside as Jackie gently took Rhasha’s right arm and Simbatu put his arm around her waist to escort her to the jeep. Confusion guided her every step.

Thamish, Thasha, and Robbie followed, and Thamish opened the jeep door so Rhasha could slowly slip inside. Everyone gathered around the jeep. Simbatu kissed Rhasha and stepped back. Looking depressed, Jackie kissed her on the cheek, then the pair moved away from the jeep. Robbie slipped in front of them, hugged and kissed his sister, and was nudged aside by Thamish, who hugged his daughter and kissed her gently on the tip of her nose. "Angel," he said, "I love you so much."

"I love you too, Papa," she said. Tears began to run down her cheeks again.

Thasha slipped in front of them and put her arms around her daughter. She could feel the pain flowing through her body.

Rhasha looked at her mother and burst into sobs. "Mama," she cried, laying her head on Thasha's shoulder, "it hurts."

Thasha hugged her tightly. "I know, sweetheart. I'd give anything to take the pain away."

After a few seconds, Rhasha gently pulled away from her mother and wiped the tears from her eyes. She started the Jeep and put the gearshift in first gear. Thasha reached out and squeezed Rhasha's hand. Rhasha painfully smiled back.

"I love you, Rhasha," Thasha yelled as the jeep pulled away. "Please be careful."

Rhasha looked back at her mother. "I love you too, Mama," she cried.

Rhasha drove past the hospital and turned right. Tears blurred her vision, and she didn't see her friends waving as she passed. She didn't know where she was going, but it didn't matter. All she wanted to do was tell Jim she loved him and talk to God.

As she drove past the park, her head was full of memories. She recalled her first encounter with Jim as though it had happened only yesterday. She could see him leaning over to kiss her on the forehead as she lay sick in the hospital, and she heard him saying, "Sweetheart, you have such beautiful eyes" as he held her hand between both of his. She remembered gazing into his eyes as he brushed her hair, and she thought of how Jim had pleaded with God for her life.

He'd been so kind to her. She smiled, and then she remembered he was gone. Tears filled her eyes and she couldn't see to drive. The jeep swerved off the road, but she quickly steered it back on.

The memories kept coming. She remembered how much fun she'd had, pretending Jim was a horse. She'd sat on his shoulders and yelled "howdy partner" to all their neighbors. She smiled as she recalled Jim threatening to buck her off. Tears again. Rhasha ran off the road and into the ditch. She regained control of the jeep, but the memories kept coming.

She thought about Jim pretending to be a stewardess, and how he'd jokingly said he was going to get her fired. And she remembered asking him if she'd ever told him she loved him, and how he'd looked at his watch, so she thought he would say, "Not in the last five minutes." But instead he'd said, "No, I don't think you ever have." Rhasha realized she would never have those moments with Jim again. The jeep swerved and veered all over the road as she wept.

Rhasha didn't know or care where she was going, but a strange force had guided her. She stopped the jeep, pushed the gearshift into neutral, and pulled the emergency brake. Wiping her eyes, she stepped out of the jeep and looked up at the building in front of her. The hangar at the airport. Jim had always said he felt closer to God when he was flying. She also felt closer to God in the sky.

Rhasha opened the hangar doors and backed the Jeep up to the plane. She towed the plane out of the hangar, climbed aboard, and started the engines. Jim had left the tank full of fuel, but Rhasha didn't even think to check. She didn't do any of the safety checks and she didn't fasten her seat belt. The sound of the engines rose unbearably as she spun the tail of the plane around to line up with the runway. Dust and grass blew all around the plane.

Rhasha thought about the first time Jim had brought her to the hangar. When Jim had asked her if she still wanted to go flying, she said, "Yes, but I'm really, really, really scared." Rhasha remembered how excited she was when she saw their house from the sky. She knew now that Jim must have seen it before she did. He just let her think she saw it first.

The plane rolled down the airstrip, bouncing over the rough runway, gaining speed. Thirty more feet, and the thumping sound on the tires ceased. Rhasha was airborne. She ascended upward as she flew toward Angel Town. She could see the village and all the buildings. Rhasha looked to her right and saw the flower garden in the park. Ahead she could see the dining hall. To her left was the hospital, where Rhasha's new life had begun. People were visible all around the village. It was a sad day for Angel Town, so no one was swimming in the pool.

This was the town Jim built, and Rhasha loved it. She could see all the straw roofs and bamboo frameworks, all the streets and how they all tied together. Something caught her attention. She burst into tears.

The little house across the street from the hospital. Her and Jim's house. Agony gripped her and she sobbed violently. The little house would never be the same without Jim.

Rhasha leveled off the plane at three hundred feet as she passed over the village. She never thought to climb higher. As the plane sliced through the sky at a hundred and forty miles per hour, Rhasha lifted her face toward heaven.

"Father," she prayed, "please forgive me of my sins and have mercy on my soul. I love you, Father, and I don't blame you for wanting Jim in heaven, with you." Rhasha paused, struggling to gain control of her emotions. "Father," she cried, "I know you gave Jim to me because you love me, too."

Rhasha felt the Holy Spirit embracing her. She released the steering wheel and wrapped her arms around herself. She felt as if she were returning God's embrace. A calmness came over her as she bathed in his warmth. She knew God was weeping for her pain. "Father," Rhasha said, "No matter what, I'll serve you as long as I live."

A tall mountain range loomed before her. Its sheer cliffs dropped down to a green valley below. Rhasha was at peace with God now, but tears remained in her eyes. Talking to God and thinking about Jim, Rhasha didn't see the mountainside as it got closer.

"Father," she said, "I wish you loved me the way you love Jim." Rhasha paused, blinking away tears. "I want to go to heaven so I can serve you for eternity. My life on earth is empty without Jim."

Glimpsing something in front of the plane, she wiped the tears from her eyes, but too late. A mountain cliff rose in front of her, no more than thirty yards away-too close for her to turn the plane.

"Thank you, Father," she whispered.

The plane crashed and burst into flames. It tumbled down the mountainside.

Angel Town residents heard about the plane crash and knew Rhasha was dead. Everyone, including, Thamish, Thasha, and Robbie, met at the church. No one felt the pain like Rhasha's mother, though everyone wept. Gloom hung over Angel Town.

Jackie sat in the park, looking upward as he prayed. Finally he rose and began walking toward the church. He stopped, and looked around the village.

He remembered when he'd sold the land to Jim. Then it had been nothing but a large clear area-no buildings, and very few trees. He'd watched Jim kneel and pray near his car. He remembered seeing the words going to heaven on a beam of light. Jackie's mother was healed that same day. Tears filled Jackie's eyes. Two of the people he loved most were gone.

Good memories replaced the sadness-walking in on Jim and Rhasha's water fight, seeing both soaked from their heads to their waists. Jackie smiled. Jim had started the water fight when he jokingly called Rhasha stinky. Jackie laughed out loud.

"I wonder if Jim and Rhasha are now angels and can see me crying. If you can hear me," he whimpered, "I want you both to know I love you." It was the first time he'd ever said openly that he loved Jim and Rhasha.

Jackie looked toward the church. The walls had been pushed out and braced up with poles, leaving the church open on all four sides. As Jackie drew closer, he noted that it was full of Africans. Some were crying and some were praying.

It was a partly cloudy day. A soft breeze brushed every face, and magic was in the air. Suddenly, the clouds began to roll quickly together in the east. Then the wind hit with the force of a hurricane. Clouds rushed across the sky. Bolts of lightning speared toward the ground and thunder rumbled though the heavens. Jackie heard a humming sound that rose until the air pulsated. After a few seconds, it faded away and the clouds rolled back, leaving a clear sky. Inside the church, the murmur of voices rose as frightened Angel Town residents prayed.

Jackie noticed a glow in the sky, well above the church. He looked at the glow and then back to the church. When he looked back to the sky again, the glow was getting bigger.

"Look, everyone!" Jackie yelled. He pointed. "Look at the sky."

All the people ran out of the church and looked up at the glow. It separated into glowing lights that became four angels. The heavenly beings appeared to be doing something with their hands. All four angels reached to one spot in the sky and started pulling the sky in four different directions. An opening appeared between them-a window into heaven that covered a large portion of the sky.

All the people watched as a bright light radiated through the opening. There was a flash, and an image of Jim appeared. He wore a white robe and sandals and he was standing with his right side facing the congregation. He held his arms out, and a young black girl appeared and ran toward him. It was Rhasha, wearing a white robe.

As Rhasha ran into Jim's arms, she threw her arms around his neck. They hugged each other tightly, smiling. They kissed, and miniature stars popped all around them.

"Sweetheart," Jim thundered in a booming voice, *"now we can love each other forever as a brother and sister in Christ."*

"Yes, Jim," Rhasha thundered, *"and I just know that somehow, God will show Angel Town we still have each other. They will know we're happy and safe."*

As Jim and Rhasha stared lovingly into each other's eyes, the image above Angel Town froze. The image of Jim and Rhasha hung in the sky as angels in heaven began to sing the song the gospel trio had sung, the day Rhasha met Jesus: *"Rock of ages, cleft for me. Let me hide myself in thee. Let the waters and the blood from thy wounded side which flowed . . . "*

As the angels finished singing "Rock of Ages," another group of angels began to sing a different song.

"This little light of mine, Lord, I'm gonna let it shine . . . "

The image of Jim and Rhasha slowly faded away. The angels drew the four corners of the opening to a single point and the window to heaven closed. A humming sound could be heard. It progressed from soft to loud. The humming sound began to pulsate. After a few seconds, it faded, then ceased. Clouds rolled, lightning crackled, thunder rumbled. Then the clouds rushed back toward the east and disappeared. Everything went back to normal, and the people at the church began to disperse.

Thamish, Thasha, and Robbie stood outside the church, their tear-filled eyes still looking heavenward, but they were content.

Jim and Rhasha were together, and in heaven.

The End

97237520R00215

Made in the USA
Columbia, SC
10 June 2018